HERE ARE L

HERE ARE LOVERS

by

HILDA VAUGHAN

With an introduction by

Diana Wallace

WELSH WOMEN'S CLASSICS

Published by Honno
'Ailsa Craig', Heol y Cawl, Dinas Powys,
South Glamorgan, Wales, CF64 4AH

1 2 3 4 5 6 7 8 9 10

First published in Great Britain by William Heinemann Ltd., London
in 1926
First published by Honno in 2012

British Library Cataloguing in Publication Data
A catalogue record for this book is available from the British Library.

ISBN 978-1-906784-44-7

Published with the financial support of the Welsh Books Council.

Cover illustration 'Miss Auras: The Red Book' (oil on canvas),
Sir John Lavery (1865-1941). Private collection, photo © Philip
Mould Ltd, London/The Bridgeman Art Library
Cover design: Graham Preston
Text design: Elaine Sharples
Printed by Bell and Bain Ltd, Glasgow

'Romanticism... a certain disease or disequilibrium of the spirit, a habitual disproportion of sentiments to their objects. It is a malady engendered sometimes by the tedium of a too straitly ordered society...'

Times Literary Supplement

To

Elizabeth Shirley

In Her Cradle,

this narrative of her mother's countryside

sixty years ago is dedicated

CONTENTS

Introduction

DIANA WALLACE

Here are Lovers opens in the spring of 1866 with Laetitia Wingfield, the young and beautiful heroine, leaning on the balustrade outside 'her father's house' in the gathering twilight and looking out over 'his country'. The title of the novel promises us romance, even melodrama, as does this painterly opening scene of a woman musing in the evening light. And, indeed, we get both as Laetitia falls in love with the son of one of her father's poorest tenants, Gronwy Griffith, a young man with a love of poetry and ambitions to be a classical scholar. On first reading, however, it's easy to miss the faint shadow cast by the gendering of the possessive pronouns in that opening sentence. Not only the house, but also the 'country' (for which we can read both Squire Wingfield's estate and, metaphorically, the nation itself) belong to Laetitia's father. The daughter of an English father and a Welsh mother, Laetitia is born into the privileged Anglicised squirearchy which rules nineteenth-century Wales, imposing its language, traditions and mores on the native Welsh tenantry. The gathering gloom foreshadows the 'little tragedy', to borrow Laetitia's words, resulting from the conflict of these 'two races and two traditions'.

'The poor are free in no country, ma'am, and under no laws,' Gronwy tells Laetitia early in the novel. His father, John Griffith, was imprisoned for his part in the Chartist riots in Newport in 1839 and now has a horror of revolutionary agitation. The spring of 1866 is a particularly significant date since it was when Gladstone (as Chancellor) introduced the Second Reform Bill, a version of which later passed into law under Disraeli in 1867. The political anxieties caused by debates around this extension of the franchise to working-class men play an important part in the text. Despite its romantic title, this is one of the few novels to centre on an election. When John Griffith, emboldened by the alcohol provided by the Tory landowners for their loyal tenants, refuses to vote Conservative at the election, he and his family are thrown off their farm by the Squire. In the resulting mêlée, Gronwy's impassioned defiance, during which he quotes Cicero in Latin, leads to his arrest for inciting a riot and his subsequent imprisonment.

It is against this background that Laetitia discovers that a woman in Victorian Britain, even if she is the daughter of a Squire, is equally trapped. Laetitia can attend the election to support her father's candidate, but she cannot vote. John Stuart Mill, MP for Westminster at the time the novel is set (dammed by Squire Wingfield as 'That blackguard Mill'), attempted to secure votes for the proposal to give the vote to women during the passage of the Second Reform Bill but failed to carry this through. His call for equality between the sexes, *The Subjection of Women*, was not published until1869. Laetitia owns neither the house she lives in, nor the clothes she wears, nor the books from her father's library which she lends to Gronwy in an attempt to help him realise his dreams of scholarship. The books are Latin and Greek classics and it is a further irony that Laetitia, despite her class privileges and her love of literature, cannot read them: as a woman her education has not included the classical languages which Gronwy deploys, albeit unsuccessfully, to assert working-men's rights. In the final analysis, not even Laetitia's body is her own to give to whom she chooses.

In this ambitious historical novel, only her second published book, Hilda Vaughan offers a biting analysis of the class and gender structures which determine who, how and where we can love. Her chosen epigraph for the novel – a definition of romanticism as 'a certain disease or disequilibrium of the spirit', 'a malady engendered sometimes by the tedium of a too straitly ordered society' – should alert us to the fact that this is more than a historical romance; that is it, in fact, a critique of romanticism. The romanticism manifested in different ways by Laetitia and Gronwy is in both cases a reaction against a society which imposes strict limits on their freedom. It is what draws them together, and what leads them inevitably to the final tragedy.

Like Jane Austen, Vaughan is interested in how people (both men and women) can be both educated and led astray by their reading, and, like *Northanger Abbey* (1818), *Here are Lovers* is a self-consciously literary and highly ironised novel. In the opening chapter, Wingfield Park, with its formal gardens and peacock clipped out of yew, is contrasted with Tinygraig, the exposed and decaying hill farm where the Griffith family eat their cawl and barley bread without a candle or lamp. The pairing of these two contrasting houses recalls that of Thrushcross Grange and Wuthering Heights in Emily Brontë's novel, another historical fiction (published in 1847, but set in the late 1700s). Moreover, when we first see Gronwy, he is reading *Romeo and Juliet* to his family. The 'romantic world' of Shakespeare's doomed lovers offers him an escape from the farm labour which is his daily life, with its blood and manure, but it also shapes his desires in dangerously unrealistic ways.

Similarly, Laetitia's reading includes the Romantics – Wordsworth, Shelley and Byron, Tennyson, and the sensation novels of Mary Elizabeth Braddon, Charlotte M. Yonge and Wilkie Collins as well as *Jane Eyre*. From their first meeting when Laetitia becomes lost on the mountainside during a clandestine night-time ride, both protagonists construct their relationship through fantasies derived from these texts. Laetitia thinks of herself as the heroine of a ‘high romance’, or ‘the escaping princess of some fairytale’, and pictures herself as a beneficent patron to Gronwy’s peasant scholar-poet. Gronwy, in turn, idealises Laetitia as a new Helen of Troy. Cathy and Heathcliff, Romeo and Juliet, Helen and Paris: with such romantic stories as templates, how can Vaughan’s lovers escape tragedy?

What Vaughan brings to her depiction of this volatile mix of high-flown romantic expectations and mundane class and gender constraints is a particularly Welsh sensibility which has its roots in her own life. *Here are Lovers* is set in ‘Llangantyn’, Vaughan’s fictional name for Builth Wells, the market town on the borders of Breconshire and Radnorshire where she grew up. Born in 1892, she was the daughter of a successful country solicitor, Henry Vaughan, who became Clerk of the Peace and Under Sherriff of Radnorshire. Her mother, a Campbell, was of Scottish and English extraction. Vaughan grew up in the house in which she was born, an eighteenth-century house of grey stone to which nineteenth-century ‘improvements’ had added plate-glass bow windows and castellated battlements. In two autobiographical essays ‘A Country Childhood’ and ‘Far Away: Not Long Ago’, she remembers the house covered with espalier pear trees and Gloire de Djion roses, with its kitchen garden and orchard, sitting amidst a green landscape of hayfields, twisting lanes overhung by hedges of dog-roses and honeysuckle, with solitary white-washed farms and the gently enfolding hills beyond. It is an enchanted and privileged childhood she describes, with dogs and a pony, a succession of governesses, including a German Fräulein and a French Mademoiselle, a cook who gives her cream and raspberries to freeze, and maids who argue in their ‘dramatic’ Welsh. It is also an imaginative childhood filled with books and stories: *Treasure Island*, *The Arabian Nights*, Andrew Lang’s fairy tales, the novels of Harrison Ainsworth, *A Shropshire Lad*, *Our Village*, *Cranford*.

These memories of a country childhood in a 'remote part of Wales' are suffused with nostalgia. This is partly because Vaughan left Wales as a young adult and never returned there permanently to live. But it is also partly because she is remembering a way of life which was disrupted by the First World War and then transformed by the encroachments of modernity: the arterial roads, motor cars and buses, bungalows and aeroplanes, film stars and loudspeakers she bemoans. During the war, Vaughan worked first in a Red Cross hospital and then as organising secretary of the Woman's Land Army in Breconshire and Radnorshire. Afterwards in 1922, while attending Bedford College for Women, she met Charles Morgan, a drama critic on *The Times* just beginning to make a name for himself as a novelist. They married in 1923 and had a daughter and a son.

According to Morgan, by the time they met 'Hilda had read a lot and against the wishes of her family had begun to write novels.'[1] He encouraged Vaughan's writing and admired her gift for narrative, telling her: 'The great thing is that you have a tale to tell and you tell it straight. It's a gift to rejoice in.'[2] In an early letter, he plans a married life which will allow them both to write: 'Oh and yes, we'll *make* each other work,' he writes, although he warns that her plan to ignore household things until after lunch will not be practicable because it will be her responsibility to provide an evening meal.[3] When in 1933 Morgan won the Hawthornden Prize for *The Fountain*, they bought a house in Campden Hill Square, and had two new writing rooms, one each, built at the top. As a couple they were part of London's literary elite. Vaughan, however, was overshadowed by Morgan's greater fame. We catch small glimpses of her in Eiluned Morgan's memoir of Morgan and in his published letters or in the diaries of contemporaries like Vera Brittain. While Morgan's job kept him in London, Vaughan found it impossible to work there and returned to Wales when possible, renting places in which to write. In all, she published ten novels, the majority of which are set in the country of her childhood.

Wales, then, was central to Vaughan's work, as setting and inspiration. Her novels offer a lyrical yet detailed evocation of Welsh rural landscapes, people and customs. She also drew on Welsh folklore, fairytale and myth: *Harvest Home* (1936) includes a chapter based on *The Mabinogi*, for instance, while *Iron and Gold* (1942), is a retelling of the old Welsh legend of the lady of Llyn y Fan Fach. *Here are Lovers*, a novel which at first glance is dominated by references to English, Greek and Latin classics, also uses Welsh folklore and customs to suggest alternative cultural traditions. Laetitia may dismiss as 'make-believe' the local legends about the 'wishing chair', a throne-like slab of rock above the river, but the wishes she and Gronwy make there could be said to be fulfilled. Moreover, Laetitia's maid Susan refers to the local fairy tales in which 'The son of a farmer, a poor small little farmer, falls in love with a princess… they meet in secret… but, of course, marriage is not for such as they, set so far apart'. Although Susan's comments are motivated by spite, the typically unhappy endings of these stories seem to promise no hope for the novel's equally mis-matched lovers.

But Laetitia and Gronwy are not the only lovers in this novel. Their secret meetings are paralleled with the relationship developing between Gronwy's brother Peter, and another local farmer's daughter, Elizabeth Evans. This less exalted love is shown maturing through the 'time-honoured' Welsh custom of 'bundling', or 'night-courting'. 'Caru yn y gwely' or 'courting in bed' was singled out by the infamous 'Blue Books' (the *Reports of the Commissioners of Inquiry into the State of Education in Wales* of 1847) for particular censure as a cause of sexual promiscuity in young

Welsh women. Night courting is used by Vaughan as a potent symbol of the clash of 'two races and two traditions' in this colonised country. Like speaking Welsh, it is one of the customs which the Anglicised squirearchy and church have attempted to stamp out. Welsh children are birched for speaking their 'uncouth' native language and maidservants summarily sacked if they are suspected of slipping out at night to meet a lover. In contrast, Vaughan's sensitive portrayal of the custom shows both its pleasures and its frustrations for a young couple who have to delay marriage for financial reasons. Visited at night in her room by Peter, Elizabeth first makes herself into 'the formless bundle of clothing' demanded by propriety. Working class and uneducated, it is nevertheless Elizabeth who has the deepest understanding of the real nature of love in the novel. 'I do vex for others as do love,' she says and her compassion is extended gratis to all who need it, whether animal or human.

It is a shame that Hilda Vaughan has not yet found a secure place in the canons of either 'English literature' or 'Welsh writing in English'. Until the republication of her novella, 'A Thing of Nought', in Jane Aaron's *A View Across the Valley: Short Stories by Women from Wales*(1999), all her work was out of print. This neglect can be attributed to the particularity of Vaughan's identity as an upper-middle-class Welsh woman, writing in English about rural mid-Wales. As Jane Aaron noted in her introduction to *A View Across the Valley*, Welsh writing in English has typically been associated with the male writers of the industrialised South Wales valleys. Thus Glyn Jones in *The Dragon has Two Tongues* dismissed Vaughan as one of the Anglo-Welsh writers who 'write about the squirearchy and its anglicised apers'.[4] The wrong class and the wrong gender, Vaughan was, as Lucy Thomas puts it in her recent PhD thesis, 'too Welsh for the English and too Anglicised for the Welsh'.[5]

A further reason, I'd suggest, is that Vaughan's novels are often either historical or set in the past. *Here are Lovers* is set, like Walter Scott's *Waverley* (1814), sixty years ago, a time-span the well-read Vaughan makes explicit in her dedication. *Harvest Home* and *Iron and Gold* are both set in the eighteenth century, while *Her Father's House* (1930) and 'A Thing of Nought' are set in the nineteenth century. The 1920s and the 1930s actually witnessed a renaissance of the historical novel in the hands of women writers like Naomi Mitchison, Rose Macaulay, D.K. Broster, Phyllis Bentley and Sylvia Townsend Warner. Vaughan's work can usefully be set alongside that of these writers. Her novels have important similarities to those of the feminist, socialist and Scottish Naomi Mitchison who used historical fiction to explore contentious issues of nationality and colonisation, encoding these through stories set in ancient Rome or Greece.

Placing *Here are Lovers* in this literary context draws our attention to contemporaneous resonances we might otherwise miss. The 1920s were a period of frequent elections (in 1922, 1923, 1924 and 1929) and a great deal of attention was devoted to the subject of the woman voter, newly enfranchised by the 1918 Representation of the People Act which gave the vote to all men over 21 and some women over 30. (Vaughan herself, born in 1892, would not have been eligible to vote in the election of 1918.) There were heated newspaper debates throughout the 1920s over the proposed extension of the franchise to women under 30, the so-called 'flapper vote'. By 1927 the *Daily Mail* was fulminating (in tones remarkably similar to those of Squire Wingfield):

> The proposal to add some 4,500,000 new voters – many of them quite irresponsible persons – to the enormous total of people already franchised is thoroughly unpopular in the country and worthy of Bedlam.[6]

In 1928, of course, this battle at least was won and women gained the vote on equal terms with men. But there were other struggles: Vaughan's novel was published in the year of the General Strike, sparked by the miners' refusal to accept pay cuts. In Wales, high levels of unemployment brought the beginnings of a severe economic depression which would dominate the twentieth century. After a noticeable lack of attention to Welsh affairs during the 1924 general election, the formation of Plaid Cymru in August 1925, although its initial membership was small, suggested the awakening of a new national consciousness. While not overtly polemical, then, *Here are Lovers* encourages its reader to make historical connections and draw conclusions about inequalities of class, gender and nationality which continue into the present.

A thoughtful and complex historical novel, *Here are Lovers* deserves to be far better known. The politics of ownership and inheritance it raises, both individual and national, were further deconstructed in Vaughan's later work, perhaps most incisively in *The Soldier and the Gentlewoman* (1932). But if we turn back from the assertion of male ownership ('*his* country') in the novel's opening sentence to read the original dedication, Vaughan has already quietly subverted the gender of nationality. For it reads: 'To Elizabeth Shirley in her cradle, this narrative of her mother's countryside sixty years ago is dedicated.' *Here Are Lovers*, which ends with Elizabeth Evans going bravely forward into the wind, reclaims Wales as 'her country' and looks to women for the future.

Notes

[1] Eiluned Lewis, ed., *Selected Letters of Charles Morgan*, London and Melbourne: Macmillan, 1967, p.17
[2] Lewis, *Selected Letters*, p.53
[3] Lewis, *Selected Letters*, p.69
[4] Glyn Jones, *The Dragon Has Two Tongues: Essays on Anglo-Welsh Writers and Writing,* London: Dent, 1986, p.42.
[5] Lucy Thomas, 'The Fiction of Hilda Vaughan (1892-1985): Negotiating the Boundaries of Welsh Identity', unpublished PhD thesis, Cardiff University, 2008, p.265.
[6] *Daily Mail,* 31 March 1927, p.10.

Further Reading

Aaron, Jane, ed., *A View Across the Valley: Short Stories by Women from Wales* (Dinas Powys: Honno, 1999)

Newman, Christopher, *Hilda Vaughan*, Writers of Wales series (Cardiff: University of Wales Press, 1981)

Thomas, Lucy,'The Fiction of Hilda Vaughan (1892-1985): Negotiating the Boundaries of Welsh Identity', unpublished PhD thesis, Cardiff University, 2008

Vaughan, Hilda, 'A Country Childhood' [1934], *Radnorshire Society Transactions*, 1982, 9-18

Vaughan, Hilda, 'Far Away; Not Long Ago' [1935], *Radnorshire Society Transactions*, 1982, 19-26

Williams, Jeni, 'The Intertexts of Literary History: "Gender" and Welsh Writing', in *European Intertexts: Women's Writing in English in a European Context*, eds, Patsy Stoneman and Ana María Sánchez-Arce with Angela Leighton (Oxford: Peter Lang, 2005), pp.156-176

CHAPTER I

Mansion and Farmhouse – In the Dark – A Fraternal Contrast

One evening, in the spring of the year 1866, Laetitia Wingfield, leaning upon the stone balustrade in front of her father's house, looked out over his country. In the valley below her, twilight was already deepening into a remote darkness, from which the yellow lights of Llangantyn and the river's pewter gleam emerged with detached fantasy, as if they had been raised a little towards her and were somehow floating above the earth to which they belonged. This trick of the night's perspective had been familiar to her since childhood. The line of the water was like a rapier blade bent upward from the ground. 'It is as if you could slide your hand under it,' she thought, 'and pull it up like a ribbon.'

The terrace was a favourite place of hers from which to watch the lengthening of the days. Though the air was still cold, with more of winter in it than of spring, the afternoons had already begun to plunge less abruptly into night, and she was pleased to imagine that the sparrows themselves hopped less stiffly and flew more joyfully than they had done three weeks ago. Even the peacock cut in yew appeared, if he were seen in full daylight, to be awakening from his black lethargy, though now in the dusk he was solemn enough, with his head still sharp against the skyline and his feet, standing in a bowl of shadow, hardly distinguishable from the sombre earth. Laetitia disliked him. He was king of the formal garden – a portentous and decorous bird. Soon, she thought, counting the months with a misgiving that sprang from her experience of that bleak countryside, summer would be come, and the stone of the balustrade be a rough warmth beneath her touch. Then the peacock's shadow, falling towards her at this hour, would be printed on the lawn with a stiff precision. Nothing would ever stir him to life or ruffle his clipped dignity.

Turning from him, she lingered still, her eyes fixed, her body inclined forward as if she were seeking some friendly shape in the gloom. There was no sound but the little mournfulness of a distant wind and the dry chatter of laurel.

'Nothing,' she said, almost aloud, and turned with a shiver towards the house.

When she was gone within, night's dark battalions continued their upward march unheeded, occupying with orderly speed successive ridges, flowing suddenly into ravines, obliterating homestead after homestead on the squire's territory, and encroaching even upon the peacock's lawn. Soon Wingfield Park itself was surrounded, an island flecked with irregular window gleams, and night passed on, still upward to the hill farms.

Of these Tinygraig was the highest, and remained visible after all else was gone. Nature, though she gave to those who lived there nothing else that they did not wring from her by their toil, gave them at least daylight's first and last. Long after Laetitia had ordered the shutters to be closed and the curtains drawn at Wingfield Park, the Griffiths of Tinygraig sat at their supper without the aid of candle or lamp. Their decaying cottage and outbuildings were huddled together close to a few lichened rocks, but received scant protection from them. The west wind, which had at this altitude a speed unsuspected by the squire's peacock, howled above the single chimney, and drove a great part of the smoke back into the kitchen, where it drifted across the supper table and, rising again slowly, was suspended in the rafters' dark.

John Griffith, who was accustomed to the ways of the west wind, dragged his chair towards the hearth, mumbling a grace for the little he had received. The words were muffled by his beard, grey, profuse, and unkempt like wild clematis in autumn, but his daughter Jane knew his pious habit. She looked at the table uncovered by any cloth, at the wooden bowls which had contained cawl and the crumbs of barley bread surrounding them, and her lips curved in a narrow smile. Mrs Griffith had followed her husband to the fireside and was holding out her hands, knobbly with rheumatism, towards the warmth. Her patient age seemed to discover no irony in the old man's gratitude for mercies so small, and Jane, with a shrug of her shoulders, turned her back upon her parents, and gathered up the bowls, the spoons and the single platter from the table. There was little to set in order and her task was soon done. She also then seated herself by the fire, and, with a log of wood to raise her feet from the stone floor and prevent her wool from rolling out of her lap, began with lean fingers the knitting of a homespun sock.

'Can't you find nothing to do, Peter?' she asked her younger brother as he lumbered across the room in his huge mud-caked boots and flung himself on to the settle.

'Ben't a man to have no rest, day nor night?' he answered. 'I've been ploughing since dawn.'

'Rest! What about mother and I? Haven't we been churning and baking and dressing fowls for market for as many hours as ever you ploughed? There's no leaving our evening's work undone on that account.'

'No, no,' Mrs Griffith murmured, knowing that she also was touched by this reproof. 'I must do a bit o' mending now.'

She rose with an effort, for her every joint was stiff, and took down a tattered coat from a nail in the wall. This was the only form of wardrobe known at Tinygraig.

'I am needing a new basket, Peter,' Jane's high-pitched voice continued. 'You could be making me one instead o' rolling about there as idle as a calf turned out to grass.'

The youth stretched himself before the fire and grinned his indifference to her taunts. His steaming clothes gave off a mixed odour of greasy wool, peat smoke and sweat; his hands, when he drew them from his pockets, reeked of the tobacco he kept there – a precious substance, too costly to be chewed every day. He had torn off a piece of it now and thrust it between his teeth.

'Go you on,' he said. 'I'm tired,' and lay still.

A lover of strength would have found his face comely. It had exposure's rich colouring, and the eyes, heavily lidded in a fashion that gave insolence to his stare, were clear with health. The forehead was low and broad, the nose short, the chin powerful. The limbs, clumsy though they were, had a slack dignity in repose.

'Come you, boy,' his father said with unexpected decision. 'We are all tired o' working, but labour is our lot here below, and if we aren't keeping at it we won't never raise the money needed for Gronwy's education.'

At the mention of his brother, Peter heaved himself up and let out a regretful breath. But without argument he fetched from an outhouse a bundle of wands such as children make into fishing rods. When he returned, his father's clasp knife was already out, and, seated side by side, they proceeded to slice each wand into two parts. Jane, appeased, continued her knitting; Mrs Griffith nodded over the coat she could hardly see to mend; and behind them Gronwy stood alone the shadows, caressing the backs of books that stood upon a single shelf.

'Is there no work for me to do, Jane?' he asked suddenly.

The four at the fire exchanged anxious glances.

'We wasn't liking to ask you,' his mother said for them all.

He advanced into the ring of firelight and laid slim,

nervous fingers on her shoulders. 'Mother, dear, this cannot go on for ever.'

She dropped her mending and peered up at him, her red-rimmed eyes moist with solicitude. 'Whatever's wrong with you tonight, boy?'

'There's nothing more wrong than usual. It's been the same now for years. You loyal folk working yourselves to death just for me. What is the use of it?'

'We have saved a few pounds a'ready,' cried Jane.

He looked at her sadly. 'The first bad harvest will swallow up your few pounds,' he said.

'But maybe the harvests'll keep good for two or three years running,' his mother answered, patting his hand.

'If they were to be good for ten years – for twenty years, d'you think you'd save enough for such an education as we dream of? No, no. 'Tis not for the son of a poor farmer.'

His father had let fall his knife. 'Maybe the boy is right,' he muttered, 'and happiness is not for us on this side o' the grave. I was looking for it on earth when I was young. Listening to the stiff-necked talk o' Chartists I was.' He checked himself, and concluded almost slyly: 'Well, well, if we do keep honest here, we shall have our reward hereafter – maybe.'

But Peter leaned forward and brought down a gigantic fist on his knee. 'We might have our reward here and now, father, if only we did keep sober and drive hard bargains. More money is to be made by that than by all your honest, dull old work.'

'Yes, yes,' Mrs Griffith agreed. 'Peter do talk sense. If only you was able to leave the drink alone, we might yet save the money Gronwy do need.'

John Griffith shook his head. His grey beard and tangle of hair swayed to and fro. 'Drink was given by God to man that he might bear his sorrows,' he said. 'If I hadn't been getting market merry once in a while, how should I have stood up against late springs and the death o' so many of our lambs and our children? 'T'as been nothing only loss since we were married, missus. First there was the fowls taken by the disease; then, in the very same year, my poor old parents – not as they was much loss, being gone too simple to work; then there was the twins and a cart mare worth a lot o' money, and a little black pig, all together did go to meet their Maker.'

His wife cut him short. 'I did have to suffer the loss o' my children sober,' said she.

'Yes, yes. 'T'as been hard on you, missus. But, as I was saying, you'll have your reward hereafter.' And once again he added after a pause, 'maybe'.

Gronwy spoke from the shadows behind his mother's chair. 'What do we know of the hereafter?'

'What the Bible do tell us, boy. Come you, and read us a chapter to lift up our hearts from our poverty.'

'I would rather read you summat o' Shakespeare's tonight. I am in no mood for piety and resignation.'

'Pity to hear you speak so,' John Griffith said. 'Once I too had a high look and a proud stomach and wanted to do as the colliers did that marched on Newport when I was young. But what came of it? Ill things came of it. Transportation. Prison.' Very low, he repeated that word, twisting it in his mind. Then, suddenly raising his voice, 'No, no, boy,' he said, 'don't you never forget 'tis written as the meek shall inherit the earth. No good'll come o' your learning if 'tis making you stiff-necked.'

'No good will come of it in any case, I fear.'

John Griffith was about to reply when his wife leaned forward and touched his arm. 'Leave the boy be,' she whispered. 'One o' his seasons o' blackness is upon him.'

But Jane spoke in a loud voice. 'Listen to me, Grono. You've been getting terrible daunted o' late because we don't get no nearer making you a teacher or a parson.'

He nodded. 'It's hopeless.'

''Tis nothing o' the sort.' Her eyes and her knitting needles flashed together. 'If we can't raise money enough ourselves, we'll borrow it off the squire.'

'The squire?' the others echoed.

'Squire Wingfield? He hasn't the name o' helping the poor much.'

'Well then,' Jane persisted, 'we'll have it off Parson Jones. *He* did use to be a kind man whatever.'

'Kind enough, yes. But he wasn't rich.'

'He'll have grown rich,' she answered confidently, 'since he's lived a good few years now near a fine place like Newport.'

At the name of Newport John Griffith began again to mumble in his beard. Gronwy caught the words 'Chartists' and 'only bringing us into trouble.' What part his father had played in the disturbances of the thirties he did not know, for the old man could never be led to talk openly of the years he had spent away from his native parish. All that his children knew of them was that they had left him with a terror of revolutionary agitation which was forgotten only when he was in drink.

'No use to dwell on the past,' Gronwy said at length. 'Shall I finish the play I was reading you?'

Peter's face brightened. 'The one about the young man as was going to climb up a ladder o' ropes to his sweetheart's bedroom? 'Twasn't a bad beginning to a story that. Go you on an' read to us about the morning after.'

''Twas written grand and scholarly no doubt,' Mrs Griffith conceded, 'but 'twasn't hardly showing so good an example as some o' them nice Sabbath tales Jane was reading me.'

'Whatever do it matter what the old play is about?' Jane demanded. ''Tis for the sake o' hearing Gronwy read such terrible big words so quick an' easy as we are listening to it. Let's have a candle, Mother.'

Mrs Griffith fetched a homemade tallow dip no thicker than a pencil, and sitting down beside her son, she began fondly to gaze at him. The others drew close and waited in silence.

Gronwy, with his fingers among the pages of the book, looked at the little group as a lonely man might look at the upturned faces of his dogs, grateful for their company but saddened by its incompleteness, wishing that they might understand the language he spoke. Not with contempt but with sad affection, this likeness of his family to dogs floated in his mind, until suddenly, meeting his sister's eyes, he realised that her attitude towards him was precisely that of a trainer towards a performing animal. She – aye, all of them – had made great sacrifices in order that he might play the scholar; now with Shakespeare on his knee – or, in different language, with a lump of sugar on his nose – he was about to exhibit his trick.

This thought gave hardness to his opening words. Poetry, which was for him a way of escape, could not on this occasion grant him swift release. He found himself thinking while he read, not of the romantic world in which he loved to wander, but of his own daily life of labour – of the pigsty's stench when he cleaned it, of the slaughterings of sheep and poultry, of the blood and manure so often mingled in the farmyard, of the slow thrusting of hunger in the belly and of cold's deep ache in the cavities of the eyes. Other words drifted across the words he was reading.

> "'It was the lark,'" said his voice—
>
> "'It was the lark, the herald of the morn,
> No nightingale: look, love, what envious streaks
> Do lace the severing clouds in yonder east.'"

But his mind, clinging yet to his own earth, repeated again and again—

"The hare limp'd trembling through the frozen grass
And silent was the flock in woolly fold—"

repeated it until monotony dulled and quietened it, and it faded, and with it faded also the remembrance of labour and pain and of all the life that was his. A slow enchantment numbed him to present experience, so that he became unaware of any listeners. He saw Juliet at her window in the dawn, her hand beneath his own, her throat engraved with the earliest shadows of day. He saw her stoop to him in farewell and, with personal echo to her foreboding, heard her whisper:

'O God! I have an ill-divining soul.
Methinks I see thee, now thou art below.
As one dead in the bottom of a tomb.'

She was his own love and to him vowed her faithfulness. She was his and for him entered the grave. It was in the churchyard at Llangantyn that they laid her. He fell upon earth there, the wet grass coldly streaked under his extended wrists, crying out to the imagined dead of his heart. His eyes were overflowing with tears, and he read with a struggle the last scene, caring little for it, down to the concluding rhyme.

A blank space of paper then confronted him. As he stared at it, he perceived that it was dirty and ragged at the edges, and was recalled by it to his own world. Slowly, as he raised his head, he became aware of the room in which he and his family passed all the hours that were not given to sleep or to labour out of doors – the open hearth heavily obscured by smoke, the damp-stained walls clammy to touch, the tiny window that never opened. His father had fallen asleep. With gnarled hands dangling and shoulders bowed he looked as he did after one of those drinking bouts in which he tried to recapture the self-confidence of his youth. 'Poor foolish old man,' Gronwy thought. His mother too was sleeping. Her toothless mouth had dropped open. In the firelight a trickle of saliva glistened like a slug's trail upon her chin and lost itself in the loose folds of her throat. The flesh had been worn off her frame, and save where the empty skin hung in pouches, the muscles and bones were laid bare as in an anatomical chart. Gronwy averted his eyes. He wanted, like the heroes of whom he had read, to feel for his mother romantic and tender admiration, and the mingled pity and disgust, which were in fact all the sentiment she aroused in him, made him ashamed and ill at ease in her presence, and caused him to turn away. Peter was scowling over a stiff withy. Poverty had already blunted the youth in him, giving an appearance of brutality to one not brutal at heart. Upon Jane it had had an opposite effect, giving an edge to what was naturally sharp in her and depriving her of whatever softness might have clung to her early twenties. 'And in this place,' Gronwy thought, 'and surrounded by these folk – God forgive me for not loving them more – I must drag out my life unless I can come by the means of escape.'

The sound of knocking brought Jane to her feet. She had crossed the room with a clatter of nailed boots and her hand was upon the latch before her parents were fully awake. A flapping of windblown skirts and a twittering like that of sparrows at dawn followed the opening of the door. 'Gels!' thought Peter, 'now we'll be having a bit o' fun for a change,' and he passed the tip of his tongue across his lips.

'No, no,' cried one of the visitors as Jane hurried her towards the circle of firelight, 'we aren't fit to be seen. The rain came on so on the hilltop. My bonnet's quite spoiled – a stylish new one too!'

'Come on and warm yourself whoever you be,' John Griffith called over his shoulder.

'Let me put myself tidy first, then,' she pleaded. 'I must be looking like a scarecrow, I declare. You haven't a glass anywhere about, have you?'

Peter began to laugh and nudged his brother; but Gronwy, who had swung round in his chair at the sound of the girl's voice, was frowning and took no notice of him.

'She's a smart little piece,' Peter whispered, as he watched her unwrapping the shawl that had given to her slight figure the appearance of a mummy, and applying dexterous pats to her hair. At last she came forward with mincing steps, swinging her bonnet by its strings and smiling archly at Gronwy.

'I dare say you've forgotten me, Mr Griffith,' she said, seating herself between the old man and his wife and according to them and their deficiencies in dress a glance of amused patronage. 'I suppose I've changed a good deal.' She looked down at her hands which were thin as the claws of a small bird, and turned them this way and that in front of the fire to obtain the greatest possible glitter from her rings.

'You're not the fine lady that you take yourself to be,' Peter decided. He did not like her pert prettiness now that he had studied it at close range, but he imagined that it would be good fun to kiss her against her will. 'She would scratch same as a cat in a trap,' he thought, grinning.

'I'm Susan Jones,' she explained, 'daughter of Mr Thomas Jones who had to take a place as a cowherd at the mansion here when he lost his money.'

'Ah, old Tom Jones to be sure,' said John Griffith. 'Well, I never heard tell as he were anything but a cowherd all his life.'

'Oh dear me, yes. He was quite a wealthy farmer once. Poor Papa! He was really too much of a gentleman, if you take my meaning Mr Griffith, to do well at anything.'

'Was he indeed? Well, well, fancy your being the little lump of a gel I mind running after the cattle as quick as our Jane here. Your hair's not changed its lively colour, I see. They did use to call you "vixen" along o' that and your small little pointy face and your sharp white teeth. Are you going by that name still?'

'Good gracious, no! I'm Miss Wingfield's maid now and treated very respectful by the other servants, I assure you. Me and the housekeeper and Mr Pink, the butler, keep ourselves quite apart from the under ones of course, and I always dress for supper in the hall every night.'

The other visitor had by now emerged from behind the settle. As she stooped to kiss Mrs Griffith, her face was seen to be round, red and wholesome as a ripe apple. Peter at once made room for her. Because she had been the companion of his childhood, his manner towards her was neither insolent nor clumsily gallant. Betty Evans was for him not like other girls. She was a friend.

'Any news, Betty?' he asked, pulling her down beside him.

She gave him a grateful glance and the crimson of her cheeks spread over her smiling face. 'Father's a bit simple like,' she answered. 'He do fret mortal for my brothers as is gone to the works.' She tried to look as sorry as she knew it was her duty to feel, but while she was sitting close to Peter it was difficult for her to be anything but happy.

'Your father have got the little lumper Benjamin growing up to be more of a comfort to him nor the others have been,' said John Griffith.

'So I do pray to God every night and morning whatever,' Elizabeth answered.

Susan began to fidget. It was low class to talk about one's prayers. Conversation under the housekeeper's presidency was strictly bound by the reticences of the drawing-room; in neither place did one speak of heaven, beds or baths in a personal relation, though God indeed was understood to be present with other well-dressed folk in Church on Sunday mornings, and large cans of water were undoubtedly carried into Miss Wingfield's bedroom on appointed occasions. But one did not mention these things when lightly conversing in mixed company. These people, Susan thought, were very poor and ignorant. Welshy in their talk, too, and common. For a moment she was ashamed of herself for having come back to them. Then she looked at Gronwy. In the presence of this unkempt labourer she could forget to be a ladies' maid; could forget, too, to be resentful of the attention that was being paid to so insignificant a creature as Elizabeth Evans.

'Your father is having you to keep house for him,' John Griffith was saying, 'and you're a tidy gel, Betty.'

'Only a gel, though. He do miss his sons.'

'True, a gel's but a gel, however hard working.'

'Betty's better nor most o' the old trash,' said Peter, and added slowly, with pleasure in provoking Susan, 'And what news has old Tom the cowherd's daughter here to give us? You haven't been back in these parts long, have you?'

'Oh no,' she answered, 'and 'tis wonderful how much of the district I've forgotten. That comes of living in higher surroundings of course. I've not been with Miss Wingfield a month yet, and I don't know as I haven't made a mistake to come – leaving a place with fine, well-up gentry down near Aberyscir.' She hesitated, stroked her rings, and at last, with a creditable imitation of aloof nonchalance, went on: 'I met your son at Aberyscir fair last year, Mr Griffith. We got talking, and that put it into my head to come back to the old place.'

'Well well,' he answered, 'Sheep, ponies and Christians do all draw home to the land on which they was weaned.'

'What a vulgar thing to say!' she thought, 'comparing me to the animals!' But, turning to Gronwy, she insisted upon talking about the fair. Did he remember what tough, common people were there? Really, she ought not to have gone to such a place. But she wasn't sorry that she had done so for once. She smiled at him, and looked quickly down at the toes of her elastic-sided boots which peeped out from beneath a fashionably voluminous skirt.

Jane shot glances from her to Gronwy. 'You never told us

nothing about your meeting when you came home,' she said to her brother.

'Didn't I?' He moved uneasily. 'There's so much to tell about a fair.'

'And so many gels one is giving the wink to that day,' added Peter. ''Tisn't likely one would keep count o' them all.'

Susan looked her disgust; the others laughed.

'So your fancy's not fixed to no one in partic'lar?' his father asked.

'No,' Peter answered, feeling very much a man of the world and avoiding Elizabeth's eyes.' There's plenty o' gels I'd go holidaying with if I thought 'em worth the price o' brandy-snaps and bullseyes. But she would have to be something out o' the ordinary as I would take for keeps.'

'What would she have to do to fix your fancy, Peter?' Elizabeth asked, and encountering Jane's scowl flushed crimson.

''Tisn't what she would have to do, but what she would have to be,' Peter announced, grinning.

'And what is that?

'Rich!'

'That's right,' cried Jane. 'I'm glad there's that much sense in one o' the family whatever. Mind you don't never go wasting your time courting a gel whose father isn't no better off than your own. There is wealth wanted for a great purpose here, and until that is served none of us did ought to go acting flighty along o' love.'

John Griffith nodded. 'You are right, gel. It 'on't do for none o' my children to be as I was in the days o' my youth, a romantical, headstrong fellow.'

Jane now perceived that Susan might be of use. 'Susan,' she said 'is the squire reckoned by his servants to be a irritable man? He's terrible distant with us tenants.'

Susan pouted. 'Mr Pink doesn't think much of him; I'm

afraid I was foolish to leave a real first-class place to come here where there's only half the number of servants kept.' She began to tell how her former mistress never wore a pair of lavender or primrose kid gloves more than once, to describe the silver-gilt dinner-service, the laced and powdered flunkies who had nothing to do but to look grand, to boast of the wine that was drunk and the food that was flung away. As she chattered, she watched Gronwy out of the corner of her eye, but he gave no sign of appreciating the sacrifice she had made for his sake.

Jane cut her short at last. 'Could you ask a favour o' the squire's daughter, do you think? If her father is a dry-faced old Englishman without a civil word for no one, she is Welsh on her mother's side whatever. What manner o' lady is she?'

Susan shrugged her shoulders. 'There's no telling. Mrs Smith the housekeeper, who's been with them for years, can't make nothing of her. She's forever reading books. Why, she'll shut herself up in the library even when Squire Lee of Rhayader Hall comes courting her, and he'd be such a good match, keeping foxhounds and the finest cellar in the county, Mr Pink says. If she fancies herself too grand for him, she deserves to die an old maid.'

'She is beautiful,' said Gronwy suddenly, and everyone turned to stare at him. 'I saw her riding a great big black horse,' he murmured. 'Looking like a lady in a picture she was. Beautiful but sad.'

'Beautiful!' Susan tossed her head. 'I shouldn't call any lady that who looks like a stone statue. And she dresses so severe, not a frill on a thing, and a case full of her mother's jewellery she never puts on. She's got no taste at all.'

'Have she any influence on her father?' Jane asked, impatient of useless gossip.

'Why, she hardly speaks to him, Mr Pink tells me. She's very queer. She lived in Italy for years with her aunt after her mother died, so they say.'

'Aye, 'tis true,' said John Griffith. 'She went away from here a little gel and came back not long since a lady. I dare say 'twas doing her no good to live among them nasty old black folk and Papists.'

Susan smiled. She was not so provincial as that. Some very good families were Papists. Really, these Welsh folk seemed to think it a crime to leave the place you were born in. 'Oh,' she cried, 'but the best gentry go to Paris and Baden-Baden. Miss Wingfield is unlike everyone else, that's all – such a pity for the gentleman who marries her. Just fancy, she's got her room full of statues without any clothes on, and…' she added, daring to be unladylike in a spiteful cause, 'when she takes her bath she often doesn't trouble about the screen when I'm there as other ladies do.'

'Gods o' Greece and Rome the statues are, maybe,' Gronwy said.

'I'm sure I don't know what they are – that or Popish images – but horrid, I call it, in an unmarried lady's bedroom.'

'If she's a scholar herself,' Gronwy went on, 'do you think she would take pity on a poor man that wanted the money to get learning?'

Susan was stung to anger by this. She had been trying to attract his attention by a variety of robinlike movements, impudent and timid. She had, as if accidentally, pulled up her skirt to display her little feet. Her beringed hands, of whose gentility she was so proud, had been fluttering in his view. In drawing her chair nearer to the fire she had touched his knee, and quickly swayed away from him with a nervous laugh that was an invitation to pursuit. She had flashed her swift smiles, her sidelong glances all in vain. Piqued at his indifference, furious with herself for having stooped to court a common churl, she snapped out her reply.

'If it's for yourself you want help from Miss Wingfield, you can whistle for it. You may think her beautiful, but I know what she is – hard and selfish like others I could name.' She turned away from him, fearing and resenting his good looks, for she knew them to be enemies of those nice social distinctions by which she set store. But she could not be angry with him long. By the time Elizabeth rose, announcing that they must be going, the natural woman in Susan had again vanquished the ladies' maid.

'Oh, but it's quite early' she declared. 'In gentleman's service, the evening has scarcely begun at this hour. And I've had leave to be out till they lock up tonight.'

None answered her. Since she had told them there was no help to be had from Miss Wingfield, a profound silence had fallen upon the whole family. Peter had ceased to take pleasure in provoking her disdain; Gronwy no longer seemed to feel the embarrassment of her presence or Jane to be jealous of her. Biting her lip with vexation at their neglect, she went to the window and exclaimed upon the darkness of the night. They made no answer. It was one of the darkest, most dangerous nights she had ever known, she said again, but still there was no answer. 'Look at my thin boots!' she said with a genteel titter, and they looked, silently, thinking of other things. But her protestations that she dared not go back with Elizabeth only for company at last attracted the attention for which she had been fretting.

Peter began to laugh. 'I've noticed that there's no gel too timid to venture out at night by herself, nor so bold but what she is wanting a young man to see her home again. Go you, Grono. I've been up with the ewes o' late and labour is a safe charm against love.'

Gronwy too was tired. Elizabeth did not fail to notice the reluctance with which he rose.

'No, no,' she said, gently pushing him back in his chair, 'I do know my way from here blindfold, boy.'

But Susan interposed. 'Oh, that *would* be kind of you, Mr Griffith. I declare I'm the timidest of creatures.' She looked up at him with the air of helpless femininity she had acquired in the houses of the rich. Peter, who remembered her running after the cattle and belabouring them with a stick, laughed once more, to which she replied with a look so spiteful that for a moment it sobered him.

'Hew! Hew!' he said under his breath. 'There's a cross-sticks!'

With a gracious nod to his parents and a promise, which they had not solicited, to visit them again, Susan hurried out after Gronwy. The darkness was a relief to her. Its concealment set her free of her pose. Tom the cowman's red-haired girl, with hot blood throbbing in her veins, might now for a little while lay aside her pretences.

Elizabeth let her pass and lingered on the threshold for a moment to look at Peter. She, too, knew that the youth she loved had little thought for her. 'Whyever should he have for the likes o' me?' she asked herself. 'I'm only a plain, ordinary piece, and, as he was saying hisself, he'll be after a woman with money.' She smiled at him and, smiling, shook her head. 'He's terrible fond o' the money is Peter,' she thought, for she knew his faults as she knew her own and never expected him to be other than he was. 'He's been kind to me tonight whatever,' she added to herself, 'letting me sit beside him, God bless him.'

Peter heard her parting 'goodnight,' but did not trouble to look round. Nevertheless she was still smiling as she went out alone.

II

'Betty!'

She heard her name called in an urgent whisper and felt her hands caught in a grip that was not weak or ladylike.

'Listen, dear. I want you to lag behind when we are clear of the fold. I have something to say to – to young Mr Griffith.'

'Is that why you was so mortal set on coming here tonight?' Elizabeth asked. 'Whyever didn't you tell me outright as you and he were courting?'

'Because we're not. What nonsense you do talk! Me and him indeed! D'you think I'd look at the likes o' him after the nice refined company – butlers and gentlemen's valets – I've been accustomed to? Hush! Here he is. You will leave us alone together, won't you?

'Oh, a' right!'

The lanthorn he had brought from the stable isolated them in a small circle of light beyond which nothing was visible.

'Oh dear,' Susan complained, 'I can't see where I'm putting my feet. I shall tumble down for certain.'

'Maybe I am holding the lanthorn too high and 'tis dazzling you,' said Gronwy, and lowered it to the full length of his arm.

Patches of the hillside's rough surface now danced between the radial shadows of the lamp, and darkness from above closed down yet further upon the little group of wayfarers. Higher than the waist nothing of them was visible, except when a chance beam, darting up as the light swung forward with Gronwy's stride, struck the tip of a chin or the hollow of a brow or the underside of a hat brim. Perhaps because she was interested by this fantastic illumination and, liking to observe its effect upon Gronwy's face, grew careless of her walking, Susan presently stumbled.

'Oh dear! Oh dear! I'm not used to such rough going. May I take your arm?'

'Yes, if you like,' said he.

Elizabeth, who was privately of opinion that Susan's stumbling had not been due to carelessness at all, now slackened her pace and allowed the others to draw ahead of her. Instantly the sound of their voices was whirled away by the wind; she would not have heard if they had turned and shouted. The wavering light she followed showed her their figures now and then; vague figures, indistinguishable from their own shadows, which swayed and revolved and crumpled in the darkness, seeming now to shoot skyward in gigantic prolongation, now to shrink suddenly into a dwarfish dance. She lifted up her hands; they were no more than a pale blur when held close to her eyes. She looked to her feet and found that she was wading in blackness. But for the pair ahead of her, she would have had no thought of loneliness on this familiar mountain. Now, for lack of companionship, she was sharply assailed. 'I do wish as Peter had cared to come with me,' she sighed. 'How happy I'd have been to walk arm in arm with him as Susan is walking with Gronwy. But there, 'tis terrible cold here, and he's snug by the fireside. That is something to be glad of, whatever.'

While she was thus engaged in her own thought, she observed that the glimmer ahead of her ceased to move forward. She approached with hesitation and halted outside the steadied circle of light. At its centre was one figure only, but soon she heard Susan's sharp voice hailing her from the opposite dark beyond the lamp's range.

'Betty! Betty! Wherever are you?'

'Here.'

'Come on, for goodness sake! I can't think what you wanted to leave us for.'

Elizabeth looked her reproach in the direction of the hidden speaker, but uttered no protest. 'Aren't you coming no further?' she asked Gronwy.

'I'm not wanted no more, it seems.'

An angry laugh rang out of the darkness. 'You mean you've had enough, don't you? It's one thing to begin a business and quite another to go through with it, isn't it Mr Griffith?'

He did not reply, and, as he swung about, Elizabeth found in his face no answering anger but a look of weary distress.

III

When he returned to Tinygraig, he found all within as black as the mountain side without. But here the wind, instead of buffeting him bluntly, found its way like knife blades through the stricken cottage, with whistling mournful as a curlew's cry. Having crouched on the hearth for a while, vainly seeking warmth, he stole up the uncarpeted stairs to the room above. Regular breathing told him that Peter slept, and intensified his sense of loneliness in a house full of labouring folk whose minds were always at rest when his began to be most active. He seated himself upon the bed he shared with his brother. Its worm-eaten frame groaned beneath the additional weight and a fragment of the tattered hangings flapped against his cheek. The floor across which he had tiptoed long continued to give forth plaintive whisperings.

Presently Peter awoke and asked in a drowsy tone, 'Well, any fun with the gels?'

The laugh answering his question was so bitter that it aroused him to complete wakefulness. He sat up, rubbing his sticky eyelids with one hand and feeling for Gronwy with the other.

''Tis you a'right is it? Whatever made you laugh so strange? You've set my inside all of a quiver.'

'Fun! Is that the word you use about the dealings of one sex with the other?'

'Why not? What else but fun is gels made for?'

'They are made, I am thinking, to allure and trouble us, as we are to pursue and to forsake them. If there be any fun in the cruel business it is to the gods whom the ancient Greeks thought mocked us from Olympus.'

Peter lay down again with a grunt.

'Go on! Now you're in one o' your poetical takings when your talk can't be understood no more than the whoso-ever-will-be-saved creed. Though maybe,' he added with pride, ''tis just as scholarly and'll bring us all credit.'

'I am not talking poetry now, boy. Poetry is kind to me. I am talking of love and life.'

'What's the matter? Wouldn't that fox-faced Susan let you kiss her?'

'Only too readily.'

'Then whatever are you so sad about?'

'That I no longer wish to do so.'

'That's her trouble I'd 'a' thought.' And he added: 'If you don't like the haughty piece, whyever was you takin' up with her?'

'When you are older, you may have to ask yourself why you were starting many a business that had been better left alone.' Gronwy rose and began pacing about in the dark. ''Tis gay at a fair,' he said suddenly, 'and you know how a drop o' drink mounts to a man's head, making him forget to look back or to look forward. That's why poor father cannot keep from it. But 'tis not drink alone do lift a man out of his poverty at a fair. There's the strange lights and shadows wheeling past him as he swings faster and faster on the roundabout, and the joy o' motion like as he were bird-free of all the air. He is growing happy and careless, forgetting the curse of Adam, and that he must till the soil all his days in the sweat of his brow. A girl's face upturned to him then is not to be denied.'

'Yes indeed,' Peter agreed, smacking his lips. 'Fairs is wonderful quickening to sin.'

'Sin? Was it sin to kiss her? I did no more. Her pointy chin was like an elf's that night. How her eyes sparkled too! It might have been with the brilliance of a soul behind them, and I, being drunk, was fool enough to think so. She told me she was there alone and frightened when I put my arm around her. "Then I'll take care o' you," I said. "For this one night we'll be sweethearts."

'That were a grand notion,' Peter chuckled, 'to have all the fun o' courting close for an evening and no harm done nor no promise given.'

'But harm was done.'

'But I thought you said as how you only—'

'Yes, yes. But I hurt her none the less. She could not rest until she had found out who I was. She wrote and told me I had made her unhappy.'

'The cunning baggage! And you were so foolish as to write back?'

'And then,' said Gronwy, disregarding the question, 'when I was taking those wethers to Aberyscir – do you remember?'

'Yes, yes. And you saw her again then?'

'By daylight.'

'And she wasn't near so pretty as what you had thought?'

'She was not the same creature.'

'Pity indeed,' said Peter.

'Yes… pity.'

'Well,' said Peter, huddling himself up under the coverlet and preparing to go to sleep again, 'there's no use to cry over spilt milk. It might have been a deal worse. You might have got her in the way.' After a pause he asked with a chuckle, 'What would she have to be like to keep you in love with her in your romantical fashion after sunrise?'

'Like her,' said Gronwy slowly, 'of whom all great pictures are the unconscious portraits, to whom all love poems are addressed, though they bear the names of ordinary women.'

'Whoever is she?'

'Helen, the daughter of Zeus, for whom Paris and Menelaus strove and Troy was burned.'

'It sounds like a prayer as you do say it,' Peter muttered, his nose in the pillow. 'I never heard tell of any o' them folks in these parts.'

CHAPTER II

Spring and Politics – In the Drawing Room – In Laetitia's Bedroom – A Ride and a Rainbow

It was the squire's custom, when he was without guests, to waste no time in the drawing-room preliminaries to a meal. At 5.30 he would go to dress, at 5.59 leave his bedroom, and at 6 o'clock enter the great crimson dining room, expecting to be instantly fed.

There, on an evening of March, his household awaited him. Already it was four minutes beyond the hour. The door was open; the butler stood by his master's chair, having withdrawn it from the table by that number of inches which would most conveniently allow greatness to be seated; and a footman, far away at the sideboard, gripped the handles of a tureen and awaited a sign. Not a sound; not a creak on the stair. All was expectation in silence, frozen and monumental. Laetitia and her brother, side by side on the hearth-rug, stared without seeing it at a vast epergne.

The spring twilights were lengthening, and the candles, in their branched silver sticks, stood up stiffly without flame. The squire, a rigid economist, disapproved the custom of dining by candlelight when daylight would serve. Through the windows, over which the curtains had, therefore, not yet been drawn, the clear evening of a wet day looked gravely in; and Charles Wingfield, turning to smooth his flaxen side-whiskers in the mirror that crowned the mantelpiece, saw his sister's head – the curve of her cheek, her neat chin, her eyelid full and long-lashed, her little ear that was made to seem a marvel of Lilliput by a drop-earring of more than its own length and by a backward mountain of braided hair – very clear cut against a steely and mournful sky.

'I wonder what can have delayed Papa,' he said, wishing to rouse her but unable to think of any remark more likely to make her companionable. 'He's so deuced punctual as a rule – and deuced angry too if I'm ever late.' Then, seeing the butler's face slide across the mirror, he turned about, and, replanting himself straddle-legged on the hearth with his coat-tails hitched up, added for the servants' benefit, 'Of course he's quite right. All the same, it's deuced awkward for a fellow after a run with the hounds to have to gallop home—'

His protest was cut short by the entrance of his father. Scowling slightly, Charles James Maitland Wingfield, Justice of the Peace and sometime High Sheriff of the County, took his place at the head of the table.

'*Benedictus benedicat*,' he rapped out, and picked up the silver ladle as if it had been a weapon. Not a word was spoken until the soup had been served and tasted.

'A touch more sherry,' the squire announced.

'You're right, sir,' Charles agreed. 'My man at Cambridge—'

'You must speak to the housekeeper, Laetitia,' the squire went on, having swallowed another mouthful.

'Very well, Papa,' said she.

Setting down her spoon, she gazed across a stretch of glossy damask at the windows which a hidden sunset had overlaid with primrose. One of the casements was open. Through it came the sound of a thrush, rehearsing his first song of the year. The sweet, shrill notes caught at her heart.

'There's a draught from somewhere,' the squire exclaimed, turning his head with difficulty. A high collar and a monstrous cravat impeded him, for in his fifty-sixth year he remained loyal to the fashions of his youth. 'Shut that window, Pink,' he commanded.

'Very good, sir… John, that window.'

When the footman had obeyed, the song of the bird was shut out. Laetitia's breast moved to an inaudible sigh; for a moment she had thought of protesting, but had closed her lips. Better to allow the routine of dinner to go on without interruption; better to enclose herself within her own thoughts than to risk her father's disturbance. She watched the tureen go and a dish of trout take its place. John bore away the huge pewter cover which had preserved the fish's warmth on its way from the distant kitchen.

Charles and his father at once became absorbed in their trout, and ate on in silence. Tired of their stolid faces, Laetitia let her eyes travel with slow scorn over the room and all that it contained – the heavy furniture contemporary with the Queen's marriage, the embossed plate, the waxen fruit grown pale beneath its glass case, the walls darkened to the colour of clotted blood, the portraits of loose-jowled Wingfields dignified by age – and returned at last to contemplate the shell-like delicacy of her own fingernails. She observed then that her brother was becoming restless. Neither she nor her father wished to interrupt their thoughts by speech, but Charles, who sat between them in space enough for half a score of diners, was growing tired of hearing only the creaking of his own shirt as he turned his head to demand claret.

'I caught these trout myself, sir,' he announced as the bones were removed.

'Indeed?'

'A goodish basket, don't you think, for so early in the year?'

'Quite good.'

'It's been deuced cold, too – fish not rising.'

'Indeed?'

'Are you coming out one of these days, sir?'

'Fishing? Good Gad, I'm far too busy. A landowner who is his own agent, as I conceive it my duty to be, is perpetually immersed in tiresome business.' The squire's lean fingers crumbled his bread. 'Upon my soul, I'm tired to death of it sometimes.'

'Then pray, Papa, why not sell some of the farms?'

He fixed his daughter with an indignant stare; but, as he looked at her, disapproval gave way to indulgence. 'Impair the estate that has come down to me from my great-grandfather? Really, my dear, really! But I suppose the sex cannot be expected to understand what his paternal inheritance means to a man. It's a great trust, a heavy responsibility.' Thinking of his many acres, he relapsed into gloomy silence.

Charles turned for encouragement to his sister. In the fading light her bare shoulders were beginning to take on a luminous pallor. Her face, too, was pale, but her lips, that seemed to be forever pouting, were richly red. Her dark hair, parted in the middle and brushed back severely from a classical forehead, formed at the nape of her neck coils smooth and glossy as those of a great snake. He remembered her wearing her hair in ringlets before she went abroad and preferred that less austere fashion. He supposed that she had now grown into what his friends called 'a damned fine woman', but she was not his ideal of a girl scarcely out of her teens. He liked them to blush and dimple readily, to laugh and chatter. Look at her now! Damn it all, if a woman couldn't talk, what could she do? In despair, he turned again to his father.

'Did the stable-boy bring back the paper from Llangantyn, sir?'

The squire's face, pale as parchment and polished as ivory across the bridge of his aquiline nose, became animated with anger. 'He did. That is what delayed me so. He brought *The Times* for March 13. The news is even worse than I had feared it would be.'

'March 13,' said Charles, struggling to be responsive. 'Let me see… March 13…'

'Damn it all – I beg your pardon, Laetitia – do you mean to tell me you have forgotten what was to happen on the twelfth?'

But Charles could recall neither a race meeting nor any other event of exceptional importance, and his face remained uncomfortably blank.

'The Chancellor of the Exchequer,' Mr Wingfield continued, having given silence time to make its effect, 'the Chancellor of the Exchequer brought forward his Reform Bill.'

'Oh, by Jove, yes, of course.'

'And you had forgotten it? Why, the whole country has been waiting for it in the gravest anxiety, wondering what this hocus pocus Government's policy might prove to be.'

'By Jove, yes,' Charles observed, placidly signing to Pink to refill his glass, 'we don't know where we are, do we?'

'If you had troubled to read your newspaper today,' his father retorted, unmindful that none but himself had had access to *The Times* since it entered the house, 'you would know only too well where we are. The Whigs have gone stark mad since poor Palmerston's death. Upon my soul, I should never have believed that I should so deplore the death of a Whig. It shows how terribly times are changed.' He was so moved that he forgot for a moment to attend to his entrée and even gesticulated with his hands as though he had been related to his Welsh tenants. 'These Liberals, as the new-fangled Whigs call themselves – Liberals! Confound their impudence, as though they were the only liberal-minded men in the country, a pack of Lancashire cotton-spinners for the most part – these Liberals, I say, are hand in glove with Bright, and rascals of his kidney.'

A sirloin of beef was set before him. He slashed at it with the carving knife. 'It's past endurance that such men – upstarts no gentleman would receive in his house – should rule the country. I don't know what the great Whig landowners are about. Why can't they see they'll be ruined like the rest of us if they play into the hands of these ruffians?'

Seeing that the beef was not getting carved as it should be, Charles interposed. 'I dare say you are right, sir; but it does no good to take a dismal view.'

The squire sighed. He seemed to grow older as the unwonted flash of animation left his face and his habitually careworn expression returned. 'No, I suppose one must check one's forebodings – especially in the presence of ladies, eh Laetitia? You must forgive me, my dear, for talking politics in front of you, but upon my soul I find it hard to keep my thoughts off them tonight. The Bill of '32 has done harm enough already. Goodness knows what will become of the old country when this new Chancellor has had his way.'

'Who is he?' she asked, rousing herself from a reverie.

'Mr Gladstone, of course. Pray do you never read the news, either of you young people?'

She glanced at her brother and smiled faintly. 'Charles reads *The Field* I believe. As for your paper, Papa, when you will part with it – a week old – I find it contains nothing but dull speeches made in the House, law reports and advertisements.'

'The world's business, my dear.'

'But ladies are not expected to take much interest in such things, are they?'

'Possibly not. Though I dare say they would do you more good than the three volume novels I find lying about all over the place, and the poetry books you take out of my library and forget to return to their proper shelves.'

She made no reply, but smiled again, this time with

eyebrows slightly raised. Jellies and pies were being handed round. Charles, helping himself lavishly, tried to start a fresh hare.

'I must order 'em to wash Jup,' said he. 'She's been rolling on a dead crow. It's rum how terriers love carrion.'

His sister gave him a disdainful glance and by his father he was ignored. His face was reddened by the wine he had drunk and the heat of a fire piled high with logs; his hair, brushed with Macassar oil into curls that met his side-whiskers, showed light against his cheeks as the horse-radish shavings against an underdone joint of beef; his heavy lower jaw was beginning to thrust itself forward. In spite of an awed respect for his father that dated from days when he had associated the library with canings, he resented being treated like a child. 'Damn it all,' he thought, 'I'm five and twenty. I drove a four-in-hand at the Varsity and I'm a member of Whites.' Staring at the cluster of glasses before him, he tried to think of what he could say that might at once show him to be a grown man, and keep his father from delivering an address on politics. Suddenly, as inspiration came, the worried look that had given him the air of a puppy listening to a strange sound disappeared, and left him smiling.

'I've been round some of the farms today,' he said brightly. 'They need new gates.'

'New gates, do they?' said the squire; and Charles's face fell as he realised that his attempted diversion was in vain. 'There'll be little enough land of ours to need gates at all, if these Radical fellows have their way.'

'Oh, come sir!' exclaimed Charles, not to be beaten yet. 'What can the pack of 'em do to us?'

'All the injury in the world. It's our goose they intend to cook. That blackguard Mill, member for Westminster, threatens land before all other property. Bright, too, has attacked large estate owners, and—'

'Let 'em yap, sir. Let 'em yap,' said Charles heroically.

But the squire was not to be comforted. 'They'll do more than yap, I promise you, if Gladstone gets his way. It's to the city mob, inflamed by such demagogues as these, that he proposes to extend his franchise. Don't you understand that? If such a calamity should come about, the country voters would be outnumbered. That would be a pretty kettle of fish for me – and for you after me. Worse for you. Landowners taxed out of existence. Agriculture ruined. It's coming; you mark my words.'

He talked on in a voice dulled by despondency. His son pretended to listen, wishing to God that he had let well alone, but eating none the less heartily for the political storm. Presently the transformation was made which nightly accompanied the serving of dessert. Glass, china and silver were carried away; the cloth, larger than a sheet, was folded by John and Pink with the accurate ceremony of advance and retreat used by stately partners in a minuet; and the beauty of plain wood, polished to the liquid transparency of porcelain glaze, was laid bare.

Laetitia leaned forward to look at the reflected oval of her face. A water lily, she thought gravely, floating in a pool. Or did not Narcissus look thus, wan with regret because he could find none worthy to love but himself? She longed to stoop down and kiss those lips which, she knew, would feel colder than her own. She liked her lips, for they smiled when she was charmed by some lyric; they quivered when she wept tears of sensibility over a novel by Miss Braddon. She was not a little pleased by their smile and their quiver. Often when her yearning for sympathetic companionship became intolerable, she sought her own reflection in one of the many gilt-framed looking-glasses with which the drawing room was adorned, and found a mournful pleasure in its assurance that neither grief nor disdain nor boredom marred her face's beauty. Its varying expressions – studied with a curiosity sprung naturally from solitude, not with the arrogance of common vanity – were unfailingly of interest to her, and she would now have continued to gaze at herself, forgetful of her surroundings and weaving a thin, wistful romance round the features confronting her, if Pink's hands, placing a fingerbowl at her side, had not shattered her mirror and substituted for Narcissus and Francesca and Elaine the red glass then in fashion, a lace doily, and a plate of Sèvres tinkling with a silver knife and fork handled in mother of pearl.

'Port, Miss?'

She made a weary movement with her head. Would they never have done eating and drinking? She raised her eyes to the window. Against an empty sky, colourless as water, the branch of a lilac bush had the precision of an etching. Every night for a week past, while her relations had been eating, she had watched the dark thicken behind it. On the first evening on which the crimson curtains had not been drawn, her father too had noticed the friendly little tree. 'Too near the house. I must have it cut down,' he had said; and she, though unprotesting, had thought, 'Yes. Here all lovely, living things are either killed or clipped into distorted shapes.' But the squire had forgotten this innocent, which seemed to have strayed into his domain from some cottage garden, and tonight it was swaying gently across the window. 'There's a breeze out there, then,' Laetitia thought. Tonight in her diary she would describe at length her love of spring. She would write of the poet's daffodils and how she had painted them last year. The sketch, she remembered, had been destroyed. Perhaps that was as well… how nice it would be to have a reputation as an artist for works which no unkind critical eye had seen! No one could now deny that Jane Eyre's symbolic pictures had been masterpieces, and the daffodil sketch, if the diary described it fully, might enjoy the same ghostly immortality. Her thought, drifting here and there, caught only at those fragments of life which romantic literature had chosen to honour – at nightingales and roses, at Gothic ruins in moonlight and love at first sight – and returned at last to daffodils once more. She murmured inaudibly the opening lines of a favourite poem – 'I wandered lonely as a cloud'. How true those words were of herself, she reflected – for, however far her thoughts strayed among the stage properties of the romantics, they always returned sooner or later to her own loneliness. She lived in an enchanted prison of self-pity, confined less by the ugly house she inhabited than by her own circle of mental mirrors.

Trying to escape from herself, she fixed her attention once more on the lilac branch, and saw that it had changed in outline since first she had noticed it a fortnight earlier. The buds had grown fuller and were ready to burst into leaf. Why, then, spring, for which she had sighed, was already here! She rose with a gesture that might have developed into a clapping of hands, so glad was she at heart.

'Time you left us to finish our port, my dear?' the squire said, glancing at the clock to see whether the correct time for her withdrawal had been reached. She, he had noticed, had a tendency to cut meals short; his son to prolong them. Sometimes he feared that if his authority were relaxed they would eat separately at their own time and pace, and the decent amenities of family life be allowed to perish. Laetitia, following his thought, was provoked into saying, as he opened the door for her:

'Thank you, Papa. I finished all I wanted to eat three-quarters of an hour ago.'

He ignored the remark. So like one of her poor mother's! Welsh both of them; and nobody could understand these moody Celts. Holding the door wide, 'We shall not take tea with you in the drawing room tonight,' he announced. 'I am teaching Charles how to manage the estate. Estate management would be Greek to you, eh?'

'Why not try to teach me something about it, Papa?' she

asked, feeling that any change from her embroidery frame would be welcome.

He shook his head and smiled at her as at a child. 'If ever you have an estate, you will have a husband to manage it for you, my dear.'

There was approval in the long look he gave her. Slim, erect, restrained in manner, yet with a promise of passion in those dark eyes of hers, she was a daughter to be proud of; a curbed thoroughbred. 'I must see about making a rare good match for her,' he told himself, but an instinct deeper than family pride, an instinct which had driven him to discourage the visits of all young men to his house, added 'not yet – not just yet.' He watched her sweep across the hall and for an instant continued to watch the corner at which she had disappeared. Then, moving slowly and unwillingly, he returned to those excellent but inferior possessions – his son and his decanter. Curious, how little use they were to him! They couldn't take his mind away from its fears for his home and his class. Only Laetitia could do that. She, like her mother before her, could make him glad or angry independently of his herd. Now that she was gone, he came back to his herd, the landed gentry; and began a dismal elegy on Palmerston – 'Whig though he was.' It bored him and it bored Charles. But there was nothing else to talk about when they were together.

II

A great fire had overheated the drawing room and filled it with the faint mustiness of a museum. Dragging back the curtains, Laetitia found the evening deepening to peacock blue. Such, she thought at once, was the evening sky of Italy, painted by the masters she loved best. She clasped her hands and threw back her head in genuine adoration, but on the instant became aware of her pose. How solitary her figure was! She alone in all the great household, intent on its port or below stairs on its cheese and beer, could turn to natural beauty from the pleasures of the table. Was the thrush, she wondered, whose song had been excluded, still singing out of doors? She opened the window and listened in vain. Soon the gardeners would tear down his nest and slaughter his fledglings. Later in the year they would kill him also if he dared the fruit garden. She was filled with melancholy by his imagined fate. No one else, she reflected, would care.

She sent away the footman who came to light the candles, and had long been sitting in darkness when, at nine o'clock, the butler entered, carrying before him a silver tray large as a shield, followed by John, this time with a lamp. Its light danced upon the great urn and its many satellites with which she was to make for herself one cup of tea. Her hand went to her reticule to find the key of the teapoy; then, after a moment's hesitation, she waved the whole paraphernalia aside.

'No, Pink, thank you. You can take them all away. And I do not wish those curtains to be drawn – or that window shut. You need not make up the fire. It is stifling in here already.'

'Very good, Miss.'

Soft footed, impenetrable of face, they began to withdraw as they had come, in order of precedence. Something in their resemblance to toy soldiers made Laetitia smile. How ridiculous was John's livery – as ornate as the fantastically shaped little chairs, covered with geometrical patterns in cross-stitch, which crowded the room! Even human beings were distorted in this house.

'Pink, 'she said, yielding to a sudden impulse.

'Yes, Miss?'

'Order my horse for me please. I am going out riding – now, at once.'

'Very good, miss.'

It was a relief to know she could shock him into a flicker of surprise. Before his lids narrowed again over his expressionless eyes, she swept past him and ran upstairs, laughing to herself and in high danger of tripping over her silks. What fun it would be to outrage the proprieties by riding alone at night! For one happy moment she forgot to be the squire's daughter and the figurehead of his house. She forgot, too – and perhaps it was the greater relief – that she was the niece of Miss Olivia Gwynne who had taught her how sad but proud a thing it is to be an artist among Philistines. She was by the grace of God in that moment, a girl of twenty in exuberant health, who had eaten a good dinner and was going for a madcap ride in the dark.

III

The bodice of her dress was rigid with whalebone and she could not reach the hooks between her shoulder blades. Her fingers, unpractised as those of a child, fumbled at the necklace and massive bracelets which her father liked to see her wear. At last she tugged impatiently at the bell rope. Was it impossible to escape from a maid's prying? Even at picnics there were footmen to carry the luncheon-baskets and uncork the champagne.

When Susan appeared, she found her mistress lighting a row of candles on the dressing table.

'Quick, Jones, unhook me!'

As soon as she was free of it, Laetitia flung her bodice on to the floor. Her slight figure rose out of the stack of her crinoline.

'Let me out of all this wire and stuff and unlace my stays… that's better; now I can breathe… now for my riding habit.'

So great was Susan's astonishment that she lapsed into her native dialect. 'Surely to goodness, you are not goin' ridin' at this hour, miss?'

'I am.'

'Then, miss, begging your pardon, at what time will you be requiring me to undress you?'

'You need not stay up. I can manage somehow without you.'

'But if no one is up, miss, and you should be out after ten, how will you get into the house?'

'Oh, I never thought of that. The keys are taken to Papa when he reads prayers, of course. Well, tell the housekeeper to leave the back door unlocked for once. Oh! that reminds me. Wait.'

She took up a pen and wrote, smiling:

'Dear Papa,
Wd you please excuse me if I said my own prayers tonight. I write this from my bedroom.

Sleep well, dear Papa.
Your affec[te] daughter
L. W.'

She folded the note, put it in an envelope which she elaborately sealed, and held it out. 'There! Give that to your master.'

Susan looked at it. 'If you'll pardon me for saying so, miss – the housekeeper, she will be in a way.'

'Why?'

'Well, miss –'Susan began to smirk and bridle. 'I don't hardly like to tell you, miss.'

'She can scarcely suppose that anyone would dare to break into a magistrate's house.'

'Oh no, miss. It's not that. But you see, she's English, is Mrs Smith, and she doesn't hold with the local Welsh custom.'

'What custom?'

'Really, I don't like to talk of it to a lady – night courtin', miss, if you must know.'

'Oh? "Bundling" don't they call it?' said Laetitia to Susan's astonishment.

'Well, yes miss, they do. Of course in the housekeeper's room we all think it very low and common. But the kitchen-maids and that lot – well, there was one dismissed without a character only the other day for keeping company with her young man in the stables after dark.'

'Poor girl. I dare say there was no harm in it.'

'Perhaps not, miss. She didn't get into trouble, not that we could find out at least. But harmless or not, Mrs Smith won't countenance it.'

Laetitia drummed on the table with impatient fingers. 'A little tragedy,' she thought, 'of two races and two traditions. And I, who am supposed to be mistress here, knew nothing of it at all. My return from Italy has made no difference to any of them.'

'You will tell the housekeeper that it is my wish that the door be left ajar,' she said, in a tone that allowed of no further comment.

'Very good, miss.'

Susan's lips were drawn tight by envy of this girl who could indulge in night adventure without risk of misrepresentation and disgrace. She was envious, too, of the luxury by which Laetitia was surrounded. Her little fox face peered greedily hither and thither, as she counted the value of all she saw. How she herself would have liked to sit where her mistress now sat to be attended by an obsequious maid! How she would enjoy wearing the bright colours that would distinguish her from those by whom she was served! She did not wonder that the quality would allow their servants to wear nothing becoming. She would see to it that *her* maid's hair was flat as the painted head of a Dutch doll; that her skirts were not inflated by a crinoline equal to her own; that all those to whom she paid wages rendered her every curtsy, 'by your leave,' and 'begging your pardon ma'am' to which she was entitled. For Susan found no fault with the system. Her discontent was with the place in it which she had been born to fill. She was no leveller; she felt only envy for Laetitia's pride; but she hated her beauty. Gronwy had noticed her riding past 'like a lady in a picture'. Susan's lips closed with real bitterness on that thought.

'Is that all I can do for you, miss?' she forced herself to ask.

'Yes, thank you.'

'Are you quite sure you would not like me to sit up for you, miss?'

'Quite.'

'Thank you, miss. I'm very much obliged, I'm sure.' She opened the door and stood beside it respectfully until her mistress was gone. Then, turning back to the room with its litter of costly clothes left for her to pick up, 'Some day,' she thought, 'I'll tell her to her proud face what I think of her, though I lose my place for it.'

IV

Somewhere in the stable yard a bucket was noisily overturned; a plunging of hoofs answered it. Laetitia stood still and drew the night air rushing over her lips. A bar of light strayed over the whitewashed buildings so that they leaped towards her like the buildings of a dream.

'If I ride alone on such a night as this,' she told herself, 'perhaps I shall see fairies.'

A bandy-legged groom, in whom she pretended to recognise a gnome, led out her horse. The lamp was carried forward by the gnome's attendant – a small lad with wrinkled gaiters – and set down clattering on the bricks. The horse would not stand. He seemed to her the horse of a giant, wheeling above her and throwing his impatient head across the sky; she saw the muscles of his flanks shine and, as he swung away from her, flakes of light slid downwards over their curves; far up in the dark, the white of an eye was turned upon her and foam glistened for an instant upon steel.

At last he stood, quivering. A wave of fear ran hotly down her spine, but she welcomed it, and, setting her foot in the hands held out by the stooping groom, she sprang to saddle.

'I shan't want you,' she called down.

The horse beneath her curvetted and snatched at his bit, and the groom, taking the lanthorn from the boy's hand, ran forward, speaking words she could not hear. His face, redly illumined and deeply cut by shadow, was like a grotesque carved in cornelian.

'You 'on't take no one with you, miss?' she heard him say at last. How ludicrously astonished they all looked at her daring to ride alone!

'No,' she laughed, tickling her horse's ribs to make him play up yet more and wondering with a thrill what would happen if he bolted with her in the dark. It was worth risking. Any sensation was better than none.

'I'll be waiting up to take your horse when you do come back then, miss,' the groom called after her as she rode out of the yard.

What a mercy he had thought of that! She had never groomed or fed a horse in her life. The thought of her dependence on the service of others stung her. 'I'll learn to do everything myself,' she declared, and pictured the horror on the servant's faces if ever she should attempt to put her resolution into practice. She remembered her old governess taking her to task for putting coal on the fire instead of ringing for the schoolroom maid. So it would always be. But tonight she would not care. Tonight she had broken free. She tickled her horse again and laughed; as she entered the wood she began to sing. Dead leaves rustled, branches cracked beneath the dancing hoofs. From overhead came the chatter of awakened birds. High up in the topmost branches of the trees the voice of the wind could be heard above her own. Horse and rider were of one mood. He, quivering with excitement, threw up his head and shied with a wild swerve whenever a rabbit scuttled across the drive. 'That's the spirit, Ajax!' she cried. 'Make the most of everything. Deceive yourself that a common rabbit is some rare monster, and you'll find this dull life quite enchanting.'

At the far end of the plantation they encountered a gust of wind from the open hills, sharp with peat and with salt from the distant sea. She drew rein and looked about her. The hillside rose in a hump against a sky but little lighter than itself. The moon was not yet up, but here and there, between ragged clouds low-flying, stars gleamed. Of the river valley below her home she could see nothing. Submerged by a lake of mist, it was now a white blur in the surrounding darkness.

'How I hate that sodden valley!' she told her horse. 'Let's make for the hilltops.'

They scrambled upward until there was spread before them an empty tableland covered with grass, through the bents of which the wind went whistling. Ahead the sky was growing lighter, turning from indigo to mother of pearl; and towards this lightness Laetitia pressed on until at last the moon rose over the edge of the wilderness. Then, dropping her hands, she stirred Ajax into a gallop, full into the moon's face. It seemed to sway above her, intermittently visible, a thin disc giving out no more brightness than a white plate hung in the sky. Then, by degrees, the wisps of cloud that had hung across it gathered and thickened until the ghost of light was obscured. The mist swirled down on every side, a heavy torrent, cold as a mountain spring. Reluctantly Laetitia reined in her horse.

'I hate going home,' she thought, 'but this is too chilly.' Physical discomfort had robbed her adventure of its charm. She began to long for the fire burning in her bedroom, for the water that would be awaiting her there kept hot beneath a cosy, and for the touch of linen sheets lately caressed by a warming-pan. Wheeling her horse about, she set him again at a gallop, but soon the darkness had so thickened that she could see nothing in front of her but his pricked ears, and was forced to check him to a walking pace, comforting herself with the thought that he would find his own way back to his stable. Before long, however, he stopped and sniffed at the ground. A touch of her whip set him plunging to one side, and the sound of water oozing up from boggy land warned her of danger. She wheeled him about again and in so doing lost her direction. The wind had fallen. There was nothing to tell her whether she was facing towards home or not – no light on earth or in the heavens, no sound, no path or visible landmark. She was enclosed by a clammy and impenetrable vapour so thick that it was rough to breathe. Ajax began to shiver violently, perhaps with cold, perhaps because she had communicated her anxiety to him. Leaning forward, she patted his neck and urged him to go on, but he was clearly reluctant to move. She was surprised – almost shocked – to discover that she must do the best she could for herself. No one was here to give her advice. No one would come running if she called for help. The wilderness was no respecter of persons. She was as likely to sink in a boghole as if she had been some poor sheep.

'We'd better stay where we are, Ajax,' she said aloud.

Her primrose kid gloves were soaked through, her hands stiff with cold. When she spoke again, telling him that the mist must soon clear away, her teeth were chattering.

'We're quite s-safe so long as we d-don't move,' she insisted, but the thought entered her mind that in avoiding bogs she might die of exposure. Time passed slowly. Her whole body grew numb, limb by limb. No longer was she sitting upright with the fine carriage that her father admired, but was pitiably huddled with her shoulders drooping forward.

Suddenly Ajax threw up his head and whinnied.

'Is anyone there?' she cried, trying to steady her voice. 'Is anyone there?'

For a moment there was silence. She thought, with a lonely dread that brought tears to her eyes, how, if this hope were dispelled, that silence would endlessly continue. And she cried once more, screaming now because she was without hope. 'Is anyone there?'

'Hullo,' came an answering shout, doubtfully given. 'Is anyone there?'

'Yes, yes! Don't go! Where are you!'

The figure of a man rose up beside her and a hand, grasping at her stirrup leather, caught her foot. Freshly alarmed, she drew back and asked: 'Who is it?' The hand was withdrawn and the alternate fear swept over her that he would go. 'Don't go,' she repeated. 'I'm lost. I'm—'

'A lady!' he muttered. 'Whoever?'

'I'm Miss Wingfield.'

'Well, well!' There was a pause; then he asked 'Can I help you, ma'am?'

Her normal life was being re-established. She gave a sigh of relief. 'Yes. Will you take me home, please?'

''Tis a tidy step from here and not over safe going in a mist.'

But she was no longer afraid. This was evidently a local countryman, such stuff as grooms and keepers were made of. 'I'll risk it,' she said, 'if you lead my horse.'

'Would you come to our house for a warm first, ma'am? Maybe the mist'll lift presently after.'

'Very well.'

She did not care where she went now, so long as she was taken. She dropped the reins and nursed her frozen fingers. In silence they moved forward until she became aware of the shapes of buildings. Then they stopped.

'Let me help you down, ma'am.'

She slid to the ground and felt deep mud engulf her feet. The man beside her was groping for a door.

'Will you be pleased to enter, ma'am,' said he. ''Tis a poor place, but somewhere to shelter.'

'Thank you.'

She pushed her way into a cavern of darkness and saw at the far end of it the red glow that had once been a fire. By the hearth she sank down exhausted.

'Jane! Jane! 'cried the man's voice. 'Come on down out o' bed – quick! Here is the squire's young lady, starved just.' Then the voice said to her: 'I'll put your horse in the stable, ma'am, and come back in a minute.'

'Thank you,' she murmured again, and waited.

There was a pattering of feet on the stairs. A black shape crouched over the embers, but no word was spoken and Laetitia was too tired to care for speech. She heard a puffing of bellows, a crackling of twigs and the little groans of one to whom stooping was a discomfort. It was a surprise, when the flame shot up, to see that it was a young woman who stood before her. At her side was the man, who had just re-entered. Both of them stared at her with the expectant gravity of peasants, but she closed her eyes, wishing to be left alone. There was, however, no sound of movement, and, when she looked up again, brother and sister were still there. This time she noticed that they both had dark eyes, pale faces and unkempt hair, black as the hair of gipsies. The room behind them, lit now by blazing wood, suggested squalid poverty.

'What place is this?' she asked.

'Tinygraig, ma'am.'

'One of my father's farms, is it not?'

She had not known he owned so poor a place. Those of his leading tenants, whom she occasionally visited, were crowded with polished oak and gay with lustre and willow pattern. 'I must give these poor creatures something they are in need of,' she decided as she sipped the tea they offered her. Returning warmth was awakening her deadened sense of adventure. This would be something worth recording in her journal. She set down the earthenware cup with a hand that was growing steady and began to look about the room with interest. On one wall hung a bookshelf. 'Strange,' she thought. 'One would scarcely have believed that these uncouth people were literate.' She rose, gathering up her gloves and whip and the long skirt of her habit. Her self-possession and her air of command were restored to her. 'I must be getting home before it grows any later,' she said. 'I shall be much obliged if you will add to your kindness by acting as my guide.'

'I'll be getting a lanthorn,' said Jane, and clattered out of the room.

Laetitia turned to the shelf. 'Whose books are these?'

'Mine, ma'am.'

'Why, you have a Latin grammar here!'

He smiled ruefully. 'Half the pages is missing. I'm not able to learn much from it.' Then seeing her look of surprise, he added, 'Books is costin' a deal o' money. I shouldn't be havin' most o' these even, but for kind Parson Jones as left me a few when he went into foreign parts.'

She turned towards him and studied him in the firelight. This was no gipsy's face, full of low cunning. Rather it reminded her of those romantic Italians she had pitied under Austrian rule. Surely she had often heard such a man as this singing in sad falsetto beneath the olive trees of Tuscany, had seen him leaning, graceful and melancholy, against some ruined tomb in the Campagna, a shepherd clothed in goatskin, yet perhaps the descendant of some great patrician. Her heart warmed towards him.

'You would like to become a classical scholar?'

The colour came into his cheeks, and he turned away his eyes and nodded.

'Then tell me what books you want and I will have them sent to you.'

'Oh ma'am, would you lend me books out of your own library? Shelves upon shelves of books I do hear you have at the mansion.'

What an intelligent, charming face his was when lit by

enthusiasm! 'Of course I will lend them to you,' she said, smiling. 'No one but myself ever opens them – poor neglected things. You would be doing them a kindness.'

'Then you do feel about books same as I do – as if they was living things?'

'They are the most living things in my life.'

He looked at her, his shadowed eyes wide with wonder. 'In that great big house, among all your relations and grand neighbours, is it possible that you feel lonely?'

'Why? Are you lonely too?'

'When I am not reading I am. But in books I find friends. I talk to great men, more intimate than I shall ever talk to my own folk.'

'Yes? Go on. Go on.'

'Indeed, ma'am, I do fear you will think me a boastful fellow.' He plucked at his collarless shirt and suddenly blurted out, 'I do know the poets better than I do know my kindred, or ever they will know me.'

'I do not think you boastful. That is how I feel myself. Their thoughts – the poets' – are *our* thoughts, are they not? Or so it seems after a little while.'

'Yes, yes. Their words, which I could not find with my tongue, have been hid in my heart long afore ever I saw them on the printed page.'

'How charmingly you put that!'

Jane had come back into the room and stood scowling beside the open door. 'Here is your lanthorn, boy. The mist is lifting. You'd best take the lady safe home.'

Laetitia started. 'Oh yes. It must be deplorably late. Pray fetch my horse and let us go at once.'

When she was mounted, he took her bridle and led her forward. A breeze had begun to stir the mist, and there was a spatter of rain.

'Why do you stay here?' she asked suddenly. 'No one cares for art or learning in this place. If I were a man—'

'If only uncle had lived, I should have made my escape.'

'And why has his death prevented it?'

'Oh, 'tis a long, sad story.'

'I should like to hear it.'

'Is it possible you can be taking an interest in such as I, ma'am?'

'I saw Shelley on your bookshelf and Byron, my beloved Byron! Go on.'

'Well, then,' he said with reluctance, as if the words were compelled, 'Uncle and father did leave this poor country when they were young, going to the works they were. But something did bring father home dispirited – he never will tell us what. Uncle though, he went on and prospered in the milk trade until he'd made a tidy little fortune and owned a dairy down in Cambridge. There he was married, but he was a disappointed husband; he never had no children. And that was how, being home on a visit, he offered to adopt me and to have me educated.'

'And your parents would not let you go?'

'No, no. They had no choice, being so poor and burdened with a good few others as have died since. I went away with Uncle, and I spent the two happiest years of my life, though Aunt was none too kind to me, even then. She had had no say in my adoption and could never forgive me that – she being a masterful woman. But I went to school in Cambridge – that was enough for me. I learned in books and my masters praised me; and I looked up daily at the great colleges in that fine place and promised myself in my hopeful, childish heart as I should one day be an undergraduate, maybe even a Fellow.' He laughed bitterly. 'I was a little lump of a boy, thinking, if I had a mind to learn, all men 'ould help an' praise me. Then Uncle comed to die. I was twelve then. I cried when I heard them hammering down his coffin. But I cried a deal more when Aunt took me away from school and made me over to the gangmaster.'

'To whom?'

'You have never heard of such men, maybe? Down in those foreign parts the farmers give them contracts to get their unskilled labour done at a low rate. They form gangs o' women and children from the poorest o' the people, glad to earn a few pence, and they drive them as the black folk was driven before the war in America.'

'Surely that is not possible in this free country?'

'The poor are free in no country, ma'am, and under no laws. My gangmaster he carried a whip. He told the gentry 'twas only to frighten the naughty boys with, but he used it freely on us all; and if we'd told on him we'd have lost our bread. At dawn he gathered us together on the village green – Aunt had moved out o' Cambridge then, and I couldn't even catch a sight of the colleges I loved. There we would form up, starved just with cold, for we were all ill-clad, and then he'd march us off to our work, sometimes as much as four and five miles distant. I used to trudge along with the rest, tellin' myself I would read my sweetheart books when I came home at night; but 'twas oftentimes eight o'clock afore I did so, and I mostly fell asleep over my supper with my head on the table and was awakened by Aunt fetching me a clip on the ear.'

'What a wicked woman!'

'Oh, come you, ma'am, she came from a poor home. 'Beggars can't be choosers,' she used to tell me when I cried, and she was right. That is the lesson us poor had best learn young.'

'But surely, some rich, kind person would have helped you?'

''Tis easy enough for the rich to meet the rich, no doubt. But I spoke to none save those as wretched as myself – girls as had lost their character and could not hope to get into service, half-starved bastards and simples, fatherless children and widows. With these I laboured in the fields six days out o' seven till I could scarce drag myself home for weariness. I ate whatever rough fare was set before me when I was not too weary to eat at all. I slept like a corpse. I arose and laboured again. Almost every day I was beaten. There was neither leisure nor learning in my life. I forgot, as those who labour continually with their hands are bound to forget, what had been learned at school. On Sundays I tried to read my books and wept to find them harder to understand than they had been in time gone by.'

'You poor child! How long did you suffer this?'

'For two years, ma'am. Then, being grown a man, as I thought myself at fourteen, I found courage and ran away.'

'And you came back here?'

'Yes. I slipped out one night and stole into Cambridge, meaning to look my last at its colleges. Then I tramped home, asking my way of those I met, begging my food, chased by farmers who set their dogs at me for trespassing, suspected o' being a gipsy and a thief just because I wasn't dressed respectable.'

'But you reached home safe at last,' she said gently.

'Yes. I came back to the place where I was born. And here I have stayed.'

His tone was so despondent that she asked: 'Were they not kind to you here either?'

'Oh yes, ma'am. They are wonderful wishful to help me. Only they neither desire for themselves nor have any understanding of scholarship. They want to make me a parson that I may wear a black coat and clean linen. But 'tis learning, not riches, as I do prize.'

'Ah,' said Laetitia, feeling that she was now launched upon high romance, 'how good it is to hear anyone say that in this commercial age! You should have been born in the Renaissance.' And she began to wish that she had been an Isabella d'Este to offer sanctuary to a poor scholar at her court.

Already, in accordance with the invariable and fatal habit of her mind, she was seeing this episode, less as a passage of life with consequences to him and to her, than as a piece for the theatre to be approached and enjoyed without recognition of personal responsibility. Deep in her heart – so deep that she would have denied its presence and believed the honesty of her denial – was a knowledge, or, more precisely, an instinctive and excited warning, that this peasant, having wrapped her in his imagination, was regarding her no more as the daughter of his squire; that respect was moving, through idealisation, towards worship, and gratitude towards another emotion less easily controllable. She might have established control. She might – at how little cost to her own vanity! – have chilled him to his senses, have shown herself once for all to be no goddess of the night but Miss Wingfield riding home towards Wingfield Park. But she let the silence endure until it acquired an intimate significance. She saw him lift his head towards her and wondered only whether he could see her eyes. If she had but spoken some commonplace, if she had said: 'The night looks like clearing, Griffith. Do you think it will be fine tomorrow?' and he had been compelled to answer, 'Yes, ma'am. Clearing wonderful. It do promise a fine day, indeed,' the spell would have been broken. But she would not break it, and he could not.

He could not, though he knew now that it was a spell that lay upon him. There came to him, even, an impulse to drop her bridle, and disappear in the darkness, and run and run while there was yet time. And it was his reason that bade him stay. He must see that she reached home safely. How should he fear a spell? Why should unreason cry persistently within him – as if his mind were as ridden by superstition as his poor, ignorant old father's – 'Run now! Run now!' She was no immortal but the squire's daughter.

But he looked over his shoulder to see if she was indeed

the squire's daughter. He saw her perched above him, dimly visible on her great horse.

'Would you have been happy if you had been born in the Renaissance?' she asked.

He smiled, a kind of charmed smile. Then, knowing that he was speaking foolishly, he said – with the expectant passion of one who speaks a wish that by some magic is to be instantly granted: 'I wish I had been born among the Greeks.'

At that moment the scurrying vapour cleared away and the moon shone out. The smile died on his lips. 'This is she whose name is Helen,' he thought with wonder, and jerked away his head that she might not see his tears.

They were come now to the gate through which she had ridden earlier in the evening. Since the moon's appearing she had allowed silence to gather once more between them – a silence full of beautiful falsities, of exquisite self-deception. She had seen his look of adoration, his tears, his swift gesture of concealment; and, though she had no desire to touch him, she did stretch out her hand towards his shoulder – and, feeling suddenly that even this contact would shake her heavenly tenure, withdrew it. Yet there was no cruelty in her; she was not playing with him, except as beauty plays that must; her mind was full of benevolent promptings. She saw him risen to the greatness of poets – herself his patroness. She saw, even, the collected edition of his works; it would have a place near her fireside where his hand could reach it; he himself would read to her, she kneeling by the flame, he looking like – like – was it a little like the portrait of Mr Tennyson? And in his biography it would be said of her—

Meanwhile he stood by her horse, stroking it, waiting.

'I must go,' she said, and repeated, 'I must go.'

But she did not stir. Before her eyes was a page of dedication. Her own initials she saw clearly – L.W. – the rest was mist. Then, glancing up, she saw a thin-drawn cloud come between them and the moon, and drift past with trailing and iridescent edge.

'Look!' she cried. 'A rainbow! A sign of promise!'

He followed the direction of her pointing hand. In a faint half-circle the colours of the rainbow visible by day were shot with silver in an ethereal blending.

'Yes, 'tis an omen,' he murmured, 'but not like the common rainbow, the seal o' God's treaty with man.'

'Of what is it a promise, then?' she asked. 'Of something happy?'

'I never heard tell as folk who saw and heard strange magical things by night came back to their own world any the happier.'

She gazed at him without speaking. She wished that he had not spoken with that foreboding. Then, suddenly ashamed and afraid – afraid for what she had done to him; afraid, too, with a little gust of fear, for herself – she gathered up her reins and said:

'I shall send you whatever books you want. Goodnight.'

'Goodnight,' he repeated, more in question than in salutation. And to himself he added: 'A rainbow night, never to be recaptured.'

He listened to the sound of riding until it was to be heard no more. The rainbow, too, was gone. He passed his hand across his eyes, turned about, and, feeling that the very earth he trod was changed, set out for his own place.

CHAPTER III

Classics – Romantics – At the Wishing Chair

Late in April, when, in the woods, the rich brown and purple that had heralded spring were giving place to green, and the open countryside was smeared with the same vivid hue, one of the squire's grooms rode up the track leading to Tinygraig. Cursing the steepness of the ascent, the stones over which his cob had stumbled and the weight of the parcel he carried, he entered the fold and looked about him disdainfully.

On a block of wood outside the cottage door sat a young woman who stared at him with the fixed suspicion of a cat that is equally ready to scratch or run away. Her hands, red and chapped across the knuckles, were busy plucking a fowl which lay in her lap. Its head, with foolishly gaping beak, dangled at the end of a long neck, stripped of feathers and lean as a hag's. The girl was dressed in the homespun of the district. Her boots were broken at the toes, and the piece of sacking she wore instead of an apron was stained with blood. The groom, cocking his head on one side, insolently returned her stare.

'Who may you be – the servant gel?'

'No. I am Jane Griffith. We do do our own work here.'

He spat to express his contempt and once more looked about him. In a slimy stream, which trickled down the centre of the fold, ducks were paddling, and his horse had sunk to the fetlocks in mud. Beneath the moss-grown roofs, the walls of all the buildings were splashed with the dirt of many seasons, for years had passed since they had received a coat of whitewash. The single window on the ground floor, through which he peered without ceremony, had been broken, and mended with brown paper. From what he could see of the kitchen, the house was as poverty stricken within as without.

'A nice place for a scholar to live in,' he sneered.

'He'll not live here always, if 'tis my brother you are making bold to speak of.'

'Making bold, indeed!' He looked down at her and burst out laughing; but she continued tearing out feathers with a succession of jerks that sounded like a hungry sheep cropping grass. 'My young lady would have done better to send you some of her cast-off clothes than what I've got here.'

Jane's glance swept over him from the cockade in his hat to the polished tips and pipe-clayed tops of his boots.

'I do prefer to wear my own clothes, poor though they be, to the livery of a servant. You think yourself fine no doubt, but you're only dressed up to make folks laugh, same as the monkey some old foreigner brought to the fair last year.'

'You'd wear gentleman's livery soon enough if only you could get into gentleman's service.'

'I serve my own.'

'A grand kind o' service that must be!'

'A better nor yours, mun, as has neither pride nor ambition in it. I could get into service right enough if I'd a mind to. And d'you think as I wouldn't earn good money, lie soft and eat my fill as you do, if I hadn't something worth scraping and toiling –yes, and starving for, to keep me here?'

She glared up at him with such fierceness in her black eyes that his lackey's contempt for poverty was quelled.

'Well, here are books for your scholar.' He threw the parcel into her lap and wheeled his cob about.

'From Miss Wingfield?' she gasped, springing to her feet amid a snowstorm of feathers.

'From our young lady, yes. It seems as she has come to hear of him somehow.'

'You'll all hear of him now just,' she answered, and, without another word, flung into the house, the parcel clasped in her right hand and the hen swinging from her left. As the groom rode away with a shrug, he heard her screaming, 'Grono! Grono, good boy! Come on down quick!'

In answer to Jane's calling, her brother's pale face and disordered hair appeared at the top of the stairs.

'What's on you, gel?'

'The squire's daughter has remembered you.'

His fingers tightened on the rail and he drew in his breath.

'And I had begun to think it was all a dream.'

'Her comin' here? Don't talk so dull! 'Tis the beginning o' your rise to be a parson.'

But to her continual exclamations of delight he made no answer. At last he held out his arms.

'Her books – give them to me.'

In the room with damp-stained walls where he had dreamed of her by night and written verses to her whenever he could snatch an hour by day, he tore open Laetitia's parcel. Inside was a note, written in the pointed hand she had learned of her Italian teachers.

'I have been expecting you to come and claim your reward for helping me as you so kindly did. But, since you have not come or written asking me for what you want, I now send you the Greek and Latin Grammars I know you lack. Also Xenophon's *Anabasis*, a small Herodotus and Caesar's *Gallic Wars*, for I do not know what other selection to make. Alas, they are closed books to me. But, that your reading may not all be incomprehensible to one who is not a classical scholar, I send you with these a fairly recent volume of Mr Tennyson's poems. It has given me great pleasure, and that, to judge by our talk the other night, affords reason to suppose that it will give you pleasure also.'

She had pondered over this epistle for many days. Should she write it in the third person as she would have done if she had been addressing a servant? No; for this youth was a would-be scholar, possibly a genius, a modern counterpart of the Stratford butcher's son. Over that dazzling possibility and the glory it would reflect on her to be the first to discover him, she dreamed for nearly a week. Then she remembered that the letter was still unwritten. Should she begin, 'Dear Mr Griffith?' Scarcely, for he was only a shepherd on her father's estate. She derided these class distinctions, feeling sure that Mr Ruskin would do so in such a special case, yet her upbringing withheld her from inscribing 'Mr', far less 'Esq', on the envelope. Finally she hid the note, unaddressed, inside Herodotus, having omitted both beginning and end. Only her signature, with the flourish which fashion required of an elegant writer, sloped across the bottom of the page. Gronwy noticed no omissions. 'Laetitia Wingfield,' he read, and murmured, 'No. That is the name of our landlord's daughter, but she who talked with me was of ancient Greece where poets were honoured and shepherds might consort with kings.'

At that moment, Laetitia was wondering, 'Was I wise to write in such a strain?' They were spring-cleaning at her home, and she was superintending the return of the family portraits to the places from which they had been taken. 'They are very ugly,' she thought; and then, 'How distressing if he should presume to be familiar! I should have no one but myself to blame. But of course he knows his place.' That was a comforting thought, and she stared at the portraits again. 'Yes, they are dull, without a spark of imagination in their long, stern faces – all so like Papa. Not a poet among them. Still, to know that one's people have been somebodies for so many generations is rather nice – in quite a different way.'

II

On the following market-day a young woman, laden with baskets which she was carrying to Llangantyn, left a letter at Wingfield Park.

'Someone begging clothes of our young lady,' thought Pink, turning over the envelope in his plump hands and dropping it contemptuously on to his salver. He was surprised by the eagerness with which his mistress tore it open when he brought it to her.

'There is no answer. You need not wait,' she said, turning her back upon him and going quickly to the window.

Gronwy's notions of polite letter writing were founded on his study of Dr Johnson.

> 'To Miss Wingfield,
>
> 'Dear Madam,
>
> You wondered why I did not venture to remind you of your generous promise. I was ashamed; for though you are so far above me that you dare stoop to offer me your friendship, your servants would ridicule my poverty and my pretensions. Only a few who are, like yourself, great-hearted, judge a man by what he aspires to be. I dared not come to your great house in my rags. Instead, I resolved to send you some verses which I hoped to make not altogether unworthy of your rare kindness and beauty. But even this I could not do. I wrote and tore up a dozen sonnets. They were as poor as myself, and as unfit to be presented, dear madam, to you.
>
> Now you yourself have sought me out and what I once hoped for in the magic wishing chair has come true. I am assured of the means of taking at least the first step in my education. For this I thank you from the bottom of my heart.

Dear Madam,
Your obliged, most obedient, and most humble servant.
Gronwy Griffith.'

She smiled a little at the termination, but read the letter many times.

'What, pray, is the wishing chair of which you make mention?' she wrote in reply. 'It seems that it has served you well. Do you think it would serve me also?'

He answered: 'It is a slab of stone down by the river. Old folks believe that it has supernatural powers. If you would so far honour me, dear madam, I would take you to see it whenever it pleased you to name a day convenient to yourself.'

She wrote back: 'I propose paying a call at Rhayader Hall next week. If the day is fine I shall drive out about noon. Should you be working at that hour near to where our drive meets the main road, I will alight and go down with you to the river, if you will really be so good as to guide me to the spot. It promises to be most delightful and romantic.'

He sent in reply the last note of the series

'Dear Madam,
You honour me beyond my hopes. There is no task I would more gladly undertake than that of acting as your guide. I shall not be working near the highroad, for my father's land is on the hilltop some distance away. But I will be at the place you indicate next Tuesday. Had you commanded me to meet you anywhere, no matter how far from my home, there you would have found

Your obedient, humble servant,
Gronwy Griffith.

> PS If Tuesday be wet or you unable to come, I will return to my post and watch for you on each succeeding day.'

'How thoughtless of me!' Laetitia exclaimed to herself when she received this letter in the drawing room one wet afternoon. 'Of course I knew that Tinygraig was miles away from the river and I ought not to waste a labouring man's time. Perhaps it is my duty to write and tell him so.'

She picked up a pen but, after playing with it, set it down and turned again restlessly to the exalted moral history of Sir Guy Morville.

'How tedious these High Church novels are,' she sighed. 'Ancient Celtic mystery and romance are far more to my taste.' Her eyes brightened and she let *The Heir of Redclyffe* slip through her fingers on to the floor. Tuesday would provide an adventure of which she herself would be the heroine. She began to play with the many-coloured silks that lay on her work table, thinking of the rainbow she had seen at the end of her night ride. With each movement she made, the wire and whalebone and stiff silk of her dress gave forth faint sounds.

'Can you not sit still, my dear?' complained the squire, looking up over the edge of his newspaper.

She leaned back in her chair. 'I beg your pardon, Papa; but it is difficult when one is young to wait for things to happen.'

'I'm sure I don't know what you expect to happen,' he replied.

A troubled look passed over her face. 'No, of course, it's quite absurd. I suppose I don't know what I expect myself.'

'Then I should continue my embroidery, my dear, if I were you.'

III

Tuesday was the first day of summer warmth. Laetitia sped at noon along the dark passage that led to the front door and was glad of the coolness of the place. Waves of muslin lapped the wainscoting as she passed by. Behind her the two ends of her lace scarf were spread out like wings by the speed of her movement. Above her head the masks of foxes snarled and grinned. She glanced up at them; then at the sunlit archway that ended the long vista of hunting trophies. It flashed through her mind that she must look like the escaping Princess of some fairytale. Smiling, she hastened on, but, soft as was her step on the carpet, the flutter of her passing was audible within the study of which the door unfortunately stood ajar.

'Laetitia, is that you?'

She stiffened with anxiety. 'Yes, Papa.'

'Come here, my dear.'

Reluctantly she obeyed, fearful lest he should notice the elation by which, she knew, her beauty was heightened. His glance, however, indicated only approval of her dress, flawlessly white down to the black slippers that peeped out beneath its hem. Such mute admiration was all she had learned to expect from him. Having surveyed her, he folded the papers on his writing table.

'You are taking the carriage to Rhayader Hall, are you not?'

'Yes, Papa. I am going to call on old Lady Lee.'

'You will be staying to luncheon?'

'Perhaps. She always invites one to stay, when one pays a morning call.'

'I will come with you,' he said, rising at once, 'I do not much approve of your driving about the country alone, though sometimes it cannot be avoided since unhappily you have no mother to care for you.'

He sighed, moving towards the door with an air of controlled weariness.

'Oh, but Papa, pray do not trouble to come on my account. I am perfectly accustomed—' She left her protest unfinished, afraid of making it sound over-vehement.

'A drive will do me good,' he said, passing a hand across his forehead. 'I have been working at estate accounts all the morning.' Then, looking again at his daughter, he forced himself to gallantry. 'I envy you young ladies, nothing in the world to do but to look cool and agreeable.'

It was the nearest approach to a personal compliment he had ever paid her, and the brief smile which accompanied it had a shy self-consciousness. He remembered her mother wearing white muslin, and his heart went out to her on a flood of memories, half sweet, half bitter, wholly regretful. He patted her shoulder, hoping that some day she might, unlike her mother, offer to kiss him of her own accord, but she did not trouble to return his tentative advance.

'You are tired, Papa,' she said.

'That is nothing unusual,' he answered, his tone sharpened by disappointment. After a moment's hesitation, he turned stiffly to the door, and, seeing that she did not follow him, added still more sharply: 'What are you waiting for, Laetitia?'

'It will tire you still further, Papa, to come on this expedition.'

'A drive in a lady's barouche! Nonsense! Come along.'

'But I have agreed to – to stop on the way.'

'To stop? Where? Nobody lives between here and Rhayader Hall.'

'Poor people do.'

He looked at her hard. 'If it is some cottager you propose to visit, you can postpone doing so until another day. I am too tired to suffer their importunities. There is always a new roof wanted or a rent that cannot be paid. A landlord gets no peace.'

'No, I was not going on an errand of mercy.'

'What then?'

'To find the magic chair and to wish.'

He stared at her. 'Upon my soul, that's a new whim of yours. Since when have you begun to interest yourself in the superstitions of the peasantry?'

He was irritable now. This was yet another piece of blue-stocking folly for which he had to thank her eccentric Aunt Olivia. He ought never to have allowed that silly woman to take the girl abroad when her mother died. His own sister, Emily, who was married and a good housekeeper, would have been a far better guardian.

'I am not a student of folklore,' Laetitia answered, smiling.

'Then what on earth do you want to visit the wishing chair for?'

'Have you ceased to wish for anything, Papa?'

Sometimes her likeness to her poor, dear mother made him more angry than sad. 'Come along,' he said, 'and don't talk nonsense. I suppose some book of your Aunt Olivia's has put this into your head, eh?'

Without answering, she followed him to the front door where the carriage and pair stood waiting. The polished metal on the harness glittered and the sleek horses shone with much grooming. The leather of the cushions was hot to touch and the still air was faintly scented by it. 'I wish I were not rich,' Laetitia thought as she seated herself and carefully spread out her draperies. 'I wish I were free to come and go like the common people. Now Papa will spoil everything with his anxiety to chaperon me.'

'Rhayader Hall,' she heard him command.

'Tell Jones to stop a moment by the river where our drive meets the coaching road, will you Papa?'

He made an impatient motion. 'If your heart is set on this folly, you can indulge it some other day.'

'But I have arranged for a guide to meet me.'

'Who?'

'I – I think his name is Griffith, a civil-spoken young man, a shepherd on the estate. He told me about the wishing chair and offered to show it me.'

She had spoken with a swift smoothness, struggling to keep her voice from showing any excitement. Her eyes were fixed on the ivory handle of the tiny parasol with which her fingers played. But for this nervous movement, she was rigidly motionless. The squire was gazing at her in astonishment.

'You arranged to meet some shepherd, of whose name even you seem to be uncertain, on the highway! And to leave Jones and John with the horses while you trapesed up and down the riverside alone with this fellow?' She responded with an inclination of her head. 'Upon my soul, you seem very unconcerned! Don't you consider such conduct exceedingly odd?'

'Surely, Papa, a mere farm lad! No one would dare to suggest—' Her lips expressed disdain, but at heart she hated herself for this pretence of an indifference that she was very far from feeling.

'Of course, my dear. I only meant that your behaviour would look eccentric. However, since I luckily came with you, no harm is done... there!' and he laid his hand for an instant on hers. 'You will come and consult me in future when you propose doing anything of the kind, will you not?'

'Very well, Papa.'

Her tone gave him no clue to her feelings. But a flash spread over her face and neck, and she kept her eyes downcast. He glanced at her sidelong from time to time, and shifted his position uneasily, fearing that she had thought him harsh. Young women were devilish sensitive. She might have known that he would not hurt her intentionally; but her poor mother had been just the same – all susceptibility. It was absurd of her to take a kindly warning as an affront. He stared ahead of him at the silver buttons on the coachman's coat. 'How the devil can I make it up now?' he asked himself.

'Why did I lie to him?' she was thinking, hot with shame, not as he supposed at his rebuke, but at her own lack of candour. Whatever was rare and adventurous in her life she would continue to hide from him. It was her instinct even to close a book of poetry she was reading when he came into the room. His comments on any subject in which for her sake he tried to show an interest jarred upon her. 'Very pretty, very pretty,' he would say of a poem which had moved her to tears or a sunset she had sought despairingly to reproduce in watercolours, and she would shrink from his words. Now he sat beside her, stiff as a dead tree from which the sap was gone. Was it strange that he could not understand the aspirations by which she was tormented? Though he was her father – no, because he was her father, she could never be intimate with him as one night's talk had made her intimate with an unknown peasant of her own age.

Her voluminous skirt half overspread the squire's knees. Now and then, as the carriage rocked on its way, their shoulders touched, and he inhaled the perfume of lavender that came from her lace and linen. Yet in his mind was stirring sadly the thought that moved her also: 'How far distant we are! How very far away!'

When they reached the main road, her eyelids were lifted with a nervous flutter. There, standing respectfully with cap in hand, was her peasant scholar. He did not look now so romantic a figure as in the moonlight. 'I have let my imagination run away with me,' she decided. 'He is only a common man in tattered corduroys, with tangled hair and dirty fingernails.' In her first disappointment, she found it easy to nod to him with distant condescension as she swept her billows of muslin out of the barouche.

'Papa, this is the young man who kindly offered to show me the wishing chair.'

The squire nodded and Gronwy touched his forelock. Laetitia turned away her eyes. This was not how she had planned her adventure. She was ashamed of her father, ashamed of her labourer friend, ashamed of herself.

'Will you please lead us to the place?' she said.

'Yes, ma'am.'

He too was embarrassed and fumbled with the latch of a gate. When he had opened it and she and her father had passed through, he followed a pace behind them as a footman would have done. In silence they descended a steep bank which sloped down to the river.

''Tis rough going for a lady,' he said at last, with obvious effort. 'Maybe I can help you, ma'am?'

'No. No, thank you.' She hurriedly took her father's arm.

'I wonder what condition the river is in,' the squire said, and she found herself responding with an unwonted show of interest. They talked of fishing until they reached the rocks between which the peat-stained water swirled.

'There is the place, ma'am,' Gronwy said. ''Tis like a throne hewn out of the rock by no human hand. 'Tis told by the old folks as whoever do sit in it and wish, telling their wish to none, shall have it come true.'

The squire laughed. 'Well, my dear, you sit down there, if you believe in such things. I shall have a look at the pool below the rapids. There ought to be a fat trout lying there.'

He turned away, leaving Laetitia and Gronwy standing opposite each other on either side of the stone. The sound of running water was in their ears, and alder trees, their branches gay with newly unfurled leaves, threw a mottling of shadow on to the moss at their feet.

'How beautiful it is here!' Laetitia murmured, forgetting the dust and disillusion of the roadway.

He did not answer but looked at her steadfastly. When her eyes met his, she knew that he was thinking only of her beauty. She felt a flush spread over her face and with difficulty restrained an impulse to cover it with her hands.

'How shall I thank you for what you have done?' he asked.

'What have I done but send you a few books – most of them not mine but my father's?'

'You have fulfilled the words of a poem I often read, but never thought to have come true.'

'Could you recite it to me?'

'Maybe if I was to do so, you would think me over-bold.'

'I wish to hear it.' She felt her heart beating violently as she spoke.

For a full minute, while they stood awkwardly face to face, he hesitated; then, in a low voice, he began:

> 'On desperate seas long wont to roam,
> Thy hyacinth hair, thy classic face,
> Thy Naiad airs have brought me home
> To the glory that was Greece,
> And the grandeur that was Rome.'

There was a long silence.

'That do express a little, a very little, o' what I do feel.' His lips trembled like those of a child about to burst into tears. 'Forgive me, Lady Helen, I – I am like a poor nightingale whose tongue has been torn out.'

'Lady Helen?'

'Have I your leave, ma'am, to call you that in my heart?'

From near at hand they heard the cracking of branches.

'Papa is returning… Yes, you may call me that. But why?' Her colour came and went, and she sank down onto the stone, and leaned back, glad of its support.

'Because the poem begins, "Helen, thy beauty is to me—"

'Well, have you wished your wish?' the squire called.

She saw his colourless face wearing the smile men assume

when humouring a child. Except the sternness which she found repellent, she knew in him no other expression than this of indulgence. Irritated, she turned from him to Gronwy. His face was pensive now, and his eyes were downcast. Long lashes rested on his cheek, and there was a bluish sheen on his abundant hair. His was the fine hair – 'of an aristocrat' she told herself; and his mouth, too, small for a man's and drooping at the corners – no, no, he was not a common working man as she had foolishly decided when he touched his forelock to her father. His looks resembled a labourer's no more than his deep, soft voice, and the language he used was not always of the Welsh countryside, but sometimes gave indication of a different culture.

'Have you wished?' asked the squire again. He was standing over her now, holding out hands that told his age. She would have to put her own hands into his, to suffer him to lift her up and lead her away from this place where her emotions had been stirred. How long she had waited for this to happen! And here was her father about to drag her back to safety and boredom. With him she would pay her call upon an aged widow, who lived always behind closed windows in a drawing room tediously like her own. When that was done, she would go home to the sombre house in which the familiar dinner would be served and the familiar evening's solitude awaited her.

Before she could control her rebellion of spirit, she had looked again at her peasant friend and had wished for love such as the Troubadours had praised, as unlike the discreet matchmaking of her cousins and aunts on the paternal side as Gronwy Griffith was unlike Squire Lee of Rhayader Hall.

She wished; and sprang up, suddenly afraid of what she had done.

As her father climbed back to the road, he observed that they had lost their guide. 'I meant to give him a small tip,' he said, 'and to ask if he was the son of old Griffith of Tinygraig.'

'I believe he is.'

'Indeed. I am told by the other tenants that these Griffiths have rather queer views for their station.'

At the top of the bank, Gronwy overtook them. 'I stayed behind that I also might wish,' he said to Laetitia.

The squire overheard him. 'What did you wish for, my man? An abundant harvest?'

'You must not tell or your wish will never come true,' Laetitia said quickly.

She and Gronwy exchanged a swift, smiling glance, but she gathered control for a coldly formal leave-taking. In the barouche, her father, touching her hand, asked playfully, 'You don't for a moment suppose there is any truth in that legend, do you?'

'No,' she answered with sudden vehemence. 'It is all make-believe – all moonshine! Oh, Papa dear, how foolish you must think me! And how much more foolish I think myself!'

He smiled at her, wondering why her tone was so earnest, and so startled the look in her bright eyes.

CHAPTER IV

Gronwy sets out – Plans are made in his Absence

The only window of the kitchen of Tinygraig was so small that a hen roosting on its ledge was closely framed by it. Through its leaded panes was to be seen, fantastically distorted by the uneven glass, the outcrop of grey stone by which the cottage and farm buildings were sheltered. To one looking out, nothing but this was visible across the slushy fold, unless, on a very clear day, the line of deserted mountain top beyond appeared in the intervals of overhanging rocks.

On a Sunday afternoon a few weeks after his second meeting with Laetitia, Gronwy stood at this window, staring up at the fragment of clouded sky it permitted him to see. When the first raindrops of an approaching squall rattled against the panes, he turned about and faced those within the room.

'Father, I have been thinking.'

The old man raised his eyes from the Bible which, because it was too massive to hold, lay propped up on the table before him. 'What is the good o' that, my son?'

Gronwy answered with a mournful smile. 'They have been practical thoughts this time.'

'If that be so, let us hear them good boy.'

''Twas Jane first put them into my head.'

His sister sat up, awakened out of the doze she permitted herself to take once a week over a volume of sermons. Her expectant face put him in mind of a terrier, awaiting a command to plunge with furious yapping into a badger's earth.

'Yes, yes. Do you tell Father what we have been talking about,' she urged.

'Well, Father, 'tis like this. Good Parson Jones is gone from our parish three years and more, and ever since he went we have been wondering whether down in the works he'd chance on some rich man who might lend us the money for my education.'

'Yes, yes. We have dreamed many a dream o' such good fortune, but I doubt it wunna come to pass.'

'So do I. But Jane here do think if ever I am to venture seeking it, 't had best be now.'

'Yes, indeed,' she insisted, 'now, now at onst, before hay harvest and shearing. If the boy goes putting it off till after the busy season, he'll let another year slip like water through his fingers just.'

Peter had arisen from the settle and was stretching himself. His hands raised above his head almost touched the ceiling. When he spoke in a voice that had not long deepened into that of a man, his mere bulk commanded attention.

'You hark to 'em, father; they are right.'

'What are you knowing about it, boy?'

'I have watched the blacksmith at work and I do know the truth of the old saying – "strike while the iron is hot." Gronwy's will is the same as iron, look you, only given a new shape when it is red hot. Let him go while he's a mind to or he'll slip back into the same old sloth.'

John Griffith looked long at his three children. 'Let it be so, then. You are young and there is hope left in you. I'll not gainsay you. Time'll show.'

He would discuss the subject no further, but returned to laborious reading of his favourite parable. Whenever appealed to, he made answer: 'Yes, yes. Venture you while you are young or you'll not venture at all.'

Seeing that he was of no use in forming a plan of action, Jane took the matter in hand.

'Well now, so that is settled and a good job too. And now, since 'tis to be, the sooner the better. Our neighbour Evans Alltgoch'll be wanting news o' his two sons as is gone down into Parson Jones's country, and Elizabeth may be'll have some small little present she would like you to carry to her brothers. Slip you over to Alltgoch, Grono, and tell them as you'll be starting for the works at dawn the day after tomorrow.'

'So soon?'

'Why not? 'Twill give mother and me time to make up a bit of a parcel to go along with you. I don't see nothing else to keep you.'

'Very well, then, if mother is willing.'

Mrs Griffith plucked nervously at her apron. 'Maybe the gel is right,' was all she said.

Thus Jane had her own way, and in the twilight of dawn two days later the whole family was gathered together in the fold to witness their scholar's departure. He was to journey on foot as poor men have done since the beginning of time. In his right hand was a long staff to help him climb hills and ford streams, and on his back a burden but little smaller than that which fell at length from Christian's shoulders. In it he carried bread and cheese enough to feed him for many days, a piece of bacon to be bestowed upon the parson, socks which Elizabeth had knitted and cakes she had baked for her brothers, and a change of clothing for himself lest his travel-worn appearance should put his host to shame.

John Griffith had been silent and morose during breakfast, and now what little of his face could be seen between his thatch of hair and his bush of beard and whiskers, worked with emotion. He laid a shaking hand on Gronwy's arm, clawing at it with ribbed nails bitten short.

'You are going into foreign parts and among colliers as

did put me wild when I was your age,' he wailed. 'Harken to thy father in the days of thy youth and do not heed those lawless men.'

'The colliers do you mean, father?'

'The Chartists among them, whatever.'

Peter broke out into a guffaw. 'Go you on, father, you are not keepin' up with the times. There's no such thing as Chartists, these days, no more nor there's children o'Rebecca as did use to break down the toll gates.'

But the old man shook his head. 'Call them Chartists, call them Radicals. Cobdenites I do believe some do call them now. Tomorrow no doubt they'll have another name. But 'tis only the name they do go by 'ull be changed. So long as there's rich and poor, and men are setting their hearts on the things o' this world, so long there'll be those as do want to make all folk equal.'

'Well, father,' said Gronwy, 'that's natural enough seeing the injustice of the social order.'

The grip on his arm tightened. 'Don't you pick up such talk as that, boy. Never give no heed to it, for 'twill only bring you to trouble. Peter here, he is hasty and hissy tempered on times, but he is in less danger than you are, for 'tis money and power for hisself as he do want, and may be after many years o' labour he'll get the both o' them.'

Gronwy searched his father's deep-set eyes which in the grey light were more than ever mournful, and, with a shudder, saw in them his own forlorn soul in the years to come.

'What is it you are afraid o' my wanting, father?'

'Justice,' said the old man, 'I'm afraid o' your wanting that; for that no man shall come by on this earth.'

Jane had begun to move from foot to foot and to flick with her apron at the fowls that were assembled on the doorstep. 'You'd best be getting along afore the sun do rise,' she interposed, when she could no longer stomach so profitless a conversation.

But his father's fingers clung fast to Gronwy's arm.

'You mind what I been telling you. Love o' justice and drink have been my undoing. Do you care for nothing only how best to earn your daily bread.'

Gronwy smiled at him with a queer twist of lip. 'Yet it is written, father, "man shall not live by bread alone." You must not blame me at twenty for seeing such visions of a fairer world as you onst saw yourself.'

He kissed his mother and sister and received from Peter a great pat on the back that sent him staggering towards the fold gate.

'Do all of you believe that this journey 'on't be in vain?' he asked, turning about with his hand upon the topmost bar.

Of the four people whom he addressed, the two youngest answered with enthusiasm. 'Yes, yes, indeed we do, boy.'

He smiled at them and, with rising hope, went out into the misty world to seek his fortune.

II

At supper that night, John Griffith sat with his huge Bible again before him and thrust spoonfuls of flummery into his mouth. The buttermilk trickled down his beard and splashed on to the clothless table, but no one took any notice. His wife's eyes were bloodshot and their lids puffy with weeping. Her sniffs punctuated the silence.

Peter, when he had finished, pushed back his chair. Having eaten all there was for him to eat, he settled his dissatisfied stare upon the hearth. There, in place of the dwindling fire which his mother's economy had allowed to die down so soon as the flummery was cooked, he fancied a lavish blaze, and a fat goose revolving on the now empty spit. How it would hiss and sizzle as the savoury juices oozed out of the browning skin! How good the sage and onion stuffing would smell, and the roasting flesh! His mouth would water when a leg was put on his plate and he would pause with knife and fork upraised to prolong the exquisite moment of anticipation before eating his fill. His mouth began to water even now at the mere imagining of such a treat. Then, with greed, envy entered his thoughts. 'If ever we do make shift with so much saving to turn Gronwy into a parson,' he reflected, 'he'll have fresh meat every Sunday – aye, and maybe most days o' the week. But what'll that profit me? I shan't have no chanst to lick the plates after him even. No indeed; I'll have to go on working my life long and keeping a peevish empty belly on me so as he may sit in the idleness o' the gentry, reading his dull old books.' He fell to making a covetous catalogue of the good things his brother might feast upon when he became a minister of religion – boughten white bread, spare rib with apple sauce, boiled beef and suet dumplings, lamb's fry in plenty every spring, cracklings, faggots and black pudding whenever a parishioner killed a pig, and turkey's eggs – larger and, for that good reason, better than those of hens. Sometimes, too, the squire of the parish would send Gronwy game or fish, but it was a consolation to know that these would lose much of their savour by not having been poached. In this last thought Peter's spurt of envy spent itself, and he was so ashamed that he hung his head and flushed as though his disloyalty had been made known to the world at large. 'Shame on me to grudge him victuals,' he told himself. There's a greedy-guts I am!'

'Father,' said Jane suddenly, 'I have been thinkin' as there is somethin' we can do to serve Gronwy while he is away.'

Peter in his contrition caught eagerly at the idea. 'Yes, yes, let us do everything we can. What was you planning in your head, gel?'

'That you and father should go to the old squire and beseech his help.'

John Griffith closed his Bible reluctantly. Only when lulled by its promises of life hereafter, or by the temporary optimism with which strong drink inspired him, was his disillusioned mind at peace.

'Maybe Gronwy 'on't need the squire's help when he do come home,' he objected.

'We mustn't be too sure o' that,' Jane answered. 'And suppose, if he should be disappointed of his hope in the works, think what a grand surprise 't'ould be for him on getting back here to find the money waiting him.'

'A heap o' golden sovereigns,' put in Peter dramatically.

'But what if he should have got it hisself?'

'Why, then 't'ould be a rare treat for the likes of us to take the nasty old squire his money back, and watch his face turn sour as buttermilk when we told him we'd no need of it.'

Peter laughed aloud at his own suggestion and Jane nodded agreement. Her eyes were bright like jet in sunlight and a tinge of pink showed on cheeks that were ordinarily as sallow as wax. John Griffith looked at his children as he had done a few days earlier, and now, as then, felt himself powerless to withstand the enthusiasm of youth. He delayed complying with it, however.

'I haven't much hopes o' the squire. He's a hard nut to crack.'

'Nuts do go harder the longer you do leave them, father. Have you never noticed that?'

'I broke my teeth trying to crack them, afore ever you cut yours boy.'

'Well, then, you did ought to know as the sooner we have a go at this one the better.'

'Well, but even if 'tis so, wouldn't it be safer to wait until Gronwy's back home? He could do more with the gentry nor you and I.'

'No, no,' Jane interposed. 'Gentry's odd. They aren't liking no one as isn't born one o' theirselves to try and rise up to their level. They don't mind the low and simple, but they can't stomach them as would like to copy theirselves.'

'Where did you come by that knowledge, gel?' her father asked.

'Ah, I've been listening to that smart piece Susan, as is ladies' maid at the mansion, and by what she's telling me the squire do like a homely, humble manner from poor folk. He'd let her old father, the cowherd, say what he pleased to him. A good simple man, he did use to call him, as knew his place, even if his talk was a bit rough. But there's tradesfolk in Llangantyn, Thomas the Tombstones and Pugh draper, as is worth hundreds o' pounds, and the squire'll treat them like dogs just.'

'Well, well,' said Griffith, perceiving a loophole for escape, 'there's no knowing how to deal with the man, then, best leave him be.'

'No, no, father. 'Tis easy enough. Do you and Peter go with your hats in your hands, very modest, like the shepherds to the manger at Bethlehem, and then maybe the nasty old badger 'ull give you some of his money.'

Still John Griffith tried weakly to resist their proposal, but Peter and Jane met his arguments one by one, and at last extorted from him a promise to go to Wingfield Park on his way home from market on the following Monday.

''Twill be a wonderful good day for us or else a terrible bad one,' he sighed. 'I'd rather have let it lie by as a distant day o' hope.'

CHAPTER V

The Squire reviews his Troops – Peter Dreams – Attempts – And is Consoled

On Sunday, while Laetitia Wingfield was being dressed in her third best gown and bonnet – the appropriate clothes in which to attend Divine Service in the country – her father's tenants at Tinygraig were preparing their petition for the morrow. So busy were they, renovating their dress and rehearsing their speeches, that they failed to go to church.

Morning and evening, through a crack in the panelling of the family pew which hid him from the common gaze, the squire reviewed his tenants and retainers. For forty years he had made it his boast that there was no Radicalism, no Dissent, no slackening of Tory Highchurchmanship on his estate. Little as he showed it and little as they guessed it, he loved those with whom he was empowered to interfere, as a martinet colonel loves his regiment. For this reason he had sworn that there should be no black sheep among them. They should be a picked – nay, a perfect team, opposing a solid resistance to the evils of the age. But what wearying vigilance he had been obliged to exercise in order to maintain discipline! What losses he had sustained of promising young men who had preferred to migrate to the mining districts or the colonies! How many girls had tarnished the good name of his estate by getting into trouble! He would have no such woman sheltered under a roof of his, and as often as not the obstinate parents chose to leave their homes rather than turn their erring daughters out of them. What havoc David

Morgan, the revivalist, had wrought in '59 even among the members of his own church choir! Hardest of all to bear was the knowledge that, although he continually took thought for their welfare, moral as well as physical, his tenants were not grateful to him. He supposed it came of their being his inferiors, not in class alone, but in race; for he was properly proud of his East Anglian ancestry and approved of his father for having stamped out the uncouth language talked in the district in his time. But even the merits of the English tongue, acquired in schools that had birched boys and girls alike for speaking Welsh, had left the stubborn heart of the people unchanged. Three generations of Wingfields had lived on their Welsh property, and the third was as English as he who first crossed the border. He could not understand why the people retained, and desired to retain, their racial characteristics. He had been unable to bring even his own Welsh wife to his way of thinking. She had died unmoulded and had left him a daughter in her own image whose thoughts were hidden from him.

As he sat in his pew on Sunday evening, he brooded over his wrongs. The Oxford scholar, to whom he had given the living, droned on above the heads of the sleepy congregation. Eloquence they loved – rhetoric, melancholy and emotional music, freedom to lift up their voices in extempore prayer, whenever the spirit moved them; but these things were not permitted on the Wingfield estate. Therefore, they slept in church and worshipped after their own manner in secret. The squire did not mind their sleeping, so long as they came to the right place for their slumbers. He noted with approval those who were now nodding in their pews for the second time that day, and observed with a scowl that no representative of Tinygraig had yawned or dozed through either the morning or the evening service. Later, when suffering from the effects of Sunday night's cold supper, he gloomily considered the rebukes he must deliver, and included the whole family of Griffith in his condemnatory list.

II

Peter, meanwhile, was gone up alone to the room he had shared for many years with Gronwy. He hurled off his clothes and leaped into bed, but did not as usual fall asleep as soon as his cheek touched the pillow. Instead, he began to recall the day on which Gronwy, escaped from his gangmaster, had come limping into the fold, his cheeks hollow, the bones of his face and body prominent, and his feet bleeding through his boots. Peter remembered staring at him in childish curiosity while his mother sobbed. He could well imagine himself coming home like a cat or a pigeon from any place, no matter how far distant, to which he had been taken; in his mind, there seemed to be nothing remarkable in this. But as he stared Gronwy up and down, he had seen books protruding from the pockets of his tattered coat – heavy volumes which must have weighed him down, for he looked a poor, weak creature. And suddenly, across his disdain for anyone not so well able to fight as himself, had flashed a disturbing thought that life held adventures, other than the robbing of apple orchards, and that the mind as well as the body might go a-journeying.

From that moment to this, Gronwy had been to him a window through which he looked out from his house of the five senses into a world beyond his reach. Of late, his increasing sense of responsibility as the most able-bodied man of the family, his growing taste for business, his hot, short-lived amours had occupied all his mind. 'A man must be working, not dreaming,' he told himself. Yet he was Celt enough not to despise the dreamer.

Now, as he tossed about his big bed, anxious on his brother's behalf, he remembered other nights on which he had crouched here, his clumsy knees, like those of a young colt, drawn up under his chin and his skinny arms twined about them, as he listened spell-bound, hour after hour, to stories of warriors and lovely ladies, of saints and outlaws and kings. His heart grew warm with gratitude. He glowed all over. 'I'll do something to pleasure *him* now,' he thought, and fell to picturing his interview with the squire.

No doubt Wingfield Park, into which he had never penetrated, was a very grand place indeed. When the young squire came of age, and there was a great feast given to the tenants, he had been suffering from mumps, and his parents had refused to let him go, as he had wished, with his head tied up in a stocking. They thought it would not be showing enough respect to the quality and pointed out that, in any case, he would not be able to swallow the food set before him. So he had been dissuaded. Now, however, his turn was come. He would be taken, not in a crowd but in no other company than his father's, into the great man's presence. There they would be, the three of them, in a room as large as a church and lined from floor to ceiling with books bound in red leather and lettered in gold. The furniture would be upholstered in crimson plush, the most genteel material known to Peter, and upon the mantelshelf, where well-to-do farm folk might display a pair or two of china vases, would be a whole set, big as drain pipes and made of solid silver. Into his imagining of the squire's parlour there entered also a vague luxuriance of pampas-grass dyed yellow, purple and pink. He had seen some in the Green Dragon at Llangantyn and had thought it 'wonderful smart'. There would be pictures, too, painted on the ceiling maybe, like those in some French king's palace of which Gronwy had told him. He 'must not be overawed by all this grandeur, but, indicating it with a dramatic sweep of his arm, must call on the squire, as the owner of such boundless wealth, to spare a little towards the education of a poor scholar. How splendid it would be if the squire were so moved by his eloquence that he seized some costly object lying about the room and exclaimed, 'here, take you this. You do want it more nor we.' On second thoughts, Peter decided that money down would be more handy. That was what he would pray for. He was growing drowsy now and loath to leave his warm bed and kneel on the draughty, uncarpeted floor. So he stayed where he was, and, staring up at the rafters, murmured his appeal to heaven.

'O Lord, do Thou be holding me up tomorrow in Thine Almighty Hand, so as I may not slip before the nasty old squire. O Lord, dunna let me be put shy an' ark'ard by his riches. Make me rich too, O Lord, richer nor ever the Wingfields are, for Jesus Christ's sake, Amen.'

Why, he had forgotten the chief part of his prayer! He rubbed his eyes vigorously and started again.

'O Lord God Almighty, give me the tongues of men and angels tomorrow, that I may make the old squire part with his money as he do stick to so tight, for Jesus Christ's sake, Amen… Our Father, which art in Heaven—' He repeated the Lord's prayer to the end as he had been taught to do night and morning. It crossed his mind that it contained nothing which was particularly appropriate to his case. 'Give us this day *more* than our daily bread,' he muttered. He was on the verge of sleep when he began to fear that God might resent his making his supplications while lying on his back.

'Damn!' he growled. 'Now may be I'll draw down a judgement on Gronwy when 'tis a blessing as I be asking for.' He tumbled out of bed and said his prayers all over again on his knees. Then he flung himself under the patchwork quilt once more, well pleased with himself for having got on the right side of God, and began to compose a speech that would put him on the right side of Squire Wingfield also. 'This'll be a more difficult matter,' he thought. 'He's wonderful sharp is the squire.' His manner must be humble but impassioned. Now that he was snug and sleepy, he fancied that he could melt a heart of stone. He dozed off, glowing with his own eloquence, and awoke with a start, exclaiming, 'Yes, yes. That ought to fetch un.' But what he had invented that was so clever he could not clearly recall. 'Never mind, 'twill come back when I am before him like little David going out to slaughter Goliath – no, surely I've got that wrong. 'Tis softening his heart, not killing him, I must be. Soften his hard heart, Lord – that's it. I have said my prayers kneeling and the Lord shall deliver him into my hand.'

He fell asleep smiling. Being excited, he dreamed a dream. In it he saw the squire seated upon a throne in the midst of a great hall, like Solomon delivering judgement in the Illustrated Bible. He saw himself, very small and brave, making a speech, waving his arms about. He felt tears of emotion running hot down his cheeks; and all at once was in the kitchen at Tinygraig, pouring golden sovereigns on to the table, as he had seen farmers pour sample grain out of a bag at market. ''Tis every penny of it for Gronwy,' he heard himself saying; and then, without any sense of contradiction, 'And now the first thing I'll do is to treat myself to a bowler hat and a roast goose for dinner; after that, I'll give Elizabeth Evans a fairing.'

When he awoke in the morning, he smacked his lips. That dream was a good omen. 'I am going to bring Gronwy his heart's desire today,' he told the reflection of his own confident young face in the cracked mirror at which he shaved.

III

There was a cow to drive to market with her calf. Frightened and bewildered, the calf tottered to and fro on its unmanageable legs. Peter whacked it mercilessly with his stick. It shook itself under his blows and staggered on, only to make another futile stand, its mild and stupid eyes staring up at the arm raised to strike again. John Griffith walked in front; a flourish of his staff was enough to keep the cow moving. She trotted on, worried but meek, looking round to low at her calf, but keeping herself always beyond the reach of man at whose hands it was suffering.

The day was sultry. The sun glared from behind a semi-opaque screen of clouds like a window of frosted glass. The hot smell of beasts and bracken as they descended the hillside, and the dust of the roadway when they reached the valley, set father and son mopping their foreheads and tugging at their Sabbath collars, which Mrs Griffith had double-starched for the occasion. Neither of them spoke much, though from time to time Peter swore at the calf.

'Poor little young foolish thing,' John Griffith said at last. 'He must be terrible sore with so much beating.'

'I'd beat him a deal more if I wasn't afraid to spoil the veal,' Peter answered.

'And yet,' said the old man, 'they be summat odd like Christians in their feelings. When I do butcher a lamb an' the blood is running hot an' red over my hands, I do often say to myself, "God forgive me, for it might be the blood of one o' my own children".'

'Go on, father. There's soft you be!'

'Yes, yes. That's what I am – soft. Now the thought o' going to see the squire today, indeed it has turned my guts all wambly. I 'on't never be able to do it, not till I've had a drink whatever.'

'No, no, father. There must be no drinking today. The squire, he's as unfriendly to drunkenness as though he were a parson.'

The old man moved his head from side to side like an animal in pain. ''Tis hard for a man to speak up without he's been heartened by a drink or two, be it his landlord, be it his sweetheart. I'd had a good drop afore I stood up in church to say "I will" with your mother, or maybe I wonner a done so rash a thing. No more'd most men, seeing the troubles o' rearing a family, if their kind friends hadn't put them a bit market-merry for the start.'

'Well, mind as you don't get market-merry today,' Peter adjured him, beginning to grow anxious. 'A man's bride may rather see him drunk than not at all, but his landlord isn't wishful to see him sober even, except on rent day.'

'No indeed,' his father answered with a sigh.

Thus they came to Llangantyn, where the flagstone's heat made them dizzy. Here was a great bleating and pattering of sheep, each flock scurrying by in its cloud of grease-scented dust. Dogs were barking, men shouting. Through the hubbub of chaffering market women, bellowing cattle and carts that rumbled into town, shrill whistles continually pierced. The lowest note, heard only in moments of relative quiet, was the steady clop-clopping of some great carthorse hauling his load. All else was high-pitched – the rapid clackety-clack of unshod hill ponies or the squealing of pigs that ran hither and thither with boys in pursuit.

Peter pushed his hat on to the back of his head, and let his breath escape through puffed out lips. 'Why the deuce be we wearing coats an' collars when 'tisn't Sunday and there's no call to be showing respect to God?'

'There's cross-eyed Edwards,' his father put in, 'there's one might buy the old cow. I'll get him to look at her.'

'Don't ask him right out or he'll guess as you're eager to sell her.'

'What do you take me for, boy?'

'I'm taking you for what I do know you to be,' Peter thought. 'I'll be keeping my head a'right today, but you'll be losing yours if we don't look sharp.'

He listened while his father engaged one doubtful purchaser after another. All found fault with the cow, and soon, Peter observed with dismay, his father ceased to point out her merits with conviction. 'He'll never make the squire believe what'll cost the squire money. I must be doing the talking,' he decided. 'But indeed, with the heat and the noise here, the fine speech I did make ready before I went to sleep last night, is clean gone out o' my head.' Trying to recall it, he neglected to watch the cow and calf, and they became mixed up with a passing drove of bullocks. Pursuit and argument followed, swearing, belabouring and disentangling. When it was over, John Griffith had disappeared. Peter durst not leave his charge to go in search of him, and grew more and more anxious as time went on. He stood shuffling his feet, and noticing with regret that the polish, so elaborately obtained that morning, was gone from his best boots. Perspiration glistened on his face. When he wiped it off, it came again and with it teasing flies. His mouth grew so dry that thirst tormented him. 'Father's in a pub for sure,' he thought. 'I'd be there myself but for Gronwy.'

At last he caught sight of his father emerging from one of the inns that lined the street. 'I have sold the worthless old cow for a tidy price,' the old man shouted.

'Don't let folks know then, for goodness' sake,' Peter answered, and asked in a whisper, 'How much?'

John Griffith told him. Peter did not think the price good, but his father persisted. 'I've done grand today an' I'll be doing grander yet come nightfall. Come on now. Let's draw the old badger in his earth.' He clapped his son on the back and the son's heart sank within him. 'Come on! Come on, boy!'

'But, father, us can't leave the cow an' calf here in the highway.'

'Well, there's dull I am! I was forgetting all about them.' He began to laugh, and went on, unable to control his laughter, until at last it stopped itself, and he stared about him, surprised and serious. 'Whatever am I thinking of? The cow an' calf. Yes, yes. The cow an' calf.'

It was a long while before Peter could make him recall the

names of their purchasers and the place at which each was to be left. More time was spent in driving them to their destinations and in escaping the double row of public houses with a friendly toper beckoning in each door.

'No, no, father. We must be going straight to the Mansion,' Peter said as his father swerved towards *The Crown, The Barley Mow* and *The Lion*, but once on the empty road beyond the town he perceived that already his father's left foot knew not what his right foot did. It would be wiser to go home. He was sullen with disappointment, but determined to put a good face on the matter.

'Come on, father, let's get back as fast as we can and treat ourselves to a wash and a drink under the pipe in the fold.'

'We've the squire to see first. Are you forgetting that, mun?'

'No, no, that I'm not. But better leave it for today. We're too sweaty to meet the quality.'

'If I'm sweaty 'tis because o' the curse God laid on Adam. And wonna he the father of all men? I'll tell the squire so to his face.'

'Yes, yes,' Peter agreed, as though humouring a child, 'but best do it some other time.'

'No. Today, I do say. Now. We are going straight to the Mansion. You was saying so yourself.'

'Look you here, father. You're drunk, mun.'

'I'm no such thing boy. I'm a man. A small little drop o' drink is making me a man. His equal in the sight of our Maker. I'll say it to his face – by God, I will.'

Peter caught him by the arm. 'Can you mind, what I say, father?' He spoke loud and slow. 'If you don't keep a civil tongue in you head, you – will – be – ruining – Gronwy's chances.'

John Griffith was startled out of his self-confidence. 'Rot my liver, yes. There's the boy to think of. 'Tis all over with me, but if I do tell them the truth as I told it them in Newport, maybe they'll cast the poor boy into gaol.' He staggered along, muttering in his beard. 'Gaol is a fearful place – a fearful place for a boy.'

Again Peter agreed. 'And that being so, father, let us turn up the track here and go safe home.'

But John Griffith pursued his unsteady course upon the highway. 'I am going to the Mansion,' he said.

'But, father—'

'Never you fear. I'll go hat in hand. I'll only be thinking my own thoughts in my head. Oh yes,' he shouted, 'I do know as 'tisn't safe to speak out. This benna a free country.' And when they had gone a few steps further, he asked in a low, mysterious tone. D'you know what they did do to them in France, boy?

'What who did do?'

'Ah, I met an ancient old man when I was a lumper had seen it with his own eyes. They cut off their heads. That was a grand thing to do.'

He straightened himself and threw up his chin. His eyes were bright beneath his stern brows. With his venerable grey beard and the staff he brandished in his hand, he looked like Moses about to strike the rock. Peter wished he could look thus when sober. 'Poor father,' he thought, 'if only he did have his sober discretion drunk, or his drunk courage sober, he'd be a grand old man.'

When they came to the iron gates that guarded Wingfield Park, he set himself before his father and clasped his hands in entreaty.

'I do beseech you not to go further,' he said, 'not while you are in your cups and heated against the gentry.'

'I've told you, boy, I'll refrain even from good words, though it be pain and grief to me, even as the Psalmist. Let me pass.'

'But, father, you can't be trusted now not to speak out your mind.'

'Let me pass. Let me pass… If you 'on't, I'll have to strike you.'

Peter hesitated. Should he, for his brother's sake, fight their father whom they both loved – here, too, under the lodge windows? Glancing over his shoulder, he saw the lace curtains stir, and knew that the keeper's wife was watching. Whatever he did to hinder his father in bringing disgrace upon the family would be misinterpreted to the squire. Moreover, ready as he was to plunge with gusto into brawls at a fair or wherever riotous youth was gathered together, he felt that the strongest man might be pardoned for fearing to attack ministers of religion, representatives of the law and the father that begot him. Seeing a staff raised, he had instinctively taken up an attitude of defence, but, looking at the hand that raised it, he stood aside. In gloomy silence he trudged up the drive.

'No muck, no signs o' labour here,' John Griffith said. Then he broke out into song: '"Passing soon and little worth Are the things that tempt on earth…"'

They passed through a second set of gates and through a yard where stable boys were lolling in the shade against the coach-house wall. They knocked at the door and, having been made to wait while capped heads bobbed out of windows to survey them, were admitted to the kitchen and bidden to wait again. By the door they sat down, Peter on the edge of his chair, stiff with anxiety. The room was cool and twilit. The crackling of a fire at its far end, the clatter of crockery and the laughter of women that came from the scullery were as pleasant to Peter's ears as distant music. Close to them a clock tick-tacked, and bluebottles buzzed drowsily upon the window panes. John Griffith began to nod. A pretty girl in a print gown that matched the pink of her cheeks brought them two tankards of the home-brewed, for which Wingfield Park was famous.

'Take it away,' said Peter. 'We don't want none o' the devil's broth.' He tried to warn her off with a scowl, but his father had awakened suddenly and grasped one of the tankards firmly between his hands. The girl turned away with the other.

'They must have mislaid the manners when they was making you,' she shot at Peter over her shoulder.

He looked at her without protest. 'If I wasn't so terrible troubled about Gronwy,' he thought. 'I'd run after you, my gel, an' kiss you for saying that – kiss you hard.' He would have been glad of a drink, too, but he steeled himself to sit quiet in the hope that his father might drop off to sleep. The pert girl peeped in again through a doorway and called into the room behind her—

'Lizzie! Betto! Come on here, *do*! Here's a pretty picture, and pretty music on my word.'

Three dimpling faces clustered at the scullery door to mock John Griffith.

'That's a nice state to come to a gentleman's mansion in!'

'Look at his mouth wide open an' not a tooth showing!'

'He's old enough to know better, judging by all that dirty grey hair. D'you think as he's ever had it cut in his life?'

'Look at his black bitten fingernails – ugh!'

They fled giggling at the cook's approach. Still the old man slept on and Peter prayed that he would remain asleep. 'Bitches,' he muttered. 'If you wasn't maids o' the squire's and under his roof, I'd warm the lot o' you for jeering at an old fellow as has only taken to drink because he do see life so hard.'

His depression and ill temper grew with every minute that he waited. At last there entered a tall footman who glanced at them disdainfully down the length of his nose.

'The master will see you now for a moment. Step this way.'

Peter arose, wondering whether he might slip in alone, but John Griffith started up and began to rub his eyes.

'This way – if you please!' the footman called from the

passage beyond the kitchen. 'I can't wait about all day for people of your sort.'

Peter seized his father by the arm and dragged him forward; to have attempted to desert him now would have led only to fuddled argument and delay. In the shadows of the passage they encountered a little man who flattened himself against the wall as he was being shown out. His crafty eyes gleamed at them above the hand he raised to hide his face.

'Red Judas the Fox o' Cefncoed,' Peter whispered in his father's ear. 'He's the squire's spy an' no friend of ours. Since he's been here before us, we'd do better to go now and ask leave to come another day.'

But as he spoke the study door was thrown open, and he found himself on the threshold of a room that put to flight his last hopes of making the speech he had planned. Neither large nor magnificently furnished, it contained not a sign of the surplus wealth to which he had intended to allude. It was as grim as a lawyer's office, and, in the midst of it, at a desk burdened with papers, sat the squire. His look of a harassed business man discouraged sentiment and prohibited rhetoric.

'Good day, Griffith. What do you want to see me about?'

His Welsh tenants were accustomed to his way of coming to the point without exchange of compliments or pleasantries, but it never failed to disconcert them.

'I – I can't rightly tell you, sir – not till I've come to myself like.' John Griffith blinked like an owl awakened in daylight and sat down suddenly, unbidden, in the nearest chair.

Peter stood screwing at his forelock and grinning in a nervous effort to placate the squire, whose eyebrows had risen. 'He's a bit overcome by heat, sir.'

'It seems to me he is overcome by drink.'

'Only a small little drop he's been having indeed, sir. Only enough to give him heart to come into your presence, sir. He is having a tremendous respect for you, sir. Yes, indeed, and it put him mortal shy.'

The squire looked at Peter and wished he had not so keen a scent for a lie. 'Why do my Welsh tenants lie to me always?' he asked himself. 'Why do they dislike me so? I try to do what is right by them. I am not an absentee landlord like Gwynne of Tretower whom they love.' And he said aloud, 'Your father has an odd way of showing his respect.'

Peter dug his thumb into the old man's ribs. 'Get up, can't you,' he hissed in his ear.

John Griffith rose to his feet and stood swaying.

'Well?' asked the squire.

There was a long silence. Peter could have cried with vexation. 'Let me be explaining, if you'll be so kind as to give me a hearing, sir,' he began, but found that his father was shouting him down.

'I am not to say a word against the gentry, nor their tyrannical government neither. What's past is past. But there's my poor boy to save now from such a life as mine has been. I'd do anything for him.' He sat down again precipitately.

'Pray make your meaning more clear,' said the squire, tapping on his desk with irritable fingers.

But John Griffith uttered never a word. Looking at him, Peter was able to see an over-sensitive man whom a life of hardship had broken – a gentle, timid creature who had sought in drink to find the normal truculence of brutish men. The tragedy of one with whom he had lived without ever, until this moment, understanding him, filled his eyes with tears. But the squire, looking at the same John Griffith, saw only a dirty, drunken sot, with a red nose and a mouth dropped open and dribbling. His fastidious nature revolted, and he turned away to confront the creature's son with the displeasure which now appeared to him as a part of his duty.

'You are surely old enough to know better than to bring your father here in such a condition?'

Peter gulped down his tears of pity and humiliation.

'He doesn't mean no harm by it – indeed—'

'That is beside the point. You have been brought up on my estate, have you not?'

'Yes, sir.'

'Then you have no excuse for pretending not to know that I disapprove deeply of drunkenness. Look at the way in which a drunkard's farm goes to ruin, the misery he brings on his family, the trouble and loss he causes to his landlord. Your father, like so many of them, tells me he can't pay his rent. He can pay for his beer, I see. What have you to say to that?'

Peter had nothing to say which could be said persuasively on the instant.

'Only this morning,' the squire continued, 'I have had to listen to complaints from one of the few really sober tenants I possess—'

'Red Judas the Fox!' Peter blurted out.

The squire's eyes hardened. 'So that is what you call him for objecting, as any respectable man would do, to your insobriety? You can go now. Whatever your father has to ask me, he can ask when he is in a fit condition to appear here. Good day.'

'*Go!*' cried John Griffith, coming unfortunately to life. 'Who was saying as I had to go? I'll not do so till I've spoken my mind to the squire.'

'We'll soon see about that, my man.'

In an instant the squire was on his feet and striding towards the bell rope, but Peter's giant bulk barred his way.

'Stop, sir, stop! Give me a hearing at least. I am as sober as yourself.'

'You may be sober, but I can't say you are particularly civil. Well, what have you to say?'

'Only this, sir. I do pity poor father and love my brother with all my heart.'

'You express admirable sentiments. May I ask what they have to do with me?'

'You are our landlord. You might help us.'

'No day passes without my being asked to help people who won't help themselves. If your father had come here sober now—'

'Talking you are, mun, as if he were often drunk! He hasn't the money to, I tell you, and a small drop do mount sudden to his head. He isn't like a gentleman as is drinking reg'lar. There's more ale drunk in your own kitchen—'

'You will do yourself no good, my man, by being insolent.'

Peter wrung his great clumsy hands. 'Indeed and indeed I don't mean to be no such thing, only you're a hard man to talk to.'

The footman appeared in the doorway. 'An old woman to see you, sir. Shall I admit her?

'What does she want?'

'She's come begging, I fancy, sir.'

'I suppose it's my duty to see her,' the squire muttered. 'Show her in – in five minutes.' He turned again towards Peter. 'Well, what is it you want of me?

'Father is wanting money to – to—' Even as he uttered the words, they seemed to him ill-chosen, and he began to stutter.

The squire finished the sentence for him. 'To get drunk with more frequently?'

'No, no, no!' cried Peter, who was red now and growing combative with the hurts he was receiving. ''Tis for my gifted brother he do want it. Oh dear, oh dear, if only I was able to make you understand!'

The squire's lip rose in a little smile. 'Perhaps I lack intelligence, but neither you nor your father there, who now seems to have fallen asleep, has been very explicit.'

'What's the use o' talking like that?' Peter shouted, losing control of his temper. ''Tisn't fair!'

'What is not fair, pray?'

'Oh, you know well enough what I mean. Why can't you

be giving me a kind hearing instead o' putting me nervous like you do do? We are wishful to make my brother a parson.'

'A parson!' The word fell on Peter in his heat like a drop of icy water. He put up his hands to cover his face and muttered through his fingers—

'He's not like us. Indeed, he's not.'

'I'm afraid,' said the cold voice, 'I have no money to spare for such a purpose. You had better go now.'

'Will you see him yourself, then?' cried Peter, uncovering his face that glowed with shame.

'I saw him only the other day. I cannot say I found any indication of his being suited to fill a station so much above his own.'

'Then you are blind – blind as an old leather bat.'

The squire pushed past him and rang the bell.

Choked with inarticulate resentment, Peter dragged his father out of the room. As they went down the passage, he bethought him of scathing retorts and moving appeals which he might have made. The saucy maids and lofty men servants stared him out of countenance. The back door closed upon him. Through the yard full of grooms he went; through one gate, then another. From beyond the high stone walls, he looked back at the mansion and knew that he would never again be able to force himself to approach it on the same mission. That was ended. He and his father between them had destroyed their loved one's chances of help from that quarter.

As they trudged back to their waiting womenfolk, John Griffith moaned. 'Oh dear, I do want to vomit. I do want to vomit terrible, but I can't, not yet.'

IV

After listening to Jane's reproaches and his mother's sobbing, Peter flung out of the house, cursing all women. Yet it was towards Alltgoch he went, in the unacknowledged hope that Elizabeth Evans would give him balm for his hurt. When he reached her house, he found the door ajar. From within came the sound of singing, so low that it scarcely rose above a hum,

> 'The sower went forth sowing,
> The seed in secret slept
> Through weeks of faith and patience,
> Till out the green blade crept.'

Peter remembered learning the parable of the sower in Sunday school. He associated it with the smell of soap and hair oil, with illicit trade in bull's-eyes, with tittering and nudging, with high spirits that no discipline could quench when he was eight years old. Even as he thought of these things, leaning against the doorpost with arms folded and head sunk, the pucker between his brows began to smooth itself out.

''Tis good to find someone with heart enough to sing,' he reflected. 'I wonder now, do she look as happy as she do sound?' He pushed open the door and tiptoed in. She was standing with her back turned to him, arranging newly washed plates along the dresser. The tinkle of crockery accompanied her singing—

> 'Oh, beauteous is the harvest
> Wherein all goodness thrives…'

The sunlight, streaming in level rays through the window, turned to terracotta the hands with which she set the homely blue and white china in its place.

'There's an honest pair o' hands, rough and red with work,' thought Peter, 'hands as a man 'ould like to see on his wife.' He watched with pleasure the movement of her full throat and of her arms, strong to labour, as she raised them above her head. Even her activity had a quality of repose. He knew that whenever he chanced to enter, he would find her thus, busy but unhurrying. The whole house bore witness to her care. The kitchen was clean and orderly. Along the windowsill were set pots gaudy with geraniums, and on the mantelpiece, among the glittering candlesticks and painted cannisters, stood a jug full of wild flowers.

'There's childish she is still, gathering them things,' he thought, but he liked her the better for it. 'She's not so sharp as Jane,' he decided, 'but there's sense enough about her for a woman, and enough foolishness – the way she's carrying on with flowers and dogs and the like – to make a man laugh. That's how the weaker sex did ought to be.'

He took a step towards her. Startled, she turned round, and for a moment they stared at each other as though they now encountered for the first time in their lives.

'There's a start you did give me!' she said, laughing. Then they were both silent, he twirling his cap, she crumpling her apron.

'Will you take a cup o' tea?' she asked at last.

'I don't mind if I do.'

She took a step backwards, away from him, with a rapidity that was unusual in her and began with lowered head to lay the table.

'Have your men had tea yet?' he asked.

'Yes, yes, they're gone out again.'

'Then you'll have to make up the fire and boil a kettle for me?'

'I don't mind that, boy.'

'You're good to me, Betty.'

'Well, well, we're old friends, aren't we?'

'Yes, yes, old friends.'

Those words restored their normal relationship. He gave himself a shake, strode over to the settle beside the hearth and flung himself down upon it.

'I'm in trouble,' said he.

'Oh, Peter, there's sorry I am!' She laid down the loaf from which she had began to cut slices and took a step towards him. 'Nothing serious is it?'

'Bad enough. But I'd rather not talk about it now.'

Her mouth dropped at the corners. 'Can't I do nothing to help you, boy?'

'Nothing but what you are doing.'

'What's that?'

'Just bein' yourself – gentle like.'

At that she went back to the table and made ready a meal suited to his vast appetite. From the corner cupboard she took the cake kept in readiness for the parson and his lady or other distinguished gentry. 'Never mind if Peter do eat the lot,' she thought. 'I'll bake another after he's gone. He's in trouble. I must give him all I've got to give.' In this reckless spirit, she piled the fire high with tomorrow morning's kindling, spread butter thick on the barley bread, was lavish with tea and sugar, and from the dairy fetched cream that was being kept for churning. When the teapot had stood on the hob until its contents was black as the heart of Welshman could desire, she set a chair for him at the table and stationed herself beside it that she might wait upon him.

'Come you on and catch holt. Maybe you'll feel a bit better about your trouble, whatever it is, after you've had summat to eat.' She would not question him and kept her eyes from his face lest they should cause him embarrassment.

'I'm feeling better a' ready,' he said, rising and smacking his lips at the sight of the feast she had spread. 'I'm feeling same as I did coming home from the dame school after a thrashing. It was mostly halfway up our hill as I did use to stop crying an' putting my hand to my backside to feel how sore it was. Then maybe I'd see a bird's nest in the bushes or, if 'twas autumn, a mushroom or some blackberries.'

She stole a glance at him and was overjoyed to find him grinning. 'Poor Peter, you did use to get birched a terrible lot.'

'Oh well,' he answered, squaring his shoulders, 'I was a tremenjous wicked fellow – always fighting with the other boys 'stead o' minding my books like what Gronwy did do… 'Tis a wonderful cake you've baked,' he added through a mouthful of it.

She began to laugh softly. 'You've not changed since them days, Peter.'

'Go on! I'm a man now.'

He had eaten his fill, and began to think about his grievances. 'I wish I'd the tongues o' men an' angels, Betty,' he continued. 'I'm a deal better at fighting nor I am at talking. An' there's folk in high places 't'ouldn't be safe for me to take my fists to, more's the pity.'

He was scowling now, and she hastened to turn his thoughts in another direction. 'I've something to show you, Peter,' said she.

'Oh, what is it?' His tone was indifferent and his look sullen.

''Tis only a small little present indeed.'

'For me, gel?'

She nodded. 'Yes… if you do fancy it,'

'Well, well.'

'D'you mind once you an' I was waiting in Llangantyn or our folks on a market day?

'No. I don't remember.'

'Oh yes, Peter. Looking in Pugh draper's shop window we did see a wool-worked waistcoat.'

'I've clean forgotten.'

'Oh, Peter! And I've been taking such trouble to copy the very same pattern because you did fancy it. But maybe, since you've forgotten, you 'on't like it now no more.'

She looked so forlorn that he was touched. 'If you've been making me a present, Betty, I'm sure to like it, gel.'

Her face grew broad with smiles again. 'I'd been thinking to keep it for your birthday next month. But I'd like now for you to have it today – because—' She found it hard to say why. 'Because you've been hurted,' she murmured, twisting her hands in her apron. But she knew that that was not the only reason. 'Shall I show it you, boy?'

'Yes, if you like, bitty.'

That had been his endearment for her when she was a child.

She searched in a drawer of the dresser, and, bringing out a parcel, thrust it into his hands and turned away. When he had unwrapped it, he stared at her gift in amazement.

'You did never do all this fine work for me, Betty?'

She answered with a laugh and would not allow her face to be seen.

'What a terrible time it must have taken!'

'Oh, an hour now and then by firelight after the rest was gone to bed.'

'And what a lot the 'ool must have cost.'

'Oh! A bit o' money I'd put by for a new gown. But I can make the one I had for grandma's funeral do another two years if I turn it.'

'Well, well, well,' he said, pushing back his chair and spreading out the waistcoat on the table before him, ''tis as fine a high-coloured piece as ever a gentleman, magistrate, High Sheriff, or Lord Lieutenant of the county even, ever wore. 'Twill be the glory of market days. No dealer'll miss to see me a mile off with that on – roses as big as pickling cabbages, red an' pink an' yellow-green leaves on a blue background! 'Tis grand! 'Tis champion!'

Still she stood with her back turned to him and laughed. 'Oh, 'tisn't all that out o' the way. Only, you being so well grown, Peter, there's room for a good few roses on your front.'

She heard him rise and come towards her. The nervous movement of her hands, crumpling up her apron, increased.

A pulse in her neck began to flutter. She could not control the twitching of her lips. Peter came closer and she shut her eyes. With a little shudder, she felt his breath hot on the nape of her neck. Thus they stood, neither touching or daring to touch the other lest the spell of this delicious moment should be broken, lest nothing should ever be quite the same again.

Suddenly from the fold came the sound of a man's voice and a boy's answering treble. Peter muttered something incoherent and swung himself to the far side of the table. Elizabeth laid her hand upon it to steady herself, and slowly opened her eyes.

'Father and Ben back from hoeing turnips,' she said. 'You'll stop and see 'em?'

'No, no.' His voice was thick. 'Good night now, and thank you for your present.'

He picked it up and strode out of the house without once looking at her. Her seeing was smudged with tears, she knew not whether of joy or disappointment.

When her father came in and saw the crumbs that alone remained of the feast she had set before Peter, she bore patiently with his reproaches. But to herself she thought, 'Yes, yes. Maybe I am foolish and reckless as he do say. But 'tis no use his telling me to act different. When I am giving, I can't give only the half.'

But Peter went his way frowning. Though, during the last hour, life had ceased to be painful as it had been earlier in the day, it was become even more puzzling. The image of Elizabeth, always hitherto in the background of his picture, had got out of focus and was now large in the foreground. It was pleasantly exciting to have his quiet little friend behaving thus, but, for his brother's sake, he told himself, it would never do. 'She's only a homely sort o' gel,' he thought. 'Nothing much to look at, an' the sight o' her, as I've known all my life, didn't ought to be no more of a treat to me than my daily bread. And she's no heiress neither, I mustn't be wasting my time in her company. No, no. Tis how best to serve Gronwy I must be thinking now. That, an' how to make money.' And, as the broken window and mildewed thatch of his home came into sight over the hill's bleak shoulder, he said aloud: 'I must have money to get out o' this. I mustn't be missing none o' the good things o' life.'

So he put away the offering of Elizabeth and it lay forgotten in an old coffer while he set about earning life's good things. In the days that followed, he worked with a fierce steadfastness of purpose and tumbled into bed each night exhausted. Yet, though he prayed morning and evening, 'please God make me rich,' and though his every action was shaped to that end, something seemed to be missing from his scheme. Tired as he was when night came, he often lay awake, assuring himself that it was only his brother's coming disappointment that made him unhappy, and with the one word 'money' stifling all the questions that had begun to stir in his mind.

CHAPTER VI

Gronwy Returns

'Gronwy'll never get his chance now, not unless good Parson Jones be able to help him.'

'He'll never rise to do us credit in the pulpit, unless he can bring back money from the works.'

Such were the words repeated daily in the kitchen at Tinygraig. Now, when she was silent, Jane's thin lips were always compressed, as they had been in the past only when she was angry.

On an evening when summer rain was falling, the old man said, 'Maybe the boy'll come back tonight.' It was more a lamentation than an expression of hope, and had become with him a customary saying after supper.

Mrs Griffith answered with a sigh. 'Indeed but I am dreading it when he do hear how you and Peter have ruined his chances with the squire.'

'Let's hope he 'on't never need the old squire's help,' said Peter. 'He may have met some kind gentleman down in the works as has given him freely all he do want.'

But John Griffith shook his head. 'Such uncommon good things don't happen only in books, and I'm afraid as our poor Grono has read too many o' them. They have put him soft, like so many parsons.'

The clicking of Jane's knitting needles stopped as she looked at each of the speakers in turn. 'Now, father, you take a pinch o' snuff.' she said. 'And, mother, 'twill do you good to do a bit o' spinning.'

'Indeed, dear, I am mortal tired after kneading the week's bread.'

Jane seemed not to think this protest worth an answer. She rose briskly and dragged the wheel towards the hearth.

'Just you finish that bobbinful. I shall be needin' the yarn for Peter's socks.'

'There's a tidy gel,' Mrs Griffith said, smiling at her wanly. 'Meaning kind by me you are, I do know. But no labour 'on't stop my heart to ache for my poor boy's misfortune.'

Nevertheless she set to work, and the drowsy humming of the wheel lulled her fears. She was looking resigned again when a knock sounded on the door, and Jane, flinging away her knitting, sprang up to open it. The wheel droned to a standstill.

''Tis only Mr Evans Alltgoch,' Jane called over her shoulder in a tone acid with disappointment.

Mrs Griffith drew her sleeve across her face and went to greet him. 'Come you in and welcome. Don't you take no heed o' me. I'm gone quite simple fretting for my eldest to come home.'

'He is coming now just!' the newcomer answered. 'He'll be here tonight.'

Mr Evans was a tall man, bent with rheumatism. His broad face, framed in reddish whiskers that were turning pepper colour, wore an almost boyish smile. He took Mrs Griffith's hand and shook it heartily, though his own was so crippled by his complaint that the grasp gave him pain.

'Our Ben here was down at the blacksmith's at Llangantyn having his pony shod, and he seed your lad come limping into town, so he galloped on up home to give us the news.' He rubbed his gnarled fingers together. 'Yes, yes. We'll be hearing summat about our boys' fortunes now. I'll have news o' my long lost two, an' the blessing o' the Lord on him as do bring it.'

'Amen,' said Mrs Griffith, the tears on her lashes.

Elizabeth and her youngest brother had come into the room behind their father. The little lad pushed past her, and his elders began to question him about his meeting with Gronwy, while Elizabeth seated herself at the end of the settle where Peter's muddy boots had lain. He had swung his feet on to the floor and was sitting upright, staring at the ashes on the hearth. Beyond giving her a nod, he had not responded to her smile and blush on encountering him. She wondered miserably whether he could have forgotten the happiness of their last meeting. She had thought of nothing else since then, and had imagined the next encounter in a hundred different ways, but had never feared that it would prove to be like this. Glancing at him sideways from time to time, she found him always frowning, as if lost in dark thoughts and unconscious of her presence.

'That's right, Ben,' his father cried, patting the child on the shoulder when his recital was finished. 'He's as sharp as a new whetted scythe, the very spit o' his poor mother. Strange, isn't it now, as my three boys should take after her, all with black eyes and fine curly hair and as quick as robins in their ways? While the gel is same as me – slow if steady, an' no partic'lar shape nor hue, but a sort o' brownish red.' He looked her over. 'Pity as you didn't have your mother's looks, eh Betty? Some man might have fancied you then. Ah well,' he added, 'maybe 'tis for the best. A father can only be sure o' his daughter behaving honest when no man do 'tice her to behave randy.'

Being in a good humour, he chuckled at his own joke, though the object of it winced and shrank into her corner.

'There's no virtue safe but that of an ill-favoured wench,' he went on, 'and to my mind none but the dark 'uns is worth trying to lead into temptation.'

Elizabeth looked again at Peter. She dared not hope that he thought her pretty, so plain had she been taught to consider herself; but he might perhaps say that grey eyes and brown hair with a copper glint in it were not altogether amiss. She waited, aching for a word on her defence, but he did not take up the challenge. Neither he nor Jane, who knitted on with unswerving industry, showed any sign of interest in the conversation, and their parents, though they asked questions of Benjamin, seemed anxious rather than glad about their eldest son's return. Elizabeth began to suspect that something was troubling the whole family. She summoned courage of her sympathy to steal closer to Peter, sliding her way inch by inch along the settle.

'Is anything the matter?' she whispered when her shoulder was touching his.

He turned a sullen face to her. 'Aye.'

Her own sorrow was instantly forgotten. 'The same as was vexing you a week ago?' she asked.

'Aye.'

'Oh, Peter, and I hoped as that was only some small little trouble like you was allus gettin' into when you was a lumper.'

'I'm a man now. Troubles don't pass off so soon.'

'Can I do nothing for you now, same as I did use to do then?'

'No. Nothing.'

She recoiled from the word as if it had been a blow, and crept back to her own end of the settle. Her father talked on of the handsome black-eyed girls he had admired in his youth, and the crooning of the wheel continued.

An hour passed. To Elizabeth it seemed like ten. Whenever she looked at Peter, she longed to throw her arms round his neck and comfort him. 'But he donna want my love,' she told herself. 'I was wrong to think as ever he did.'

Suddenly the door was opened and every face turned towards it. Gronwy entered with rain streaming from his clothes. Elizabeth had time to notice that he looked worn and dispirited before a chorus of greeting broke out and his mother took him in her arms.

'I'm all right,' he said, trying to smile. 'Only a bit tired by so much walking. 'Tis a heavy day.' He sank on to a chair. 'No, no, Mother,' he protested, as she knelt to unlace his boots, but he was too weary to check her.

'Light the fire an' make him a strong cup o' tea quick,' Mrs Griffith commanded.

'I am 'doin' it a'ready,' Jane answered, from her knees on the hearth.

Old Evans had drawn his chair close to Gronwy's. After prolonged fidgeting, he broke out—

'Starved you may be, boy, but if you be able to speak at all, why don't you tell me about my sons? Are they alive? Have you seen them? Are they well in health? Have they met with no accident down in them nasty old pits?' He paused, and added wistfully, 'are they coming home soon to look for their old dad?'

Gronwy's closed eyelids parted. Elizabeth watched the brown eyes that were not bright and hard like her brothers', but sad as a dog's, rest pityingly on the old man's face. Her hand went up to her heart, for she knew by his look that Gronwy brought evil tidings.

'Poor father,' she thought without a trace of resentment, 'what good'll my love be to him if his men children are lost?'

'Your two sons are alive,' Gronwy said.

The old man began to tremble. 'They have neither of them lost a limb?'

'No, no.'

'The Lord be praised! Why wouldn't you say so at onst?' Tears ran down his cheeks and hung like dewdrops among the white and sandy hairs of his whiskers. 'Tell me more, mun.'

'What more is there to tell?' Gronwy asked.

'Are they rich?' piped Benjamin.

'They are earning high wages,' Gronwy answered with a hardening of expression, 'but you, Ben, had best stay here to help your father.'

Old Evans caught at the boy's shoulder and drew him close.

'Yes, yes, Ben 'on't never leave his dad, will you little 'un?'

The child pouted and hung his head.

'He's the last o' my children as is left to me,' his father sighed.

'What about Betty?' Peter demanded suddenly.

'Oh well, the last o' my sons, I do mean… Now, Gronwy good boy, when am I to set eyes again on the others?' As there was no answer, he added: 'They will come home some day, 'on't they?'

'Oh yes, they will come home when there's a strike on, or they are out o' work.'

'Then we'll all be rich an' have fresh meat and a pudding every day,' said Benjamin.

Gronwy made no reply, and to all further questions his answers were evasive.

'The boys is not saving nor living a Godfearin' life,' Elizabeth decided in heaviness of heart. 'I must try to make up for them to poor father, so much as a gel can do whatever.'

When at length he rose to go, old Evans looked down at the traveller with disappointment.

'You haven't told us nothing o' what you do think about the works,' he complained.

'I didn't think much o' them.'

Benjamin looked his incredulity and his father gave up his questioning in despair. There was nothing to be got out of Gronwy tonight.

'Here, Ben good boy, give me your shoulder to lean on,' he said, and limped out into the dusk. Elizabeth followed.

'Good night all!' she said, and, receiving no reply, went out alone.

When the door was closed behind her, John Griffith asked Gronwy. 'What's on you not to tell Evans more free like about his boys?'

The others pressed closer. Jane had set aside her knitting and Mrs Griffith passed her hand over her son's steaming clothes to feel how they were drying on him.

'How could I have broken the old man's heart?' said Gronwy. 'He loves those good-for-nothings as much as you love me.'

'Good-for-nothings! What is the matter with them? They were tidy boys when they went away from here.'

Gronwy's eyes brightened with anger. 'The system – that is what's the matter. If you saw how folk do live down in the works, you wouldn't be surprised at their taking to drink.'

'Drink!' Peter looked at his father. 'Drat the stuff – devil's broth, that's what it is. If they are drinking, they'll never keep what money they do earn, no more nor others I could name.'

'No collier ever does,' said Gronwy. 'He is defrauded of his wages at the truck-shop to start with, and then he finds himself, with what little money is left, among men who will drink with him, gamble, fight or go poaching with him, but never join him in leading a decent life. They have had no chanst to know better, I suppose. There are public houses in plenty, but not a church or a chapel or a library such as the growing population do need. The children are not sent to school, for they can earn money for their parents when they are so small 'tis a pity to see them going down into darkness. I met few as could read, but they can all blaspheme. The women get drunk like the men. 'Twas thought a rare joke what I saw one day – a fight in the street between two near naked gels as had torn the clothes from each other's backs.'

Mrs Griffith threw up her hands. 'What a lack o' shame!'

''Tis small wonder they grow up without shame, mother. Privies there are none in many o' the houses. Crowded as poultry pens they are – men an' women of all ages sleeping huddled close together in the same room. And when the colliers do come home from the pits, you may see them any day taking their baths in the kitchen with the door open on to the street.'

Again she threw up her hands in horror. 'In a Christian country!'

'Christian!' Gronwy laughed. 'What do the owners care whether those by whose sweat they do grow rich ever hear the word o' Christ or no?'

'Then whatever is the parsons and preachers about?'

'Our good Parson Jones for one is doing all he can. But hundreds o' people flock into his parish every year, and his church was built only to hold the few farmers as lived there formerly. He is single-handed now as he was then, worked to death just, and living as poor as we do ourselves on account o' giving so much away.'

John Griffith and his wife exchanged glances. It was Jane who had the courage to ask the question that was in their minds.

'Then Parson Jones can't do nothing to get you your education?'

'Bless you, he has scarce time to christen an' bury. How could he interest himself in a would-be scholar who is not even o' his parish? He could only spare me half an hour, an' then his talk was all about the sin and wickedness o' mining towns. No, no, poor Parson Jones can never help me.'

The tears welled up in Mrs Griffith's eyes. Her husband cleared his throat and gazed fixedly at his feet. Peter spat into the ashes. It was Jane who spoke up once more.

'Can't you make no money then for your own education? 'Tis to be had in the works, whatever you may say against them.'

Gronwy had drunk his tea. He pushed away the empty cup and rose.

'Yes. That is what I was meaning to do when I went down

there before I had seen them. “If none will lend me money for my start,” I thought, “I must work for it myself, no matter how long it do take to earn.” But now that I have seen under what conditions money is made, I know ’twould break my spirit long before I had saved the half o’ what is needed. I do believe as it do kill the soul to lead a collier’s life.’

His mother interposed. ‘Indeed, yes. You mustn’t try no such thing – you aren’t near strong at the best o’ times.’

‘I am not over strong to labour – that is true, mother. I am dropping tired before Peter here has begun to sweat. But ’tis not o’ the work underground that I am afeard. That might kill me may be, but there are worse things than dying.’

‘Don’t talk like that, boy,’ she cried.

‘Why not? Do you think o’ death as a calamity?’

Four pairs of eyes stared at him in astonishment.

‘Are you not thinking o’ death with fear?’ Peter asked in awe.

‘No.’ Gronwy turned his back on these folk who loved him so deeply, but in whose midst he was always lonely. Leaning against the mantelshelf, he stared down into the fire. ‘’Tis life I do dread. ’Tis life as can do all the wrongs to man he need never fear from death.’Tis not the chanst o’ dying young, nor yet o’ being crushed or burned to death as some colliers are, that keeps me from the mines. ’Tis the filth an’ darkness that I do dread – the ugly life, the ugly towns, the ugly people. I’m afraid – afraid with a sickening I dursen’t show even to myself – o’ living to lose my love o’ beauty an’ my hope that’s in my heart. May I die first. Haven’t I wasted years enough a’ready, labouring with my hands an’ letting my brain rot? My old schoolfellows at Cambridge must have their minds stored now with precious knowledge, yet there was not one among them so promising as I. And am I now to be sold into bondage more degrading nor ever my work with the gangmaster? Now, when a being from a happier world has looked down on me—’

He broke off, and those in the room behind him looked at one another in troubled perplexity.

'No,' said Gronwy. 'I must waste no more time before I begin my studies in earnest. Struggling alone with a Latin grammar at the end of a day's shepherding 'on't make a scholar of me. I must go to college. And to that end,' he added, 'I must humble myself before the squire.'

Their silence alarmed him.

'You think 'twill be o' no use?' he asked.

'You tell him, Peter,' John Griffith said.

'What have you done?' Gronwy cried, as his brother remained speechless.

'We have spoiled your chances,' said Peter. 'We have done you a terrible wrong – we, as did only mean to serve you.'

His face was crimson, his head hung down and his huge fists were clenched. Gronwy went to him, pitying his helpless strength, and laid a hand, that could never guide a plough straight, on the massive shoulder.

'Never mind, boy. Only tell me what has happened.'

Peter told him.

'An' now,' said Jane, rocking herself to and fro, ''twill be no manner o' use for none of us to go begging to the old badger. Having spoken, he 'on't never go back on his word. 'Tis well known he's as obstinate as a boar pig.'

Gronwy had listened quietly to the blundering recital of his father's and Peter's failure. Standing erect beside his brother's chair, he had made no movement. Only his mother noticed through her tears that hopelessness had settled on his face.

'Why did you not beg help of her instead?' he asked.

'Of *her*?' John Griffith repeated.

'Of the squire's daughter.'

They stared at him. 'But the maids at the mansion don't think much of her.'

'What do they know of her sort?'

'What do you know of her yourself, boy, come to that?'

He did not answer at once. 'She lent me books,' he said at last.

'Oh, aye,' said Jane, 'I remember. She came here one night when I was abed and sent you some books after by a groom. But the loan o' books is one thing. The loan o' money is another. She'd have done better not to raise your hopes.'

Gronwy lifted his hands to his eyes, 'No,' he said with a fierce intensity that startled them, though the word was spoken scarcely above a whisper. 'I have seen a light shining in darkness. That I shall never, never regret, though darkness tenfold close over me again.'

Slowly he began to grope his way towards the door.

'Wait till I fetch you a candle,' Jane exclaimed, relieved that this talk in the twilight was over.

For answer, he laughed in such a fashion that his mother shrank from the sound.

'No, no. Leave me be,' he said. 'I must accustom myself.'

CHAPTER VII

The Shearing

The activity of shearing day came as a relief to Tinygraig. That morning, before the diamond-paned window of the brothers' room had begun to pale in the darkness, Jane's voice was heard outside their door.

'Wake up! Wake up!' she cried, beating vigorously with her fist. 'Have you forgotten what day it is?'

Peter leaped into wakefulness and tumbled out of bed. 'A'right. I'll be down now just… Are you awake Grono?'

'I've been awake for hours.'

'You've not slept much then?'

'I never do these days.'

'That's bad, mun.'

But Peter was too busy fumbling with his bootlaces to say more. The rims of his eyes felt sticky and his limbs were heavy to move. The temptation to return to bed was strengthened by his having awakened in the midst of a pleasant dream. His forehead was puckered by his effort to remember what it had been about, but, except that Elizabeth had figured in it, he could recall nothing. If he had dreamed of any other girl on the night before shearing day, he would have chaffed her about it in public, but he was aware of an unusual shyness in his thoughts of Elizabeth. It was with mingled regret and relief that he turned from them to the business of the day, and clattered downstairs.

'You were astir early, Jane, to get a kettle boiling for us so soon,' he said, pouring his cupful of tea into his saucer that it might cool the sooner.

'O' course I was. There's work to be done an' poor mother gone so simple.'

She snapped out the answer without raising her eyes from the potato she was peeling. Over her dress of Welsh flannel she had spread a sacking apron, and in her lap was a bowl piled with earth-stained potatoes. On the floor beside her stood a three-legged cauldron into which she splashed each one when it was peeled white.

'Pity indeed as you should have to work yourself tired today,' Peter observed. 'Maybe as some young man'll offer to sit up with you tonight.'

She glanced up, and the firelight gave a red glint to her eyes.

'Shame on you, boy! Which of us would have the heart for such foolishness with Gronwy's future to think of? Work – that's what you an' I got to do. Work, an' make money, an' save every penny of it to pay for his education.'

'Yes, yes,' Peter agreed, rising from the table with a sigh. 'I was only joking.'

Gronwy had come into the room. 'Sometimes I think you would all be happier if I were to throw myself into the river,' he said.

'How can you say such a thing? 'Jane cried. ''Tis proud we are to serve you.'

'Your pride is costing you dear. Why should four honest folk deny themselves every pleasure for the sake of a discontented dreamer?'

'You 'on't be discontented once you've risen to be a parson.'

'I've no hope of that now.'

Peter seized him by the arm and dragged him towards the door. 'Come on, an' I'll tell you a plan as I've struck on for getting us out of our poverty.'

Gronwy's answer was a sad, incredulous smile, but he allowed himself to be led out into the fold. A shock of cold air and a noise of sheep greeted them. Part of the space between the outbuildings had been enclosed by hurdles. Here was penned the flock that had been brought down from the mountain the night before.

'How strange and insubstantial they do look in the dawn,' Gronwy murmured.

'Too small they are,' was Peter's practical comment. 'But come you I'll persuade father to try a better breed afore long. Our bit o' grazing'd carry more 'ool an' more mutton than he do make it.'

He fetched the ponies from the stables and in silence they mounted. The light was gaining in strength as they rode along the tableland that stretched beyond the Tinygraig rocks. The valley beneath was hidden by mist and the sky was without colour; but around them they could see a vast expanse of grass so heavily laden with dew that it had an encrusted texture and seemed more grey than green.

'Sheep,' said Peter, after a long silence. 'That's my answer to our troubles.'

Gronwy, startled out of a reverie, turned to stare at him. Peter was looking very knowing.

'Ah, you may think as I don't see no further than my day's work,' he said. 'But, mind you, my head is as busy as ever yours is with your old book-learning. Now, mark my words, we'll see a wonderful change in farming in our lifetime and those as is sharp enough to act according 'ull prosper; but those as is biding in the old way – ruined they'll be.'

'What makes you think that?'

'Why, bigger ships, iron ones they do say, an' railways bringing cheap food from foreign parts, an' the moving o' folks away from the countryside into the cities, 'twill send the price o' home-growed corn down an' the price o' country labour up. That farmer'll be the best off as is paying little wages and turnin' his ploughland into pasture.'

'Maybe.'

'But I'm sure of it boy. and I'm going to act according, I tell you.' His massive under jaw shot forward. 'Father, he can go on spudding thistles in the wheat and pleaching fences to pleasure the old squire – damn him; an' the boys o' the district can sweat theirselves weak practising to show off at ploughing matches; but not a stroke more tilling the soil will I do than I'm driven to. Breeding better stock, renting more hill land, followin' the markets so as I can buy cheap an' sell dear – that's my game.' After biting his lips, he broke out again. 'Father's been labouring with his hands, same as Adam after the fall, all his life long, an' he's as poor now as when he came back from Newport an' started to rent the place. What's the good o' that?'

'He's lived honest.'

'Aye. But I am meanin' to die rich.'

The cold light was now changing its quality. A warm radiance spread over the sky and golden rays struck upward from behind a range of bills to the cast. Presently the sun itself appeared and at once the whole tableland across which they were riding gave out a million specks of diamond brightness. Down in the valleys on either hand, banks of mist, white as curds, were revealed. Their edges quivered as the sunshine touched them, and there began a slow, eddying dispersal which left visible in every valley a silver streak of river. Peter stretched himself, filling his lungs with the crisp air, and a confident smile spread over his face.

'Yes, yes,' he said, 'I'll be a rich man yet.'

A moment later his expression changed to one of anxiety.

'Damn me! I forgot to say my prayers this mornin'.There's a bad beginning for shearing day! Something's sure to go wrong afore nightfall. There's no time to get off an' say them now,' he went on. 'Do you think 't'ould be wrong, Grono boy, to ask a blessing o' God on horseback?'

'Suppose you sing a hymn. There could be no harm in that,' Gronwy answered with a smile.

'Yes, yes. That would be more seemly than praying in the saddle,' and in a harsh voice Peter broke into the first hymn that occurred to him. It had been in his mind since he had heard Elizabeth sing it at Alltgoch.

'One day the heavenly Sower
Shall reap where He hath sown,
And come again rejoicing…'

While he sang, his eyes, wide open now, scanned the horizon where a bog aflower with cotton reed showed white as a patch of snow.

The singing ceased, and his brother looked at him wistfully. 'You sound wonderful happy, Peter. What is it you do find to be so thankful for?'

Peter licked his lips. 'A good appetite.'

'Yet you often have little enough with which to satisfy it.'

'Come you, 'tis worth having for the hope it do 'rouse. I like to want things as I do lack, to be young an' have a long life before me in which to fight for them.'

'What if you do fail to get them?'

'I am not going to fail, mun.'

'Then you are wanting things as are easier to get than those I desire.'

Peter was too full of his own ambitions to challenge that statement. 'Meanwhile,' he went on, ''tis good to rise up as a giant to run his course, and to lie down tired to rest; to feel muscles strong under my skin; to grip a colt between my legs, an' feel him rear an' jump, an' know as he can't unseat me, try how he may. 'Tis good to master beasts an' men – that's my delight… Hi! There's the sheep. Go you round on their left with Bob, an' I'll be gettin' behind them from the right with Prince an' Dio. Here Prince, here Dio, good dog!' And he set off at a gallop towards the distant white dots scattered on the green.

Gathering together the flock and driving it down to Tinygraig was an exacting business and allowed no more talk until they were in sight of the homestead.

'Look,' Peter exclaimed then, 'a good few neighbours are come. But mind you, there'll be thrice that number when I've increased our flocks.'

In a little field below the house, they could see more than a dozen horses grazing, and the voices of men came up to them from the fold. Peter's eyes brightened.

'There'll be victuals enough today,' he said, as they were driving their flock into the pen where the sheep of last night's gathering were already huddled together. At the opposite entrance stood a man who caught them as they were required, and carried them, struggling helplessly, to the benches of the shearers. This man's sleeves were rolled up, displaying arms tough and brown as the gnarled branches of an oak tree. So soaked with sweat was his shirt that it stuck to his back. Peter watched with approval the muscles that rose on either side of his spine as he stooped to battle with a plunging ram.

'I 'ouldn't mind trying a fall with him,' he reflected. 'He's one worthy to wrestle with me.'

Shouting a greeting and a challenge, he strode across the fold, which was full of young men shearing the sheep, stamping them with his father's initials in hot pitch, and branding the lambs on their noses. The air, now growing warm, was heavy with dust and the oily smell of wool. Sunshine poured down upon the red faces, and arms glistened with perspiration. Peter was enjoying himself. Followed by Gronwy, he made his way across the panting bodies of bound sheep into the house. The kitchen was crowded with women who laughed and chattered shrilly. He was abashed by the presence of so many of them. 'One gel at a time I can do with well enough,' he thought, 'but there's no handling them in a drove.' He flung himself down in a chair and kept his eyes fixed on the table.

'Give the boys a bit o' the best ham for today,' he heard his mother's voice say.

He took courage to glance up, and saw Jane, very trim and angular in the black gown she had now put on, surrounded by a group of girls whose bright eyes were an invitation to amorous adventure. He winked at one of them. She would be pleasant to kiss, he decided, but she was less alluring than the smell of frying ham which reached him at that moment from the hearth. He was rubbing his hands together, anticipating first the meal and then the kiss, when he became aware of Elizabeth setting a cup of tea before him. He was disconcerted, feeling as he had done when detected in mischief as a child. She fetched him sugar, then bread and butter and a plate.

'Thank you, Betty,' he muttered, thinking that she was kind, but not so exciting as the girl opposite. When she brought him the ham, he ate it ravenously and ceased to think of any counter attractions. He was licking his chops for the last taste of savoury grease when his father entered the room.

'Have you done eating, boys?'

'Yes, father, more's the pity.'

'Well then, Gronwy, do you go up to the hill again and take back the sheep as is already shorn. And you Peter, along o' your strength, can carry the wool up to the towlod.'

They followed him out, but on the threshold Peter paused to look over his shoulder. Now that he had overcome his shyness, he was loath to leave the women. Their whispering in corners, their high-pitched laughter, their sidelong glances and swift colour, set his pulses beating.

'Just you wait till this evening,' he threatened the girl with the tempting mouth. 'But I must do a bit o' work before I do claim a treat.'

He had not laboured long, counting and recording the number of fleeces, making them up into huge bales and carrying them on his back up a ladder to the loft over the stable, when a halt was called for dinner. His exertions had renewed his appetite and he clattered into the kitchen with the others who had breakfasted earlier. The men and boys seated themselves at table, stretching their tired limbs, and boasting of the work they had done, while the women ladled out cawl from the vessel suspended over the fire. When the steaming bowls were set before them, the men ceased to talk, and nothing broke the silence but sounds of supping and the satisfied smacking of lips. After the cawl came mutton and vegetables, and not until this course had vanished did conversation begin. Then the women cleared a space for themselves and began to eat what was left, hindered by much nudging. The giggles of the morning had given place to shrieks of laughter, and Peter contributed to the fun by clutching a girl in each arm and vowing he did not know which of them he would court that night. At last John Griffith who, having drunk, was enjoying his guests' mirth, arose and announced that there was yet work to be done.

'Father don't see me safe here,' Peter cried, as he moved towards the door. And amid winking and jostling they all trooped out again.

The afternoon was oppressively hot, but the promise of supper with cider in abundance and of the singing and lovemaking that should follow it kept them blithe at their toil. Having cleared the table and laid it ready for the next meal, the girls took off their aprons and strolled out into the fold, two or three together and arm-in-arm for shyness' sake. From his loft, Peter could hear increasing outbursts of laughter, feminine cries of protest and snatches of song. 'I'll be down with them an' enjoying myself grand in a few minutes,' he told himself, but suddenly the cheerful sound ceased. He heard instead the clatter of horse's hoofs. 'Whoever can that be?' he wondered, and went to the loft window to look out, but a projection in the upper part of the building prevented him from seeing the newcomer. A group of girls, however, was in sight, and, as he craned forward, he saw them bob down, dropping curtsies of varying depth. The colour heightened in his face. 'The squire, sure to be. Blast him for daring to show his ugly old snout here unasked after he's treated us so mean.'

Driven by angry curiosity, he slid down the ladder, careless of a fall, and reached the ground in time to see his father touching his forelock and wiping his hand up and down the seam of his trousers before offering it to the squire. 'Tisn't fair,' thought Peter. 'There's poor father like a hedge'og he's so humpty in the back, an' there's Betty's father, too, coming up so respectful, though he's hardly able to drag hisself along the fold he's that stiff with rheumatics – an' both of 'em younger'n better men nor him.'

'Come you on out, missus!' he heard his father call, and saw his mother hasten to the door and drop a curtsy. He spat on the ground to express his unutterable disgust.

'Jane, come you an' pay your respects to the squire,' his father called again; but Jane did not appear, and Peter grinned.

Having received the salutations of those who were not too shy to come up to him, Mr Wingfield made a tour of the fold and spoke in turn to each of the shearers. Peter noticed that wherever he went, he was received with a courteous touching of caps and listened to with an air of deferential restraint, but that, when he had passed on, the lads exchanged furtive grimaces. The solemn inspection over, the whole company trooped into the house, for Mrs Griffith had announced in a voice that quavered with nervousness that supper was ready. Peter followed in the rear of the others, but, before he could enter, Jane came running out to him.

'Stop where you are,' she panted. 'He's asked for Gronwy. Maybe he do mean to help us after all. You'd best not show your face after angerin' him so.'

She put out her hands to steady herself by the doorposts.

Her spare bosom rose and fell, showing her to possess a virginal charm of which Peter had been unaware. Her sallow cheeks were flushed and her eyes bright as a robin's. He looked in surprise, and, beholding that she was fair, was suddenly proud and fond of her.

Taking her by the shoulder, he asked, 'Are you thinking there's a hope, gel?'

Her body quivered; she dared not answer.

'Where's Gronwy?' he asked.

'Not come back from the hill yet. Wait you for him here to warn him. I'll save you a nice bit o' supper, good boy.'

'Never mind my supper, gel. Oh, Jane, Jane, if help should come at last!'

Her eyes were softened by tears and he shook her with rough good nature. 'Now then,' he said, 'don't you be acting foolish same as other gels. 'Tisn't like you.'

Nevertheless, he was glad she had betrayed so much feminine weakness. They exchanged a grateful glance, and, with a sniff and a dabbing of her face with her apron, she hurried back into the house.

Peter remained without and peeped in through the window. On either side of the long table sat men and boys as they had done at dinner time, but now they were mute as mourners at a funeral. They did not open their mouths except to put food into them, and even this they did without much relish, for they were trying to eat genteelly. At the head of the table sat the squire with his host and hostess edging away from him. The girls, who had laughed and chattered as they waited on the men earlier in the day, were now subdued by their anxiety to behave like young ladies. Their natural movements had become self-conscious and ungainly. Elizabeth went about her work quietly as before, but, of the others, those who had been most boisterous were now most bashful.

Peter was hungry, but, more than food, he coveted a deep

draught of cider to quench his thirst. Most of all he longed for the singing and hilarity that had always distinguished this crowning day of the shepherd's year. He envied the feast less than he resented the gloom by which it was spoiled. 'If only someone was to sing now,' he thought, 'I 'ouldn't feel my belly so pitiful empty.' To his astonishment, the squire rose, glass in hand. 'Well I never! Is he going to let hisself be jolly for once?'

But Mr Wingfield did not delight the company with a hunting song as his hard-riding, hard-drinking father might have done. There was nothing of the eighteenth or early nineteenth century in him. He was a flower of that serious-minded age which had been inaugurated in the 'forties by the Queen's consort. Therefore, having risen to propose a toast, he took the opportunity to make a lengthy speech. The older men listened politely but without enthusiasm. They roused themselves only to shake their heads at the boys, who began to fidget. The women, awaiting their supper, stood propping themselves against the wall and yawned behind their hands. They had all laboured since dawn and were in no mood to listen to exhortations to do their duty as citizens. Still the squire persisted. Here was a chance to state his case to a tenantry which he knew was disloyal to him. 'They think me a hard man – this John Griffith and his son especially,' he had thought before setting out on this comfortless expedition. 'Now, if only I could make them understand that I was acting on principle, they would not suspect me of avarice in refusing to lend them money. Everything I have done that has made me unpopular with my tenants was done on what I believe to be a right principle. My poor dear father would fling away his money when in a generous mood. The result was a mortgaged estate which it is my duty to set free. I have tried to act providently by my children, justly by my inferiors. If every man did as much the whole country would prosper.' And now, standing at John Griffith's table, he strove, without seeming to defend or excuse himself, to demonstrate the basis of his conduct, and produced, not sympathy, but at first tedium, then active resentment.

Fragments of the speech reached Peter through the window, and caused him to move impatiently from one foot to the other. 'Duty,' he heard repeated many times, and then the name of Gladstone coupled with 'a menace to the established order'. The squire was bitter against Gladstone because he feared him. The Liberal administration of Russell had fallen in June, brought down by that Reform Bill of which the squire had so strongly disapproved. But Reform was by no means dead. Subversive organisations called Trade Unions were for the first time giving definite signs of political activity. The cause of the Franchise might be stayed, but the ex-Chancellor of the Exchequer, whom the squire regarded as the evil genius of the whole agitation, was still powerful, and the dark forces behind him were gathering strength. The great man's shadow lay over the feast at Tinygraig. He was, said the squire, a renegade, a betrayer –'albeit an unconscious betrayer' – of all their 'ordered liberty'.

'I'll be voting for that Gladstone some day, whoever he may be,' Peter thought. 'By God, I'd vote for the devil hisself if the squire was making such a dull old speech against him – not a laugh in it nowhere.'

At last the monotonous voice paused. Then it commanded: 'Three cheers for the Queen!'

With a clatter of overturned chairs the company rose to its feet, and cheering, more expressive of relief than of loyalty, made the crockery rattle.

'Now then, my men, three groans for that seditious rascal Bright.'

Three half-ironical groans followed, and Peter saw several youths nudge one another and grin. 'Old fool!' he thought, 'fancying folks do agree with him because they daren't tell the truth to his face, 'fraid he'll turn them out o' their farms.'

A hand was laid on his arm. Swinging round, he saw Gronwy.

'Man! I am glad to see you at last! The squire is within, an' Jane do think as he might help you after all.'

Gronwy's face became so white that Peter seized him by the arm. 'Are you able to go in an' speak with him? Or shall I fetch you a drink first?'

'No, no. That was father's undoing. I'm calm enough, only – Peter you can't guess what this do mean to me. Pray for me, boy – you are believing, like a child, in prayer – so pray for me.'

He went into the house, and Peter, turning his back upon the window, covered his face with his hands and whispered over and over again, 'Please God, soften the nasty old squire's heart. Please God, make our Gronwy a champion scholar, for Jesus Christ's sake, Amen.'

After what seemed to him an eternity of agonised waiting, he heard a step behind him.

'Is that you, boy?' he asked, without venturing to look round.

'Aye.'

The tone struck a chill through the listener.

'No, no,' he cried. 'The squire can't have refused, not once he was seeing you so sad. He can't never have been so wicked.'

'He spoke kind enough. I don't think he means to be cruel.'

'Damn him! What's the good o' that? Did you beg an' pray of him?'

'How could I, before them all?' Peter turned to expostulate, but Gronwy cut him short. 'Oh, you don't know my position. Even if I'd seen him alone, I couldn't have told him my chief reason now for longing to rise in life.'

'Whyever not?'

'Because I daren't tell it to no one. I scarcely dare confess it to myself.'

A clatter of hobnailed boots warned them that those within were about to come forth. Gronwy turned to meet them with a look of despair.

'Father told me that you were to keep hidden till the squire was gone,' he whispered at parting.

'Damn him!' Peter retorted. 'So I'm to lie hid like a murderer in my own father's house because that old miser isn't liking to see me.'

He strode across the fold, kicking one of the many dogs that lay there so that it fled yelping. Up the ladder into the loft he climbed and paced about like a caged lion. As his tramping to and fro brought him for the tenth time to the window, he caught sight of Elizabeth in the fold below. There was no thought of gallantry in his mind now. The tempting girl was forgotten. But Elizabeth, he knew, could lessen the hurt of his anger as none other could do.

'Betty,' he called, 'come on up here.'

Seeing his face flushed and distorted with passion, she set down the pail of water she was carrying and climbed up to him. He looked terrible in his fury, but she was not afraid for herself.

'You was there,' he began, grasping her by the arm. 'What excuse did he give, with all his money, for not helping our poor Gronwy?'

'Who? The squire?'

'Yes, yes, o' course. Can't you answer a plain question?'

She tried not to wince under the pressure of his fingers. 'He did say a deal about every man doing his duty in his own station o' life.'

Peter released her arm angrily as though she had been to blame. She stood where he had left her, and followed him with sad eyes while he paced to and fro, calling down curses on the squire.

'You are agreeing with all I do say?' he asked at last.

'I am sorry for you,' she answered, 'terrible sorry.'

'Is that all?'

'Isn't love and pity enough?'

''Tis more nor I do deserve, losing my temper so,' he said, coming to a standstill beside her. 'But, look you Betty, 'tis enough to drive a man mad, now isn't it?'

Her grave regard made him ashamed of his violence and he sought to justify it.

'Look,' he said, pulling her by the arm to one side of the loft where the rafters, festooned with cobwebs, sloped down to meet the floor. 'I dursn't stack no wool here, for the old boards is gone so rotten. 'Tis the same with every one o' his farm buildin's – falling to pieces just – while he is living snug as a tick in his great big mansion.'

As she still made no reply, he added with great vehemence: 'Look at that!' and stamped with all his might, so that the board on which they were standing cracked.

'Get back! 'Tisn't safe!' he cried, hastily withdrawing a pace.

Elizabeth was not so quick. Before she could retreat, the worm-eaten board beneath her feet crumbled away and fell with a crash into the stable below. She vanished from sight up to her armpits, and saved herself from falling further only by extending her arms and clinging desperately to the planks which still held on either side of her. Peter rushed forward and seized her hands, but to drag her up was no easy matter. The rotten timbers groaned. A second shower of powdery wood followed the first. He heard a horse below give a shrill squeal of terror, and was sickened by an imagining of Elizabeth's face crashed beneath its hoofs. The sweat poured from his forehead. His heart beat so wildly that he wondered whether it was going to burst. But with a final effort that taxed all his strength he swung her up beside him and carried her in his arms to safety.

After the immediate dread of losing her was over, he leaned limp as a newly dead body against the bales of wool. He was aware of nothing but their yielding softness and the astonishing weakness of his own knees. His arms remained round Elizabeth, and, when he himself was a little recovered, he noticed that she was trembling. He opened his eyes – which, it seemed, he had closed without knowing it – and found to his surprise that she was flushed and smiling.

'You don't seem terrible frightened. Then why are you shaking so?'

"Deed I don't know.'

'Well, I've had a fright. It has turned my guts clean upside down. I'm as giddy as if I'd had tenpennorth on the roundabouts.'

He continued to hold her to him, and neither of them moved.

'Betty,' he said after a while. 'I've been in fights an' seen a powerfuller fellow bear down on me with fists like great big loaves upraised. I've had the squire's keeper come after me when I was a lumper an' I've knowed how he could lay on a horsewhip to boys as he caught poaching. I've had a bull turn nasty on me in his stall an' I've tamed young horses other men was afeared to go nigh.'

'You are wonderful brave,' she murmured.

'Well, I'm telling you the truth now. Nothin' I've gone through did ever give me such a turn in all my life as this has done.'

'Why is that?' she murmured.

'I was dreading to see you hurted.'

'Peter!' She hid her face in his shoulder.

Feeling her body quiver against his own, he pressed it yet closer. A gentle warmth stole through his limbs. He tilted his head that he might see as much of her flushed face as was not nestled into his coat. The sun's last rays, slanting through the single opening in the loft, fell upon her. All the latent richness of her colouring was made manifest. He beheld her brown hair touched with gold and shot with strands of burnished copper. The nape of her neck was not white now but overspread with the soft hue of apricot. Her hands, that clung to the lapels of his coat, were rosy. Slowly he put a hand under her chin and looked down into her eyes. They swam with tears, but her lips were smiling. Then he saw that her mouth was more beautiful than the mouth of any other woman. He longed to kiss her, yet he, who had been bold to make light love to others, was now afraid. He was at once happy and awed as he was when he heard 'Eternal Father strong to save' sung to the accompaniment of an organ's deep notes.

'Peter,' she whispered, 'can it be that you are loving me?'

His lips closed upon hers. She shut her eyes and abandoned herself in ecstasy to his caresses. He strained her to him, uttering little wordless sounds of delight. He let her go that he might seize her hands and cover them with a shower of kisses.

He knew now that he loved her and had been growing in love of her for many years past. Having found what he had sought to hide from himself, he was at peace. How long they had stayed in each other's arms, neither of them could have told when a sharp voice from below recalled them.

'Peter, are you up there? The squire is gone. I've saved you a bit o' supper.'

'A'right, Jane,' he shouted back, his arms tightening about Elizabeth.

'Come on down then, quick! I do want to clear the table. The neighbours is wishful for a concert.'

'Damn the old concert!' He let go of Elizabeth and, retreating a pace, stared at her. 'To think as I didn't guess how I was wanting you this long while!' he exclaimed, and, like a man dazed by a great light, groped his way to the ladder head, and left her standing alone.

She did not follow him at once, but sank on to her knees and buried her face in clasped hands. That so splendid a being as her childhood's hero should stoop to love her was an overwhelming miracle. The tears began to trickle through her interlaced fingers.

'O God,' she prayed, 'as Thou hast been blessing me so, give me strength to serve him faithful all the days o' my life.'

CHAPTER VIII

Elizabeth Refuses Company – A Time-honoured Custom

Throughout the long days of summer, Peter laboured that his family might prosper. Only at night when he lay down to rest did he allow his thoughts to pass from work to love, whereupon sleep straightway overcame him. He was too tired to dream of Elizabeth when he slept, too busy to visit her when awake. Yet the fear never crossed his mind that by neglect he might lose her. That she would be his wife was certain, for thus he had decided it should be. He was so sure of her assent that it never seemed necessary to him to ask it. He talked no longer of seeking a rich wife and suffered no more passing gusts of passion for pretty girls. The thought of Elizabeth as his future bride steadied and contented him. But he was firm in his resolution not to dwell on that thought to the detriment of his brother's prospects. To toil that Gronwy might have money for his education was a duty; to visit the woman who loved him was a temptation to which he must not often yield.

Thus it was by chance that he met her on a certain market day and stopped to exchange a few words.

'You do look that 'ticing today,' said he, ''tis a hard job for a man not to pick you up an' kiss you.'

She was not wearing the tall hat of the older women, but a little bonnet that made a circle like a halo round her face, and showed her sleek hair parted in the centre and brushed down on each side of her forehead. A tight-fitting bodice, full short skirts and a small red shawl completed her demure equipment. Her hands were clasped at her waist and a basket was in the crook of either arm. When Peter spoke, she did not move away or giggle as most country girls would have done, but her cheeks flamed and her eyes grew bright with joy.

'Oh, Peter!' she protested. 'You 'ouldn't never kiss me where everyone could see us?'

'Don't you fear. I'll behave respectable enough with your father's eye upon me. But I'll come courting you one o' these nights, an' then you'll see a difference.'

'When?' she whispered, studying the toe of her boot.

'So soon as ever I can spare time from my work… Damn! There's them sheep broken away down that side street.'

He hurried off without another glance at her, and she saw him again that day only in the distance, talking to his father's customers. His face had become flushed. From time to time he wiped the sweat from it with his coat sleeve, and thrust his cap back on his head. His hair had been oiled for the occasion until it shone with the gloss of a well-groomed horse. She noted with pride that he was taller by a head than most men around him, and that the coltish clumsiness of boyhood was changing to the self-assurance of a man aware of his power. Content to watch him, herself unobserved, she sighed only when her father ordered her home.

'What are you hanging about here for if the butter an' eggs is all sold?' he demanded. 'Get you on back, gel, an' put supper ready for your brother an' me.'

She went, wondering whether another week would pass before she again had sight of Peter. As she passed the Green Dragon inn, a young man was leading his pony out of the yard. She was vaguely aware of his wink and hurried on with her head lowered. But he followed her, shouldering his way through the throng of farmers and their shrill-voiced wives.

'Whyever wouldn't you stop to say a civil word?' he asked, overtaking her and jogging her elbow with his own.

'I was thinking o' something else.'

'Go on! You can't allus be thinking in your head so deep that you can't neither see nor hear me. Three times now I've whistled like a peewit around your house at night.'

'Oh, that was *you*, was it?'

'O' course 'twas I. Didn't I tell you at John Griffith's shearing as I'd come courting you?'

'Well, I do remember your whispering some foolishness when I was waitin' at table.'

'An' you never thought no more about it?'

'I thought you was only joking,' she said.

'No, I do swear by the land it has been no joke to me.' He looked at her beseechingly. 'It has been goin' hard on me when you 'ouldn't so much as look out o' your window.'

'Indeed though, I did look out.'

'Then you did see me in the moonlight?'

'I did see some strange man. I didn't rightly know who 'twas – only – only not him I was expecting.'

She nerved herself to look him steadily in the face. He was a slight, well-proportioned youth with features less massive and more regular than Peter's. She recognised his good looks and reflected that some people might have thought him more prepossessing than her lover; but to her he was only one of many fellow-creatures whose appearance aroused goodwill.

'Well, well,' he sighed, 'so that is it!'

'Yes. That is how it is,' she answered, sorry to disappoint so agreeable a man. ''Tis not as if I didn't fancy you – I, I mean as if I might not have been fancying you, or your like, if – well, 'tis very kind o' you to have paid me the honour o' coming courting me at night, an' I'm much obliged I'm sure, but—'

'But 'tisn't no manner o' use for me to do so, as there is someone else afore me. Is that it?'

She nodded. 'Well, good day now, an' thank you all the same.'

She walked on, but in gloomy silence he kept pace beside her. At length he spoke again.

'You 'on't give us both a chanst?'

She looked up at him, puzzled.

'We could keep you company,' he explained, 'turn an' turn about. Then you would come to know which of us you did like being kissed by the best.'

She suppressed a smile. ''T'ouldn't be hardly seemly.'

'Oh, but I would give you my word, sober now, indeed an' indeed, not to fight him, nor to cause no trouble whatever – only to take my turn o' courting you.'

'But I am not wishful to be courted by none but him. I shouldn't like the feel o' none other touching me.' She felt this explanation of her loyalty to Peter to be inadequate, but it was the best she could give.

'Oh well,' he sighed. 'It don't seem much use my trying to come anigh you now just. But you do know whose son I am, an' where you can find me if you should be giving up this other fellow after a bit.'

'I 'on't never give him up.'

'But maybe he'll give you up,' he suggested brightly.

''T'ouldn't make no difference to my love for him if he did.'

Her firmness chilled him. 'If that's how 'tis, then I'd best try not to think o' you no more.'

He mounted his horse and rode away sorrowfully. She trudged on uphill alone, wishing more than ever that Peter would come to her. 'If he should never marry me, I shall be terrible lonely,' she thought. 'I can never love no other man now, nor want to bear children to none but him, an' I'd dearly love to feel a baby at my breast.'

She turned about to watch the receding figure on horseback. Already it was small upon the road. As she watched it diminish, she became aware that she too, viewed from a distance, must appear a small and insignificant speck on this desolate stretch of highway.

'I am sorry I had to refuse the company of a fellow traveller,' she thought. 'Maybe I should have been glad of it before the journey is done.'

II

Several more weeks passed before Peter visited her. One day, when he had been occupied less than usual by his work, the desire for her grew in him until it could be suppressed no longer. Gronwy had gone out after supper.

'Let him be,' his mother said. 'He has been terrible daunted by this disappointment, an' do like to go scowling about the hilltops alone. 'Tis eating my heart to see the poor lad so pale as he is growed o' late.'

'And yet,' Jane observed, 'I do catch a sort o' tranced smile on his face on times, like as if he had seen that light shining in darkness as he told us of hisself that night he spoke so queer.'

'Ah,' said Mrs Griffith, 'what he meant by that 'tisn't for us to tell.'

'No, no,' John Griffith agreed. 'Scholarship is a fearful an' wonderful thing. We should thank the Lord as honoured us with a scholar in our family, though, mind you, 'tis bringing us nothing only trouble an' expense.'

They discussed the barren glory of learning until Peter's patience was exhausted.

'Let's leave the door unlocked an' go to bed,' he urged.

His mother was reluctant but was at last persuaded. Peter clattered upstairs after her, yawning an elaborate pretence of sleepiness. Long controlled passion surged within him, making his mouth dry and the palms of his hands hot. As soon as heavy breathing from the two rooms across the landing told him that Jane and his parents were asleep, he stole downstairs, carrying his boots in his hand. On the doorstep he put them on again, and, having crossed the fold on tiptoe, vaulted the gate with a great bound of joy at finding himself free. His impatience to reach his sweetheart drove him into a lurching run across the uneven ground. Brambles, invisible in the darkness, snatched at his ankles; once he put his foot in a rabbit hole and fell sprawling. The palms of his hands were grazed, but he picked himself up with many oaths and ran on again.

As the white shapes of Alltgoch appeared in the gloom ahead, a dog darted forth barking. Peter ran on, regardless of the snarling at his heels, until he felt the corduroy of his trousers held in a grip intended for his leg. Then he kicked out vigorously, his foot encountered a soft body and the dog vanished with a yelp of pain. Its yapping from the safety of the hillside awakened other dogs within the buildings. As he entered the fold, he heard them fling themselves against the door of the shed in which they were imprisoned. 'Ha! Ha! you villains,' he laughed. 'You are warning me, are you, that courting by night is a dangerous game? But I can defend myself against man an' beast. I am not afeared o' nothing.' He groped his way between the ricks and searched for a ladder. None was to be found. 'There's a nuisance!' he muttered, and added to himself: 'Damn it all! I'll not go home now without a kiss, not if I have to pull the slates off o' the roof to get at her. But maybe she'll come down to the front door an' let me in.'

With renewed hope he felt his way round to the other side of the house, swung his legs over the low wall which enclosed the scrap of garden, and, picking up a handful of loose earth, threw it with a true aim. The window was opened and Elizabeth's voice sounded close above his head.

'Is that you, Peter?'

'Aye indeed. Who else should it be?'

As he spoke, it occurred to him for the first time that other lads might seek to woo her. 'Come on down an' let me in quick,' he commanded, his tone sharpened by jealousy.

'Is anything the matter?'

'No, only I do want you.' He suspected her of laughing. 'Come on down!' he said again.

'I mustn't come dressed like this whatever.'

He heard her withdraw from the window and waited impatiently for her to descend the stairs. No doubt she was making herself into the formless bundle of clothing which propriety required of a modest girl who received her lover by night.

'She needn't take so long about it. There'll be no shape of 'oman to be felt at all when she's done,' he thought. He took a turn round the garden, kicking at the stones.

'I 'on't wait here no more,' he decided suddenly. 'Damme if I will.'

He strode over to the porch and, seizing the rope-like stems of white jasmine with which it was festooned, dragged himself up on to the leaded roof. From there he could just reach her windowsill. Careless of a fall, he hoisted himself upon it, holding on to the lintel for support. With his disengaged hand he pushed open the lattice and thrust his head into the room.

'Betty!'

She made no answer, but he fancied that he heard a quick breath not far from him. He began to force his way in, though the window was scarcely wide enough to admit his broad shoulders. When, after prodigious effort, he had wriggled through and stood panting within, he found the silence and darkness disconcerting. Not even the faint luminousness of the sky on that cloudy night served to guide him here. He was as helpless as a blind man.

'Betty!' he whispered again, holding out his arms. Slowly he brought them together. They closed upon nothing. He hugged them to him with an aching disappointment. Her unsuspected power to inflict pain surprised him. Her face had been upturned to receive his kisses the first time he had desired to bestow them, and it was this easy yielding that he had imagined ever since. Now, perceiving the potential cruelty of love, he immediately appealed to Elizabeth like a child that has been tricked and is afraid.

'Why are you teasing me so unkind when I do want you so?'

She came towards him with a patter of naked feet on the uncarpeted floor, but stopped beyond his reach.

'No, no, indeed and indeed, I was not meaning to act unkind. You munna think no such thing.' She hesitated. 'I was only turning shy.'

Her voice died down to a whisper and he imagined her hanging her head. Reassured, he groped his way forward, caught at her, missed her, and suddenly found her fast in his arms. His relief at having her there was so great that for a while it stilled his passion. The pressure of his arms was gentle, and gentle the cheek he laid against hers.

'I have missed you something odd.'

'Yet you have not been near me for such a terrible long time.'

''Twasn't for not wanting to. You forget I be growed the man of our family now, with father gone so rheumatic an' Gronwy such a scholar. 'Tis I do have to do all the work.'

'Yes, yes. I am not blaming you boy, only Peter—' She put up her hands to his face and felt it over with her fingertips. 'You are so strong an' so weak too.'

'Well, what is it you are being so solemn serious about?'

'I was thinking as I would never blame you, not all our lives long. If ever you do hurt me—'

'But I 'on't never do so, you gully. I do swear it.'

'Oh, Peter, don't you be swearing so ready, same as your namesake was doing in the Bible, or maybe you'll betray me like he did do his Master.'

He felt her body quiver. 'What is all this sad talk about,' he asked, 'seeing I love you so?'

'Yes, yes dear, you are loving me after your own fashion.

But I do know well enough as our two loves ben't of the same fashion.'

'Go on! Love is love all the world over. Don't talk so dull!'

'Well then, what would you do if you was to find me unfaithful to you?'

'I would make a fine mess with my fists o' the fellow as tried to come atween us.'

'Even if I did love him?'

'Why, all the more then, o' course!'

'There now! That is just where our loves do differ,' she said. 'Neglectful you may be, yes, an' taking up with another 'oman, but I should not be able to raise no anger against you in my heart. 'Tis not for your love o' me as I am loving you. I was doing that long afore ever you looked on me to desire me. 'Tis you, not what you do do, as I do love, an' I could not find it in me to hurt you – no, nor no one as was dear to you neither… Peter, are you thinking as I am talking dull now?'

'No, no,' he answered, 'only I don't know what you are being so afeared of.'

'Nothin' in partic'lar. Only we are young yet, an' there's no knowing what may come to pass. That is why I was wanting to say this to you, dear – no matter what you do do, if 'twas murder, there's one as'll never turn from you, for her love, not being builded on your actions, cannot be brought down by them.' Her hands clasped him about the neck. 'You will remember that? And you 'on't never be afraid or ashamed to come back to me? Promise?'

He moved uneasily. 'Yes, yes. I do promise, only don't let's be so solemn sad, same as if we was in church.'

'Well, but 'twas an act o' worship on my part, the very same as if I had been kneeling at the Lord's Table.' She tried to laugh at herself. 'Oh dear, there's irreligious I am! Come you an' sit down, an' tell me about the work you been doing.'

Glad of her changed mood, he caught her up in his arms

and felt his way with her to the bed. There he laid her down and stretched himself beside her.

'Shall we be pretending as we are man and wife a'ready, Betty?' His question, muffled by her hair in which he had buried his face, set her trembling. 'Indeed an' I wasn't meaning no wickedness,' he reassured her, 'only as we should play a make-believe in our talk.'

'Very well then, boy. Shall we fancy as we are old folks or young?'

'Middle aged,' he decided, 'old enough to have our children growing up, an' not so ancient but what I am still courting you like this.'

He pulled her to him and kissed her. The game was never begun, for with each kiss their breath came faster and at last the silence was broken by a sob as she pushed him away.

'Let me go, sweetheart!' she cried, and, as he obeyed her – 'No, no, don't you leave me like that. I only meant—'

'Oh, I know, I know. Seeing as we can't be married for years to come, I must be acting respectable.' He had risen and moved away into the darkness.

'Peter,' she pleaded. 'Come you back and say as you're not angry with me.'

It was a minute or two before he would consent to sit down on the edge of the bed, and when he did so he still spoke gruffly.

'A gel is having to take care of herself, I suppose.'

'Indeed and indeed, dear, I didn't think only o' myself. I reckon as you would be sorry too if – if—'

'A'right. A'right. I'll do you no harm.'

''On't you come back, then, an' hold me in your arms?'

'No I 'on't. I'll bide by here.'

'Very well, boy,' she sighed. 'Now shall we play as we're married?'

'What's the use? 'His voice was sullen. ''Twill be years an' years afore ever we can be.' He drummed on the floor with his heels. 'Money!' he exclaimed suddenly. 'That's what we do lack. Folks as do lack money dursn't give way to love. 'Tis reckoned a sin in them as can't pay for it.'

'Pay for it?' she echoed.

'Yes, pay! 'Tis the old whose blood is cold as can afford to buy what they don't need. The young must burn and consume theirselves.'

She felt along the coverlet for his hand. 'No, no, Peter. Love can't never be bought. Only bodies can. Love is given free to rich an' poor alike, same as mine was given to you.'

His fingers closed upon hers. ''Tis all very well for you to say such honey-sweet soft things,' he grumbled. 'I'm a man, an' I do want my wife.'

He threw himself down beside her again. His arms met round the bundle of coarse woollen material in which she was encased. He could smell flannel and household soap, honest smells associated with her.

'Oh, my little sweetheart,' he whispered, 'don't you understand as I am longing to bring you home my bride an' have you to sleep in my arms every night instead o' visiting you once in a while like this, an' having to go just when I'm most yearning to stay? I do want you by night to love, an' by day to see you about my home with your quiet slow ways, an' the weeds you're bringing in from the fields, an' your pretty foolishness to the beasts.'

'I'll make your home a happy place some day.'

'But I do want you now – now!' he cried. 'I'm wanting to see our children grow up around me while I am yet hearty.' His voice sounded thick with swallowed tears.

''Tis hard to wait an' wait an' see no end to my waiting.'

'Yes, yes,' she murmured, stroking his hair, ''tis hard on you.' Her fingers passed over his face with soothing caresses until he grew calmer and presently sat up, brushing his forelock from his eyes.

'Well, well,' he said, 'since I mustn't be giving them to

you now, let's see how many children you are going to bear me. Give me your hands.' He took them both in one of his. 'We'll try the left first. That's the gels. We'll keep the best till the end. But how shall we tell if you are to have more nor five of each sort?'

'Maybe some o' my fingers would crack twice then,' she suggested.

'Ah, I suppose … I've never tried this way o' reading the future, though I've often heard tell of it. Have you?'

'Never,' she answered. 'I never did wish to try it with none but you.'

He took her fingers one by one and pulled them about in their sockets till he hurt her and she protested, 'You mustn't try so hard to have daughters. 'Twill happen natural or not at all.'

'Well, well, they're not for us seemingly,' he said at last, laying down her hand. 'I would have liked to see one growing up the spit o' her mother. But there, the boys is the cream, the gels is nothing but skim milk after all. If you'll give me five fine boys, swamping fellows as can fight the neighbours off our bit o' pasture, I'll not say nothing about the lack o' gels.'

He took her right hand and cautiously tried the thumb. It gave no sound. He tugged at the first and second fingers with increasing firmness, but they were equally silent.

'Damn me!' he exclaimed. 'I am not going to be a lucky father.'

He pulled the third finger almost out of joint. Elizabeth uttered a little cry of pain, but there was no sound of cracking. Peter was depressed.

'Well,' he muttered, 'I'm blessed if you aren't going to be a barren. I never would have feared such a thing of a healthy gel with a fine shape like yours.'

'Try the little finger,' she urged. 'One child is better than none whatever.' She forced a laugh when he hesitated, though she was as anxious as he for the good omen. 'I do believe you are afeared.'

''Tis the last chance, look you,' he answered. 'And think what a loss o' wealth it is for a farmer to beget no sons.'

''Tis a loss o' love for a woman to bear none.'

'Maybe; but you can't want them so much as I do.'

She held his hands fast. 'Peter!'

'Yes, gel?'

'Suppose as a prophet should rise from the dead an' tell you as I would never conceive, would you sooner be free o' me?'

He swept her up into his arms. 'No, no, indeed! Strong sons do help a man to rise in life. But you – why I would give you the run o' your teeth in my place even if you was all cost an' no profit, my little bitty.'

She nestled against his shoulder. 'I'll not be that.'

'O' course not. But don't you go thinking there's nothing I do care for only money.'

'You do care for it a powerful lot, Peter.'

'Well yes,' he admitted. 'And mind you, I do mean to have it too. Now where's that small little finger o' yours?'

He felt for her right hand and pulled the joint that was their last hope. A faint crack delighted them both.

'We'll have one boy at least,' they cried in unison. For a long time they paused in their kisses only that they might draw breath to kiss again.

'I must be getting back along now,' he sighed at length.

'Aye,' she agreed in a subdued voice, 'we both of us have our work to do in the morning so soon as it is light.'

'Never mind,' he said, giving her a final hug, 'when we are married, I'll be staying close to you, closer nor ever you have let me come yet, an' then there'll be no more rising hungry from table. I'll take my fill o' sweets as is denied me now.'

He parted from her with a dozen playful threats that made

her cheek grow hot; but the cold walk home sobered him. Like a man who has been over-confident in his cups, he was made doubly despondent in the reaction.

'Rachel she did ought to be called for the many years as I'll have to serve for her,' he reflected.

From a distance an owl uttered a long-drawn screech and its mate in the branches of a tree dimly visible above Peter's head answered with a succession of sharp little cries.

'I-do want her-now. I-do want her-now,' were the words suggested to his mind by these sounds.

'Aye. I do wish as I didn't want her so tormenting much,' he said, almost aloud. 'I do wish I did live like Gronwy in a scholar's dream, loving only some legend o' the Lady Helen, not a woman o' flesh an' blood like my Betty.'

CHAPTER IX

Susan becomes a Spy – Laetitia promises Help –And is Frustrated

One day, towards the close of that summer, the solitary figure of a woman emerged from the woods surrounding the squire's house, and began to ascend the hillside to its rear. Above the lively green of the beech trees was spread a belt of gorse aflower with gold. Higher still, where the tall bracken grew, was green of a deeper shade, and near it purple heather and fegg grass burnt apricot by the sun. Clouds, round and white as puffballs, sailed across a blue sky, their violet shadows chasing one another on the earth below; and larks darted up singing on every side of the climber. She, black clad and with head bent, was intent only on preserving her skirt from the brambles, and on picking her way daintily between the rabbit holes. She noticed nothing but the dangers threatening her clothes. When she was not absorbed in avoiding these, her thoughts, because they were so vehement, formed themselves into phrases, broken as the breaths she drew.

'Why hasn't he come to see me? Even if I am a servant, I'm not so poor as his folk … Make haste, she'll be back from her ride, and ringing for me to dress her up again for dinner. Always at her beck and call, I never get a chance to meet him. What has changed him so? Another woman?'

Her chin was thrust forward and the line of her lips contracted to a thread. With a strength born of jealousy, she redoubled her efforts, and, reaching the summit at last, leaned exhausted against the trunk of a May tree that clung there. Her back was turned to the valley from which she had come. Before her stretched a wide tract of grassland, broken only by outcrops of rocks and showing no sign of any living creature but the grazing sheep.

As she rested, a man appeared on the horizon to her left. First his head became visible, then his shoulders, and finally his long legs. Though some way off, he seemed a giant, for he was the only upright creature emerging from the long undulations of the tableland. The stick he carried and the dog accompanying him suggested that he was a shepherd. A whistle, borne by the wind to Susan's ears, confirmed this supposition, and produced a movement among the sheep, who were clearly familiar with its warning. They began to move rapidly from the sheltered hollows where they had congregated to the higher ground on which it was the shepherd's business to make them graze in fine weather. Susan noticed the letter G stamped in tar upon the white flank of one of the nearest ewes.

'They are his,' she thought. 'Yes, 'tis his father's land I am on now, and that is sure to be he coming towards me.' She flattened herself against the tree, intending to surprise him by stepping forth when he had drawn closer. 'He'll be kinder today,' she told herself, feeling as he approached a need of reassurance. 'I've got on my best black; that's in the very height of fashion. He said I had the daintiest shape in the fair that first time he set eyes on me. Such honey-sweet things he said then! I thought him quite the gentleman. Surely he'll say them again today, meeting me here alone like this.' She readjusted her bonnet and gave a pat to her curls. As he strode towards her, it seemed with increasing haste, she became more self-confident. 'I'm looking my best now, I declare I am, all flushed with climbing. He'll see me different to the night I was foolish enough to visit his father's house when I was out of curl and wet with the storm. I do wish I had her silks and jewels, though. Then I'd make sure of him!'

Suddenly she saw him raise his arm as if in salutation.

'He's seen me,' she murmured with a throb of delight, and started forward, but was arrested by the sight of another shape appearing on the horizon to her right. This was of a woman on horseback. Susan retreated beneath the overhanging branches and awaited the intruder's advance. Even at a distance she was recognisably not a farmer's daughter, nor was she mounted from a farm. Having put her horse to a canter, she was riding straight towards Gronwy, the long skirt of her habit and the veil that hung from her tall hat streaming behind her. Susan's eyes widened in astonishment. 'It can't be she! Yet there isn't her like in the county. Why is she riding alone, and how is it he seemed to be expecting her? Whatever business could such as they have to bring them together?'

Suddenly the flush died from her face. The rider had reined in her horse beside the shepherd and his arms were raised to receive her.

'Oh, the randy piece!' Susan exclaimed beneath her breath.

But the figures outlined against the sky did not embrace as she had expected. Gronwy helped Laetitia to alight and, while she seated herself on a rock, remained standing respectfully, holding her horse. Hope revived within Susan. Perhaps her first wild impulse to rush out and denounce them had been absurd. At any rate it would have been fatal to herself. She had her living to earn and must suffer in silence. Trying to make the best of this bitter reflection, she assured herself that one so proud as her mistress could have none but a business interest in a man so far beneath her in station. But what could this business be?

When Laetitia waved Gronwy to a place beside her, Susan winced; when he seated himself a yard away, she drew breath again. Upon the patch of sky visible between their two figures, a little cloud sailed past.

'Why has she bidden one of his class to sit in her presence if they are not courting? Yet why, if they are courting, dursn't he touch her?' Susan could conceive of no relationship between a man and a woman that was at once emotional and physically remote. The longer she watched the tantalising drama being enacted beyond her hearing, the less could she understand it.

Unsatisfied curiosity became so painful that it would have driven her away if it had been possible for her to move unobserved, but to have ceased spying on her mistress now would have been to betray herself. In despair, she closed her eyes. 'I can't bear to look at them no more… Suppose if he is kissing her now?' The thought stabbed her into a desire to see, no matter how the seeing might torture her. She clenched her fists and opened her eyes. The figures on the rock were unmoved; the strip of sky between them was as wide as ever. 'Strange,' Susan muttered. 'If only I could hear, I should understand.'

II

Though Susan had heard, she would not easily have understood.

Laetitia's head was turned away from Gronwy, but she was aware of his gaze fixed upon her with a reverent admiration impossible to resent. A faint smile hovered about her lips. His unspoken homage was mildly exhilarating like the soft breeze that stirred the grass about them.

'How good this is!' she exclaimed. 'How different from my home! Look – there is nothing which is not beautiful in the whole wide world as we see it from here.'

'And no one as is not sympathetic.'

She answered only with an inclination of her head.

'Harmony!' she murmured after a while.

'Harmony!' he echoed with a luxurious sigh.

When she spoke again, it was with a nervous increase of animation. 'That is the special charm of our friendship – the sense of harmony – how shall I express it?'

'There are no words in which to do so.'

She shot a smile at him. 'And you a poet?'

'If I am more of a poet than other men, 'tis only in knowing better how little can ever be said…' he paused, gazing at her, '…about – about the holy an' lovely things in life.'

She turned away her eyes. 'Then let us discover what our friendship is not,' she said with a forced gaiety of tone. 'There are words for that at any rate. It is not practical. There is no money concerned in it, no social advancement to be gained by our meeting with only the sky and the earth to witness. Down there…' she pointed in the direction of her home – 'they could never understand – this.'

'Because 'tis not anything as can be touched.' he said looking at her ungloved hand lying within his reach on the rock. 'It arose from no forethought, an' will lead nowhere, nor leave nothing behind to show as it ever was. None will know of it but you and I. 'Tis like the moon-rainbow we saw together that first night when the rest o' mankind was asleep. There is no mark upon the earth to tell where that thing o' passing beauty once was. It came. It vanished. We cannot show others how fair it was. But we two know. When you and I are gone our separate ways along the high road an' the low wherein our feet were set at birth, a recollection is all as 'ull survive o' this, this miracle.'

She dared not look at him and for a time no word passed between them.

'Come,' she said at last. 'What shall I teach you today?'

She had assumed a little air at once complacent and brisk, suited to the part of governess, but his answer disconcerted her.

'Whatever you like – or nothing at all. 'Tis much the same. Just to be near you, Lady Helen, do learn me all ever poet could desire to know.'

Though her colour heightened, she answered stiffly: 'Last time we met, I told you about Sir George Scott and Mr Ruskin, and the Gothic revival in architecture, do you remember?'

'I am storing in my heart your every word. No one of them shall ever be more cold than it was upon your lips.'

She began to play with the silken tassel on her riding-whip and to talk rapidly, keeping her eyes fixed on the ground. In the shelter of the rock upon which they sat, the sheep had by long rubbing worn away the grass and a patch of earth was exposed that the sun and wind had dried. Upon this natural blackboard, she drew illustrations to her lecture – the pointed arch of 'the paramount style which dear Mr Ruskin has described so enchantingly' and the rectangular lines of classical architecture which she confessed to finding 'a little formal and unromantic'.

Gronwy looked from the diagrams to the slim hand that traced them, and thence to Laetitia's face. To him she was, as she had always been, ideally lovely, but the ideal was less coldly remote than it had been. Her lips were more full and red, and her expression had softened; her eyes, when they rested upon him, were filled sometimes with a shyness that made him afraid, so clearly did it proclaim her to be woman; her cheeks, too, were warmer and more rounded than they had been, and he fancied that perhaps she smiled now more often than she had hitherto. While she spoke and he gazed at her, the breeze had been growing into a wind. Suddenly it swept down upon them, raising a swirl of dust.

'Oh,' cried Laetitia, 'my temples and palaces have all vanished! Look, there is only dust left there in their place.'

'That is how it will be with my ambitions.'

'Oh, no, no. They will be fulfilled.'

He shook his head. 'Such dreams as mine do not come true for those in my station.'

'But other great men have risen in life.'

'Those who have done so were given help when they needed it. There is none to help me but your father, and he would not.'

She stared at the dusty patch beneath her feet. 'Perhaps if I were to ask him,' she said. 'I have not dared. He so disapproves of ladies interfering with his business, but I will try. Yes, I will help you. You shall not say there is none to do that.'

III

As she rode homeward, she repeated the words to herself. Across the springy turf of the hilltop, the scent of flowering gorse drifted up to her from the lower slopes, and presently a sheet of gold came into view. Slackening her rein, and half closing her eyes, she drew in the perfume.

What would be the end of this idyll? Some day, she supposed, she would marry, but not until a man altogether different from her father's friends appeared. Marriage had been the one hope of escape from the monotonous days she had had to live. In winter, sitting at her embroidery frame and longing for any employment that should keep her mind – or was it her emotion? – as busy as her fingers; in summer, strolling idly in a garden whose neatness seemed to say 'there is no work for you here', she had imagined herself in the cultured London world to which marriage alone could give her access. On the gravelled terrace before the house, where no figure but that of some patiently stooping gardener ever intruded upon her solitude, she had in fancy moved among a crowd of distinguished guests. There, suave ambassadors had paid their tribute to the genius of artists whom it would be her special delight to honour. Great ladies had lent the sparkle of their jewels, wits their sprightliness, scholars their dignity, to assemblies richer in talent and beauty than any that was ever gathered in this world.

Now, these fancies had been superseded by an actual interest. Her new friend and pupil absorbed her thoughts. Not until this moment, when she asked herself whither their companionship would lead, had the prospect of marriage re-entered her mind. She tried to visualise her husband, only to find her imagination occupied by the man she had just left. Some day she would lead him to that inevitable husband and would say, 'This is the friend of whom I told you.' Then the two men, the one so clear before her, the other mistily imagined as many years older and benevolently unobtrusive, would smile at each other. 'She taught me all that she knew of the arts,' Gronwy would say. 'She lent me the books which first formed my taste. Hers was the faith that inspired my early poems, and hers the encouragement without which I should have despaired. She risked the contempt of family and friends in condescending to one who was of simple birth and without means. It was through her brave intercession with her stern father that I obtained my university fees.'

She had reached the drive gate. Beech shadow and sunlight shaft rippled across her face as she cantered up to the house. Bright-eyed she reached the stable-yard and threw the reins to a boy.

'Is your master in?' she asked of a maid encountered in the hall.

'Yes, miss. And, if you please miss, he was asking for you now just. He's in his study, miss.'

Laetitia knocked at his door.

'Come in.'

He glanced up from a lease that lay spread out before him on the littered desk. She was familiar with that look of worry, hardened into severity. It was inauspicious, but a glance at her reflection in a mirror made her confident of her power to soften him.

'You sent for me, Papa?'

'An hour ago at least. Where have you been all this while?'

'Out riding, Papa. I have only this moment returned. Pray forgive me, if I had known…'

He did not return her smile, but frowned, and fidgeted with his lease. She longed to seize his hands and stop their irritating movement, but kept control of herself while the clock ticked away and her courage began to ebb. At length he delivered himself of the speech with which he had been in travail.

'I was displeased to discover today that you were out riding alone. I met Thomas in the yard and asked him why the deuce he was not with you. To my astonishment he told me that you frequently ride unattended. It is the first I have heard of it. Will you kindly tell me what makes you do such a thing?'

Her fingers tightened on the ivory handle of her riding whip. 'Thomas is getting stiff and old, Papa. I have not the heart to order him out.'

'Nonsense! He is quite capable of as much hard riding as a lady is ever likely to undertake. Besides, if he were not, there are the younger grooms. Why could you not have taken one of them?'

'I did not think you would object to my going up on the hill behind the house alone.'

'I do object – very strongly.'

'But you know I go gathering flowers in the woods alone, Papa.'

'That is quite a different matter from being seen riding without a manservant behind you. You are not a child any longer, and you ought to realise what is becoming in a young gentlewoman. Upon my soul, I shall be obliged to engage a companion, a middle-aged lady who will have my authority to forbid your doing conspicuous things, if you cannot be trusted to avoid them for yourself.'

'Oh, pray Papa, do not think of doing that. It shall never occur again, I promise you.'

'I should think not! The idea of a daughter of mine gallivanting about the country like a farmer's wench going to a fair! You will have farm lads offering to escort you next.'

She coloured so deeply that the lobes of her ears, peeping from beneath her dark hair, showed pink as coral.

'Please, Papa…'

'You think me harsh? Recollect that not long ago you arranged to meet one of my tenant's sons, by no means a desirable family either, and to go scrambling down to the river's bank with him. It was only by chance that I found out about this escapade. I begin to wonder how many more of the kind you have planned.'

'Papa!'

'Be so good as to listen to what I have to say without interrupting me. It adds greatly to my already overburdening anxieties to discover that you are such a madcap.' He tapped the lease; then a copy of *The Times* that lay beside it. She knew that he was thinking of the July rioting in Hyde Park and of the Reform speeches that were now being made throughout the country. His talk had been of little else since the fall of the Liberal government which she had hoped in vain might have reassured him. 'It's like him,' she thought, 'to vent his temper on me.'

'I should have thought,' he continued, 'that your poor dear mother's sister would have taught you to behave with decorum, if she had taught you nothing else. But she seems only to have put a lot of nonsensical notions into your head.'

Laetitia stiffened. 'She is dead, Papa; and I loved her. I loved her more than anyone living,' she added with passion, her eyes flashing daggers.

'Very well, very well. I have not a word to say against the poor lady but that she might have brought you up better.'

He had not intended to become embroiled in a discussion

of his sister-in-law. He respected loyalty to the dead – though why his own daughter should have shown so much more fondness for that blue-stocking spinster than for himself, he could not for the life of him understand. It was improper and perverse. A girl ought to love the author of her being more than anyone else. In any case, he must assert his authority; that was his duty.

'There is another matter,' he said, 'in which you will oblige me by being more discreet. I consider your familiarity with your inferiors most ill-judged. Do not interrupt me again. I know what you were about to say. Nowadays it has become fashionable for ladies to visit the poor. I have no objection to your doing so occasionally, though in my dear mother's time that would have been considered an occupation more fitted for an elderly widow or a pious spinster than for a girl of your age. I have no great liking for your hearing all manner of coarse topics discussed by the common people. My sister would never dream of allowing her little Lucy to acquire an undesirable knowledge of life by going in and out of their homes. Send soup and jellies by all means when they are ill. My dear mother always did so. You have my fullest approval in doing whatever our station requires that you should do. But you need not allow the tenants to take liberties.'

'But Papa, I scarcely ever speak to one of them, and as to visiting their homes…'

'Then how comes it that you have been lending books to the Griffiths of Tinygraig?'

'Is it a crime to lend books to those who are longing to read them?'

He paused for control before answering. 'Do you think it becoming or dutiful to use sarcasm to your father?' he asked. 'I am not discussing crime. I am warning you, for your own good, that your conduct is conspicuous and likely to prove harmful to yourself and to others. We each of us have our duty to perform in our appointed station of life. I have never aped those who are in a higher position than myself. I have tried to live as a country gentleman of moderate means should live, attending to my estate and to my responsibilities as a magistrate. I do not, therefore, expect my tenants to envy or attempt to copy our class. The nobility, gentry and common people of this realm have each their proper sphere. In my opinion, it would be the ruin of England to change this. Each class is best fitted to carry on the work to which it has been accustomed, and all this nonsense about universal education would, if put into practice, result only in making the agricultural labourer discontented. Let those whose lot it is to follow the plough, follow it and keep their minds on it. They will be worse labourers and less happy men, if you fill their heads with other matters.'

'But, Papa, there are exceptions surely – rare spirits.'

'Rare spirits be…' He checked himself with difficulty. 'Upon my word, I've not time to listen to such romantical girlish nonsense. There is nothing to be gained by discussing general principles with a woman. I ought to have known that.' He cast an angry glance at the portrait of his dead wife. 'Let me make myself perfectly clear and stick to facts. I missed several volumes from my library.'

'Did you want them to read?'

That mocking voice might have spoken from the grave. His temper rose.

'What has that to do with it, pray? There were vacant spaces on my shelves. Upon enquiry, I found that you had been lending books of mine – of mine, mark you – to a common labourer who has probably spoiled them with his unwashed hands. You will be so good as to get the books back immediately. You will further oblige me by not again disposing of my property without having the courtesy to ask my permission.'

She said nothing. That had been another of her mother's

tricks – to enclose her disdain within a rampart of silence unnatural in a woman.

'This Griffith of Tinygraig,' he burst out at last, 'is an unsound fellow. He was suspected of being a Chartist in his youth. He drinks like most of his class and had the impudence to come here when he was drunk and tell me I ought to make a parson of his elder son. He brought with him a younger one who proved himself to be an insolent fellow; and now I am informed by the groom who took my books to Tinygraig that the daughter also is most disrespectful to her betters. The other tenants tell me that the elder brother is a conceited good-for-nothing. He is universally disliked.'

'People do dislike their intellectual superiors.'

'I have no wish to discuss the intellectual superiority of these people. In my opinion, you are putting them out of their place, and I forbid you in future to have anything to do with them. That, I trust, puts an end to the matter.'

'Is that all you have to say to me?'

'That is all.'

Her face had lost its flush of eagerness and was pale with curbed resentment. She covered him from head to foot with a slow look of contempt, and turned away. He watched her cross the room, and was proud, even in his annoyance, of her regal carriage. His study, half office, half gunroom, would become an unattractive place when she was gone. He had intended to admonish her, but not to drive her away. Incomprehensible though she was to him always, and infuriating sometimes, he had a need of her presence, a hunger for the tenderness he repelled. Perhaps he had been too harsh. He was sorry, and felt awkward. She was in the act of closing the door behind her, when he called her back.

'Letty!' She turned without advancing. 'Come here and kiss me.'

He had meant to say more, but the words of reconciliation were checked by her immobility.

'Come here and kiss me, my dear.'

His tone now was nervously peremptory. She mistook its intention, and hated him for humiliating her.

'Well?' he said, wondering what little present he could make her that would win her forgiveness.

With compressed lips she came to him, stooped, and touched him coldly on the cheek. She knew that such a kiss was less satisfying to him than an angry refusal. Her eyes were smarting, but the thought 'he would enjoy to see me cry', kept back the tears. But, once upstairs in her room, she flung herself down on her bed and wept with passionate abandonment. 'Miser!' she thought, 'with all his wealth that he spends on such dull, stupid things – food, and his cellar, and keeping up this hateful place – to deny a poor genius his chance in life, to grudge him the loan of a book even. How shall I tell Gronwy Griffith? It will break his poor, poor heart.' But, in the midst of her grief, she raised her face from the pillow to see how it looked when wet with tears. 'They don't suit me,' she decided. 'I am most beautiful when I am happy.'

Susan, who had hurried back from her hiding place, knocked at the door.

'Go away,' the voice from within answered her. 'I am not coming down for dinner tonight.'

Susan allowed her retreating footsteps to be heard, but returned more quietly and listened at the keyhole. She heard nothing but a sigh and the turning of a page. Laetitia, having bathed her eyes and re-arranged her hair, was reading sad poetry consistent with her mood.

CHAPTER X

A Meeting and an Encounter

As summer and autumn passed, the squire, awakening now and then from worried absorption in affairs, noticed that his daughter rode abroad less often than had been her custom. The discovery gave him no kind of satisfaction. He had told her to ride accompanied, not to abstain from riding, and was more inclined to blame her change of habit for what he considered its sulkiness, than to praise it as obedience. She had always been the same – fractious and stubborn. Even when he had told her, as a child, not to disturb his quiet by rustling the pages of a picture book, she had closed the book rather than enjoy it in any way of his choosing. It was an irritating method because it was open to no reproof. He could not then compel her to read; he could not now compel her to ride. Whenever she did take out a horse, she was attended as he had ordered; towards him she was coldly deferential. With that, though it pleased him little, he had to be content.

One afternoon towards the end of October, he set out in his carriage to inspect the staking of a stream which he thought poachers were netting. No sooner had the sound of the slow, high-stepping of his horses died away, than Laetitia came out of the house. A sunny haze gave to the landscape the vague richness that it would have presented to one who looked at it through amber glass. No wind shook the branches of the trees; they drew as rigid and almost as formal a pattern on the sky as the wrought-iron gates which a Wingfield, long since dead, had brought home from his grand tour and set up at the park entrance. From time to time, however, one of the few remaining leaves became detached and floated down to join those that were already thickly piled, brown and crisp as brandy snaps, round the moss-padded roots of the trees.

The skirt of Laetitia's gown licked up these leaves as she passed and set them crackling. Even so little sound alarmed her, and she paused abruptly, turning her head this way and that, and using her dark eyes with the suspicious alertness of a thrush that hops in timid jerks towards a dangerous fruit garden. A flapping of wings set her heart beating quickly, and she was scarcely reassured when, glancing up, she saw a flock of wood-pigeon in rapid flight. A distant shot gun told her that they also were in peril. Charles and the beaters were out and were near.

She went forward nevertheless. Though her secret meetings with Gronwy entailed now more risk than in the past, they were for that reason no less attractive to her. Danger, indeed, gave them in her eyes a colour that she was powerless to resist, and, when she found Gronwy leaning against the gate which gave access to the hill behind the house, she saw in his quiet figure a symbol of her own defiant adventure. Her colour rose, her lips quivered into a smile, but her eyes remained anxious.

'I feared I should not be able to come,' she said. 'My brother and Sir Edward are shooting over the home farm today. I did not know of it until an hour ago when it was too late to send you a message. We must not stay and talk. The woods are full of beaters.'

'My brother is one 'o them,' he answered. 'The young squire sent word last night for us both to come an' beat for him.'

'And you came to me in spite of him?'

He smiled as one who had no need to speak his thought and she was proud of his loyalty.

'We have both of us taken risks,' she said. 'There—' She

thrust a couple of books into his hands and turned to go. 'These are all I can afford at the moment.'

He stared from her to the books and back at her again. 'Afford – how is that?'

She frowned in vexation at having let him know the truth.

'It is nothing, I assure you; I can manage to get a little money next month, and I am not denying myself anything I want in buying you books.' Her smile was less imperious than any she had given him; it was timid, almost beseeching.

'But,' he began, 'but you – you to be in need o' money! I don't understand. I never guessed.'

'Oh, you need not fear that I lack any luxury money can buy. But it pleases my papa that I should have to beg for a new bonnet or a pair of slippers every time I need one. I suppose, as parents go, he is very generous; I ought not to talk like this. But I would rather have a tenth of what he spends upon me and be allowed to do with it as I pleased.' She glanced down at the massive gold broach fastening the collar of her bodice. 'I am tired of being treated like a child, and sad that I can do so little to help you. I would sell my jewellery if only I knew how to do it. But,' she sighed, 'there is no one I could trust with so compromising a business, and I am at a loss how to set about it myself.'

Gronwy's eyes were full of brooding trouble. ''Tis horrible,' he broke out at last. 'You are like the bewitched princess in the fairy tale, living in a palace an' having all you can desire save that which living people desire most – their liberty.'

She smiled at him wistfully. 'You always think of something to say to me that makes my lot endurable,' she said. 'At home I am made to feel more like a naughty schoolgirl than an enchanted princess.'

He was silent for a while, his dark brows drawn together. 'Why did you have to buy books for me at all?' he asked. 'You did lend them to me out o' the squire's library when first you favoured me in my ignorance. Why has that changed? Was your father missing his property?'

'Yes, his property!' she cried. 'That is just what he called the books I lent you, books he could never appreciate as you do.'

'So he forbade you to lend me more?' And when, by her shamed silence, she had assented, he exclaimed in a voice changed by pride: 'I do wish as I had never touched one o' his books. Wanting them as I did, I would never have laid a finger on them if I had known.'

'Oh, don't – don't!' she said. 'I am ashamed enough already. I wanted you never to guess.'

Because there were tears in her eyes, there awoke in him a tenderness he had not dared to feel for her before. He leaned over the gate towards her. Indications of woman, inviting mortal love, he had perceived in his divinity of late, but it was the brimming of her tears that revealed her to him. He was overwhelmed with joy, and longed to seize her hands and kiss them. But it had been an accepted symbol of their relationship that neither should touch the other except in some formal way; he had never taken her hand except in helping her to dismount, and the habit, though the spirit of it was destroyed, held him now. But she was aware of change in him. With a nervous movement, she brushed away the tears which had accomplished so great a revolution and stepped back from the gate.

'I must go,' she said.

He awoke out of a trance. 'No, no – not now – not just when—'

'Yes, now,' she insisted. She turned swiftly, but as swiftly came back with a look of entreaty in her face. 'You will keep my books, will you not? Tell me that you are not proud and resentful against me?'

He would have fallen upon his knees before her, protesting his devotion, but could neither move nor speak. She waited, looking up at him, no longer aloof.

'Whatever you bring me I – I will accept,' he stammered at last.

The words, when he had uttered them, coldly touched his heart. What could this love bring him but despair?

'When shall I set eyes on you again?' he cried, seeing her move from him.

She paused and glanced back over her shoulder. There was no pose of hers, he thought, that had not an enchanting grace, but this he would everlastingly remember.

'It is difficult,' she said. 'I am not allowed to ride alone, and at this season of the year my brother is always patrolling the place with his gun.'

'But,' he implored her, 'do you contrive it somehow.'

'Yes. I will send you a message whenever it can be arranged.'

'Soon?'

She smiled at him, but there was no hope in her eyes. Away she went speeding, out of his sight between the tree stems, like a kingfisher flashing downstream. Somehow, at some time, he would see her again for a few minutes. He looked forward now to nothing in life but these rare meetings. In the spring of the year, he had still clung to the hope that means would be found, or might be earned, to pay for his education. That faith, so long and obstinately held, had died within him, and nothing else remained.

'The life of a country lad do offer no rewards to such as I,' he thought. 'My hunger is not for such food as the labour of hands can procure. Nor am I thirsting to get drunk at market, and shout my lungs empty as I race my neighbours home on horseback. Neither would the soberer joys o' the older men satisfy me. There is no red-faced wench I wish to see sitting at my fireside, rocking a never-empty cradle.'

The longings and regrets of years and the bitter disappointments of the last nine months weighed heavily upon him as he leaned on the gate, staring at the grass where Laetitia had stood. His mind went out into wild places. Only his helpless love for Laetitia, he told himself, now held him to life. But for this, and the happiness he had in reading the books she gave him, there was no pleasure he might expect – no hope, and therefore no reason, in continued existence. And to linger for this pleasure that was a torment? His grip loosened on the bar and he drove his nail into the ingrained moss.

A shout of laughter interrupted his gloomy reverie. Turning with a sudden twist of hunched shoulders as if to protect himself from a blow, he saw two young men coming towards him with the easy strides of those who live in the country but are not bound to the plough. Behind them a party of estate labourers trudged along, laden with dead rabbits and birds that swung from poles carried across their shoulders. As they approached, a rustling of fallen leaves drew Gronwy's attention from them to the path by which Laetitia had disappeared. He turned in swift alarm, but found, instead of the woman he had feared to see, a wounded rabbit dragging itself into cover to die, with broken hind-legs that trailed upon the ground behind it. He was familiar with these sights, but they never failed to move him to disgust and pity. His anger was now directed against the squire's son and his friend. He did not move out of their way when they reached the gate. Charles Wingfield looked him up and down in surprise.

'Hello! Aren't you another of John Griffth's sons?'

'Yes, sir,' answered Gronwy, sullenly staring at the trail of blood left upon the leaves by the mangled rabbit.

'Then why the devil weren't you out beating for us? We missed a lot of game through being short of beaters.'

Gronwy surveyed the approaching group with their load of carnage. 'You did kill more than ever you want to eat,' he observed.

'What the hell d'you mean? I asked you why you were not out with us?'

'I had other work to do.'

Charles's pink face was unsuited to express any emotion but sulkiness or complacency, but the blond eyebrows went up and the lips were pushed out in contempt. Gronwy, following the scornful glance, saw that in his own hands were clasped the books Lactitia had given him. He thrust them into his pockets.

'That doesn't look much like work,' the young squire said, and his companion laughed his approval.

Gronwy looked from one to the other of them. Both alike seemed to him sleek, well fed animals. In the shallow blue eyes with which they stared at him, there was no more power of speculative thought than in his own brother's, and they had none of that fine leanness of form and manliness of expression which the discipline of a hard life had given to Peter. Peter, he knew, had nothing in common with himself, but he loved and admired him. The two young men before him, he despised; and, being sore at heart, he did not trouble to disguise it.

'Not all work is manual,' he said. 'There's just a few of us do work with our brains.'

The young men exchanged a glance of amusement. He noticed with regret that his irony did not make them wince.

'I should have thought manual labour pretty important in your case,' said Charles. 'You hope to earn your living on a farm, eh?'

'My father and my brother do that.'

'Oh, I see; and you live on their backs?'

'No, I do not. I do work every day as you an' your friend there 'ould find a rough change after your bit of idle sport with servants to carry your game for you.'

They stared at him, astonished by his insolence.

'If I do take a bit o' time off once in a while,' he went on, ''tis in the hope of rising to be something better than one o' your tenants.'

'You won't be that long, I can assure you, when I come into the estate,' Charles retorted, moving on through the gateway into the wood.

'Impertinent good-for-nothing, pretending to be an undiscovered genius, lolling over a gate all day long with a closed book in his hand.' Gronwy heard the words and the laughter that greeted them. Peter also heard. He was at his brother's side with a bound, and flung down the rabbits he was carrying.

'Let him come back an' fetch what he has had the fun o' killing,' he cried. 'I'll never be a beast o' burden to him no more.'

Gronwy's face was still pale with resentment, but there was a triumphant curl to his lips.

'No need to vex yourself, boy. I could tell that coxcomb something as would make him hang his head lower than ever he thinks to bring mine.'

Peter stared. 'Whatever is that?'

'His sister was here not half an hour since talking to me, as she do often do in secret.'

The other labourers passed them with inquisitive glances. Peter's mouth had dropped open in dismay, but he kept silence until the last of the beaters was out of hearing. Then he asked in a bewildered voice:

"Tisn't true as you do often meet the squire's daughter?'

Gronwy nodded. His instant of furious scorn having passed, he was full of remorse for his betrayal of Laetitia's secret.

'By accident?' Peter asked with increasing distress. Gronwy shook his head. 'Then you an' she are sweethearts?'

There was no answer.

'Oh, boy, boy,' Peter cried. 'Wherever can such madness lead to?'

'My love for her?' said Gronwy. 'What need is there for it to lead to anything beyond itself? 'Tis the most perfect thing ever I knew. Is that not enough?'

Peter looked at him apprehensively. 'Don't talk so wild,' he said. 'Think, man, whatever will become o' your courting such as her?'

'What becomes o' the rainbow?' Gronwy answered. ''Tis here for a time, transforming the hills with its loveliness. And then 'tis gone.'

'But we are not speaking o' rainbows,' Peter persisted, 'but o' love o' man and 'oman. That, if 'tis fortunate, do lead to a home an' children.'

Gronwy hesitated; then, with raised voice, asked almost angrily: 'Do you fancy as I'd ever dare to think o' Miss Wingfield as a – as a possible – wife?'

'How ever do you think on her, then – a keepmiss?'

'You'd not understand,' Gronwy answered.

'No,' said Peter, angry in his turn. 'I do not understand. I do want my sweetheart to sleep with, an' so do any other man that is right in his head.'

'Come then,' Gronwy replied with a weary smile. 'Let us go home, and say no more about this.'

CHAPTER XI

Laetitia Refuses and Meets with Refusal

Throughout the first fortnight in November, rain fell steadily with a soft kissing sound. Day after day, Laetitia awoke to hear the dripping of water from the eaves, and, when she looked out, to see the beech trunks as slimy and black as the slugs that crawled along the garden paths.

She went out little, for she could not drag her unwieldy skirts and petticoats through the mud that covered every road with a thick carpet, and on horseback the presence of a groom spoiled what pleasure she might have had in riding between drenched hedges under a putty-coloured sky. She tried to amuse herself instead with the fashionable cross-stitch and the painting of still-life groups; but already her father's house was overfull of such amateur decoration. 'There is no demand for anything I can do,' she thought, and neither paintbrush nor needle could satisfy her long. For an afternoon she found mild excitement in reading Byron's forbidden *Don Juan*, but it was not to her taste, and her old favourites, which had enthralled her during the previous winter, pleased her no more. Even Mr Tennyson would slide from her lap and leave her to gaze through the streaming window panes and long for the return of spring.

At length there came a night of frost and on the morrow a gleam of straw-coloured sunshine. With a fur tippet over her shoulders, she went out on to the terrace and leaned with folded arms on the stone parapet. Perhaps, if the weather held, she might soon meet Gronwy again. Then she started up with sudden resolution. 'Why should I not go to him now?' she asked herself. 'He may be out shepherding on the hill where we can talk without fear of detection. What a relief to have someone to talk to, someone who understands!' Her decision taken, she turned to execute it, and saw her father coming towards her from the house. His steps were short and hurried, and his perpetual frown was deeper than usual. 'I have done something to displease him again,' she decided, her lips, which had been smiling a moment ago, contracting into a hard line.

'I thought you were going to the magistrates' meeting at Llangantyn after breakfast today, Papa,' she said.

'So I was, but young Lee called unexpectedly and detained me.'

'So early?'

'He had some business – rather pressing. At least, having made up his mind to it, I suppose…' He paused, drumming on the parapet. 'He had something rather important to say to me.'

'Indeed?'

Her studied indifference added to his embarrassment. 'It concerns yourself, my dear. I may as well tell you at once.'

Her first feeling was of relief; his ill-humour was not for her, then, 'You mean that Sir Edward asked you for my hand in marriage, Papa?'

He started. 'Well, upon my soul, he did not give me to understand that you knew anything about it. He has spoken to you himself, the young rascal?'

'No. He hadn't the courage to do that,'

The anxious lines about the squire's face relaxed. 'You don't like him, eh? I told Charles that in my opinion you had never given the fellow the slightest encouragement.'

She had feared that her brother's friend might have found an ally in her father, but, far from being disappointed, he was, it seemed, relieved by her coolness. She took her cue.

'What is your advice, Papa?'

That pleased him. The question had been put in a submissive tone, but she was inclined to laugh at its result. Her father tugged at his iron-grey whiskers, adjusted his cravat and cleared his throat. She had seen him go through the same movements a dozen times on the platform. 'If only I dared be myself with him for once,' she thought, perhaps he would be natural with me in return, but I must not risk angering him now.'

'Of course it is my wish to see my only daughter happily settled,' he announced.

'But you would not care much for Edward Lee as a son-in-law?'

The squire seemed to struggle with himself. 'He is not a bad match,' he forced himself to say. 'Comes of a good family; has a respectable property adjoining our own. Your brother is strongly in favour of your accepting him.'

'Oh, so he has been consulted already?'

'Young Lee naturally appealed to him to use a brother's influence.'

Laetitia's lip curled. 'He has not put himself to much pains to appeal to me. That, I suppose, was not necessary since the properties adjoin.'

'It was only right and proper, my dear, that he should ask my consent before attempting to win my daughter's affections.'

There was an awkward silence.

'Well?' the squire said at last.

'Well?' she echoed.

'Are your feelings…' he hesitated, '…inclined favourably?'

'I am not in love with him, if that is what you mean, Papa.'

'Love?' Her father shook his head. 'I don't know about that. This is an important question, my dear, highly important. We must all take a common sense view of it.'

The emotional agitation which clearly accompanied this speech amused her. How bravely he was struggling to be fair to the robber!

'Think it over,' he said.

'I have done so, Papa. I guessed long ago that this was coming, though I tried to prevent it.'

'You would prefer to remain single for the present?' In spite of himself, his tone was eager.

'I have no wish to marry Sir Edward,' she answered.

Suddenly he took her hand in his and gave it a convulsive squeeze with his bony fingers. He was unreasonably happy. The thought that he was not to lose her made him giddy for a moment; then drowsy with content, as he had been when, as a young man, he led this girl's mother, undemonstrative as Laetitia herself, down the aisle of a village church. He recalled a glimpse of his bride's face as they walked together across the graveyard, and, looking at Laetitia, saw the same hint of latent passion in the red lips and the dark eyes, whose meaning he could never fathom. She was there, close to him still, and she did not wish to desert him. He wanted to laugh aloud with relief, like a man released from pain. The struggle to behave as became an English gentleman had racked him. Somewhere among the unacknowledged roots of his being was a primitive desire to keep this girl for himself. It had surprised him by making him absurdly jealous of a young man whom he had liked until this morning. For an embarrassing moment he wondered whether he would dislike equally any man who attempted to take his daughter from him, but thrust the difficult thought aside. He wanted youth near him to sustain his old age, and Laetitia was young and good to look upon. That was all, he told himself – and natural enough. What father did not love his daughter? But an instinct, which he had striven to suppress, cried out that he had more than ordinary need of her. Charles, too, was young, and his reasoned affection for the heir to the Wingfield property was altogether different from his feeling towards Laetitia.

'Sometimes you complain of having a dull time here, my dear,' he said, taking her arm. 'I tell you what I will do – invite my sister Emily and little Lucy here for Christmas and give a ball. How will that do?'

Laetitia looked at him in silence, seeming to weigh her answer which he had hoped would be an exclamation of pleasure.

'Come now, will that satisfy you?' he said, patting her hand. 'You shall have the handsomest gown money can buy, and wear all your poor mother's jewels. I have kept the best of them for you in the bank. There is a fine set of rubies I gave her on our wedding day. And we will send out invitations to the whole county. You and Lucy may go to the Hunt Ball too, if your aunt will chaperon you. You ladies like to show off your fine feathers, eh?'

'Papa, dear,' she began and hesitated, visibly more nervous now than when she had received news of Edward Lee's proposal. 'Do you really wish to do something to please me?'

'I do, my dear.'

'Then I had far rather you gave me the money to spend on something else. Would you do so? Oh, Papa, you cannot guess what pleasure you have it in your power to give me.'

'What is it you want? A new piano? A pony chaise to drive yourself? You shall have it, if it is anything within reason.'

'I want nothing for myself, Papa.'

'That's strange for a woman, isn't it?' he asked with chilling suspicion.

'Now and then a woman wants to help someone else.'

'Well, then, what is it you do want?'

She felt the arm that touched her stiffen. He was beginning to suspect her of 'some odd notion'. How much easier her task would have been, she reflected, if it had been entirely selfish!

'You remember that young tenant of yours who wanted to be educated—'

He cut her short. 'Upon my word, when I offer you a treat for Christmas, I do not expect to have it made an occasion to re-open that discussion. I told you once for all that it was closed.'

'But, Papa, you would be doing me a favour, you would be giving me the greatest possible treat, in helping one…' Her father's cold stare made her stammer, '…one in whom I – for whom I feel – sorry.'

'What made you recall that good-for-nothing fellow? Have you spoken to him again? I forbade you to encourage any of that Griffith family. Charles tells me that the young man in question was most insolent to him the other day.'

She did not answer his questions. Because he was her father, she dared not tell him the truth. Phrases of earnest entreaty formed themselves in her mind, but she was afraid to utter them. Her eyes smarted with unshed tears and her lips trembled, but with an effort she regained control of herself.

'It seems a pity that the young man should not have his chance if he is deserving,' she said.

On the squire's face was the set look she had seen there when a servant tried to explain why it had been impossible to obey one of his orders.

'Listen to me, my dear. I am not refusing to pay for the young man's education only because I can ill afford it, but because it is against my principle to put him out of his place.'

She knew then that it was useless to argue any more. She gave a little sigh and turned away, but her father would not release her.

'If this young man,' he said, 'were able by his own exertions to rise into a class above his own, it would be a different matter. I will concede that there are men of genius here and there who have a right to be accepted as equals by their social superiors. But they must establish such a right for themselves.'

'How can he possibly do so when he is so pitifully poor?' she interrupted.

'Kindly allow me to finish what I was about to say. If this young man cannot rise in life without first taking money from those towards whom he shows so little respect, then he had better remain in his own station and learn to do his duty there. You forget that his father and grandfather before him have been ignorant shepherds. It stands to reason that the lad is unlikely to make a successful scholar.'

'There have been peasant scholars,' she answered. 'There are many of them in Wales today.'

'Then why can't he do as they have done? Tell me that. Have they all been nursed by their landlord?'

'No, but they have been helped by their own chapels. You know that they are nearly all non-conformists. The Griffiths' difficulty is that they are Church people. They must be helped by members of our class, if they are to be helped at all. Papa dear, why should we allow it to be said that English landlords and parsons discourage education? There must be poor people on churchmen's estates whom it would be worthwhile to help forward.'

'A few rare cases, there may be,' he conceded. 'But you mustn't look for genius in every farmhouse. Breeding tells after all. Bless my soul, if you had spent a lifetime, as I have, in the breeding of stock, you would not doubt the principles of heredity on which I base my objection to this new-fangled nonsense of putting everyone out of his place. Let the labourer's son continue to till the soil, and the descendant of generations of trained rulers govern the country. They will each do their own work best.'

There was a desert of silence.

'Come, come,' said the squire, feeling that he had been unjustly treated, 'let us talk about something pleasanter than social problems of which you fortunate young ladies know nothing. Are you pleased with the idea of my giving a dance at Christmas, eh? Are you going to thank me for it?'

He waited hungrily for her to speak. At last, like a child pushed forward to recite its lesson, she answered: 'Thank you, Papa. I ought to be very much obliged to you, I am sure.'

CHAPTER XII

Guests arrive – Mamma and Miss – Susan delivers a Letter

The approach of that year's Christmas made Wingfield Park busy with more than ordinary preparations. On the day of Aunt Emily's arrival they were in full swing. Snow had fallen at night and the morning was heavily overcast, but at noon the sun pushed its way through and suddenly all the world was a-glitter. The whitewashed ceilings of rooms habitually dark became lit from below by a reflected brilliance, and even into the warren of passages that lay between the dining room and the kitchen a cold and austere twilight penetrated.

Laetitia, standing at the entrance to the storeroom, could see the black-clad figure of the housekeeper moving about between the sacks that stood in orderly rows upon the floor. These – and her breath shortened at the remembrance – these were the sacks of Joseph's brethren; as a child, she had peeped into the mouth of each to find the money hidden there. In this quiet, strangely scented room where her mother used to give out the weekly stores, she had played a thousand games which now rose up before her with a ghostly melancholy. What a place of enchantment it had been! In that dark corner had sat the old fairy who spun gold upon her spinning wheel. Never, never, Laetitia thought, would that imagined wheel turn again.

With a rustle of silk she came into the room and raised the lid of the tea-chest. There was the lining of tin foil that had once seemed to her so costly. Upon the shelves, just as she remembered them, were ranged the prosperous looking pots of jam and jelly, each bearing on its paper lid a title and the day, month and year of its manufacture. Next to these were blond jars of honey. The pickles stood apart, making a swarthier show, and the boot-blacking, candles and all kinds of housemaids' property occupied a lower shelf, from which hung nets containing lumps of soap she had longed to eat, believing them to be monstrous caramels. There, too, was the cask of paraffin. Even this had lost its magic. Once, in the days when she knew that a touch would transform it into a sheet of flame, there had been a thrill of exquisite terror in every flattened journey between it and the wall. Now it was vilely safe. She turned away from it to the vessels that contained the dried fruits that were used in Christmas puddings and, wishing that she could not see into them so easily, lifted the lid of each in turn. Currants, raisins, candied peel – all of them hers for the taking. She let the lids fall again. She had never been particularly greedy for sweet things, she remembered; Charles had been the greedy one. Charles had always been making himself sick by over-eating. If he, as she did once, had hidden himself behind the dreaded cask and been accidentally locked into the storeroom, he would not have missed so splendid an opportunity. He would have eaten and eaten. He might even have died of it – poor Charles – and the Wingfields have lost their heir among the sugar plums. Well, by the history books, kings had died without more dignity… But she had been different from Charles. She had exercised moderation even towards the damson cheese and had not eaten too much of anything. Instead she had climbed very cautiously upon an upturned bucket lifted on to the seat of the chair. There, perilously perched, she had gone, like the Athenians, in search of new things; feeling, looking, and guardedly tasting her way along the upper shelves – slimly on tiptoe.

In the midst of her daydreams, the housekeeper approached her and waited sourly for orders. When she had given them, she idly watched a group of maids, under Pink's majestic direction, setting sprigs of holly behind the engravings of Lord-Lieutenants and High Sheriffs of the county, which were hung in the dark passage leading to the servants' hall. Already the greater part of the house had been transformed, by many days' labour, into a prickly mass of evergreens. Bunches of mistletoe hung from the galleries and dripped their sticky berries on to the polished floor. The furniture reeked of beeswax. For a week past the under housemaids had been running as if there were not a moment in which to walk, and the flapping of dusters and aprons had put Laetitia in mind of a rookery at roosting time. Country girls, imported to work in the scullery, lost their way among the corridors, and, encountering the lady of the house, flattened themselves against the walls, hanging their heads or giggling with red hands clapped to their mouths.

Leaving Pink and his High Sheriffs, Laetitia glanced into the butler's pantry. A footman in his shirtsleeves was polishing the additional mass of silver that was now unpacked from the chests in which for years past it had been stored. Beads of sweat were on his forehead; he was coughing in a cloud of bone dust; but, when he had breath enough, he hummed a tune. Everyone but herself for whom the dance was being given, and her father, who was giving it to please her, seemed to be agreeably excited. They were busy; she alone had to look on. 'My life here will be like this always,' she thought, 'the life of an indifferent spectator. And if I were ever to marry Edward Lee, what would the change signify? I should superintend the dusting of ugly portraits every spring, but they would be dead Lees instead of dead Wingfields. I should order the same plate to be taken out for county celebrations, but it would bear the Lee crest instead of Papa's. The footmen would have livery of a different colour;

the eternal drawing room would have been furnished by his mamma instead of mine. What a revolution! But perhaps, as a bride, I might be privileged to alter things a little. I should have a new damasked suite if I begged for it prettily. But nothing, of course, foreign or "outlandish", as Charles would say!'

'Laetitia! Laetitia! 'cried Charles's voice. 'Hello! Where are you?'

'Here I am,' she answered. 'Here!'

'Oh, there you are!' he said, striding towards her. 'They've come.'

'Who have come?'

'Why, Lucy – and Aunt Emily. Didn't you know they were expected today? I thought all these preparations were for her – I mean, for them.'

'I had no idea they would arrive before nightfall.'

'Oh, I'll tell you how that was. They found the train service so bad from Buckinghamshire that they were forced to start a day earlier and put up last night in Hereford. I was down in Llangantyn, pitching in to the gunsmith, when I happened to see them alight at the railway station. Wasn't that fortunate?'

'Very.'

'Yes, by Jove. I don't know what they'd have done – two ladies without an escort – only a maid with them – if it hadn't been for me.' He stood smiling, and slapping his top-boot with his riding whip. 'I hired a carriage – the best I could get, but a musty old thing, not fit for her to set foot in – and I drove up with them myself.'

'You left your horse in Llangantyn?'

He stared at her and burst into a shout of laughter. 'Well, upon my soul! I gave him to a lad to hold and I'm dashed if he's not standing in the middle of the street still! Gad, I clean forgot I had a horse! I had better send a groom down for him before Papa finds out. He's quite upset as it is by a sister and a niece of his having to drive up from the station in a hired fly. They did send a flimsy, you know, but those blockheads at the post office have only this moment delivered it. Some ladies would have been in hysterics, I dare say, arriving like that with no one to meet them. But Lucy was splendid – treated it all as a joke.'

'That *was* splendid of her!' said Laetitia.

Charles rushed on, undeflected by irony. 'Yes, wasn't it? Laetitia, she *has* altered. She's grown deuced pretty. I'd no idea she'd develop like that.'

'But I thought she was always your favourite cousin when you were children?'

'So she was, but—'

'But now you like her for other reasons? Then, I remember, it was because she used to save the raisins out of her cake and push them into your pinafore pocket when nurse was not looking.'

He laughed. 'Oh, she's quite a grown-up woman now. Come and see for yourself.'

He took her arm, as he had not done for months, and hurried her towards the drawing room. She wondered whether he had decided to fall in love with his cousin. He had often echoed his father's phrase – 'a man wants a fine-looking woman to sit at the head of his table.' Lucy, it appeared, had become qualified to fill that position, and, from what Laetitia could recall of her, it seemed that she would make a comfortable as well as an eminently suitable match. 'What Lucy's dear Mamma and kind Uncle Charles desire her to do she will manage to find pleasure in doing,' Laetitia thought. 'It's a pity my emotions are not equally well-regulated.'

Mrs Bodley-Booth, looking for all the world like a broody hen in her speckled brown silk and her ruffles of cream-coloured lace, received her niece's salutation sitting; Lucy, as befitted her age, rose and fluttered forward, seeming to hasten, but keeping careful control of her features, her bonnet-strings, her frills, her floating draperies and her reticule. She greeted Laetitia with a smile, a light pressure of the hand, and a yet lighter kiss, each suited to the occasion and perfected by practice under her mother's instruction.

'She is certainly thoroughly well-trained,' Laetitia said to herself. 'How coldly those china-blue eyes would stare if their owner knew the story of Gronwy!' For a moment she almost envied Lucy her decorous security. Then her heart rebelled and spoke to her, as hearts have always spoken to ladies who favour the romantic tradition: Life, it said – and the dark eyes now looked scornfully, pityingly into the blue – life was worth living only if it were lived dangerously – in the grand manner!

II

Breakfast at Wingfield Park was scarcely less formal than dinner. It had a ritual of embraces performed with a nice care for precedence. Aunt Emily's night was found upon enquiry to have been 'exceedingly comfortable', though she had feared, when she lay down, that she might have been a little over-fatigued by her journey. Lucy, more briefly, had 'slept like a bird, Uncle dear,' and Charles, exploring the contents of many silver-lidded dishes, very pleasantly imagined her bird-like slumbers and thought the simile entrancing. Meanwhile Laetitia, who was guilty of forgetting Aunt Emily's taste in sugar, presided over tea and coffee. There was beer, too, a decorative piece of conservatism in a Georgian flagon – beer for breakfast, as there had always been. No one, except Charles in his first Cambridge vacation, had touched it for years. The squire himself had once thought tentatively of abolishing it, but his heart had failed him. 'A pleasant old custom if I may say so,' Pink had said, and Pink, having conquered a master willingly persuaded, still carried off each morning the spoils of victory. Besides, it tickled the squire to be asked questions about that flagon by young guests who had known no monarch but Victoria. If it went now from the breakfast table, it would – well, it would leave a gap.

'I must do my morning round of the stables,' Charles announced when he could eat no more. His eyes rested upon Lucy with the critical approval he bestowed on good horse-flesh. For this attention she thanked him with a dimple, and he added, as carelessly as possible, that he might look into the drawing room later in the day to see how the ladies were amusing themselves. Then, with a glance of defiance at Laetitia, of whose smiling observation he had become aware, he strode from the room, and his female relations were able to cease toying with the crumbs of a meal they had long since finished. They made an organised departure. Aunt Emily led the line, a flagship in full sail, but Laetitia and her cousin hesitated. Each urged the other to go first, until Laetitia, wearying of formality, caught Lucy by the arm and attempted the doorway in line abreast. The channel proved too narrow for their crinolines and their disentanglement was at once prolonged and polite. Indeed, when they were at last free and smoothed down, they went off to the drawing room with all the apologies and laughter that courtesy required. But Laetitia understood, and was intended to understand, from the look in Aunt Emily's eye, that Lucy would never have been so roughly impulsive. Aunt Emily was surprised.

In the drawing room, a suitable chair and footstool had to be found for Aunt Emily and the beaded firescreen to be adjusted so that the logs might not scorch her. When her tatting had been fetched by Lucy, it fell to Laetitia to entertain her with conversation. She soon found that it was easier to let her guests choose their own topics than to tempt them vainly with hers. How shamefully, Aunt Emily said, ladies' maids ill-used old lace! How clumsily housemaids treated old china! Really, it was more than carelessness. Often, Aunt Emily thought, the damage was spitefully done –

in jealousy inspired by radical teaching, for always it was the most valuable thing they chose to destroy. They were ignorant creatures, talkative and frivolous. They had no notion of the difference between good porcelain and bad; they'd be as well pleased, she was sure, to deck themselves with some florid imitation as with her own *point de Venise*. And they were too lazy to learn.

'But if they do not know, Mamma,' said Lucy unexpectedly, 'how can they choose the best pieces to destroy? I feel sure Martha Grigg was not spiteful when she broke my shepherdess' crook. She was most repentant when you sent her away.'

'Yes, my love,' her mother answered. 'But in saying that you show – and I am glad of it – that you have as yet a very imperfect knowledge of the world. You must allow that my experience has been the greater, and – Lucy darling – not dispute what I say with that quick little tongue of yours. Of course Grigg was repentant when she was found out. You forget that she attempted, in a most underhand way, to stick the crook on again.' Mrs Bodley-Booth laid down her tatting. 'Fortunately,' she added, 'it did not adhere, and by ridding ourselves of her we protected ourselves no doubt from more serious losses.'

Lucy, blushing under affectionate reproof, was learning that it was unwise to detect flaws in the maternal logic. And, indeed, poor girl, she had intended nothing of the kind, but only, by one of the questions which were from time to time required of her, to prevent her mother's speech from becoming too conspicuously a monologue. The question, unfortunately, had been over-intelligent.

'I beg your pardon, Mamma,' she said. 'I had forgotten Grigg's deception.'

Laetitia found it hard to endure. Would they talk of nothing but their servants and, their possessions? She dared provocatively to wonder whether Mr Swinburne's critics were justified in attacking his notorious *Poems and Ballads* as they had done – or rather, she added hastily, in quite the terms they had employed. Mrs Bodley-Booth looked at her, looked at Lucy, looked back at her again – that was enough for Mr Swinburne. Laetitia stumbled into the safer paths of Mr Tennyson only to find that Lucy's tutored rapture made her suspicious of her own enthusiasms. And suddenly she yawned – an incredible, unpardonable, uncontrollable yawn. The gods concealed it from Aunt Emily, but Lucy saw.

'Sleepy, Laetitia dear?' said she.

'Sleepy within an hour of breakfast?' said Aunt Emily, looking up. 'How could that be?'

'Well, Mamma,' said Lucy, 'she…' The temptation was almost irresistible, but Lucy nobly resisted it. After all, it might be unwise to anger Laetitia before the ball. 'Well, Mamma,' she began again, 'sometimes a hot fire is very affecting.'

At this moment Laetitia saw her father ride past the shut windows on his way to the home farm. Now at last she might leave her guests without fear of encountering him and being reproved for incivility. Making an excuse of household duties, she fled to her own room.

She had not been there long, however, enjoying the peace of a snowy landscape, when a knock on the door made her turn with a nervous start, as if detected in guilt. Her gaze had travelled down the white slope to where a line of trees marked the river's bank. She had been trying to identify the position of the wishing chair. 'This is too childish,' she thought. 'I am too much alone. I dwell on romantic absurdities. It's a good thing I have someone here of my own class to talk to at last.' Yet, as she called 'Come in,' there was so much more of irritation than of welcome in her tone that her cousin hesitated.

'They told me you had come upstairs, dear. You are not busy, are you?'

'As though I were ever busy!'

'Aren't you?'

The eyes that stared at Laetitia, opaque and shallow as little blue china plaques, grew rounder than ever. Round – then doubtful. Their owner had detected irony in Laetitia's smile, and decided to treat her strange speech as a joke.

'But why do you laugh?' Laetitia asked, looking straight at her cousin with disconcerting gravity. 'Are you ever busy?'

'Why yes, of course, dear. Mamma does not approve of my being idle. So I am always employed.'

'At what, pray?'

'Oh, fancy work and—'

'Don't you get tired of that? I do.'

'But I do so many other things. I collect wildflowers and press them – that is when we are in the country. In town there are always cards to leave. One spends half one's day driving from door to door. And the dressmaker and the milliner take up so much time. And when we are going out to evening parties I have to lie down in the afternoon. Mamma is so particular about my not looking tired. Oh yes, there's always a great deal to do.'

'I wish I found it so.'

'You would, dear, I assure you, if your papa did not live here in such seclusion.' A note of patronage crept into her voice. 'You really must persuade him to let you come and stay with us in town next season. Mamma took a house in Mecklenburg Square last year because I was coming out – in spite of the fear of cholera in London, too. Wasn't it sweet of her? She says that, like the poor dear Queen, she would never have been seen in public since Papa passed away if she did not consider it her duty to go out for my sake. You've no idea how truly unselfish Mamma is ... It was ever such a fashionably furnished house with an imposing suite of reception rooms – so delightful for my coming-out dance.

And the stabling was so good too. If your papa would allow you to bring your own horse and groom with you, we could ride in the Park together.'

'It is very kind of you to want me,' said Laetitia, and she tried to feel grateful. But she found herself turning away towards the window, looking once more at that black scar that split the landscape. The pause was broken at last by her asking, 'Lucy, what people does Aunt Emily permit you to meet in London – what sort of people, I mean?'

'Oh, everyone! All the nicest families one meets at the Hunt Ball at home.'

'The same people always?

'Yes, most of them. You know there is quite an exodus from our county for the season. Of course we are so much nearer town than you are here.' Again that note of patronage. 'In Wales, you county families become quite rustic, I dare say.'

But the little scratch did not seem to have its intended effect on Laetitia.

'Do you never meet artists?' she enquired.

'Artists? Well, Mamma had my portrait painted by a Mrs Ward last year, in my first ball frock. My dear, I wore—'

'But she is not a friend of the family's?'

'What, the painter? Oh no, she was paid for her work.'

The corners of Laetitia's mouth twitched. 'Like the other tradesmen?'

Lucy looked blank. 'Oh no, dear, she is quite ladylike. The Queen often used to visit her studio.'

'I suppose,' said Laetitia with a smile, 'you never meet Mr Rossetti or Mr Millais or any of the giants of the Brotherhood?'

Lucy shook her head. 'Mamma is rather exclusive. Some of the Whig hostesses entertain men of no family, painters and people of that kind, but Mamma does not visit at their houses. She always likes to know whom she will meet, especially when she is taking me with her. It's natural, isn't it?'

'In case you should hear expressed any original view on any subject?'

Lucy tried not to look puzzled. 'I don't care much for conversaziones and musical evenings. I prefer balls.' Her face resumed its usual complacency. 'We go to a great many balls.'

'If Aunt Emily were really so kind as to take me to town next year, should I go night after night to balls, precisely like the one Papa is giving here on Tuesday? The same sort of people would be at them, I mean, only they would be up for a few weeks of the season instead of staying all the year round on their estates as we do here?'

Lucy, too polite to say that therein lay the whole difference between country bumpkins and the best people, adroitly diverted the conversation, which had made her feel vaguely ill at ease.

'Oh, that reminds me, dear, of what I came to ask your advice upon.'

Laetitia turned round from the window with an eagerness that alarmed her cousin. Lucy's face was hopefully searched for whatever secret might lie beneath its smooth exterior. It was both soft and hard, as only the face of a naturally virginal and artificially sheltered girl can be. It bore no trace of love or hatred or fear, of pity or suffering.

'If I can help—' Latitia faltered. 'Shall we try to be friends, Lucy, and tell each other things?' There was no reply. 'I am rather lonely sometimes,' she added.

The cold eyes grew round once more. 'What, with your dear papa and your dear brother?'

'But I have no girl friends. It would be such a relief to have someone to whom I could talk freely… And you?'

'Oh,' said Lucy, 'what I came to ask you about was only what wreath I should wear at the dance.'

Laetitia went to the window again. 'Fool!' she told herself. 'Fool to expect anything else. She'll suit Charles to perfection.'

'I thought pink,' Lucy was saying. 'My dress is white, of course. But I have brought both pink and blue ribands.'

'Why not wear both, then?'

'Oh, Laetitia, do pray be serious. I prefer forget-me-not blue, but there are no flowers to be had in winter that would match it, are there?'

'I'm afraid not,' Laetitia answered, her back still turned to her cousin. The snow had obliterated all the small hollows and minor ruggednesses of the landscape, leaving visible only the vast outlines of the hills. 'How a few blue ribands would brighten this outlook!' she exclaimed. 'I wish I saw ribands wherever I looked.'

Lucy was increasingly puzzled, but she maintained a polite appearance of good-humour.

'How droll you are, dear! Now do tell me. Would not pink roses out of your conservatory look sweet with my pink ribands? I have a knot of them to wear on each shoulder, and one for the centre of my bodice.'

'That sounds quite correct.'

'You really think so? I am so glad. I was afraid that real flowers worn in the hair were just a trifle out of date. The Princess of Wales used to wear them when she was first married – when was it – three years ago? So of course everyone else copied her. She is so lovely! Have you seen her?'

'No.'

'I have, often. What was I saying? Oh yes. Now the fashion is all for plain chignons, very large.'

'Then surely you ought to wear a plain chignon, very large, too?'

Lucy pouted. 'I suppose I ought, but a wreath of flowers round one's head is so becoming. I should so much like to wear one if you do not think it would make me look conspicuous?'

'I don't think you would be in the least danger of being that.'

'Then I shall wear a wreath. Is your head gardener clever at making such things?'

Susan now appeared carrying a box.

'The carrier has brought this, miss.'

'Oh, my ball dress.'

'How exciting!' Lucy cried, jumping on to the edge of the bed where she sat with her little dangling feet just visible beneath the frills of her skirt. 'Do pray open it, my dear and let me see.'

'Certainly, if it would amuse you. You may open it, Jones.'

The maid's fingers were quick to undo the string and lift the lid. She and Lucy bent their heads over the dress when it was spread out upon the coverlet. Laetitia watched them, half contempt, half envy.

'I wonder whether anyone here will like it or if I was a fool to waste my time designing something unusual.'

'You designed it yourself!' Lucy cried. 'How clever of you, but how daring! It is unusual – quite without trimming – not at all like my last frock that came from Paris. But never mind. I am sure the artists, in whose pictures you are so interested, would admire it very much.'

'None of them will ever see it.'

'Indeed, miss, you will look like a bride!' Susan interposed, darting up at her mistress one of her fox-like glances. 'What a lot of smart goings on there will be the day you are married to Squire Lee.'

'Don't talk nonsense, Jones.'

'I beg pardon, miss. I'm sure I meant no offence,' said Susan; and she added, with a quick, forced giggle which, if Laetitia had been of her own class, would have been the winking nudge that facetiously excuses all amatory jesting – 'But, if you won't have him, then, by your leave, there's a higher-up gentleman perhaps?'

Laetitia winced, and Lucy, though more than a little surprised that, even in Wales, such familiarity was possible, exclaimed, 'Come, confess! Is there? Is he to be present at the dance, that rather particular somebody?'

'No,' said Laetitia, and a rebel thought came: 'I wish he were. He may be their social inferior, but he worships beauty of which they would know nothing.'

'Oh,' cried Lucy, 'but he ought to be there, whoever he is! There is always a Prince Charming as well as a Princess in the fairy tales.'

'Not in the ones they tell in these parts, miss,' Susan put in.

Lucy looked at her, her blonde eyebrows slightly raised. Her Mamma's maid would not have ventured to speak without being spoken to. Cousin Laetitia, she feared, allowed these talkative Welsh servants to forget their place. Nevertheless, curiosity prompted her to ask: 'What happens, pray, in the local fairy tales?'

'The son of a farmer, a poor small little farmer, falls in love with a princess.'

Lucy looked incredulous. 'Then the story ends sadly for him?'

'And for her too, miss. They meet in secret. She is as sweet on him as he on her. Yes, indeed, that's how the old story goes. But, of course, marriage is not for such as them, set so far apart. In some of the tales, 'tis true they do marry after a fashion, but it is always ending the same – her going back to her own folk and leaving him broken-hearted to die or to lose his reason. That's what comes of loving out of your station… But there, miss, 'tis just a lot of nonsense the old folks used to tell us when we were children.'

'The moral seems to be quite a sound one,' said Lucy. 'But our fairy tales, which all end with "And they lived happily ever after" are much nicer, I think… Now, I must go back to Mamma in case she wants me.' At the door she paused to cast a glance of doubtful envy at Laetitia's satin. 'I wish she would not always dress me in white muslin with pink or blue ribbons, but, of course, she says it's the correct thing for one's first season.'

'Your gown will be much more admired on Tuesday night than mine,' Laetitia assured her, and, as she spoke, she thought, 'only Gronwy Griffith would recognise its classical beauty. They will all think it eccentric – the worst thing a woman's dress or manner can be. What does it matter if I am a failure here? Why do I let it hurt me? If only I could be utterly indifferent to their opinion or else learn to conform to it in all things! What folly and weakness to dress with distinction in order to please myself, and then to be disappointed because here, among the Philistines, I please no one else!'

'My figure is not fashionable, I'm afraid,' she told Lucy. 'Charles often complains of my not pulling in my waist enough.'

'He admires a small waist, does he?' Lucy's hands went up to her own before she could restrain the tell-tale impulse. Her cousin began to laugh, and she hurried from the room with a look of injured modesty. When she was gone, Laetitia pressed her forehead against the cooling pane of glass. What was the use of all this pretence? She did, like other girls, desire to be thought beautiful. Now that it had been put into her head, she wanted Gronwy Griffith to see her in her ball dress.

'Shall I hang up the gown in your closet, miss?'

She started at the sound of Susan's voice. 'No. Leave it there… You may go.'

Left alone in the room, she went to the bedside and touched the glossy folds of her dress. Presently, a voice outside called her: 'Laetitia, are you there?'

'Yes, what do you want?'

A heavy tread approached. 'Come in,' she called impatiently, and the door was thrust open.

'Hello!' said Charles. 'Preening your fine feathers ready for Tuesday night?' He grinned at her with unusual good humour.

'Do you like it?' She raised the dress and held it against her.

'Umph! A bit outlandish isn't it?'

She threw it down on the bed.

'I dare say it's all right,' he said, seeing that he had vexed her. 'I don't know much about these things, but you never seem to dress quite like other women.'

'You and papa would wish me to be like all the rest of them in this neighbourhood?'

'Well, dash it all, a fellow doesn't like his sister to seem eccentric. But I dare say it will do. Ask Lucy's opinion. She's the person to go by.'

'Indeed. Then you admire her rows of flounces and her knots of riband that tie up nothing?'

'I'm blessed if I know what I admire about her dress,' he laughed. 'But I thought the one she wore last night remarkably pretty, didn't you?'

Laetitia hesitated.

'Oh the sex! I suppose you are jealous.' Then, with a change of tone, he added. 'Letty, will you come for a ride? That's what I came to ask you. I'm going to Llangantyn.'

'What, in the snow?'

'It's thawing fast. If we take the horses gently, it won't ball much.'

'You are very eager about it on such a wretched day.' He looked awkward and did not reply. 'And it's something new for you to want my company,' she added.

'Lucy—' he began.

'I can guess, thank you. Lucy's mamma said she might go for a ride with you if I went too.'

'That's just it.'

'Well,' she said, 'I have my own amusements. I have learned to depend on myself for them, you know.'

She turned her back on him and swept across the room to her bureau.

'Upon my soul, you're a queer sort of sister,' he muttered, becoming very red.

'To a brother who has suddenly become most loving and attentive,' she retorted.

'I don't know what you have to complain of.'

'Only that you took not the least trouble to make my life pleasant here when I came home from Italy,' she answered with a warmth that astonished him, 'and that you have scarcely said "goodnight" or "good morning" to me since I refused to marry the first man who promised to rid the house of my presence. Oh yes,' she cried as he attempted to interrupt her, 'don't pretend that you ever showed the slightest fondness for me or that your manner has not remarkably changed in the last twenty-four hours.'

Abandoning herself to the angry impulse of the moment, she caught up a pen and began to write.

'Lucy will be deuced disappointed,' she heard her brother say.

'Have you ever cared how much I stayed indoors alone?' she demanded without looking round.

Charles stalked out of the room with a jingle of spurs. Laetitia addressed her envelope, sealed it with trembling fingers and carried it downstairs to the housekeeper's room.

'Is there anyone who can take a note for me to one of the farms?' she asked.

Her eyes were bright with excitement and her breath came fast. The housekeeper rose with evident unwillingness.

'All the men are busy putting up extra stables for Tuesday night, miss. If it's anything very important, I dare say your own maid here could take it.'

Laetitia was reluctant, she did not know why, to place her letter in the hand that was stretched out to receive it, but she could find no excuse for refusing the civil offer.

'I'll go with pleasure, miss,' said Susan, 'if you can spare me.'

'Thank you.'

The letter was no sooner surrendered than Laetitia wished it back again.

'Begging your pardon, miss, is it to one of the nearer farms?' Susan asked, her eyes fixed on her mistress's face.

'The address is on the envelope. You can read it. It's Tinygraig,' Laetitia replied.

Something in the ensuing silence made her ears burn, and she found herself foolishly offering an explanation.

'I lent some books to the farmer's son, who is quite a scholar, I am told. And I want them returned.'

There was no answer from Susan, and Laetitia left the room. Her head was held high and the dignity of her carriage would have quenched any flicker of impertinence. But secretly she was ashamed. Vanity had tempted her into betrayal. Betrayal! That was an ugly word. For a time she paced up and down her room trying to argue herself out of her growing belief that she had done wrong. Betrayal might be a fantastic word to apply to her innocent attempt to give pleasure, to receive admiration, but other equally unpleasant words thronged up to reinforce it. The phrase, 'a vulgar piece of coquetry' arose from some half-forgotten conversation with her Aunt Olivia.

'She would pardon my meeting him in secret to talk as we do,' Laetita thought. 'She would understand the innocence of that as papa and the others cannot. But this sending for him to see me in my ball dress would seem to her unworthy.'

She ran down to the housekeeper's room again.

'I have changed my mind about that note,' she said.

The housekeeper eyed her with deepening suspicion. 'Your maid has gone, miss.'

Laetitia turned away with a nervous laugh that had in it both anxiety and relief. 'Never mind, then.' And she added to herself: 'As the country people say, "it was to be".'

III

On the brow of the hill where she had watched her mistress and Gronwy meet, Susan saw her sweetheart of a single evening coming towards her. She did not hide now beneath the branches of the May tree. Leaves and blossom were gone, leaving them black against the sky like the twisted limbs of a many armed and many fingered dwarf. When last she had stood upon this hilltop, the country had been aflower and in her own heart hope had still waited. Now the torturing suspicions of many months were confirmed by the presence of the letter she had thrust into the bodice of her gown. The sharp edge of the envelope pricked her breast like a knife point, and she pressed it to her, glad of the hurt.

As she walked, her shawl was so fiercely blown that it gave her scant protection, and the hands that held it to her were icy. The tempestuous wind was in the west. Already a rapid thaw had overlaid the countryside with black mottlings. Rain threatened if the gale should slacken, and the river valley was stained by the approach of a sullen twilight. Night, when it came, would be wet, cold and impenetrably dark. Susan's whole body shivered and for a moment she shut her eyes. But the bleakness of the scene, so terribly in accord with the wintry hatreds that had made barren her own soul, was not to be shut out. Shrivelled bents and bracken – all that survived of the living green of summer – whistled sly and shrill in the ground wind, tormenting her continually with their little tunings of despair.

It was the face of a woman in an extremity of envious suffering that she turned to Gronwy when they met.

'Why, Susan,' he exclaimed, 'whatever is the matter? Are you ill?'

'Much you'd care if I was dead.'

He stared at her in distress. 'Why do you talk like that? Weren't we friends once?'

'No!' She spoke so fiercely that he stepped back a pace. 'Don't lie. There's no such thing as friendship between a man and a girl. You and I have been lovers; now we are enemies. False you've been to me, and I'd rather as you laughed at me and went your way than pretended to be a friend and kind – you hypocrite, you.'

He looked at her sorrowfully but attempted no self-defence. 'We are all in the grip o' fate,' he said.

'Oh, have done with your scholar's talk! Fate you may call it, but plain, honest folk would say as you had jilted a poor girl.'

'Susan, don't drive me to say harsh things. I never made you any promise.'

'You kissed me often enough, whatever.'

'Your every look and action on the night we first met asked for kisses as light-heartedly as mine were given.'

At that she burst into a passion of tears, 'Oh God!' she cried, 'it has been no light-hearted matter with me since.'

He came close and laid his hand on her arm, but she flung it off with a violent gesture.

'Don't dare touch me! I hate you now as much as I was loving you once.'

She continued to cry, her face hidden in her hands and her whole body shaken like a sapling in a gale, while he stood beside her, pitying but mute, full of remorse for the pain he had caused, but knowing that reparation was impossible.

'Listen,' he said, when her angry sobbing was less, 'we met and made love. 'Twas done half in jest by both of us. Then we both changed.' She tried to deny it, but her voice failed her. 'Yes, yes,' he continued. 'I am speaking the truth. You changed as well as I. We both demanded that the game should cease – you, because it had become serious, and I because – because it was played out… You think I said that wantonly to hurt you. Susan, all this is disillusionment and humiliation to me. But that is the end of much earthly love. Let us face it and be brave… Come now, could you wish on such a footing to renew our intimacy?'

'Why not?' she cried, looking up with a greedy eagerness that filled him with sudden disgust.

'No, no, Susan, you said just now as you hated me.'

'I didn't know what I was saying. Indeed and indeed I was beside myself.'

She followed him and touched his shoulder. With difficulty he resisted an impulse to shake off her hand as roughly as she had shaken off his own.

'We should be more often hostile than in harmony,' he said, forcing himself to stand rigid and endure her caress. 'There never was nothing between us but an attraction pitifully short-lived.'

'Other folks have married on less.'

'That is where man do often make so bitter a mistake. The beasts are wiser, Susan. They do not mate for life because of a moment's desire.'

'Aren't we no better than the beasts?'

He could not answer the irrelevance of that, nor did she seem to expect an answer. She had said it for the sake of saying something. Presently she added in a tense whisper: 'You are done with me, then?'

He bowed his head. She did not wrench herself away or speak wildly as before, but stood close to him, with a certain menace in his closeness, and her white face working with fury.

'Oh, that I should have humbled myself to beg love of you,' she said in a low, quivering voice. She turned from him, but had not gone ten paces when she swung round again. 'Here, I've a letter for you from your sweetheart. Maybe it will please you that I am the one ordered to bring it.'

The word 'sweetheart' roused him out of a melancholy reverie. She was violently tearing open her bodice and exposing a white breast. The letter came fluttering towards him from her hand.

'Much joy you'll have of her as cares only for your flattery and is ready to break your heart same as you've broken mine so you serve, like her other suitors, to feed her vanity. You'll rue the day ever she smiled on you.'

She left him, and made such reckless speed down the hillside that the wind seemed to have whirled her away.

CHAPTER XIII

Invitations – Laetitia is dressed for the Ball – The Kitchen – Gronwy looks on

Having undertaken, in a moment of rashness, to give a dance for his daughter's pleasure, the squire had determined that it should be of such a kind as was consistent with his high reputation in the county. Though a father's fondness might prompt it, the giving of an entertainment by one in his position was no light matter. None must be left out who was entitled to an invitation or any invited whose presence could possibly give offence. The decorations must be elegant, the refreshments plentiful, the liquor above reproach; the servants must be finely liveried and exact in the performance of their duties. 'I rarely open my doors to any but young Lee, the rural dean and one or two intimates,' said he. 'When I do entertain, I must entertain handsomely.' So he had sat down to his desk with that crumpling of a parchment forehead and that tightening of thin lips which accompanied all his anxiously contrived social services. Thus, some weeks ago, Laetitia had found him.

'This will cost a great deal,' he had said, looking up from his calculations.

But she, thinking of the only gift she had ever begged of him, kept silence. Not until he began to count those for whom his best port must be produced did she protest.

'I thought this was to be a dance, Papa. They are too old to walk through a cotillion even, and they have no young people to bring with them.'

'Never mind, my dear; they have a right to be asked.'

She ran her pencil down the visiting list. 'Lady Ballenger. She is nearly eighty. Has she a right to be asked …? Colonel Lloyd. He lost a leg in the Mutiny and walks with a crutch. Has he a right to be asked…? Judge Williams. He detests youth and is said to have disinherited his own children. Has he a right to be asked? Isn't this a party in honour of the young?'

'Don't talk nonsense, Laetitia. When I am known to be giving an affair of this sort, everyone expects to receive the courtesy of an invitation.'

'Everyone?'

'You know perfectly well what I mean.'

'Very well, Papa. But why call it a dance that you are giving for my pleasure?'

'You young people will dance.'

'If the old ones leave us any room.'

There the useless conversation had been ended by the squire's taking the list out of her hand. 'You will oblige me,' he had said, 'by seeing that cards are sent to the following. I am putting crosses by their names.'

II

On the evening appointed, the Lord Lieutenant and the High Sheriff, with their ladies, were to drive over in time for six o'clock dinner. The Vicar of Llangantyn, who, having had the living presented to him by the squire, was English and a gentleman, if an indifferent priest, had been bidden to meet them. Laetitia, jangling a bunch of keys in the hope of impressing her aunt who was growing more politely critical with each day of her visit, went into the dining room before going up to dress. She must make sure that the flowers and silver had been heaped upon the table in the way her father approved. Chairs and floor, steel fender and fire irons, plate and glass – all shone with cleaning. Pink and his assistants, modestly triumphant, hovered at her elbow, but she forgot to praise them.

She pictured the solemn procession that would file in here in a couple of hours' time – men and women walking arm in arm gingerly and not for pleasure's sake as did the country people on Sunday afternoons. Her smile at the thought set Pink soaping his hands in anticipation of her compliments. 'In our class,' she reflected, 'it is proper for a woman to take a man's arm only when she has no natural inclination to do so. Aunt Emily would never allow Lucy to stroll about the place arm in arm with Charles, though he is her cousin and will probably marry her. And it would be quite incorrect for the High Sheriff's wife, who adores her husband, to go into dinner with him. No. She will sit on Papa's left and the Lady Lieutenant, of course, on his right. "Of course!" – how Lucy and her mamma love the phrase … Papa calls the Lord Lieutenant's wife a skinny old harridan and the High Sheriff's wife bores him because she is always trying to overhear what her husband is saying to the ladies on the farther side of the table; but it is proper that they should sit on either side of their host. And their husbands will sit on either side of me. I must not seem to talk more to the one who can hear what I say than to the other who is deaf. Charles, as son of the house, will have to take in the High Sheriff's wife and sit between her and Aunt Emily, who will not relish a chit of a child like myself taking the head of the table. But she can't openly resent it because my being there is quite the correct thing – of course! And Lucy, marooned between the Vicar and my deaf cavalier, will enjoy herself even less than the rest of us. That ugly, overloaded epergne will make it impossible for her even to exchange a smile with Charles. Nor will her boredom, or his, or mine, be short. Dinner tonight will be twice as long as usual. How I hate all this food and this formality about the serving of it!' Rebelliously she turned away from the dining table without a word. Pink and the others stood aside deferentially and watched her go. Then in unison they rolled up their eyes towards heaven and made that clicking sound with their tongues which is more expressive of disgust than all the words ever spoken.

In the hall the housekeeper waylaid her.

'Excuse me, miss, might I trouble you to step this way and see how the ballroom looks?'

Laetitia went wearily. The room was already too hot, for her father had ordered huge fires to be lighted, lest his elderly neighbours should take cold. Banks of hot-house flowers protruded into the floor space. 'Dancing will be difficult,' she thought. 'This is more like a lying-in-state. We need only the coffin and the Grenadiers.' From the flowers she turned her attention to the sofas that lined the walls. 'There is room at any rate for all the dowagers to display their diamonds,' she murmured.

'I beg pardon, miss?'

'Nothing. I only wondered whether there were quite enough room for the dancers.'

'Well, miss, the master said—'

'Quite right. I am sure he will pronounce the arrangements admirable.'

'I hope so, I'm sure, miss. We've taken that much trouble for this evening!'

'I wish it were over.'

The housekeeper stared. 'You will enjoy it surely, miss?'

Laetitia nodded. 'I suppose so… One moment of it… But I must make haste.'

She went to her room and rang the bell. Susan answered it in a flurry of excitement.

'Oh, miss! What do you think? Her ladyship's come, and she's gone up with her maid to dress, and their coachman says she and Sir Percy are in a terrible way, they being the first in the county to hear of it, after the doctor and widow, that is—'

'To hear of what?'

'Our member of Parliament – he's dead.'

'Sir Robert Johns? Why, he was to have been here tonight.'

'Yes, miss, to be sure. They say it was a cruel shock to his poor lady, though I have heard the maids tell how they did used to quarrel. He being such a well set-up gentleman and so high-coloured, no one would ever have thought it of him, but Doctor Pugh told him months ago, they say, that there was fat all round his heart like a mutton kidney, and if it were to meet that would be the end of him. He was a wonderful man to eat, the coachman was telling us, and to drink by all accounts, but of course now he's dead an' gone it wouldn't be hardly Christian to think of that.'

'There will be an election, I suppose,' Laetitia put in while Susan paused for breath.

'Yes, miss. That is what her ladyship's coachman said. Sir Percy said to him as he got into the carriage, "Davies," he said, "this is a bad business." And he said, "Shocking bad, sir." And then Sir Percy said, "That Radical stands a…" excuse me, miss, but what he said was, "a damned good chance of getting in if we don't hurry on an election at once." And her ladyship put her head out of the window and said. "Oh Percy, d'you think it right to go to this dance with poor Sir Robert lying dead? Oughtn't we to ask Mr Wingfield to send away his guests?" she said. She had to shout it twice, the Lord Lieutenant being so deaf, miss. So all the servants heard and thought perhaps they wouldn't have to go out or sit up tonight after all. But when Sir Percy understood what she was talking about, "No. Drive on," he said to the coachman, and they heard him telling her ladyship, "everybody will be there," meaning here, miss. "We'll call a sort of informal committee meeting," he said, "and talk over what's to be done."'

'The prospect of tonight's dinner and dance grows more

and more gay,' Laetitia thought. 'Well, there is still an hour before I need appear to receive Papa's guests.' And she said aloud: 'Draw the curtains, Jones. Shut out this dismal twilight. Now light the candles – all of them – I want an illumination.'

In the joy of newsbringing, Susan had forgotten her enmity; but, as she undressed her mistress and prepared her bath, hatred rekindled within her. The emotion was not now consciously related to its cause. She was no longer simply envious of a luxury denied to herself or simply jealous for Gronwy's sake; she had ceased to connect her angers, her humiliations, her burning resentments directly with their source. To see Laetitia, to serve and obey her, to stoop in some menial action at her feet, was a hurt so violent that it cried out for relief in an opposite infliction of physical pain. Lighting a candle and seeing Laetitia's back turned to her, she found herself actively tempted to thrust the flame against the bare arm. She wanted to drag at the hair she took down and to score with her nails the flesh she uncovered. Above all, it was an agony to her to unfasten the clothes that Laetitia's limbs had warmed. Her head swam with the scent of them, and the close scent of the exposed body. Laetitia was much freer with her maid than Susan had known other mistresses be. They had been in the habit of banishing her from the room at the moments when she thought it proper that she should be banished, and had been extremely careful for the adjustment of the screen behind which they had their baths. Laetitia seemed to care for few of these niceties – a fact which Susan found it easy to explain on the ground of proved wantonness. She continued, however, to do her work with the dexterity of a practised maid – to do it with so much outward quietness that her mistress was unaware of any kind of mental tension surrounding her. This indifference of Laetitia's, her whole air of standing there to be stripped by a submissive machine incapable of private torments, produced in Susan first an added irritation, then a feeling that she – the wrath, the stifled indignation, the emotional writhing that were her inner self – was standing somehow apart from the scene, and that it was another woman whose knees pressed the floor, whose hands tried the water's heat, whose voice at last said, 'yes, miss,' when her mistress asked if all was ready.

'Poke the fire,' Laetitia said, 'I want to feel the flame on me.'

Susan stood away, watching the flame on her, hearing the water trickle from her shoulders. Again she had refused the screen – wanted all the light there was, she had said. The room was so large that the two centres of light – the stiff row of candles mirrored above the fireplace and the glitter of silver and glass on the lace-flounced dressing table – had little power to penetrate its darknesses. The great half-tester was overlaid with shadow, streaked here and there by a vertical line where a fold of its crimson hangings was touched by a direct beam; the ceiling's dulled whiteness was fantastic with shapes thrown by the fire; in the distance, nothing stood out from the gloom, but the wardrobe mirror's pallor and a needle flash from its bevel. Susan, withdrawn to the foot of the bed, remained staring, with one thin hand caught up to her breast. The fire fell in the grate; the flame weakened. Laetitia's curving body, her moving arms, her head, the loosening and tightening of her breasts as she stooped and raised herself, became now indeterminate silhouettes, which, as Susan gazed, shifted their personal significance. They were a hated pattern, representative of her own mind's confusion, which so mingled with the thwarted longings that ranged within her that Laetitia, as Laetitia, was for a moment forgotten, and nothing remembered but the kisses Gronwy had once bestowed and the intoxicating pressures of him on her own arms and her own breasts. And what had begun in memory flashed into imagination. The caresses she felt were not the caresses of fair-night, but other and more passionate touchings, ghosts of her brain, exquisite and stormy anticipations.

Then, without knowing that she had moved, she found herself on the hearth, wrapping her mistress in a towel, rubbing the hot limbs. Her head was aching; there was a trembling stab in her eyes. But she brought powder and applied it; fetched clothes, warmed them, held them out; answered, when it was required of her, in a voice steady and deferential, 'yes, miss, a bath is wonderfully refreshing.'

Dressing followed its calm routine. Laetitia, seated by her mirror, held out her slim hands, examining the fingertips.

'More of that paste, Jones. And polish the nails again, please. I want them to look like mirrors tonight.'

And when no further criticism could be made of her finger nails, Laetitia said, 'Now my hair. I want it brushed for a long time. And put on some of that French pomade that smells so sweet.'

'Yes, miss.'

There was no sound but the tiny crackle and hiss of brush and comb, and a little sigh of pleasure from Laetitia, and the ticking of a table clock.

'Now my scent spray. Yes, my eyes are closed. Some on my lips – so, that will make them look redder.'

'They are the reddest ever I saw in a pale face, miss.'

'Are they?' Laetitia stood up. 'Shall I do, do you think, Jones?'

'You look lovely, miss. No one could say different.'

Laetitia leaned forward smiling, and looked into the reflection of her own eyes. They were bright with excitement, their pupils enlarged. 'I am not pale tonight, Jones. Look, I have quite a colour.'

She, whose careless putting on of the same dress day after day had seemed to Susan the pose of a blue-stocking, was careful now for every detail. Did she, then, value the admiration of her father's guests whom she had always pretended to despise?

'There's no making her out,' thought Susan, watching her glance from clock to mirror, pick up her silver-backed hand glass, study herself from every angle, and insist, as she had never before insisted, upon this change and that. Her lips were parted; her face, generally masked by indifference or scorn while Susan applied her skill, wore now an expression of almost sensual eagerness.

'Now, I must have something to show up the blackness of my hair. Just one white rose, I think… No; no fluffy ribands or feathers… There!'

'And your poor mother's jewels, miss?'

'No. Not those clumsy things – not unless Papa misses them. I shall wear only this string of pearls. Their sheen matches the satin. Aren't the lights beautiful, Jones, along the edge of each fold? … Yes, it is all rather beautiful, I think.' She spoke slowly, surveying the completed picture. Then, without seeing with what eyes Susan regarded her, she said, 'Thank you, Jones,' and went from the room.

III

She went downstairs with light step and clear purpose. The rooms prepared for her father's guests were now a still and dazzling emptiness; an army of candles, unquivering in the sheltered air, saluted her. Beyond them, in the waste places of the house, was a darkened labyrinth where oil lamps shone feebly on the doors of lumber-rooms. Through this she passed until she encountered, at the end of a black passage, light streaming from a door ajar, and with it the laughter and uplifted voices of men and women, and snatches of song. 'They are young and happy in there,' she thought, and entered, eager for her share.

Instantly there was silence. Then, on the undersuck of surprise, rose sounds of stifled exclamation, of breath suddenly drawn, of laughter caught up. There was a scraping of chairs as those who had been seated rose.

'Where is cook?' she asked, her voice clear in the hush. 'I promised to let her see my ball dress,' she explained, forced to apologise for the presence that had wrought such havoc. Rounded eyes stared at her, mouths were agape. None dared speak. At last, upon her embarrassment, there broke out a chorus of awed admiration.

'Indeed to goodness, miss, 'tis a grand dress!'

'Well, dear, dear, nothing so stylish has ever been seen in the district!'

'There's champion it is!'

Mechanically she revolved before them, her arms raised a little from her sides. 'You like it?' And, as she spoke, she looked into the eyes of Gronwy who stood alone, clutching the back of a settle as if he needed its support. She had known of his presence when she entered the room, but had lacked confidence to challenge him. Now, as she raised a smiling face to his, she was shocked by his rigidity and exceeding pallor. His eyes, in their deep sockets, were full of angry scorn. Her smile at once stiffened; she must not show that she was afraid. Catching at a chair to steady herself, she gave a nervous laugh. 'I am glad you like it. I hope you will enjoy yourselves this evening. I am going to order wine for you all to drink my health in… Goodnight.'

'Thank you, miss. Indeed, you're too good!' they cried as she turned to go back to her own place.

'We'll be drinking the health o' your sweetheart too,' some wag called out, and the girls began to giggle.

'You'll put the halter on one o' the highest-up gentlemen in the county,' said another.

And a third, greatly emboldened, added: 'If that gown isn't getting you off miss, nothing won't.'

She found herself smiling that joyless, stiff smile again, but she did not look any more towards the settle.

When she was gone, gossip, jesting and lovemaking broke out afresh. The anglicised upper servants were in the housekeeper's room sipping cordials and vying with one another in gentility, These in the kitchen were the Welsh, the stuff of which faithful retainers are made, ready to fight for their master, to get drunk toasting him, to oblige him by doing anyone's work but their own, to add to his wealth by stealing from his neighbours, to amuse him, flatter him, and on occasion shrewdly tell him the truth. Since Squire Wingfield would permit them to exercise none of these gifts, they appeared at their worst in his service; thwarted and bewildered themselves, they were at daggers drawn with his precise English housekeeper. But tonight, out of her hearing, good comradeship and native wit abounded. Only Gronwy took no part in it. He heard the sallies on that 'proud piece', Miss Wingfield, on her naked arms and shoulders and deductions therefrom. He heard them discuss her probable lovers, and whether they would venture to do this and that, and the remarkable softness of her bed. The humour grew more broad, the roars of laughter louder, but his white face and burning eyes never changed their expression. No one noticed him, however, until he could endure it no more and laid his hand on the outer door. Then someone exclaimed: 'Holt man! You're never going afore you've drunk the lady's health an' that o' her bridegroom?'

His lips twisted into a grimace, as though he had tried to smile and failed. Without answering he lifted the latch.

'What's on you, mun?'

'Whyever was you coming here tonight, if you're not staying for the fun?' demanded a stable boy.

'I came because I was summoned.'

'What for?'

'To learn my lesson, it seems.'

So bitter was his tone that those about him stared, but he had no sooner gone out than the cook began to scream, 'Out o' the way, there, the lot o' you! Dinner is to be served. I can't have you great lumps o' boys under my feet no more. Where's the soup tureen? Where are the fried toasts, you gaping gels? *Cooch*, dog! *Whiskit*, cat!' and, in the lively commotion that ensued, the youth who had made so surprising a departure was forgotten.

IV

Later that night, when the servants were clustered in the gallery, looking down into the hall and nudging one another whenever a couple crossed it, a solitary figure stood in the darkness outside the ballroom window. Through plate glass and velvet, the music came muffled to his hearing, but a curtain not quite drawn left a slit through which he was able to peep, 'like a leper', he told himself, 'forbidden to join the congregation, watching the rights o' religion from the graveyard.'

'This, indeed, is the place o' death for me,' he thought, 'where such pure love as I had for her lies buried. There she goes smiling within a foot of its grave, caring more for an hour's vulgar flattery than for all the true homage I paid her.'

She had danced across the parallelogram of light which was open to his observation. Another man's arm was about the waist he had never dared to touch. She was not adorably sedate as was her wont with him. Reckless and hard, she seemed now, laughing, flushed, with head thrown back and eyes brilliant as diamonds. Her whole personality was changed. She was become more beautiful than ever but with a tormenting beauty.

'How has she the heart to be so gay while I do suffer so?' he muttered, fancying in his pain that she knew him to be watching her and had added this to her other cruelty. 'Why is she more lovely, more alive now than ever I saw her before? Is it maybe because she do thrive, same as the vampires I've read of, upon the sucked life o' her victims?' Fury and desire wracked and sickened him. Her low-cut bodice and her tiny puffed sleeves that slid away from her shoulders fascinated and shocked the Puritan in him. He thought himself a devotee of the classics; in truth he was the son of John Griffith who yearly spelled his way through the Bible and the *Pilgrim's Progress*. Other ladies, he knew, wore dresses cut as low as hers, but until tonight he had never seen them save in pictures. In her it seemed a deliberate and evil flaunting. His eyes lingered on the soft dividing of her breasts, and his heart cried out against her as a wanton. Now he wanted to hurt her whom he had longed only to serve. A common flirt she had shown herself to be when she had made him stand among a crowd of menials to admire the finery she had put on. As a common flirt he would treat her from henceforth. He vowed it, biting his nails to the quick. Overhead in the branches of the beech trees the wind was singing a dirge. He was ashamed, but could not look away or stay the processes of his mind. A sense of sin fed his lust, and he forced her and lay with her in his heart. Then, with cold impulse, he turned into the dark. ''Twas a tender, glorious thing, the love she killed, the love I bury here tonight,' he thought. And, covering his face with his hands, he wept.

CHAPTER XIV

The Election

'Oh, mamma!' Lucy exclaimed as the carriage rolled into Llangantyn on election day, 'the people are shouting so – do you think the horses will bolt?'

She laid a hand on Laetitia's arm, and Laetitia, who was tired of sitting in the musty carriage while her cousin trod on her toes and peeped out first from one window, then the other, had difficulty in not shaking her off with angry impatience.

'There is no need for alarm, Lucy,' Mrs Bodley-Booth replied. 'Your dear uncle would never have permitted us to come if he had anticipated the slightest danger.'

'No, never,' Laetitia agreed.

How troubled men were for their women's safety, and yet how little, it seemed, they cared for their happiness! Since the night of the ball, she had been fretting her heart out. Blaming herself for what had happened that night, she had sent another parcel of books to Gronwy which had been returned next market-day without thanks or explanation. She had written to him but had had no answer. So troubled had she been that she had feared that her father might notice too much, but he had noticed nothing. Preparations for the election had absorbed his energy. All day he was out. When he returned, he was bespattered with the mud of political meetings and would talk of nothing but the campaign. Planted in his old position before the fire, he would interminably rehearse the villainies of his opponents.

'The fellows' flagrant corruption of the people is a

disgrace,' he said. 'It ought to be put down. Now there *is* a reform for which I stand – the abolition of bribery.'

And when he was gone to have his clothes cleaned, Charles would take up the same tale to a different tune.

'These new Radicals from the north,' he would say with a wink, 'have raised the cost of an election a bit more than's convenient. The Governor and his friends don't like having to foot the bill. And small wonder either. The Radical candidate's wife has fallen in love with all the cats in the county. A guinea apiece she pays for them, and tips 'em into the river at nightfall.'

After dinner, unless her father went out again, it had been Laetitia's fate to read the local papers to him – ill-written political leaders, reports of speeches full of abuse and empty of reason. If she flagged, she was accused of disloyalty.

And now, with Aunt Emily and Lucy as companions, she was being driven in to witness the triumph. The grooms on foot, the coachman with his whip, and the plunging of the horses forced a way through the crowd. The streets were blue and crimson with angry posters. From the public houses, which had been thrown open to wearers of the right colour, groups of men emerged now and then, to form themselves into a wedge and drive it through the reeling mob in quest of an enemy banner or in rescue of a friend. A banner was torn down and trampled upon close to the carriage step, and a rotten egg, hurled from a distance by a straggler in retreat, hit and broke upon the windowpane. Its greenish fluid spread on the glass.

'Oh, the brutes, the brutes! cried Lucy, bobbing in her seat.

'My dear,' said her mother, 'even on such an occasion, your excitement—'

'And if it was one of Papa's eggs, Lucy?' said Laetitia.

'Oh, but it wasn't. Our side… It wasn't. It couldn't have been, could it, mamma?'

'Certainly it was a very bad egg,' said Mrs Bodley-Booth. 'But we will not discuss it. Make sure, my dear, that the window is fast, and sit back a little.'

Laetitia looked out no more until they drew up at the door of the *Nelson*. Within the walls of this most respectable Tory inn, many ladies of the Party were already assembled, safely tucked away in a big first-floor parlour, whence they had access to the balcony over the Doric porch. A sharp spurt of chatter greeted Squire Wingfield's ladies, for on that day, above all others, the squire was a great man.

'From here,' they were informed by the agent's clerk who conducted them to the balcony window, 'you will be able, ladies, to see all the fun of the fair.'

The fun became tedious as the day wore on. Even Lucy ceased to clap her hands when, for the seventh time, Mr Bright was burned in effigy. 'Cobden now!' someone shouted.

'What was that?' said the squire, who happened at that moment to be behind the ladies.

'Mr Cobden,' said Lucy. 'Mr Cobden, Uncle!'

'Hush, Lucy dear,' her mother put in – 'not too excited, remember!'

'What about Cobden?' said the squire.

'They are going to burn him, Uncle.'

'Come, come, that won't do,' said the squire. And, turning: 'Here, Tackley, go down and stop our fellows if you can. Tell them from me – not Cobden. Can't burn Cobden. He's too lately dead.'

'Oh, Charles!' said Mrs Bodley-Booth, shaking her finger. 'Isn't that rather squeamish of you? After all, Cobden was a commercial traveller of some kind.'

'Nonsense, my dear,' said the squire, a little beyond himself that day. 'Must have a clean fight. Any burning of Cobden there is to do, we can safely leave to the—'

'Charles! Charles! Remember Lucy!'

'Quite,' said the squire. 'I beg your pardon. But you must allow me to give my own orders during this campaign.' And he sat down, breathing hard.

Laetitia watched the 'clean fight' with a weariness that forbade any quickening of her pulse. Now and then, fragments of Radical speeches, delivered from above the portico of the *Green Dragon*, came across to her, and, for want of better occupation, she tried to listen, but the Tory brass band, blaring patriotic airs, successfully prevented her or anyone else from being poisoned by such seditious stuff. If one of her father's supporters attempted to speak, the Radical band, heavily escorted, moved to counter attack. From time to time bodies of voters marched into the town with their squires at their head, and fought their way gallantly, through sticks and stones and the refuse of gutters, towards the polling booth.

So the day wore on. The candidate was introduced to Laetitia, but he said only what her father had said in front of the fireplace every day for weeks. The most enthusiastic ladies grew tired of repeating the party gossip they had been taught, and began to chatter far more pleasantly of bonnets and romanticised obstetrics, a subject of annual interest. Sir Edward Lee brought Laetitia a slice of seed cake and a glass of sherry wine. It ought, she told herself, to have been embarrassing to talk to the man whose offer of marriage she had refused, but he spoke only the political formulae she knew by heart and neither perturbed her nor seemed himself at all perturbed. When he had drifted away, other friends of her father's hurried in, waving their tall hats, to announce the hopeful state of the poll. Presently she saw her father himself leading a group of farmers through the throng below. There had been a hush and he seemed safe enough. But suddenly noise broke out afresh. This uproar had a new note of anger. Someone, of whom she could see nothing but long arms waving, was making a speech that drew the whole mob towards him and lashed it to madness. Everywhere between the Nelson and the Green Dragon was tumult. Men who could have heard nothing of the speech except by the lightning report that runs through crowds were dragging at their neighbours' throats. One face, lifted for a moment, was covered with a sheet of blood.

'Oh, Gracious Heavens! Someone has had his head cut open!' cried the ladies. 'Murder! Murder! They are killing one another! Whatever is it all about?'

The gentlemen were urged to run out and ascertain the cause of this increased commotion, and, in the same breath, to stay where they were and expose themselves to no such risk. They obeyed which entreaty suited their inclination, some running to the door eager for a fight, others clapping their hands behind their backs, pacing the room in the utmost agitation, and saying: 'This is serious! This is really serious!' The ladies were more ready to applaud rashness than discretion. The Radicals, they thought, who were certainly responsible for this ruffianly behaviour, needed a severe lesson – 'and they'll have it, by Jove!' cried Edward Lee, glancing at Laetitia as he seized his cane and rushed out. Above the portico, Mrs Bodley-Booth's smelling salts were in great request and Laetitia found herself compelled to assist a swooning acquaintance to another apartment where her stay-laces could be cut.

When she returned to the parlour, her father was seated on its largest horsehair settee, having his head bound up. With a thrill of admiration, she thought, 'So at last one of my people has done something rash.' Never had she liked him so well. But, before she could reach him, Lucy was clinging about her waist.

'Don't faint, Letty darling,' she cried. 'It's all right. Your dear papa is quite, quite safe. Really it is nothing – the merest graze from a turnip one of those ruffianly Radicals threw. The special constables knew him of course, so they made a ring round him and escorted him back here in safety. They have arrested the wicked fellow who was the cause of it all, and Sir Edward, who admires you so and was very, very brave, has just been in telling us that the magistrates are sure to be as severe as possible. Nothing is worse, he says, than disloyalty to a landlord.'

'But what happened? 'Laetitia asked, trying to shake off her cousin's embraces and to reach her father, though, now that she knew him to have been hit only by a turnip, he had lost favour in her sight.

'Oh, of course,' Lucy answered. 'I forgot you were out of the room while Uncle was telling us everything. Why, it was a son of one of his own tenants – wasn't it disgraceful? The young man's father was not among Uncle Charles' men when he mustered them this morning. So Uncle made enquiries as soon as he reached town, and – what do you think? – the horrid creature had been drinking at our expense in one of our own inns – one of those the Conservatives have opened to their supporters I mean. At first he said—'

'Who said? Who is it you are speaking of?' Laetitia interrupted.

'Why, Uncle's tenant – the father of the young man who caused the struggle, the young man they've arrested.'

'What was his name?'

'His name? Uncle Charles did say, but I've forgotten.'

'Well?'

'Well, he went into one of our inns as I've told you. And at first he said he was waiting to join his landlord's party when they came in; but the more he drank – so the barmaid told Uncle Charles – the more openly Radical he became, and at last he swore – oh, with some dreadful oaths which, of course, Uncle Charles did not repeat –that he wouldn't vote Tory to please anyone. And would you believe it – he is known to have voted for that Radical man who, they say, beats his wife.'

'Well,' said Laetitia with growing impatience, 'what if he did vote for him?'

'But, my dear, of course Uncle Charles had to tell him that he would receive notice to quit his farm next – oh, I don't know – whenever it is one can turn one's tenants out.'

Laetitia's foot was tapping the floor. 'That's nothing unusual,' she retorted. 'Lord Willborough, the great Whig landowner, ejected scores of tenants for voting Tory at the last General Election. Our side complained about it then. I think myself it's an odious piece of tyranny, whoever does it.'

Lucy stared. 'Oh, but my dear—'

'Never mind my views.'

'Well,' said Lucy, swallowing her amazement, 'the old man made a speech – he was very intoxicated – and admitted he had been sent to prison in his youth for being a Chartist. Fancy! And your poor, dear papa has been harbouring him for years. It has upset him terribly, more than the blow from the turnip, even. But it was the creature's son who was the more insolent of the two. He jumped up when his father had done. It was his speech caused the riot. He said the wickedest things about his betters. Sir Edward, who heard him positively inciting the people to rebellion, declares he was quite eloquent for a man of his class. He referred to the history of Rome and actually quoted one piece from a Latin author – Cicero or somebody, Sir Edward says. Why, Letty darling, you are going to faint!'

'Do you mean that he spoke words in Latin?' Laetitia asked. She had grown so white that she was instantly surrounded by ladies offering her sal volatile. She pushed them aside and went swiftly to her father.

'What is this, Papa?' she demanded. 'Whom have you had locked up for making a speech? I thought everyone was at least permitted to say what they thought today. Listen to that howling mob out there. Why have you not had them locked up?'

He blinked at her, dazed and bewildered.

'What are you talking about? That is the customary thing at elections. This fellow – the fellow you wanted me to help, by Jove! – wasn't drunk. He was dangerous – seditious.'

'I can guess what he was – a man of intellect among that besotted, filth-flinging rabble!'

Her pale face and flashing eyes drew the attention of those who stood near.

'She's beside herself on her poor father's account!' someone exclaimed.

'She's going into hysterics,' said another, trying to soothe her.

But Laetitia forced her way through them on to the balcony.

'No, no, no,' she cried to the pursuing Aunt Emily. 'Leave me alone. All I want is air.'

In the street below, the triumph of the Tory candidate had just been announced, and all those who had got drunk at his expense were cheering themselves hoarse. She heard her father's voice behind her, leading cheers in reply. And suddenly she remembered standing in a balcony six years ago, watching a crowd seethe past, listening to its shouts of victory. Ah, but how different it had been! She had been a child then whose delight in the emancipation of her beloved Italy was unclouded by any fears for the future, and she had flourished her scarlet favour and clapped her hands as Garibaldi, the great Republican, drove past at Victor Emmanuel's side. By contrast, this triumph was sordid; liberty was mocked in it. Liberty, in fact, was marched off to gaol.

Ladies were crowding behind her on to the balcony, fluttering kerchiefs and scarfs of the victorious colour, laughing, chattering, blowing kisses, and shaking hands with perspiring members of committee. Only Mrs Bodley-Booth had time to notice her niece.

'My dear child, do pray come in and lie down.'

'I assure you I am quite composed now, Aunt Emily.'

'I must beg to differ, dear. You cannot be yourself. You are showing no enthusiasm whatever over our victory. It looks exceedingly odd in your father's daughter.'

Laetitia burst out laughing. 'We have bought up more of the votes of this *canaille* than our opponents could afford. That's all, isn't it, Aunt Emily? However, let us keep up appearances by all means.'

She thrust herself into the forefront of those rejoicing, and, leaning perilously over the balustrade, brandished the squire's favours in a manner afterwards described as 'a trifle too conspicuous in an unmarried lady'.

'Steady, Laetitia,' said the squire, tapping her shoulder. 'Steady! Steady! I'd no idea you'd be so pleased.'

CHAPTER XV

The Witches' Fowl – A Wild Thing Goes Free – Susan Spies Again

On the white marble mantelpiece in the squire's drawing room a clock stood in a glass case. During every pause in a desultory conversation, it made its fussy ticking heard, and at each hour and half hour its little bells rang a chime that reminded Laetitia of the nursery musical box.

'I hate it,' she exclaimed, rising suddenly and letting fall from her lap a cascade of silken skeins.

'What do you hate, pray, my dear child?' Mrs Bodley-Booth asked.

'That clock.'

Laetitia swept down upon it and laid her hand on the case.

'My dear, you will never be so rash as to stop it? No clock of value should ever be stopped.'

Laetitia's hand dropped to her side again. 'No, perhaps it is not worthwhile. Time wouldn't pass more quickly.' She was tempted to quote a poem which had often drawn tears to her eyes:

> 'It might be months, or years, or days,
> I kept no count, I took no note,
> I had no hope my eyes to raise…'

No hope! In all her future there was nothing to which she might look forward. Nothing would ever change. Her glance travelled from wall to wall. There, in a florid gilt frame, hung a picture of her mother, insipid as that in the squire's study; no portrait of an individual woman but the conventionalised representation of a lady. So long as the canvas lasted, those painted lips would wear that vapid smile of which the living woman had never been guilty. There, too, were her own childish watercolours, preserved by parental pride. Nothing had changed since they were first hung there. The ghosts of roses on the wallpaper which her mother had chosen mocked her whichever way she looked, for this room was sacred to her mother's youth and in it her father would lovingly bury her own youth also.

How she detested sitting here day after day making polite conversation to her relatives! Every Saturday morning they spoke of going; every Saturday evening they consented to stay, until, after each decorous hesitation and yielding, she was prompted to cry out, 'Oh, for goodness' sake, say you are going to stop here until Charles proposes to Lucy, and have done with it!' Their comfortable acceptance of the room made her hate it more than she had previously hated it. The little chairs and fringed tables, the cross-stitch, the gimp, the bulging or twisted legs, the accumulated ghosts of dead gaieties trying still to preserve an arch triviality in the tomb, whipped her to disgust. They gave the place the air of an ancient coquette, mournfully flirting behind a fan. Laetitia tapped the fender with her toe and the fire irons rattled. If only her thoughts would not go round and round like a blinded horse at the cider press! If only she could escape, sleeping or waking, from memories of election day!

'Laetitia, my dear child,' said Mrs Bodley-Booth, disturbed by the clatter of tongs, 'I must speak to your papa about your seeing the doctor. For the last three weeks you have not been looking quite so rosy as a young lady should.'

'There is nothing the matter with me – nothing that Doctor Pugh could cure.'

'You will allow me to know better, my dear. You are

suffering from anaemia. Now do pray go and lie down for an hour.'

'More rest is the last thing I want, I assure you, Aunt Emily.'

She picked up her fancy work again and Mrs Bodley-Booth's lips tightened in disapproval. Anger was an emotion and therefore must not be displayed, but she suffered herself to say, 'I wish I had you under my charge, my dear. You are rather too young to make wise decisions for yourself.'

Lucy felt that good manners demanded of her an attempt to make peace. Laetitia was not quite what she could have wished Charles's sister to have been. She was clever, she was moody. At times she was almost eccentric. But, even though their hostess were guilty of this last offence – than which there was but one worse in a young lady – it behoved mamma and herself, as guests, to disguise their disapproval. That at least was what she had been bred to believe, and it puzzled her to observe how frigid her mother's manner was becoming. Really, it was quite conspicuous!

So she began now playfully to tease Mamma in a manner timid enough to be disarming. All her little sallies were made so that she might retreat if she found herself in danger of giving offence. Naughty Mamma, she said, was always a year behind the fashions. Saying it, she shook her finger as a kitten shakes its paw. But this time there was no response – not a wriggle in the basket, not a maternal purr. It was a favourite theme that Lucy had chosen, but Mrs Bodley-Booth would not smile indulgently as was her wont. Nor would she thaw to flattery when it was suggested that she would look entrancing in a short sack coat. Instead she administered a rebuke intended to silence the prattle of which at times she grew so heartily tired.

'My love, you are sitting near the fire again. How often must I tell you that such self-indulgence will ruin your complexion?'

'Forgive me, Mamma dearest, I forgot.'

Lucy moved away from the warmth but, still smiling affably, began again to praise little jackets and porkpie hats. 'Don't you agree with me, Letty? Shawls are quite gone out of fashion, are they not?'

'Really, my dear, you can scarcely expect Laetitia to be a judge of what is worn or done in society, living as she does down here.'

A scornful smile was Laetitia's answer, but, with the heroism of ignorance, Lucy began again. Mamma was a darling, but why *must* she make her wear bonnets? 'All the younger ladies wear hats now, and I declare it makes me look quite dowdy to go about in a bonnet. Letty has the daintiest little hat with plumes in it, Mamma. She let me try it on the other night – didn't you, dear? – and she said it suited me better than anything she had seen me wear.'

'I think I am the best judge of what suits my own daughter.'

'Oh, Mamma dear, you must not be vexed with me for quizzing you about your taste in dress. We all know it is excellent.' Laetitia's eyebrows went up. 'I was only joking, of course, but bonnets—'

'Bonnets?' said the squire's voice. 'What's this about bonnets? I believe you ladies talk of nothing else when we are out of hearing.'

Charles followed him into the room. Both, booted and spurred, took up their position with backs to the fire, coat-tails over arms, hands thrust into breeches' pockets, feet far apart – in poise and manner reflections of each other. Charles, poor blunderer, in the half-facetious tone appropriate to the drawing room, swore that Lucy's bonnets were deuced becoming, by Jove! His father and her mother exchanged a smiling glance. Lucy blushed, and exclaimed: 'You naughty, naughty Cousin Charles! You have said quite the wrong thing! How like a man—'

Laetitia rose abruptly and went to the window. Scraps of their standardised jesting reached her across the ottomans and she drummed on the window ledge with fingers that had lost their power to be still. She did not observe Pink enter and approach her.

'Excuse me, miss,' said he. 'A farm lad has brought you a howl.'

'A what?' she said.

'A howl, miss,' he said. 'The bird, if you understand me, miss.'

'Oh, yes, Pink. Whatever for? Who brought it?'

'He didn't give no name, miss. He said he'd understood you had a fancy for wild birds – so I'm informed, miss. I didn't see the young man meself. He wouldn't come into the light, I understand, on account of frightenin' the howl.'

'I did tell some of the tenants last year I wanted a raven—'

She was speaking listlessly, thinking of other things. A raven – yes, it was Poe who wrote of the raven, and it was Poe, too, who had written: 'Helen, thy beauty—' Her drifting thought checked upon a sudden suspicion. This owl. This man who wouldn't be seen. She stiffened at once and turned towards the door. 'I'll see him myself.'

'What's all this?' the squire called out.

She explained hurriedly. 'I'll just go down,' she said, 'and let the poor creature fly away.'

'Better send him to young Evans,' Charles put in. 'They're confoundedly destructive of game.'

'And don't forget it's nearly time to dress for dinner,' her father admonished her.

'And be sure to take a shawl if you are going near an open door,' her aunt added. 'Dear Laetitia is so careless; really not fit to be trusted alone. I wonder you do not find her a mature companion, someone of responsible age, someone…'

But Laetitia had made her escape and the smooth voice was cut off by the closing of the door.

'Oh, what do she and all her sort matter now?' she thought as she sped downstairs and out into the yard, shawl-less. And then, with quickening pulse – 'If it be he, what shall I say? Will he accept my pearls? If only we knew where to sell them, they would bring money enough to take him abroad – to give him a new start. How I should miss him! Selfish … Will he be too proud after all he has said against us? Oh, I want to know what he has been thinking of me this long, dreary age!'

In the twilight of the yard, only the young man's bulk was to be distinguished, but it was enough to show her at a glance that this was not Gronwy. The sharpness of her disappointment shocked her.

'Good evening,' she said, controlling her voice with difficulty. He did not speak, but seemed to be studying her from beneath a pulled down hat brim. 'You have brought me an owl, I hear? That was very kind of you—'

He startled her by breaking into a laugh, loud and harsh, which snapped off unfinished.

'He's mad!' she thought, retreating a step.

In a moment he was close upon her. 'Here! Don't you try to get away. I'm going to speak to you.'

The yard was empty at this hour and darkening. Behind her she had closed the back door. From the stables came gleams of light and thin whistling, but the men there were not easily within call. She made no attempt to cry out. Someone who was not herself but kindred to her said within her: 'This is going to be an adventure. You are afraid, but you are glad.'

'I shall be most happy to hear what you have to say.'

'No you 'on't.'

This was disconcerting, and she tried at once to re-establish the values of the drawing room.

'I think you forget to whom you are speaking. There is no need for insolence.'

'I am forgetting nothing, nor forgiving neither, an' 'tis no manner o' use your trying to play the great lady with me. I do know what you've been – my brother's sweetheart: and a nice one, knowing you'd never marry such as he, to go leading him on to his ruin!'

Her fear had gone now and anger was cold upon her. She spoke slowly, letting each word drop like water from an icicle. 'So that is the interpretation which common people put upon my action in trying to help a poor scholar?'

He caught her by the wrist, and for a moment she was terrified into exclamation. 'Don't!' she cried, struggling like a trapped bird. 'You're hurting me! Let go!' Then training and tradition reasserted themselves. Fiercely ashamed, she stiffened and stood still. He had wrung her wrist so that she could not keep the tears from her eyes, but her teeth were bitten into her lower lip and she made no sound. When she ceased to fight, he peered at her in astonishment: then flung her away. If she had been released a moment earlier, she might have fled. Now she reeled, but stood her ground, and, drawing her breath with difficulty, asked: 'Well? Now perhaps you will be so good as to explain your behaviour.'

The return of her courage seemed to shake his. 'Why can't you leave him alone?' he cried, almost in entreaty. 'If you wasn't keeping him here, he'd go off to foreign parts tomorrow, where folks 'ouldn't point him out for a gaol bird. What are you doing it for? You do know as it can't end in nothing only shame.'

'I don't understand.'

'Oh, don't lie to me. I do know all about your meeting him.'

'Where? When?'

'Here in the garden by night, ever since he was come out – a fortnight pretty near. D'you think as we haven't missed him every night from his bed?'

'Well?' she whispered.

'Well, last night I followed him. An' that's where he came –

there, to that summer-house, or whatever you do call it, in your front garden. That's where he do come every night, sure to be.'

'Every night?' she replied under her breath.

'Watching the house he was for hours. I suppose as you'd seen me in a bit o' moonlight as caught me crossing one o' them terraces, or you'd have comed out to him?'

She tried to read his face in the gathering dusk. 'Every night, you say, every night since—'

'Don't you pretend as you don't understand,' said he. Then, with reversion to his tone of pleading – 'Let him go, miss. We've talked an' reasoned with him for hours, but we can't none of us make no sense nor shape of him. Bewitched him, you have – he's like a man that's seen his own corpse-candle.'

'Is he ill? Does he seem—'

'You are knowing well enough how he do seem. An' 'tis you as is keeping him so.'

A groom had come jauntily from the stable, whistling a tune. There was a clatter of buckets and a bar of light fell across the yard.

'I'll be gettin' back home,' Peter muttered. Having turned to go, he came back irresolutely, and spoke low, abashed by the servant's presence as he had not been by Laetitia's. 'Let him go, miss. Don't you go playing with him no more for your sport, same as a cat with a mouse, till he's worn to death. If there's no pity in you—'

'That is what you think of me?' As she spoke the flash of a passing lanthorn showed her clearly to him, and he thought her beauty diabolical. 'Tell your brother from me,' she went on. 'No, I will tell him myself.'

The stable boys were coming back from the well and touched their forelocks respectfully in passing. 'Good evening, miss… . Good evening, miss.' A gardener shambled up with mixed curiosity and deference.

'Good evening, miss,' he said. 'If you'll pardon me speaking to you, miss, I've sent in them there roses you wanted from the hot-house – the finest I could force for you, miss, this time o' year.'

'Thank you, Williams.'

'Thank you, miss.'

It was useless, Peter felt, to appeal to her. His recent boldness now appeared an outrage and he was cold.

'There's the bird as served my turn,' he said. 'You can wring his neck if you don't want him. They're said to bring a death, are them witches' fowls.'

She watched him disappear in the darkness and heard his dragging footsteps die away. Then, summoning a groom, she told him to cage and feed the owl, which still lay in a sack at her feet.

'A bit o' raw meat, miss? Very good, miss. But maybe I could catch him a live mouse. He'd fancy that better.'

'Perhaps. Will he play with it, as a cat does, till it is – what was the expression – worn to death?'

'That I couldn't say, miss, not knowing much about them goodyhoos, to say the truth, only that they're nasty things.'

'Have you ever heard them called "witches" fowls?'

'I have heard a bit o' talk about them, miss.' He cleared his throat. 'If you don't mind my mentioning it, miss, I wouldn't have nothing to do with him, if I was you.'

'No, I shall set him free tonight.'

As she passed through the house on her way to dress, she saw Mrs Smith's head thrust out inquisitively from the doorway of the housekeeper's room. Laetitia passed on; then, pausing, gave over her shoulder an order in level tones.

'Do not lock the back door tonight, Mrs Smith, before sending in the keys to your master. I shall be going out after prayers to see an owl I have just had brought me. I will bolt the door myself when I come in.'

'The keys is to go up as usual, miss, but the door is to be left unfastened?'

'Yes.'

'I beg pardon, miss, but in case the master should disapprove—'

'It is my order. That is enough.'

'Thank you, miss.'

'And tell my maid that I shall not need her.'

'Very good, miss.'

II

Since the coming of guests to Wingfield Park, a new formality had been added to the evening's routine. In the interval between dinner and the serving of drawing-room tea at nine, whist was regularly played. The squire and his son now remained but half an hour over their port and afterwards joined the ladies at a card table. Laetitia was not required to take a hand. Sitting in the shadows, she let her embroidery and a volume of *Armadale* lie neglected in her lap.

At last ten tinklings of the clock indicated that the time for prayers was come. On a silver salver, protected from scratches by a square of baize kept for this nightly ritual, the keys were brought. Two footmen extinguished the candles and folded the card table. Twenty-two chairs were then arranged in two rows, a long row of seventeen for the servants and, facing it, a short row of five for their betters. Five hassocks were laid by the five chairs, and a large piece of baize upon such of the seventeen as were intended for the lower servants, who had, as the housekeeper said, a nervous habit of fidgeting which did no good to silk upholstery. Five books of devotion bound in Russia leather were then presented on a salver that now fearlessly risked its polish, and seventeen books of the same devotion differently bound were distributed on the seventeen chairs. All being ready, Pink opened the door, and the staff, which had assembled in the passage, poured in. Mrs Smith made a separate entry so that all might know that she had not been waiting in the crowd of Welsh menials.

When the squire had told his Maker what he and his household required of Him, he rose from his knees and nodded a signal of release. Men and maids filed out of the room in order of precedence, the head servants going first, well-spaced and unhurrying, the newly caught herding together like sheep, as if each was fearful of being the last to leave the pen. Pink only remained. To him, prayers were a duty discharged; he awaited his dismissal.

'That is all, Pink,' said the squire.

'Thank you, sir,' said Pink, and withdrew.

Everyone was now embraced. 'Why Laetitia, how hot your cheek is!' In the hall, candles were lighted. Stairs creaked. Guests were escorted to their bedroom doors. 'Sleep well, Aunt Emily!'

'Goodnight, Laetitia, my dear!'

And the squire's lonely voice from down the passage: 'Good-night, Letty, and God bless you!'

She waited in her room until there was no sound in the house but the ticking of clocks. Then, with a shawl wrapped round her, she crept down through a darkness that leaped from her candle. In the kitchen, where the raked-out embers still had a sleepy life, a lanthorn had been set for her. She kindled it and went out.

The night was so still and watchful that she thought of it as of some nameless beast ready to spring. It was warm, too; the air had a thick softness. The snow, when her feet touched it, was soft as fur, without grinding of heel. Frightened by the silence and by the dark air of threatening expectation in all around her, she hesitated; then, gripping her lanthorn, forced herself to cross the yard.

In the harness room she found the captive, who stared at her with great eyes, beautiful and savage. 'You shall go free, you wild thing,' she murmured. 'You shall go free.' But the owner of the eyes only stared his defiance.

She carried him in his prison to the yard, and there, setting him down, extinguished the light. When she was accustomed to the darkness, shapes of buildings grew out of the sky. 'This is as proper a night as could be to loose the wild,' she thought as, with increasing excitement, she fumbled at the cage door. Suddenly it opened and she withdrew her hand in haste. There was a pattering, a flutter, a harsh cry, a tempestuous beating of wings. A pale form rushed up past her face, giving her the wind of its passage. Soon, from the black mass of trees beyond the house, she heard again the wild bird's cry. It was repeated from the hillside and echoed in the invisible valley. Something in her own heart stirred to answer it, some influence of magic that set a pulse leaping in her throat.

The fingers with which she lifted the empty cage were trembling, but when, having returned it to the stable, she emerged again, she received a warning to go no further that seemed to have an origin outside her own fears. It was, she would have said, as if the night itself had laid a hand upon her shoulder and bidden her stay, and as if, when she went forward nevertheless, a voice near to her had whispered: 'Go if you must. But you go knowingly. You know to what it leads.' Yet she did not know. Why should this adventure lead to disaster? The tale of the magic of owls and the groom's belief in it were alike ridiculous. Though she went now, she need never go again. Her will, she told herself, was free.

Yet, for all her excitement, for all the stirring of defiance within her, for all her picturing of herself as a solitary and romantic figure moving to a courageous escape, her heart was heavy. As she crossed the yard, another owl – or, the very one she had liberated – passed close on level wings, silent as a vast snowflake drifting in the wind. It disappeared in the direction by which she must go, and she seemed, therefore, to be following it. Her mind swung suddenly into fairy tales of witches that had taken the form of beasts and birds to lead human beings to their doom, and she looked back to her father's house as if she hoped to find reassurance in its solidity. It seemed to have receded beneath night's black arch and to be shrunken to a little part of its natural size. 'A doll's house,' she said, 'and all the dolls asleep.'

By contrast, her own way was expanded. The steps from the terrace, slippery with softened snow, were multiplied and enlarged; the stretch of lawn was wider than ever it had been by day; and the summer house, when at last she approached it, assumed the shape of a giant's beehive, slashed with luminous streaks of snow. Here she paused and listened. 'He is not here,' she thought, 'or he would have seen me coming. I am saved from this madness.' Knowing not whether to laugh or cry, she stood swaying, her eyes half-closed.

Then suddenly she stiffened and was alert. A sound had reached her from within, such a sound as told her that he was there and that his face was buried in his hands. Pity so sharp that it made her breasts ache assailed her and her mouth was dry. She entered, feeling before her with her hand.

'Gronwy!' she said; then, with lips that moved hardly to form the ghosts of words, 'Oh – my darling – forgive me.'

An indrawn breath answered her. An overturned chair crashed on the floor. She could not see, but felt him come close to her. His hand, touching hers, sent a shudder through her body, and stole up her arm, with incredulous fingers, from wrist to shoulder.

'My God! Can it be?' He caught her to him. 'What do I care,' he cried, 'why or how it happened – if I be mad or this a dream…? God, let this madness last till I be dead! My beloved! My beloved!'

When she withdrew from him, her face was wet with his tears. Neither of them could speak. Like children afraid, they tightened the clasp of their hands and dared not move lest they should set time moving. They stood pressing close in the dark, feeling each other tremble.

The terror of an irreparable loss was upon Laetitia when

she closed her eyes and waited, with head thrown back, for his farewell.

'Goodnight,' she said.

'No, no.' He clutched at her. 'Why are you going – now – so soon? Stop – oh, my sweetheart – just one small little minute… . When shall I see you again?'

'I don't know.'

'Where?'

'Here, perhaps. I haven't thought.'

'Nor we haven't talked of – of all that has happened—'

'The past?'

'An' the future, too – we haven't said nothing o' that.'

'Oh, my dear,' she whispered, breaking from him and leaving his hands empty, 'God knows what there is to say.'

III

Next morning, very early, Susan stole out of the house. Like a pecking bird she moved to and fro across the yard in jerks, starting at every sound from the stables. In the trampled slush between the buildings, she could not find what she sought, and was still peering at traces of hobnailed boots when a boy swung round the corner of the coach-house and caught her unawares. He gaped to see so genteel a creature trailing her morning gown of holland through the puddled snow. But Susan was a resourceful woman.

'My lady has lost a brooch,' she explained.

His red face broadened. It was not often that an upper servant deigned to address him. 'Maybe I can help you find it, Miss Jones?'

'No, no – thank you. I don't wish to trouble no one.'

''T'ould be no trouble at all, Miss Jones.'

She turned suspicious eyes on him. 'Go on with your own work, please.'

He glanced at her little elastic-sided boots, shook his head, scratched it, shrugged, and began to sweep the back-door step. When he looked up again, he saw her with head down swiftly following a trail that led out of the yard and across the drive towards the terraces. She whisked round the corner of the house and was lost to his sight.

Once more he shrugged his shoulders. Two scullery maids had joined him at the door.

'Fancy our young lady walking abroad in the snow when she's a comfortable parlour to sit in by the fire,' said one.

'Fancy that proud piece Miss Jones being so eager to find what she's lost,' added the other. 'There's never no telling what the quality'll do next, but ladies' maids – they *are* partic'lar.'

'You're all queer cattle – gentle and simple alike,' thought the stable boy, resting on his broom. 'I've been thinking a lot about you o' late and I do find you wonderful strange.'

And for the third time that morning this student of women shrugged his shoulders and scratched his head.

CHAPTER XVI

Charles is Almost Rash – Midnight Discovery – Afterwards

A few days later Charles Wingfield dressed for riding with even more than his usual care. Yet, in spite of his macassared ringlets, his laboriously tied stock, his jewelled pin, his gay waistcoat, his perfect breeches and his boots which had, in the polishing, caused three menservants to sweat and swear, he did not seem satisfied by his appearance. He examined it in every mirror he encountered while prowling uneasily up and down the passage and through the hall. He scowled at it, smirked at it, and, inflating his chest, struck an attitude as if about to address a pack of recalcitrant electors. Maintaining this dignified bearing, he paused, not for the first time, outside the door of his father's study. There his spirits sagged, and, after a moment's hesitation, he retreated towards the hall, his eyes turned with longing upon the flight of stairs that offered him retreat to his own room. Everywhere the masks of foxes grinned at him, seeming to relish the discomfiture of one who had pursued and slaughtered so many of them. Their glassy eyes, some of which had witnessed his hesitations before that self-same door in years gone by, reminded him of how on a glorious morning long ago he had gone forth unbidden on his father's horse, and had let it down, and had suffered for his crime. He tingled at the thought. Damn it all! His father could not still cane him. The very request he was about to make proved him to be a man. Tugging at his blond whiskers, he again passed the study and again checked himself, wondering this time whether the granting of the request he had to make would, in fact, be in his own interest.

Of course a man must settle down some day and beget an heir to the estate – confound those foxes, how they grinned! But to make the irrevocable choice at five and twenty – well, it was a bit of a twister. It was different for a woman. She couldn't look forward to much variety in any case, and the sooner she was provided for the better. Laetitia, for example. If he were his father, he'd put his foot down and make her marry Lee. But to throw away his own freedom before he'd had time to look round – was that wise? Wisdom be damned! He wanted Lucy. He wouldn't be happy till he'd got her. In the heat of that realisation he had stridden up to the formidable door when the knob was suddenly turned beneath his hand and out came the housekeeper.

'I beg pardon, Mr Charles, sir,' she gasped. 'I heard a step and "that's one of them listening at the keyhole", I thought. I'd no idea it was you, sir.'

She curtsied an apology and bustled away with that look of mingled detestation and gusto which virtuous women wear when they are on the tracks of their less discreet sisters. 'Hullo!' thought Charles. 'Who's the wretched housemaid she's got her knife into now?'

'Come in, come in,' exclaimed the squire, seeing him hesitate. 'What is it you want?'

'Nothing of any importance, sir – that is, I mean – it *is* important in a way – but it can wait if you are busy.'

'No,' answered the squire. 'I certainly hoped that I had finished with my worries for today. But something troublesome is always happening unexpectedly – in my own household, too, this time – one of the maids—'

Charles had begun to grin. 'Another increase in the population, sir?'

'No, no. At least, I trust it is not as bad as that.'

'Then what's the matter?'

'The housekeeper, a most worthy and conscientious creature, has been in to tell me she heard a window being unbarred last night after all the doors were locked – nothing easier, of course, than for anyone inside to get out through one of those opening on to the terrace.'

'But, dash it all, sir, if she saw nothing—'

'She saw a man crossing the garden from the summer house to the wood.'

'What of that?'

'Come, come, Charles. Who would enter a gentleman's garden at midnight with any honest purpose? He was either a thief, a poacher, or – or one of the maids' followers.'

'After our property in any case,' said Charles; but his grin died as he looked into his father's face, for he found there the same expression which he had seen in Mrs Smith's. She, he thought very much to the point, was 'Mrs' only by virtue of her rank, and a vague hostility towards these sapless guardians of girls' morality awoke within him. Why shouldn't the poor devils have followers if they chose?

'It's a recognised local custom,' he said, 'this courting by night, you know.'

'My dear boy, there is nothing whatever you can tell me about the Welsh. I am perfectly well aware that there used to be such a disgraceful custom. It was admitted and deplored even by their own dissenting ministers. But it has now been stamped out—' Charles made a face expressive of incredulity. ' …at least on the estates of landowners who, like myself, take an interest in the moral welfare of their tenants.'

'But I don't see, when it leads to no harm—'

'It always leads to harm. These people have to be guarded against themselves, and I consider it my duty so to guard any young woman as long as she remains beneath my roof… Tonight I shall post one or two of the older men, who can be trusted, in the shrubbery. Then, if we hear a sound in the house, you and I will go out and try to catch the fellow.'

'And if we succeed, what will you do?'

'Give him a piece of my mind and tell him that he richly deserves a thrashing.'

'And the girl?'

'Ah, if I find the guilty one – beyond doubt, mark you, for I intend to be scrupulously just in this distressing business – I shall be obliged to dismiss her.'

'Without a second chance?' The squire inclined his head. 'That seems a bit hard, sir.'

'No, Charles, no. No young person is received into my service without being warned of the penalty attaching to misconduct of this kind. These Welsh girls ought not to enter such a house as this if they are incapable of behaving themselves in accordance with its rules.'

With a rare flash of sympathetic vision, Charles replied: 'Depend upon it, sir, they wouldn't do so if they could earn a living by any other means.'

The squire started. 'Good God, Charles, your attitude towards the whole thing astounds me. One would think you were condoning immorality.'

That settled Charles. He had gone too far and retreated abashed. 'Oh no, sir! Dash it all, I was only trying to – to—'

'To what, pray?'

'To – understand, trying to understand, just for argument's sake, their point of view.' He turned away from his father's angry stare. 'I don't mean to say for a moment that they're right,' he caught himself saying, but he longed to cry out, 'Damn it all! I know what they feel. I've been feeling it myself for the last month. And if ever you knew, you've forgotten!'

Charles was making great strides in imagination. Now, as he fidgeted with his correctly tied stock and wished that he had not, at this juncture, offended his father by advancing an opinion of his own, another disconcerting revelation was vouchsafed to him. He perceived that desire may be starved into atrophy as it had been in his father and in his father's approved servant, 'Mrs' Smith, or fed to satiety – as a premonition painfully warned him his own would be after some years of marriage with the obliging Lucy. He saw, too, that, with desire, toleration often dies. 'All men and women,' he thought, 'are probably potential lovers at some time of their lives, but those who've lost the taste for it are like reformed drunkards, most bitter against those who still enjoy it. They see sex everywhere and hate it everywhere. Poor devils, how they must loathe the spring! For then the birds in every tree are mating. The lambs in every field must remind them of last autumn's tupping. They probably hate the bees, matchmaking from flower to flower. Spring must be hell for the Mrs Smiths of this world!'

But spring and sex weren't hell for him, or for that wretched housemaid, whoever she was! He'd like to have Lucy in the spring – next spring – that was what he had come about. He'd like – his hand tightened on the edge of his father's desk. He must not think like that. There was no knowing to what deeds such thoughts might lead. As it was, he found it hard enough to avoid pretty housemaids who might get him into trouble. If he gave himself rein like this—

'You will oblige me,' his father said, 'by sitting up tonight. We will come down and meet again here after going upstairs – no need to let the ladies know about so unsavoury an affair.'

'Just as you like, sir,' said Charles, trying to feel self-righteous. 'I am ready to do as you wish.'

II

The softness and deceptive warmth of snow were gone. That night a bitter wind drove cloudy squadrons across the sky. Now the moon was clear, sliding on the wet edges of all it touched; now, across its face, came a galloping mass of darkness. Hailstones pinged like bullets against the study window panes, and for a while nothing could be discerned of the garden without.

In one of these inky interludes, the squire laid his hand on his son's arm. 'Hush! I thought I heard a sound—'

'The wind, sir.'

'No, no. A shutter being unbarred – one of those on the French windows of the drawing room.'

'We can't see anything. We can't possibly make sure,' Charles said, and began to gnaw his thumb. Keeping quiet in a darkened room with his father was a damnable way of spending the night. He remembered regretfully a rowdy conclusion to last year's Derby day in company with fellow 'swells' and girls who, though they'd never have passed in Aunt Emily's drawing room, had been rare good company at Cremorne.

'The moment this storm is over,' the squire whispered, 'we'll go out and search the garden.'

Charles said nothing. One would think the old boy enjoyed it, though it seemed a job more fit for a police officer than a gentleman. Anyhow it was useless to protest or stir.

They waited while the wind screamed and the windows rattled throughout the period of darkness. At length the moon came out. The shuddering trees, the terraces, the stone steps; the geometrical flower beds, box-edged; the path leading to the summerhouse, the clipped laurels by which it was flanked – every object in the garden sprang into the watchers' vision, neat, hard, black and white as the squares of a chess-board.

'There she goes!' cried the squire as if he had been tally-hoing a fox. 'There she goes!'

Charles followed the direction of his pointing finger and saw a woman, muffled in a shawl, hurry across the topmost terrace. Down the first flight of steps she went and across the second terrace, moving forward in brief advances like a pawn pushed across the board. 'God pity any one in love,' thought Charles.

'Go and tell the housekeeper to see which of the windows has been opened and to take her stand beside it. We must have all the likely earths stopped. You'll find her waiting for orders in her sitting room. Be quick. I shall wait here and keep watch till you return.'

Charles hesitated, but decided to obey. He did not, however, hurry back to the study, but loitered on his way downstairs until he heard the quick, fussy footsteps, which he knew to be his father's, cross the hall. 'Thank God, he's gone out to do his dirty work without me,' was his first thought, but a second pressed close upon it: 'All the same, there'll be the deuce of a row if I'm not in at the death.'

Shouting came up to him from the shrubbery as he strolled out, dawdling and reluctant, on to the terrace. In an instant, curiosity had overcome good nature and he was running down the steps as people run to see a street accident. The shouting increased. He saw his father ahead of him, hastening towards the summerhouse from behind which the uproar came. Suddenly the girl they had watched descending thither dashed out of the laurels with one of the gardeners in close pursuit. She screamed, bolting like a rabbit to right and to left; then, coming round the summerhouse, she ran into the squire's arms. Charles heard her cry of despair, saw her recoil and huddle her shawl about her. Her face was young, stricken with anguish, pitiably drawn. She was beyond hope of escape now and drooped limp as an empty dress upon a peg. 'It's a damned shame,' thought Charles, but still he went on. Another gardener had emerged from the laurels and fragments of the two men's breathless conversation reached him.

'Yes, yes, sir. Griffith Tinygraig's son – him as has been in gaol for speaking so disrespectful o' the gentry… Yes, yes. We saw him – now just. In your own garden, sir.'

The squire turned to the girl. Charles saw her sway like a stalk in the wind. She was so frail that it seemed absurd that such a storm should break upon her. He heard his father's voice rumbling, and was half angry, half inclined to laugh. 'I'll give her a tip when it's all over,' he thought.

'I am beyond measure astonished,' the squire was saying, 'that Miss Laetitia's own maid should have behaved in a manner disgraceful even in a scullery wench.'

'I've done nothing wrong, sir,' she gasped out.

'How have you the effrontery to say so? To meet your young man, clandestinely, might—'

'I never did, sir. I swear—'

'Do not add perjury to your other offences. You have been in the habit of creeping out here when all respectable persons were abed.'

'No, sir, indeed and indeed, I never did before.'

'Do not attempt to deny it. I have come to know that someone has broken the rules of my house before tonight.'

'It wasn't me, sir.'

'Will you kindly hold your tongue.'

'What a fool the girl is,' thought Charles. 'Why can't she take her licking?'

His father was rumbling on, more thunderous than before. Suddenly Charles found his pomposity, and the gaping gardeners, and the very youth of the diminutive offender, irresistibly funny. 'What a solemn farce, and all about nothing!'

'The young man,' said the squire, 'with whom you have dared to behave in this way is the worst character in the district—'

'I never so much as saw him tonight, sir. I only came out to see—'

'The moon, I suppose? I have no patience with liars. You will leave my service tomorrow and you need not apply to my daughter or myself for a reference.'

'Oh, for God's sake, sir,' she sobbed, 'don't turn me away like that. My parents are dead. I've nowhere to go. And I never did what you're accusing me of.'

'If you had told me the truth, I might, in the circumstances, have considered keeping you on until—'

'But I *have* spoken the truth. I never met him here. It wasn't me he came courting.'

'Oblige me by going to your room and packing. I cannot pardon these deliberate lies.'

The girl was beginning to protest again when a new voice interrupted her.

'She is not lying. Gronwy Griffith came here to see me.'

In the doorway of the summerhouse, framed in its blackness, stood Laetitia. Charles stared – at first with mere surprise and interest, as at the brilliant *dénouement* of a play. On the terrace below him were grouped the actors, gazing like himself at the central figure. The stagecraft was perfect, reminding him of the Screen Scene in *The School for Scandal*. But Laetitia had come forth of her own accord. Looking at her white face, he perceived the torturing power of her pride. It had not suffered her to let a servant be blamed for that of which she herself was guilty. He perceived, too, in one of those flashes of intuition by which, during these few months of his life, he was troubled, that no matter what agony it cost her or to what humiliation it might lead, she was exulting in this playing of a sensational part. And how superbly she played it! He, who had been indifferent to them, felt now the force of her beauty and dignity. He was compelled to admiration.

For a moment, he was, indeed, proud of her as never before. Then he looked at his father. The piece being played before him instantly lost its glamour. It had been comedy once; then tragedy that could be watched with an impersonal pity; now it was catastrophe befallen his own people.

The squire seemed to have shrunk. Like last season's walnut within its shell, he had shrivelled, and his clothes hung upon him loose and creased. Charles covered his eyes with clenched hands. His father had been powerful – like God, able to punish and reward. Now it was as if he had seen his Creator grovelling at his feet, and he was terrified and sickened.

When he could wrench his hands away from his face, his first thought was –'Confound those gardeners! Why are they allowed to stand gaping at him?' Then, as his eyes fell upon the little girl who had seemed like a stalk in the wind, he saw her terribly transformed. What the devil was the matter with this moonlight? It was making him see hidden truths about people, horrible, indecent things. He closed his eyes but could not stop his ears. The girl was laughing; she was crying; she was shrieking with inhuman shrillness and penetration.

'Now you see for yourself! Now you see for yourself, you old rat!' Was she thrusting that devilish pointed face towards his father's? Charles could not look. 'Your fine haughty daughter!' the voice went on. 'The spit of her mother, was she? Who knows if her mother didn't treat you the same way? Only you never found her out, courting a common ploughboy. Proud of her, were you? Are you proud now? A grand sort o' lady, isn't she, to rob one of your own servants of her sweetheart? He was mine – mine, d'you hear? Oh, she's welcome to him now he's been in gaol. She can have my leavings – and she's eager to get them seemingly – coming out here after him at night when "all respectable persons are abed". That's what you said to me, isn't it? That's what you were going to send me packing for – an' I needn't ask you, nor your fine lady daughter, for a reference. It's a good job for her she needs none. Where'd she be if she had to earn her living like me you treat as dirt? On the streets – earning it as a nightwalker, playing the harlot for her keep as she's been playing it here night after night just for a bit of spice. That's the sort your daughter is – your daughter you fancied—'

Charles plunged like a wounded bull into the midst of them. 'Stop her talking, sir,' he shouted. 'Get rid of her.'

But the squire only stared at Laetitia with lifeless eyes, while his hands, which he was accustomed to move with so much restlessness when he was angry, hung loose at his sides.

'Can't you speak, Laetitia,' cried Charles. 'There's been some hideous mistake.' And then, because he knew that it was not so, he turned in fury on the men whom his father had set to trap the offender. 'Damn your impudence – spying on your mistress. Get out, all of you.' And, when they had shambled away, grinning behind their hands, 'Letty, for God's sake go! Don't stand there listening – it's – it's intolerable.'

She went, carrying her head high, but Susan's frenzied screaming mounted up the steps from terrace to terrace after her. Charles saw her shudder at the ugly words and bite her lips. Reaching the topmost terrace, she disappeared into the darkness, and Charles turned again to his father. The old man – he looked a very old man now –had not moved. He was still staring at the place where his daughter had stood.

III

As she moved towards the house, every other thought in Laetitia's mind was overwhelmed by a desire to escape from moonlight. Entering the drawing room, 'Oh! God bless the darkness!' she murmured, stretching out her hands. But even as she plunged into it she became aware that this darkness concealed a human presence.

'Who's there?' she cried, starting back. 'Why are you hiding – watching me?'

'I beg pardon, miss.' It was the housekeeper's voice. 'I was on the lookout for one of the maids. I never guessed – not for a moment, miss—'

Laetitia passed on. 'No,' she thought, 'nor did I ever think it of myself.' Then, suddenly – 'I must have water. I must wash.'

When she reached her room, she laid hold of the bell rope, but, remembering that she was now without a maid, let it drop. 'How like me to summon someone – a servant – anybody, when I am lost… Like that night on the mountain top – that first night.'

Through blinds and curtains, a little of the hated moonlight forced its way in. Dimly reflected in the many mirrors, she saw on every side – herself; ghostly portraits of Laetitia Wingfield, standing irresolute, twisting a lace handkerchief in her hands. At last she went towards the washstand, but turned from that as she had turned from the bell; and, suddenly flinging herself on to her bed, cried aloud: 'Oh, my God! As though I could ever wash myself clean again.'

CHAPTER XVII

Laetitia Alone – Aunt Emily Understands – Deadlock

Laetitia had been alone in her room all day. Now, as the light that entered it through rain-smeared windows began to fail, she was more than ever aware of that active silence in which only gentlefolk and prisoners can be engulfed. The cheerful clatter of the kitchen could not reach her here; from its communal labours, as from those of the yard, she was too far removed. Such footsteps as had passed her door during the morning had been muffled by a thick carpet.

When, weary of hearing nothing, she looked out from her window, she saw the terraces which last night's vulgar drama had defiled. There stood the summerhouse where, in her madness, she had allowed a peasant, her own maid's discarded lover, to take her roughly in his arms, while far away from it, in the valley's misty gloom, the tarnished silver of the river recalled the folly of her girlish wish. It had been early summer – blossom time – when she had asked the fates for romance. Now, having been answered, she wished that she had never left the shelter of the garden, full of standard rose trees uniform and sedate. What had been her quarrel with them? Only that they were so well pruned. They blossomed the better for that and would have furnished Lucy with wreathes for her hair. Now there were no flowers in the formal beds. She remembered having seen great slugs crawl out of their box edgings. Wherever she looked, the paths seemed befouled with slime. She could walk in that place no more without shuddering; was ashamed even to look at it. She turned back into the room. That also, in one long day, had become hateful to her.

Early in the morning, a servant had brought her tea and lit a fire. Lying with face hidden in her pillows, she had heard the clatter and believed it to be insolently loud. The final banging of the door had, to her inflamed pride, suggested another affront. She had jumped out of bed and run to see if she was locked in. Much as she dreaded that indignity, it was almost a disappointment to know that she was free. All night she had tried to comfort herself with the thought, 'Next year I shall be twenty-one. No one will have the legal right to shut me up then.' But no one thought it worthwhile to shut her up even now. 'They know I lack the courage,' she had told herself; and, locking her own door, had leant against the wall and wept.

After a time she had begun to shiver, and turned to the tea tray. The tea was cold. She had twisted the cup round in her hands and vaguely admired its transparency. In the poorer farmhouses, they drank greasy leek broth out of wooden bowls. Long soaking made them sodden and gave them a musty smell. 'It's true – I haven't the courage,' she repeated; then, pacing about the room, had begun to whisper fragments of her thought in a voice which, when she heard it, frightened her.

'Sordid poverty – starvation perhaps – for both of us… *Her* lover; I wonder if she spoke the truth – and what she meant? Poverty, and the contempt of all my class. Never to speak to gentlefolk again. I'd grow coarse with labour – and ugly. I'd lose in the end the love for which I had flung everything away… When – when I let him kiss me, I never for an instant contemplated such a thing. Truly I didn't. Not marriage. Not living together always. I never pictured it so. It was only a madness – a moment! If I hadn't been found out—'

A flood of self-contempt had swept over her, tossing her, like a drowned thing, on to her bed. There sick fancies had assailed her. She remembered reading of a torture applied to prisoners who would not confess. They were stretched on the floor of their dungeon, a board was placed upon them and great weights piled on it until they spoke or died. She was being put to the torture while she lay staring up at the ceiling. So heavy was the load upon her breasts that she could hardly breathe. It was choking her. She cried out, and sprang from the bed, knowing not at first whether she was waking or asleep. A childish curiosity possessed her to see how she looked.

A mirror had shown her a face swollen out of its own delicate shape. 'I cannot keep my beauty even for a few hours,' she thought, 'when life is not made easy for me. How could I hope to retain it then? Oh, but I have gone over all that before, last night – hour after hour. It's settled once for all.' Yet, through the day as through the night, passion and fear, pride and shame, the longing for love and the fiercer longing to receive homage, fought within her. Once or twice someone had knocked on the door.

'Would you like anything to eat, miss?'

'No. I am not hungry.'

Now that the dusk was stealing upon her, she came back for the hundredth time to her bed and dropped down upon it, cold and faint. Was it her dizziness, she wondered, that made pieces of furniture, isolated as small islands in the darkened ocean of the room, assume fantastic shapes? The canopy of the bed was a vast tent, its mahogany posts were trees that towered above her. She was small and chill – the corpse of a queen lying in state in mid-forest.

II

Hours afterwards she was awakened by renewed knocking at her door.

'Who is there?' she cried.

'Your Aunt Emily.'

Recollection rushed back. She wanted to scream and scream, but she dragged up the coverlet and thrust her face into it. The knocking began again. At last she said with control.

'Pray, come in.'

'Your door is locked or I should have done so.'

'How foolish of me to forget!' She dragged her cramped limbs out of bed and groped her way to the door. Having opened it, she stood aside.

'How cold it is in here,' her aunt complained. 'Have not the maids kept up your fire?'

'I did not let them in.'

'That was a mistake. One should always keep up appearances before the servants. Now let me light a candle or two so that we may see each other while we have a talk.'

Laetitia watched the flames arise. 'What hands my aunt has,' she thought, 'smooth as moulded wax, yet somehow commanding. They never make nervous movements.'

'My poor, poor child,' said Mrs Bodley-Booth in a tone of extreme sweetness. 'Have you not washed or dressed today?'

'I forgot to dress.'

'A young lady forget to dress!'

Laetitia found herself hanging her head as she had done long ago when told that little ladies did not suck their fingers or cross their legs or whistle like ploughboys. Up went her chin in defiance, but the movement was forced.

'Now go and wash your face,' Aunt Emily said, 'and brush and braid your hair.'

The sting of cold water revived her pride. When her hair hung in two plaited ropes, making a black frame to her pale cheeks, she was able to meet her aunt's scrutiny at least with outward composure.

'Sit down, my dear.'

They sat facing each other, erect, with hands clasped in their laps. The stately pose of the elder woman had been given ease by long habit; that of the younger had an unnatural rigidity.

'I know all,' Mrs Bodley-Booth said slowly.

Laetitia quivered like a filly touched with the whip. 'It was very kind of you, then, to come and see me.'

'It was my duty to come.'

There was a heavy silence.

'What has he decided to do?' Laetitia asked suddenly. The knuckles of her clasped hands had grown white.

'Your poor, dear, broken-hearted father?'

'Yes. But is there any need to speak of him as if he were dead?'

Her aunt's mouth hardened. 'It is evident that you have not yet realised the extent of the mischief you have caused.'

'Have I offended him so deeply?'

'Offended is scarcely the word. He simply cannot understand—'

'He never could.'

'But,' said Aunt Emily, 'I have tried to make him do so.'

'You?' Laetitia stared into the impassive face. 'What have you ever—' she was about to say 'felt', but checked herself, and her aunt's smooth voice continued:

'You should have no need to ask, Laetitia. I never did anything to cause my dear parents a moment's anxiety, I am thankful to say. When I sat at my poor papa's deathbed, I was able to do so without self-reproach, as you, I fear, my poor child, cannot hope to do.' She paused that this statement might have time to cause its smart; then proceeded benignly: 'But, perhaps, though only a woman, I do know more of the world than your dear father. His is so upright, so noble a nature, that he cannot comprehend the temptations to which baser characters are subject. The love of vulgar admiration and excitement, the flightiness to which young girls, if not carefully controlled, are apt to yield, seem to him incredible, and, let me warn you, my dear, unpardonable.'

Again she paused, looking for a break in Laetitia's pride. The girl's beauty, which she had come near to hating during the last few weeks, was now so marred by suffering that she found it in her heart to pity her. Laetitia's unspoiled youth had provoked her enmity, but there was no cause for envy in this Laetitia. Because she had never recognised – and would, indeed, have contemptuously denied – that an ageing woman's rivalry had lain at the root of her dislike of her niece, Mrs Bodley-Booth found a great deal of Christian satisfaction in the kindlier sentiment she was now able to feel towards the same niece, pleasantly humiliated. For Mrs Bodley-Booth was not a vindictive woman. She had no disposition to trample on a rival whom God had rebuked. He could be trusted henceforward to keep Laetitia in her place; it was the part of her aunt, who was His ally, to help her to bow patiently to the divine decree.

'I have offered to take you away with me, my dear,' she said with a momentary approach to genuine kindness, 'to be responsible for you as though you were my own little girl.' Yes, if she could succeed in teaching Laetitia to be, like Lucy, sweet and submissive, if she could dress her inconspicuously as she ought to be dressed and keep her in the background to which she properly belonged, then she might grow to love her. She was moved to generous self-approval by the thought of all she would do for her niece. It would mean trouble, of course; but she had never been afraid of trouble that led to the improvement of others. She was a good woman and had never felt more sure of it than at this moment.

'I have seen to everything,' she said brightly; 'with the full approval of your dear father and brother, of course. I have taken what steps were possible to ensure the silence of that insolent creature who, I am told, so far forgot her place as to be exceedingly rude to you last night. If anyone worth considering should hear of the servant's gossip, we must hope that they will attribute it to the malice of one who – as I am letting everybody know – has been discharged for untruthfulness. No one in my own county will credit any scandal about a young lady whom I permit to associate with my own Lucy.'

'Are you not afraid to risk it, Aunt Emily?'

There was a hint of the old irony in that. The girl was far from being cured yet, Mrs Bodley-Booth decided.

'I am glad,' she said, 'you are sensible of the fact that I am taking a risk. Lucy has never read a word which I have not previously pronounced suitable. She has overheard no objectionable talk. When one of her girl companions, of whom I most approved, became married, I gradually discontinued their intimacy. When Lucy herself becomes a married woman she will of necessity learn by gentle experience things it is better for her now not to know. You will understand, Laetitia, that I have mentioned all this only that you may realise that I trust you in her presence to keep silence on certain matters.'

'I see,' said Laetitia, 'as though a bad woman should be allowed to mix with chaste ones on the understanding that she would never allude to her past life.' Even as she uttered these words, she was made by her aunt's lifted eyebrows to blush for her lack of taste. 'I am sorry, Aunt Emily,' she added. 'I am upset by what has happened.'

'That is over. In a day or two you will start life again.'

Mrs Bodley-Booth had intended to be kind, but her lips narrowed at Laetitia's answer: 'Turn back from life, you mean, do you not?' The girl was going to be a hard case.

'My meaning,' her aunt replied, 'ought to be apparent to any but the deliberately perverse. It is that you will start to live again as becomes a gentlewoman.'

Laetitia's moment of rebellion was ended. She sat with

bowed head, thinking of the years before her in which she would be denied even the solitude and comparative freedom she had enjoyed in her father's house. With aching regret, she remembered riding across the hilltop to meet Gronwy. The swing of the horse galloping beneath her, the throb of hoofbeats exciting as primitive music, the wind singing a shrill accompaniment in her ears, had compensated her for the loss of those jewelled Venetian nights of which she had never ceased to dream. What compensation would she have when ambling between the railings of the Row with Lucy for companion? How would she endure the protracted meals, the nightly card-playing, the daily hours of needlework that served no useful purpose and had no artistic merit? Sometimes, 'for a change', they would visit other ladies who were similarly employed in similar drawing rooms. On the drive thither, her aunt would sit facing the horses, smiling and nodding unheedingly at Lucy's babble, as if to say, 'Isn't it nice? One never has to listen to the dear child. One knows that whatever she says will be quite harmless.' She herself and Lucy, seated side by side opposite their supervisor, would wear twin bonnets chosen without regard for their widely differing tastes and looks. For, in this life that awaited her, convention would crush individuality, until guarding her face from freckles became her most serious concern. 'But what does it matter, since I shall never meet him again wherever I am?' she asked herself. 'Let them crush me into their mould – it's all I'm worth if I lack courage to be myself.' In this mood of self-scorn, she said aloud in a voice as toneless as a nun's: 'Since you are good enough to wish it, Aunt Emily, I will go with you.'

'I am glad. And I hope you will put yourself under my direction, my dear, and will realise that I am a better judge than you, alas, have proved yourself to be of how you should behave.'

'Yes. Aunt Emily.'

'That is right. Now go to bed and get some of your sorely needed beauty sleep. I have persuaded your poor father to see you in the morning, so you will be required to appear again as usual. Lucy has been told that you were indisposed. Remember to say your headache is better when she inquires after your health.'

'I'll remember – and that I must lie to everyone from now on.'

'No, Laetitia, no! Not lie, my dear, but be discreet … goodnight.'

She had risen and was going from the room composedly, as if nothing more unusual had happened than the giving of one of the many orders she was accustomed to have obeyed.

At the thought of being left alone again, a yearning for sympathy surged through Laetitia.

'Aunt Emily,' she cried, 'what did you mean when you said you had tried to make papa *understand*?'

Mrs Bodley-Booth paused. A scarcely perceptible stiffening of her figure and tightening of her lips might have warned Laetitia that she was hardening herself to repel any emotional outburst. 'Still,' Laetitia thought, 'when she spoke of the temptations to which baser natures than my father's are subject, she implied, however unwillingly, some sort of kinship between herself and me.'

'Tell me,' she urged, hoping desperately that this woman, with whom she was henceforth to live, had, like herself, known the torment of parting from her beloved. 'Tell me what you meant, Aunt Emily.'

Mrs Bodley-Booth took up a candle before answering and held it at the level of her breast. The neat little wrinkles about her mouth were revealed. Her eyes, with a motionless flame reflected in each, seemed darker now than by daylight.

'We are all anxious to think as leniently of you as possible,' she said at last. 'We feel that you could never have stooped to – to what you have done – meeting a young man –

of any class – alone, at midnight—' Her composure seemed to desert her. 'We feel that this would have been impossible unless your intentions towards him had been of the most serious.'

'Only my having definitely intended to marry him would have justified me, you mean?'

'Nothing could justify you. But, when your poor father expressed his disgust at the thought of a lady bred as you have been contemplating a runaway match with a common labourer, I tried to mitigate your offence in his eyes by making him realise how blind is a young girl's innocence.'

'Innocence? Why do you use that word of me?'

Mrs Bodley-Booth lowered her eyes. 'There are matters, my dear Laetitia, of which no woman of refinement cares to speak; but perhaps on this occasion it is my duty … To my mind, you have proved conclusively, my poor child, that you can have no conception of what marriage entails. As I said to your father, "she probably fancies it would be romantic to share a cottage with a peasant poet. That is all." She made a motion with one hand, too slight to be called a gesture, as if brushing aside an offensive gnat. 'Of course,' she continued with evident effort, 'I found it most distressing to discuss such a subject with two gentlemen, but, for your sake, my poor, motherless child, I brought myself to do so. I placed myself in your position.'

'How do you know what my position is?' Laetitia asked, surprised that her aunt had not wrongly assumed the worst.

'I judged by my own ignorance when I married.' A little spasm of remembered fear ran over her face before she could control it. 'You may talk wildly, as you did just now, about chaste women and bad women – you foolish little girl, sheltered as you have been, you can have no idea of the meaning of such terms, unless, indeed, natural depravity—' Another slight flicker of dismissal completed the sentence.

Laetitia averted her burning face. 'Natural depravity?'

Was she, in whose veins the blood ran warm, naturally depraved? If her aunt had known or suspected the passionate secrets of her mind, she could have given but one answer. But it was not her aunt's opinion that perturbed Laetitia now; she could, she thought, have stood firm against that or against the opinion of any Wingfield. They, though she bore their name, were of a race different from her own, and she held their prejudices in no honour. Her mind was, however, stabbed, in this moment of self-discovery, by the fear that the only two women whom she had ever loved – her mother and her mother's sister – might have passed upon her a judgment scarcely less severe than Aunt Emily's. One had been a cold, reluctant wife; the other had shrunk from all the pleasures of the body. Abstinence and aloofness had been their creed, and in theory this creed was hers also. Was it for this reason that her joy in Gronwy's company had been overshadowed always by a vague, unrecognised cloud? Had that cloud been a sense of guilt, of betrayal, of pollution of ideal? If these two women would have condemned her – or, rather, turned from her in disgust – ought not she to despise herself? Yet she was not, in fact, ashamed of the passion she had felt. The woman in her declared that it was a glorious, not a contemptible or evil thing, if she but had the courage of it. Natural depravity? She did not know. But she knew now the Wingfields' name for love.

'This ploughboy,' her aunt was saying, 'whom you may perhaps have privileged to touch your fingertips, would, as your husband, have the right – the right – to kiss your lips – to, to, to kiss you – undress you – caress you with his dirty hands. He would be your bedfellow. You would share a room with him. All the little mysteries and reticences, about which you have been so fastidious, would be exposed before him. Why, even I, who was blessed with a husband of my own rank, the most considerate of men, was sorely shocked by the unavoidable intimacies of married life during our honeymoon… I think,' she said with sudden energy, 'it was the least happy period of my marriage… But of course you cannot have imagined the surprises, the – the discomforts—' She was speaking with such increase of speed that she forgot to round off her sentences. 'No,' she said positively, 'that you should have contemplated giving your – your person to this common, unwashed labourer would be, as your father finds it, monstrous, if you had guessed what complete self-surrender – but I will say no more.'

Laetitia retreated from the light of the candle. She closed her eyes, remembering how Gronwy's kisses had fallen fast as a hot shower of rain on her eyelids and her throat. She remembered too, those longer kisses that had crushed her lips, inflicting exquisite pain, arousing an insatiable longing for more such blended delight and suffering. He could have done with her then as he chose. She knew it, and quivered, not only with the recollection, but with a ghostly anticipation of passion… 'What would *she* think, who stands there with her hateful light, if she knew how I long, even now, to be in his arms…? What would *they* think?' Remembering again how her heroines of childhood had been withdrawn from desire, she felt that all pure womanhood must be as cold as they and would shrink from her in loathing. 'Thank God they are dead,' she thought, 'my dear ones. I could not live deceiving them as I must always deceive her.'

Mrs Bodley-Booth saw the tears that glistened on her lashes. 'In speaking thus bluntly, I fear I have shocked you,' she said. 'I am sorry, my dear.' But there was satisfaction in her tone.

Laetitia opened her eyes and stared in horror at the speaker. 'I thought for a moment that she could understand,' she said to herself. 'I thought she had come to make me a generous offer, at least according to her lights. Now I know. It's because I'm beaten that she wants me – because I can't resist … Merciful God, I shall have no means of escape from her – ever. I have closed this house to myself as I closed Rhayader Hall. No other will open its doors to me except with her consent. From henceforth I shall be always the disgraced niece to whom Mrs Bodley-Booth has been so kind. I shall not have a friend in the world or be allowed to find one. She will never let me forget that I am under observation and an object of suspicion so long as any vestige of youth or beauty remains.'

She said aloud: 'When does this new life you are offering me begin?'

'Your papa and I will settle that tomorrow… Now, my dear child, go to bed at once. You are in danger of taking cold.'

Aunt Emily inflicted a little kiss of departure. When closing the door behind her, she thought she heard a sound that was half sob, half laugh. 'Hysterics,' she said to herself, and added, thinking of Laetitia's past defiance: 'A good cry will do her no harm.' Then, reproving herself for uncharitableness, she allowed her good woman's heart to have its generous way. 'Poor, silly little thing,' she murmured, who was always sorry for the physical discomfort of her relations, 'I'll make her have my smelling salts.'

III

Though Laetitia went downstairs next morning, her father made no allusion to what was past or what was to come. He avoided her as far as courtesy would permit, and did not brace himself to receive her formally until the late afternoon. She went then to his study, summoned by Charles in an awkward whisper.

How sad, aged and bewildered her father was! She pitied him. But it was too late now. Nothing could heal the wound she had dealt him. He was no more angry with her than he would have been if she had become insane and homicidal but avoided her eyes with that tortured embarrassment that paralyses men confronted with their loved ones gone mad.

'Your aunt is taking you away,' he said, speaking in a sickroom voice. 'There maybe a few days' delay, however, which will necessitate our all braving it out.'

'Why, if I am going, Papa, can I not go at once?'

'Because your aunt has allowed some of her servants to go home. She will, of course, have to order them back to Simpton Lacey before she can leave here.'

'Of course!' she said.

It was her aunt's word, Lucy's word. Why had it come so readily to her lips? She had wanted to break out into protest, 'What does it matter if she has not quite so many people as usual to wait upon her? If you knew what it is for me to stay in this place where I have failed my lover and am at every turn reminded of him, you would take me away yourself – now.' But all she had said was 'of course'. After a pause during which he rustled his papers, she added, 'Is that all?'

'That is all, Letty.'

The corners of his lips twitched as he spoke. Was he also longing to speak his mind, to cry out, 'Why did you stoop to love this common farmer's son? How could you do it? Tell me. I was so proud of you. I don't understand.'

She waited, knowing that if he could break the icy reticence that numbed them both she would throw herself on her knees and sob out to him as much of her story as she herself understood.

But, when he spoke, it was only to say, 'I hope you will show proper gratitude to your Aunt Emily. She is taking a great deal of trouble on your behalf.'

'Yes,' said Laetitia. 'She enjoys taking trouble of that kind.'

He gazed at her, too sad, it seemed, for anger. Touched by remorse, she turned her back on him and went towards the door. He opened it and let her pass.

That, perhaps, was the last interview that he and she would ever have. Even now, if she turned back – what was he doing behind that closed door? Fingering his papers? She went on to her own room, and, before evening brought darkness without sleep, read herself into a melancholy trance. He meanwhile went about his business, and presided at his table, and asked for more sherry in his soup, trying not to remember the moment when his wife had first allowed him to hold their daughter in his arms.

CHAPTER XVIII

A Determined Messenger – Charles is Rash

On the following day, Laetitia, having ordered breakfast in her room, found herself visited by her aunt before her tray had been removed. She was, however, already dressed and opened the door at once.

'Good morning, Aunt Emily. Pray come in.'

'I was coming in, my dear. We have all been distressed by your absence from the breakfast table. You know your papa likes to see you at the head of it.'

'I am not feeling well.'

Laetitia turned towards the window and began to play with a silk tassel. The voice behind her at once assumed the tone in which a kind but firm nurse speaks to a naughty child.

'Come, come, my dear. No matter how you feel, you should endeavour to resume your household duties until I take you away. We must not appear to give in.'

'Why not?' asked Laetitia. 'What is the use of trying to deceive servants who are already undeceived?'

Mrs Bodley-Booth refused to argue. 'It has stopped raining,' she observed. 'Put on your bonnet and shawl and come out with me for a stroll.'

Laetitia yielded. It was better to yield at once than after defeated rebellion. In silence she went to her wardrobe and took out a shawl.

'Now your bonnet, my dear.'

'I never wear one in the garden.'

'Then you ought to change your practice. Think – if anyone should see you with your hair all blown about.'

Without answering, Laetitia took a bonnet from the peg on which it hung and tied the strings under her chin.

'And your gloves,' Mrs Bodley-Booth ordered. 'I was sorry to notice the other day that you had made your hands quite rough by going out with them exposed – in this cold wind, too.'

Laetitia returned to the wardrobe, unfolded a parcel wrapped in tissue paper, and held up a pair of lavender kid gloves. 'Will these do?'

'Surely not quite new ones for the garden.'

'As you like, Aunt Emily.' She drew on another pair as she spoke. 'These have been worn once before. That is a proper compromise, perhaps?'

The weak irony with which she had been wont to sting her father had no effect now. Soon she found herself following her aunt downstairs and sedately pacing beside her on the terrace before the house.

'This is a gloomy place for a walk,' she said.

'It is drier under foot here than elsewhere,' was the answer.

Dim sunlight filtered through the misty air and raindrops gleamed pale topaz on the leafless branches. The wind had fallen. Only the sounds of dripping and of footsteps crunching on the gravel broke the winter's hush. But already from the sodden earth arose the smell of spring. Peeping up through the chocolate loam, white shoots, like blanched almonds, showed where another summer's flowers would bloom. Laetitia thought of the spring that was gone. Of those that were to come, she dared not think; for the scent of sap and of moist soil warming to the sun would be to her a recurrent torture, unless, she told herself, she could be schooled to live each spring again in memory, without present desires.

They had walked the length of the house a dozen times when a maid came towards her.

'Please, miss, a young woman has come to ask a favour of you – partic'lar, she said; she wouldn't go away—'

'I cannot see her.'

'Very good, miss.' The maid turned to go, but Mrs Bodley-Booth stayed her.

'One moment, please … Laetitia, dear, you have not asked the young person's name or business.'

'Elizabeth Evans, ma'am,' the maid answered. 'She's a daughter of the master's tenant at Alltgoch, she said.'

Mrs Bodley-Booth inclined her head to show that she had heard, and, with eyes on Laetitia's face, asked, 'What sort of person is she – respectable?'

'Very, I should think,' Laetitia answered indifferently. 'Old Evans is a favourite tenant.'

'Wait,' Mrs Bodley-Booth commanded the maid, and, taking her niece by the arm, propelled her out of earshot. 'My dear, it is surely your duty to hear what this young person has to say. Do you not see that you must behave before these people as though nothing had happened? If you receive her with your former composure, she will contradict any rumour that may have been spread among the working class.'

Weary of struggle, Laetitia made the easy answer, which, as she spoke it, seemed an echo from her own future; 'Perhaps you are right, Aunt Emily.'

The maid was sent to fetch Elizabeth Evans, and the two ladies stood together, their gloved hands clasped before them, composed in demeanour, ready for contact with the common world.

But when Laetitia looked into Elizabeth's eyes, she knew that here was a woman, warm-hearted as herself and far more sincere, whom it would be difficult to deceive. She had stopped a few paces from the ladies and dropped them each a curtsy. That service rendered, she set down the baskets she was carrying, and, disregarding Mrs Bodley-Booth, spoke her mind to Laetitia.

'Please, miss, I do want to speak to you alone.'

'My good girl, I am Miss Laetitia's aunt. You can talk quite freely in my presence.'

Elizabeth's eyes turned on the speaker. When she had a task to perform, her concentration upon it overcame the shyness she had been taught to feel in the presence of her betters. 'Thank you, ma'am,' she answered firmly, 'but I'd rather not, if you'll excuse me. Miss Wingfield has grown up among us, but we are seeing you very strange.'

'I grew up here myself, my good girl. But of course you are too young to know that. What is it you wish to ask my niece for?'

'I am not wanting to ask her for nothing, ma'am.'

'Well, to tell her, then?'

Elizabeth was silent.

'Well?'

'I must speak to Miss Wingfield alone, ma'am, or go away without speaking.'

'Very well, if you have something you are ashamed to tell in my hearing—'

Mrs Bodley-Booth looked with suspicion at the sturdy figure bundled in its flannel petticoats and shawl. Then, with a swish of *moiré antique*, she sailed off down the terrace like an indignant brigantine. No sooner was her back turned than Elizabeth, with unexpected swiftness, drew a letter from under her shawl and thrust it into Laetitia's hands.

Laetitia looked at the envelope in amazement. Instantly the little colour that was in her cheeks vanished. She had thrust the letter into the front of her bodice before her aunt reached the far end of the terrace and magnificently went about.

'Quick,' Laetitia whispered, 'before she can hear—' Her gloved hands were at her breast. How her heart beat! And she had been trying to make herself believe that, for her, emotion was a thing of the past! 'Speak for heaven's sake. You had this from him? How is he? What has become of him?'

'He is very near mad, miss, talking to me like a ghosts' friend o' takin' his own life. And it seems he's been in that way ever since he came to know—'

'What? What does he know?' Had he guessed that she had in secret been a traitor to their love? That she had wished to escape from everything that recalled it? 'For God's sake—' she pleaded, and broke off with a glance of fear. Oh! Was she still afraid of her aunt's disapproval, even in this instant when her love for Gronwy had rushed back into her heart? 'What does he know?' she asked, turning again to his messenger.

'That you were found in the garden and blamed for all after he had fled away. He had met you in the arbour, hadn't he, miss?'

'Yes.'

Elizabeth waited in silence until the *moiré antique* had come and gone.

'As he was leaving the garden,' she said then, 'some o' the squire's men set on him, but he took to the hills, never doubting they was only after a poultry thief or a poacher. But now he has come to hear how 'twas after he fled, an' as they are taking you away. "I will never see her no more," he said to me, miss. "Go you, Elizabeth good gel, an' beg o' her to send me three small little words by you that I may die in peace."'

'What words?

'I forgive you.'

Laetitia's eyes filled with tears. 'Forgive? It is he who must forgive,' she exclaimed. 'Tell him that – no, tell him I will beg forgiveness of him myself. I cannot go from here – I will not go until – listen. Tell him I will contrive somehow to meet him – let me think—'

'When, miss? At what hour?' Elizabeth asked.

'I don't know. Some evening before I am taken away. I will manage to slip out. Tell him to wait each evening about dusk.'

'At dusk, miss. But where?'

'Say – say, "Helen will meet you at the place you showed her."'

'Where is that, miss?'

'Never mind. He will understand.'

Elizabeth nodded and repeated slowly: 'Helen will meet you at dusk in the place you showed her.'

'Well?' said a smooth voice. 'Have you completed the confidences I was not trusted to share?'

'Yes, Aunt Emily. I have been hearing a very sad story.'

'Indeed. I am sorry this young woman should not have thought me capable of helping to right the matter, whatever it was... No, my love, you are not wanted here just now.'

Lucy had come out of the house and her mother went hastily towards her. Elizabeth gathered up her baskets.

'I'll be going, miss, an' telling him what you do say.'

'No – stop.' Laetitia felt a need of this strong, simple creature, whose life, she rightly guessed, was lived consistently with fulfilment of clear purpose. 'How did he come to make you his confidante?'

'To tell me o' his love for you, miss?

'Yes.'

''Deed, I don't know, miss. Men an' beasts do often come to me when they are hurted.'

'Oh, my dear!' said Laetitia, deeply moved. 'How happy you must be!' Then, with swift thought, she added: 'But you are taking a risk now. If your father knew—'

'He would beat me no doubt.'

Laetitia stared. 'Surely he couldn't beat you – a grown woman!'

Elizabeth showed that she was puzzled. 'Oh, an able-bodied man, like what father is, could beat any woman, I suppose.'

Laetitia's lips smiled. 'Go now,' she said sadly. 'They are coming back.'

II

For the first time for several days Charles Wingfield ran upstairs whistling and passed the door of his sister's room without dropping his tune. His father and aunt, he knew, expected him to be ashamed of Laetitia, and, when the united family sat in mournful silence at meals, he was indeed shocked by what she had done. But the eyes of his elders were not upon him now, and Lucy had offered to show him her album of pressed ferns if he came early to the drawing room before dinner. He must lose no time in changing or the old lady would be there before him. So he rushed to his dressing room, banged the door, flung down his hat and riding whip, tore off his coat, and began to fumble with the straps that held his spurs.

Pressed ferns. He couldn't help grinning as he recalled how grave an interest he had expressed in the damned things. Bless her! What did it matter whether the pages that her pretty fingers turned for him were covered with the pitiful skeletons of plants or with her favourite quotations from the poems of Coventry Patmore of which she happened at the moment to be making a collection in a kindred volume bound in red plush and tied with ribands? It was the little hands themselves, so plump and white, that pleased him. As long as they did no work to make them 'mannish', he cared not a rap what they collected. Their chief function in future, he liked to think, would be to wear the gold and jewelled rings he hoped to set upon them. This thought led him on to wonder when his father would die. Instantly he became conscience-stricken and began to swear at his boots. They fitted too damned well. He was striving with a boot-jack when there sounded a knocking at his door.

'Come in,' he cried irritably, and, turning round, saw Laetitia.

While he stared in astonishment, she entered swiftly, closed the door behind her, and locked it. His sulky, sidelong glances at the dinner table had warned him that she was growing each day more pale and that deepening shadows of sleeplessness were gathered about her eyes. Now he saw that she looked really ill. Her locking of the door proved her to be overwrought. She could not stay the twitching of her lips or the convulsive intertwining of her fingers. Charles was seriously alarmed.

'My dear girl, whatever's the matter?' he blurted out. 'Yes, yes, of course, I know. But you mustn't take it like this. Here, sit down.'

She stood, swaying perilously. When she tried to speak, she failed.

'Get me some water, please,' she managed to whisper at last.

In blundering haste he fetched a glassful from his washstand, spilling half of it as he limped across the room with a boot on one foot only.

'There you are, my dear.' He watched her drink it and sink down on to a chair. 'I say, hadn't I better call some of the women?'

She started up trembling. 'No, no – for heaven's sake – they'll drive me mad with their veiled insolence.' And suddenly she burst into tears.

'Good God,' he muttered. 'This is awful.'

She had dropped down again on to the chair. Leaning her arms on its back, she hid her face and sobbed. He stood beside her, first on one foot, then on the other, giving her shoulder an occasional pat, racking his brains for something kind to say. At last, embarrassed beyond endurance, he left her, and strode about the room scowling at the sporting prints that adorned its walls. There, in that masculine company, hung a small watercolour portrait of Laetitia as a child, her eager face framed in the ringlets he used to think so pretty.

Poor little Letty! They had been good playmates then, before she went abroad among the damned foreigners who were to blame for all this nonsense.

'Charles,' she said, 'I – I'm sorry. Will you forgive me? I haven't slept for nights. You see, I can't eat either and then one gets foolish and light-headed.'

'Poor Letty!' he muttered. He was genuinely sorry for her, but wished all the more for that reason that she would go away. Any woman who made a scene was bad enough, but when you cared for her – well, it made his eyes sting. Devilish uncomfortable. These were precious moments, too, and Lucy was wasting them alone. Lucy was leaving soon. It would be months before his father would let him visit her at Aunt Emily's place. Some other fellow might step in meanwhile, for there was no definite understanding between them. By Jove – suppose he were to lose her through not having popped it tonight! Why the devil couldn't Laetitia have chosen some other time for thrusting her infernal troubles upon him?'

'Look here,' he said as gently as he could, 'won't you go back to your own room? You ought to lie down, you know, and take some smelling-salts, or whatever it is you do.'

'What's the good? I should only stay awake all night thinking. If you would take a weight off my mind, I think I could sleep.'

Impelled to rid himself of her by any means within his power, he grasped her hands and lifted her up. 'I'll do anything I can to help you – there now. If only you'll go—'

She cut him short, looking into his face with such piteous entreaty that he winced. 'Oh, Charles dear, do you really mean that?'

'Yes, yes. Anything you please.'

'I was right – I guessed – I knew you would understand and befriend me now that you are yourself in love.'

'I wish she'd stop talking so hysterically and go away,' he

thought. 'There won't be a chance of my seeing Lucy alone if she stays here much longer.' Aloud he asked: 'What is it you want me to do, my dear?'

'Take me for a ride tomorrow evening.' She watched his face with agonised anxiety. 'You know that I am being taken away the day after. You must tell Papa – he trusts you – that it will look better for us to be seen out together. That will appeal to him. That's all they think of – how to keep up appearances. Little they care if I lose my reason.'

'Come, Letty, you know that's not true. We're all fond of you.'

'Prove it to me, then. Prove it.'

His face began to show suspicion and increased discomfort.

'Why d'you want to go for this ride?'

Her hands, which had lain passive in his, caught at him, and clung to his shoulders.

'Charles, don't deny me this. I'll say anything I can in your favour to Lucy – to Aunt Emily.'

He saw that she might be useful in that respect, though her talking of it thus openly made him ill at ease.

'Listen,' she continued, 'there is nothing I will refuse you, *ever*, if you will make it possible for me to meet Gronwy once again. No, no, don't interrupt. Only once – only for a moment. He has written me a heartbroken letter. I have been the wretched thoughtless means of ruining him and his. I can't go – I will not go without one word of forgiveness, one word—'

'No, Laetitia. It's impossible for me to have anything to do with this.'

'You don't love Lucy, then. You can't know what love is.'

'The cases are entirely different.'

'If you really loved her, you would pity him and me.'

'I do pity you. But – oh, damn it all, it's not fair on a fellow!'

The door leading to his bedroom stood open. He moved towards it, meaning to shut her out; but she clung to him, and broke into renewed sobs he could not endure to hear.

'No! No! No!' he shouted, all the more vehemently because he felt himself weakening. 'I tell you it's not fair on me. If Papa found out—'

'Must I believe your fear of him is greater—'

'I'm not afraid of him – not in the least.'

'Charles,' she said, 'this is the last thing I'll ever ask of you. You will never have a chance to befriend me again.'

He paced about his big room, considering the matter. What harm could there be in it, if no one knew? Besides, if he refused, he would make an enemy of Laetitia, and Laetitia was going to live with Lucy.

'If you'll go quietly now, I'll agree to think it over,' he conceded.

'No,' she said. 'It's everything to me.'

Among the Surtees novels at his bedside was the handsomely bound Bible which the squire expected each room in his house to contain. Laetitia pulled it out and held it above her head.

'Look. If you say "yes" I will swear solemnly on the gospel never after tomorrow to seek an interview with Gronwy Griffith. They are parting us for life. All that I ask is to be allowed to say goodbye.'

'For Goodness' sake, put down that book and don't be so theatrical,' Charles exploded. 'Do go and dress for dinner.'

'Say "yes", and I will go this instant.'

'All right, all right, then. Have it your own way.'

God bless the woman! She was crying again, and hanging on to his shirtsleeve.

'O Charles!' she said. 'Thank God for that! Thank God! You will take me tomorrow?'

He felt tears on his hand. 'I've said so. I've said so. Tomorrow.'

'Damn tomorrow,' he growled as she left him. 'She's spoiled my chances for tonight.'

CHAPTER XIX

At the Wishing Chair Again

In February, when cows due to calve during the spring had begun to go dry, and eggs were scarce, Elizabeth never went to market. Her father rode into Llangantyn weekly, whether or not he had business there because, as he told her when she chided him for coming home drunk, it was 'needful for a farmer to follow the prices'.

'Do you keep sober an' come home early, Father dear,' Elizabeth said on one of these occasions. 'I'll have a grand supper ready for you – pigs' trotters – there's something to tempt you back!'

'Come on, Father,' cried Benjamin, and struck his pony a smart blow with the palm of his hand. It bounded out of the fold in a series of bucks that nearly unseated him, making him shout with laughter as he clung to its mane.

'That's the sort o' spirit I do like to see on a boy,' said old Evans, picking up his reins and clapping heels to his ancient horse. 'Ben is promising to be just the same as his elder brothers. There'll be a yelling an' a singing an' a galloping an' a kissing o' maids when they do come back from the works with their pockets full o' money!'

'I dare say,' Elizabeth answered, 'but don't you grieve me tonight by staying out late – there's a good, kind father.'

'A'right, a'right. Don't you tell your father how to behave, gel.'

He urged his skeleton of a horse into a trot and hurried after his son. Elizabeth shook her head as she watched him. About her feet was a swamp of mud and manure. Rain had fallen throughout the night and the moist air was cold enough to draw steam from the dungheap piled high against the stable wall. Low-hanging clouds were a leaden roof to all the earth, and the hillside above Alltgoch was dark with dead bracken and wet slate.

'Well,' she thought, 'it's no use standing here fretting about what I can't alter.'

She went indoors. Removing her apron, she tucked up her skirts and tied a piece of sacking across her. This done, she set upon the fire a three-legged cauldron, and, while the water in it was growing hot, clattered about the kitchen and the adjoining dairy, sweeping the floors. A little later there arose a noise of splashing and scrubbing; and by noon the squeeky sounds of polishing and the smell of beeswax and turpentine filled the house.

At midday she cut herself a hunk of bread and cheese, stood propped against the dresser to eat it, wiped the crumbs from her mouth with the back of her red hand, and straightway returned to her labours. The early twilight of winter was darkening the interior of Alltgoch when at last her work drew towards its end and she came downstairs from the bedrooms she had been dusting to open the backdoor.

'You may come in now,' she called. 'The floors is dry.'

An old dog that had been unable to follow the horses came limping across the fold, faintly wagging his tail. As she stooped to rub his paws on the bracken that served as a doormat, two cats leaped on to her shoulder and fled into the house.

'Ah, you saucy villains! You do make bold with me when there's no man nor boy about.'

She followed them into the kitchen and flung a log upon the fire. Flickering lights and shadows began to dance over the white walls and ceiling. On the stone mantelshelf, which bore battered tracings of carving, were arranged a few pewter platters behind the canisters and candlesticks. She noticed that they were in need of cleaning, and, though her back and arms ached, stood on tiptoe and lifted them down. With wood ashes scooped from the hearth she began to scour the largest of them.

'I do never like to leave a job half done,' she informed the dog, who replied with a beating of his tail upon the floor.

'I do have to do a thing with all my heart or not at all. That's how I do love Peter.'

Another series of taps answered this speech.

'Are you liking to be talked to, as the cows are at milking time?'

He responded as before.

'Very well, then. I'll tell you how I am able to keep working when I am terrible tired. I am making believe as 'tis all for Peter's sake, as this is his house, and as he'll be coming in for his supper at the end o' the day, an' praising me for what I've done.'

The dog laid his pointed muzzle on her foot and uttered a moan of satisfaction at the attention he was receiving. She went on talking to him in a low voice while she rubbed the dish.

'Peter'll have to go from this neighbourhood along o' his folk when they are turned out o' their farm. 'Tis hard for me to think o' parting from him.' Her eyes smarted with tears, but she blinked them away. 'I have been promising to myself an' him as I on't fret. For since we are loving each other faithful, 'tis only a matter o' waiting for better times to come, an' then he'll fetch me to be his wife.'

For a moment her hands lay still in her lap and she stared with wide eyes into the fire. 'I would rather wait all my life long for Peter nor have a fine house o' my own tomorrow with any other man living.'

Again the dog whined and crawled closer, nuzzling her feet. One of the cats, which had been sitting erect on its haunches surveying him with jealous eyes, circled round him and sprang suddenly over his body into its mistress's lap. She laughed aloud at the air of triumph with which it stared down upon its grovelling rival, and at that moment Peter opened the door.

'I looked in at the window an' thought as you were alone.'

'I *am* alone,' she cried, jumping up.

'But you were talking an' laughing when I opened the door.'

'Only to the beasts here.'

She held out her arms to him, but he stood and stared incredulously at her.

'Are you telling me the truth now?'

The colour rushed up into her face. 'Oh, Peter! As if I 'ould tell ought else to you.'

'No, no, o' course not,' he said. 'I don't know what's on me these days. I'm gone terribly nasty tempered with all this trouble. I could be thinking ill of you even.' He caught her by the arm. 'You 'ouldn't never take up with another man an' have him here in the house keeping company with you behind my back?'

She looked up at him so steadfastly that he was at once ashamed of himself and released her.

'There's childish dull you are to go talking to the creatures,' he said.

She meekly accepted his rebuke. 'I doubt I am. But they are so wonderful kind to me when I am here day after day alone. Are you ever thinking as may be they have souls the very same as our own, only smaller like?'

'Souls! Don't talk so foolish. You are going on like as if you was only a small little lump of a gel.'

He had no sooner spoken than he repented him and put his arms about her.

'Betty, my little bitty as I did use to call you, don't you take no notice o' me if I am speaking unkind. I dunna mean it, indeed an' indeed; only worse ill luck is fallen on us nor ever, an' mother is weeping an' rocking herself to and fro, an' father has drunk hisself dull same as he do allus do when he is hurted in mind or in body, an' Jane is so curst, storming an' banging about the house like a mad 'oman, an' I can't bear it no more.'

He stooped and nestled his hot, unshaven face against her neck. His chin, which had put forth a sturdy growth of beard, scratched her, and she staggered beneath his weight. But he had come to her thus in his hour of need, like a child to the mother it has never learned to fear, and she cared for nothing else.

'Sit you down beside me on the settle,' she said. 'There. Now put your poor throbby head on my breast an' tell me what has happened. Maybe as I can help you?'

'No one can't do that now. 'Twas bad enough before, with Gronwy disgracing us by getting hisself into gaol – not as I do blame him for a word he said against the gentry – but a man as has been gaoled, no matter what for, is marked for life. 'Tis same as if he was cross-eyed an' red-haired, no one 'on't employ him, not if they can help it.'

'Come you,' she said, 'when your folks do take him away into another district, 'twill be forgotten.'

''Twill come up against him sooner or later wherever he may go. "Peter," he said to me last night. "No poor man should ever learn to read or write. Indeed, if I had never learned to speak 'twould have been better for all of you. 'Twas my power of eloquence," said he, "made me noticed by the gentry in a way as will never be forgiven me so long as I'm above ground."'

'He'll not be known by the gentry in some other county.'

'I have been into another county since I was seeing you last, seeking a farm for father to rent. But farms is scarce, more partic'lar such as we could pay for when we've lost all we shall lose by having to turn out an' sell our stock on bad times.' He looked up suddenly, his face so contorted with fury that she shrank from him. ''Tis a wicked blasted shame as a landlord can turn a tenant, at six month's from Michaelmas, out o' the farm he's worked on all his life. Father has toiled an' sweated early an' late, an' made corn grow where onst there was only fern. When he took over our place much of it was no more than a barren bit o' hill land. By the labour o' his hands he's doubled its value – not for hisself, mind you, but for the owner. But old Wingfield shan't benefit, damn him, by putting up the next tenant's rent – not more nor I can help whatever. I'll undo all as can be undone o' poor father's life's work in the time that's left us.'

'That 'on't do you no good,' said Elizabeth sorrowfully.

'No. But 'twill do the squire harm,' Peter answered with gusto.

'Well,' she said, anxious to change the subject, 'what new trouble is come upon you?'

He hung his head. 'I'm ashamed to tell you, though I've knowed summat of it myself this long while.'

She took one of his huge hands and curled her fingers round it. 'You can tell me surely, boy?'

'No. I'd not tell you even, only one o' the squire's gardeners did see it all in the garden by night, an' when he was drinking at the Green Dragon an evening or two ago he was making a joke of it. That's how all the neighbours got talking an' the story comed round to poor father.' He faced her again, his brows contracted and his lower jaw thrust forward. 'I'll make pulp like porridge just o' that gardener's face. 'Twill bear the mark o' my fists down to the grave.'

'Oh, Peter, whatever has made you so cruel angry?'

When he answered, it was with hesitation and in a low voice. 'Have you ever heard strange talk o' lads as did fall asleep with the moon shining on their faces, an' others as did speak with the fairies in the old tumps on the hill tops?'

She looked up perplexed into his face that was at once so strong, so troubled, so helpless. 'Whatever are such stories to do with you?'

‘’Tis poor Gronwy I am thinking on. I do believe he is ’witched.’

‘But why?’

‘Because he has been beguiled by that strumpet, Wingfield’s daughter, into courting her.’

He expected Elizabeth to utter some exclamation of astonishment. As she remained silent, he demanded; ‘Well, aren’t you even so much as surprised?’

‘I knowed that a’ready,’ she answered quietly.

The pendulum of the grandfather clock swung leisurely to and fro a dozen times before Peter moved. Then he rose to his feet and stood towering over Elizabeth, his head lowered and his expression as blank as that of a bullock which draws near to some strange object in a familiar field.

‘How did you get to know? Was the talk going out about Gronwy’s folly afore ever it comed to my ears?’

‘No, no. He came here hisself after he’d been found in the squire’s garden an’ told me the whole story.’

‘You! Why should he tell you?’

‘How should I know? Some folks do like to come to me in time o’ trouble. It do seem strange, but that’s how ’tis.’ Still Peter stared at her. ‘Maybe,’ she added, ‘he knew as I should be sorry for him.’

‘Aren’t we, as are his own flesh an’ blood, sorry enough for him?’

‘Aye; but he guessed as I should be sorry for her too.’

Peter spat into the fire. ‘Oh, so the poor fool came here to talk to you about that false witch as has beguiled him?’

‘About his sweetheart – yes. An’ to beg me to carry a letter to her.’

The sullen surprise of Peter’s look turned to anger. ‘You didn’t dream o’ doing no such thing?’

Flinching, she forced herself to answer, ‘I did as he asked.’

She saw the red deepen in his cheeks.

'Whatever was you thinking on,' he thundered, 'to go abetting what you must have knowed I would do all in my power to stop? Why, if I wasn't afeared to swing for it, I'd take a gun to any one o' them for the vermin they are. Crows an' goodyhoos, jays an' magpies isn't living more harmful lives nor what they are. An' you – you – you o' all others to go carrying love letters to the one o' that damned breed as has caused the chief mischief. My own sweetheart to play me false!'

'Peter,' she murmured, ''tis just because you an' I are sweethearts that I do vex for others as do love.'

Her humble tone mollified him.

'But our case,' he said, 'is different from theirs.'

'So each of us do say of our own.'

She went to him and pushed herself with gentle insistence into his arms. ''Tis the small little differences atween folk as do make them able to harden their hearts one against another. But if you were onst to see the great big likenesses o' all human folk, you 'ouldn't be able to hate your enemies no more.'

A torrent of protest rose to his lips. He hated Miss Wingfield because her victim was his own brother and because she was one of 'the quality' who were all selfish and cruel in their dealings with the poor. His angry words, however, remained unspoken.

'You are wrong to pity bad wicked people, partic'lar such as are rich,' he said.

'No, no, boy,' she answered with unexpected firmness. 'If I have done wrong in this – and, mind you, I have prayed over it many an hour – if I have done wrong, 'twas in asking Miss Wingfield to take a mortal risk.'

'Whatever do you mean?' growled Peter.

She began to twist her apron in her hands. ''Deed, I don't hardly know, boy. But poor Gronwy has been put wild by love. He might do hisself a mischief. He might 'tice her to do herself a mischief, too, so set is he on their living or dying together.'

Again Peter spat into the fire. 'She'll let no harm come to *her* o' her love; 'twas nothing only play to her.'

'He's having the tongue of a preacher and the eyes of a hunted dog,' said Elizabeth. 'There's no knowing to what madness he might win her, she being already so daunted by loneliness and he maybe meeting her secretly in some dark, romantical place … But Peter, honeyseed, you'll forgive me for doing what I did reckon right by them?'

'Well, well,' he grumbled. 'What's done is done. You have carried a letter from Gronwy to that witch. Let's hope as 'twill be the last as will pass between them?'

'Then you'll not blame me for an act o' kindness to two poor sweethearts as must be parted?'

'No. I'll say no more. You are too gentle soft to be blamed.'

He kissed her first with dry lips; then with lips moist and warm. At last he kissed her with his usual rough passion, and, finding himself softening into universal forgiveness of spirit, broke away from her with an effort.

'You are making me tender like yourself, an' a man did ought to be hard.'

'Why?' she asked.

He thought the question stupid. 'Because of having to fight for his own o' course. An' I am going to fight the gentry in whatever part o' the country I an' mine are driven into. An' some day I shall rise to be feared by them as do spoil the poor.'

Thinking of future struggles, he began to pace up and down the room.

'Come you on out with me,' he exclaimed. 'I do hate to be under a roof as is owned by one o' them. Let's have nothing over our heads, only heaven as is free to all men.'

Without protest or comment, she banked up the fire with sods of peat, and, taking her shawl from a peg, wrapped it about her, and followed him into the fold. He strode past the faintly luminous buildings and on to the open hillside, while she kept close to his heels and the old dog to hers. Thus they went on for a time; then, stopping abruptly, Peter allowed her to overtake him.

'Where are you going?' he asked.

'Indeed, dear, I am going wherever you do go,' she answered, 'but I don't know where that will be.'

The dog crept close to her and thrust a cold, wet nose into the palm of her hand. Thus they stood, the man irresolute, the woman and the beast awaiting his decision. About them, advancing night had cloaked the dead bracken and faded grass in a common blackness.

'We'll go down there to the wishing chair,' said Peter at last. Thought, word and action followed one another so quickly that he was plunging downhill before Elizabeth understood his purpose.

''Twill be dark,' she gasped, as she scrambled after him.

'Not so dark but what those as is wretched may wish for better times.'

Nothing more was said. He descended headlong, leaping over rocks, sometimes slipping on wet moss and stumbling into rabbit holes. The valley, when he reached it, was a cup of darkness, overlaid by a close, black sky, pierced by few stars. Jumping down on to the main road at a point close to its junction with the squire's drive, he paused, and waited for Elizabeth, trying to decide what form his wish should take, and what magic he should invoke against the Wingfields. He had surprised Jane in the making of a mud image of the squire that she might run needles through it. It should have been made of wax, he had told her, so that it might melt, and had laughed at her witchcraft. It was odd in Jane. But he had been awed while he laughed – awed because it was Jane, who did nothing from which she did not expect results.

But with the sound of Elizabeth's footsteps on the road

behind him came the practical thought – 'What's the use of a poor man trying to fight with a rich one? Only prison an' ruin comes o' that. Gronwy ought to be a warning to me to let be such wild ways. I'll get rich first, an' then I'll be able to strike our enemies a very different blow from the one he struck. 'T'on't be words as they'll have to fear from me.'

When Elizabeth came close to him, she peered up into his face and was alarmed by what she saw there.

'What are you doing,' she asked, 'standing here by the squire's gate so silent?'

'I am promising myself a treat.'

'Oh, Peter, you 'on't do nothing rash?'

'No, no, gel. I'll be grinding slow – but exceeding small, same as the mills o' God.'

She shuddered. ''Tis cold here an' dark.'

From the direction of the river came a long-drawn 'hello-o-o,' which awoke melancholy echoes. 'Hello-o-o-a!' it sounded again, but there was no answer. Peter started forward.

'Come on. We'll go an' wish for better times.'

'But maybe you an' I 'on't wish for the same things. What if your wish be for vengeance an' mine for loving kindness 'twixt you an' the squire's seed?'

'Come, come, you 'on't act so foolish as to wish no such thing. An' we mustn't be tellin' our wishes whatever, or they 'on't never come.'

He drew her hand through his arm. Close together, forming a single shadow, they crossed the pale road, pushed open the gate through which Laetitia had once passed with her father and Gronwy, and clambered down a steep path that led to the river. The noise of its rushing over rapids and gurgling in deep pools came up to them out of the darkness, but the gleam of its water was hidden by the alder trees that fringed the bank. As they approached these, a figure detached itself from the black mass and barred their way.

'Who's there?'

The tone was one of authority. Elizabeth felt Peter's arm stiffen under her fingers. He took a step towards the speaker.

'Who's there, I say? Are you deaf?'

Peter answered: 'Who are you yourself?'

The other ignored his question. 'You can't get down to the river this way tonight.'

'Oh, indeed! An' who makes bold to say as I can't?'

'I do – Charles Wingfield.'

Peter was shaken by a gust of silent laughter. In his loudest rages, Elizabeth had never feared him as she did now, when he neither spoke nor raised his fist.

'Peter,' she whispered, 'come away.'

He pushed her from him. 'So this piece o' common land, where gipsies graze their donkeys, is yours too, same as the birds o' the air, an' the fishes in the river yonder?' He purred over the words like a cat devouring raw meat.

Charles Wingfield was taken aback. 'What the devil d'you mean. Who are you?'

'One as you be turning off your estate because his brother spoke out the truth o' you an' your class. But you shan't order me off here, where you can't claim the power o' the law to help you in your tyranny. On this bit o' land which is no part o' the Wingfields' ill-gotten estate, we are equals as God made us, an' if you do fancy as you're the better man, come on, an' we'll soon see if you are or not.'

Charles Wingfield did not move, but spoke with an effort, as one who had nerved himself to make a humiliating confession. 'You are a Griffith of Tinygraig?'

'Aye, an' you'll not forget my name in a hurry if you stand in my way. Get out o' the path, damn you!'

'Look here, my man, d'you know why I'm stopping you?'

'No. Nor I don't care neither. Get out, I say, or I'll strike you, mun.'

Charles seized his arm. 'Listen. My sister and your brother are down there together.'

'The devil!'

There was a pause, heavy with angry breathing. When Charles spoke again it was with the same painful effort.

'They have met for the last time to say goodbye. She and I rode together. We were to have come earlier but couldn't. Your brother's been waiting since dusk, it seems… Now do you see the reason? It's their last meeting, I tell you. Go back the way you came, and, if you value your brother's interests as I do my sister's, speak of this to no one.'

He turned from them and was instantly swallowed up by the alders' shade. They heard him crashing through the undergrowth, and once more his forlorn 'Hello-o-oa!' awoke mocking echoes among invisible rocks and hills.

''Twas he we heard calling a long while ago,' said Peter, in a flat voice.

'There are horses tied to a tree nearby,' Elizabeth answered. 'I can hear them stamping.'

Neither moved. There had come into Elizabeth's mind the message she had carried without understanding – 'Helen will meet you at dusk in the place you showed her.' Gronwy had been waiting since dusk, Mr Charles had said. Still Elizabeth did not understand, but the riddle had sadness and terror in it, and she trembled. Peter was trembling too. They stood side by side, unspeaking, stricken by vague, unadmitted fears. Then the shouting ceased, and they heard the squire's son fighting his way back to them through the snapping branches.

'He is in haste,' Peter muttered.

And Elizabeth answered below her breath. 'Then he's failed to find them.'

When he was close to them, Charles shouted out furiously: 'They are gone! What devil's trick is this? Did you come here to keep me talking while they ran off together? Gad! You shall pay for your insolence!'

Peter sprang into activity and tore off his coat. 'Come on,' he cried, 'if that's what you do think. I'd have seen the bitch in hell before I'd have helped her to run off with a brother o' mine; but one o' your damned lies is as good as another to fight you for.' Elizabeth clung with both hands to his raised fist. 'Get out o' my way, gel,' he shouted, 'or you'll be hurted too,' and he shook her off so that she fell to her knees upon the ground. She saw Peter led away to prison for this night's work. He was the stronger, and if he should give the squire's son 'an unlucky blow' it might even be a gallows matter. She prayed for strength to stay his folly, and, in a desperate effort to gain time, she screamed – 'Stop! Don't stay here fighting. Maybe as they are not fled together but drownded.'

'Drownded! 'Peter's fists dropped to his sides. 'Is that possible?'

He awaited no answer, but, with a great push, sent both Elizabeth and Charles Wingfield staggering out of his way. 'Grono!' they heard him calling; and farther off 'Grono! Grono, boy! 'Tis I calling you. 'Tis Peter. Come on out if you are hiding. Show yourself alive for the love o' Christ!'

The echoes reawakened, and from every side voices, growing fainter and fainter, cried plaintively. 'For the love o' Christ! For the love o' Christ!'

Elizabeth stole up to her companion in the darkness.

'Have you any matches, sir?'

He started. 'Matches? What for? What are you talking about?'

'Have you any on you?'

'Yes. But what—' He passed his hand across his eyes. 'Is this a damned nightmare, I wonder?'

'Oh, sir, come on down to the river quick an' let us be searching. Maybe without knowing it I spoke the truth.'

'You don't really think—'

'Who can tell? They was both of them terrible unhappy.'

'Good God!'

She seized his arm, and together they stumbled forward. Peter's desperate shouting sounded now from very far away, but only the eerie voices answered it as before. 'Grono!' came from across the river— 'Grono ... Grono... Grono!' from upstream and down.

'Where did they meet?' Elizabeth asked.

'Here by the wishing chair, I think she called it.'

'Strike you a match, then.'

A spurt of flame showed his sheltering fingers and his face, boyishly flushed and troubled, with pouting lips and slightly protruding eyes. Instantly, Elizabeth stooped to examine the rock. Before the night wind had blown out the light, she had seen something unusual lying on the brink of the stream.

'What is this,' she asked, groping for it and holding it up. ''Tis a riding whip.'

His answer was hardly audible. 'My sister's.'

They stood like figures of lead with the whip held between them, listening to the sucking of the pool.

'This place is horrible,' said Charles. What are we to do? Oh, my God, what can we do?'

Pity had freed Elizabeth from her normal shyness. She laid her hand on his arm and tried to steady it. Presently they heard Peter crashing and stumbling towards them.

'They are not here,' he cried, as soon as the two indistinct shapes by the wishing chair were recognisable. 'Whatever can have happened, mun? Whatever can have happened?'

Elizabeth answered in a tone of quiet authority. 'Go you down to the rapids below the pool an' wade in so far as it is safe for you to go.'

'Why, gel?' There was a shudder in his voice.

'You may be finding summat caught in the rocks there,' she steeled herself to reply.

He set off at a lumbering run. While they waited, she looked up at Charles and saw that his face was hidden in his hands.

'Are you praying?' she asked in a whisper, feeling as intimate with him now as if he had been her own brother.

'Good God, no! If only I could—'

Simply as a child, she raised her eyes to the dark heavens which she had been taught to believe were the dwelling of God.

'O Lord, let there be some mistake. Let Miss Wingfield and Gronwy come back to us safe.'

Her prayer made Charles self-conscious and ashamed. He uncovered his face.

'Look!' he cried. 'Here he comes!' And a moment later, to Peter, 'Well, speak, man! What have you found?'

'This.'

Three heads bent together over a bedraggled rag which Peter clutched in his hand.

'What is it? Only a bit of water weed.'

'No, no. Feel it, mun.'

'A woman's veil,' said Charles. 'Her veil. It's the thing she wore dangling from her hat. This, and the whip at the water's edge – She's flung herself in. She's drowned.'

'Aye,' said Peter. 'He's drowned.'

Charles took life suddenly. 'We must call help. Torches. Ropes. Men to drag the pool. It can't be too late to do something.' And he added: 'I must tell my father. I must tell him – God help me!'

He plunged into the alders, and a moment later they heard the thud of hoofs galloping over wet turf and the neighing of the horse that had been left behind. The moon was rising, though hidden as yet by a mountain range across the river. In that quarter the sky had begun to lighten and the stars to pale.

'Peter, Peter, my sweetheart,' Elizabeth said, 'you are wet an' shivering like as if you'd got an ague. There's no good to be done here now. Come you home with me.' He made no reply. 'Peter, you'll be catching your death o' cold. An' if you too should come to mischief it'd break my heart… for my sake, come,' she urged, and in despair flung her arms round his neck. 'If you love me ever so little, come home with me now.'

'I'll bide here.'

His teeth were chattering so violently that he stammered. Elizabeth pressed herself against him, trying to shield his body from the wind.

'My little one,' she cried, straining up to reach his big, bowed shoulders, 'is my love o' no comfort to you in this dark hour?'

'They have murdered him, those Wingfields. On them an' on their class I will wage war – on the Bible I'll swear it – so long as there is breath in my body, so help me God.'

He spoke as a man obsessed. His limbs were rigid between the fits of shivering by which they were continually shaken; but Elizabeth persisted in her attempts to soothe him. Laying her cheek on his, she called him fond and foolish names, and told him of her love in words that had never before been hers to command. She wiped the cold sweat from his forehead with hair that had fallen down about her face, and crooned over him as a mother over her child, raising his hands to her lips and kissing warmth into his numbed fingers. With all the tenderness she had ever shown him, with more passion than she had dared hitherto to disclose, with feminine cajoleries of which she had not known herself to be capable, she tried to win him from his black mood, but he would not answer her.

A slice of copper coloured moon now tipped the opposite hill. New lights and shadows leapt up around them. Peter was staring over Elizabeth's head at the pool in which his brother had met with death. She could find in his eyes no recognition of herself, and at last her lips began to quiver and her eyes to fill with tears.

'Do my love mean nothing to you?'

He shifted his gaze, and began slowly to stroke her hair.

‘Aye. ’Tis meaning a deal,’ he answered absently. But his face remained set. Her hands unclasped and dropped wearily from his neck. He seemed no longer to be the boy she had known.

CHAPTER THE LAST

Politics and Spring – A Prayer in Conclusion

Laetitia's lilac tree, which she had watched through the dining-room window just over a year ago, was putting out buds again. The squire passed it on his way from his front door for a tour of the garden. 'Too near the house!' he said aloud. 'I must have it down. I've been meaning to a long time.' At that moment a gardener passed him, but he had not the energy to give an order.

The approach of spring gave no promise to him, and he went his way without scent of it. The last few weeks had aged him. It was with difficulty now that he held himself erect, and he used his cane and arm stiffly as the buttress to an old building. When his eye fell upon the gravel sweep, he scowled at it. There, in spite of hoeing and raking, tiny blades of grass were sprouting.

'When I am not about, my servants neglect their duty,' he thought. 'It's the same with my tenants – ungrateful, disloyal.' He tried to check his thought there, but it persisted. 'My children too.'

He walked painfully through his gardens, forcing himself to give orders and administer rebukes. The slipperiness of moss-grown paths, threatening him with a fall, and the showers of raindrops that fell on his neck and face as he pushed his way under overhanging boughs did not daunt him. At all costs, he'd do his duty, and it was long before he dismissed the head gardener who had followed him like a beaten dog, cringing and sulky.

When the man was at last gone to vent his temper in thrashing the youngest garden boy, the squire stood alone by the gate leading into his beech wood. Rumours had reached him, as he sat brooding indoors, that John Griffith and his surviving son at Tinygraig were 'taking it out of the land,' and letting the fences fall to pieces before their tenancy expired. 'I ought to go and look round the place,' he reflected. 'I hate to go near it, but I've been indulging myself in grief too long.' But still he stayed within the walled garden which gave him a feeling of security that would be lost outside. The hostility of his inferiors, and the possibility, usually remote, that they would insult him, had once inspired him with a lofty satisfaction. Now it was painful to him –painful, as if there were some justification of their enmity. 'Weakness,' he muttered. 'Moral cowardice.' But his lean fingers continued to play with the latch of the gate.

How steep the drive looked, and how sodden with last year's leaves piled in drifts of slimy brown! Why hadn't the gardeners swept them up for leaf-mould? Why – but he was tired of these questionings. He had lost his old pleasure in organisation and command. In the library was a comforting fire of logs. In the drawing room – though he didn't like the drawing room now – was another; his sister would be waiting for him, toasting his slippers. Though she said little, he had found her composed presence in the house very soothing since the catastrophe. He didn't know what he'd have done without her.

Then he squared his shoulders impatiently. 'Bless my soul!' he thought. 'I must be getting old – wanting to spend time with the ladies!' This would never do. And, because rheumatic pain shot through his limbs and the longing for warmth and for quiet domesticity was almost a torment to him, he forced himself to open the gate and to toil uphill between the beech trees.

Having passed beyond reach of their drippings, he was attacked by a new discomfort. A spiteful squall swept down on him from the hilltop where the stunted may trees were all stretching their branches away from the prevailing wind. He paused, buttoned his collar about his throat, and laboured on.

After the storm came a glint of sunshine. First the horizon was rimmed with light; then the glory flowed towards him and over bog and moor cloud shadows chased one another away. In every gully, torrents sparkled, and the sedge-rimmed pools and the peat-cuttings threw up the washed blue of the sky. Spring, impetuously gay, had broken out all around him, but the squire, with no more welcome to it than the turning down of his collar and the undoing of a top button, went steadily on.

When he raised his eyes, it was only to see how far he was from his odious destination. While making one of these surveys, he discovered, not far away, a figure on horseback. 'That's Charles,' he thought. 'He's seen me – aye, and he's swerved to avoid me.' With a sour pleasure in the exercise of his power, he hailed his son and watched his reluctant approach. Since the day of Laetitia's funeral they had spoken only for form's sake in the presence of Lucy and her mother. For the squire had upbraided Charles in terms not easily to be forgiven, directly charging him with responsibility for his sister's death. Thinking of it now – that painful scene – he decided that he had been right in speaking as he did; it had been his duty. He would not, even if he could, take back his words. All the same, he wished the boy wouldn't look at him like that. Such resentment was unlike Charles, and the squire found it hard to bear from the sole heir of his body, for whom he had worked and worried all his life. It wasn't fitting, he told himself now, that he should be the first to break silence between them. Yet he broke it – with an ill grace.

'Where are you off to in such a hurry?'

'Only exercising my horse, sir.'

Silence fell on them. Charles stared at his saddle peak, the colour in his cheeks deepening.

'Going home?' the squire asked, prodding holes in the turf with his cane.

'I suppose it's about time.'

'Better turn round and come a step of the way with me.'

'Aren't you going home, sir?

'You can see I'm not.'

Charles said no more, but dismounted and began to pace uphill beside his father. Now and then he glanced anxiously at the horizon and once consulted his watch. Neither spoke. When their elbows touched, Charles said, 'I beg your pardon,' and withdrew a yard. Once the squire brought up his head with a jerk and opened his mouth as if to speak. But he closed it, and, when his lips moved again, his words were those he spoke daily at the dinner table: 'Have you seen the paper?'

Charles showed relief. He had feared that something personal, and therefore embarrassing, would be said.

'No, sir,' he hastened to reply. 'You had *The Times* when I came out. It contains a report of the debate on Dizzy's new version of his Reform Bill, I suppose? He was to bring it forward on the 18th, wasn't he? What d'you make of it now?'

The squire frowned. 'This time last year,' he said, 'we were all facing the common enemy – Gladstone. Now it is one who calls himself our friend who makes almost the same mischievous proposals. In my opinion, Cranborne, Carnarvon and General Peel, as sound Conservatives, were right to resign when they did.'

Charles demurred. 'Well, I don't know, sir. I think they'd have been wiser to back the Jew, even if they don't like the shape of his nose. He's what the Party needs – a clever strategist. I admire him for dealing the Whigs such a blow –

with their own weapon, too. It's a damned amusing situation.'

'It's a damned dishonourable one,' the squire exclaimed with so much vehemence that Charles stared at his careworn face.

'Aren't you pleased at his making the Whigs smile on the other side of their faces, sir?

'I despise the manner of it.'

'I thought that particularly sharp.'

'Sharp enough, I grant you – worthy of the man's low cunning.'

'Hang it all, sir, it's more than that. He's a brilliant statesman.'

'I dare say; but he is not an English gentleman. And therefore, in my opinion, he's not fit to govern this country. Let him offer his reforms to the Medes and Persians. What is his idea, I ask you? To pander to the city mob – to give it, in the name of Conservatism, just what its own radicals had promised.'

'Well, you know, sir, the franchise was bound to be extended sooner or later.'

'I don't believe it – not if the best elements in the community had steadfastly resisted attack. But there are always traitors, ready to lower their own class.'

The squire stopped suddenly and bit his lip. Good God! That struck pretty near home – he might have been talking of his own family! Disloyalty to the old tradition smote at him everywhere, and he could have cried out in the bitterness of his heart. But, as he uttered no word, Charles noticed nothing amiss and went on talking. He liked Dizzy, he said – gave one something to laugh about in the Parliamentary Debates. Of course he wrote novels, and was said to have worn rings outside his gloves, and all that – a Jew, but a genius in spite of it. He'd be useful. He'd succeed in making the Party popular.

The squire frowned at the word. 'Even in politics,' he said, 'votes aren't everything. There are such things as right and wrong.'

'You take the whole business too seriously, sir. I look on it as a game.'

'Yet in a game, even, I trust you would not betray your own side and would scorn to cheat – that is,' the squire could not refrain from adding, 'if anything of all my teaching remains in you.'

Charles shrugged, and slouched along beside him. Silence heavier than ever closed upon them.

'Why did I say that?' the squire asked himself in vain, 'just when we were on the verge of a friendly discussion?'

It was long before he could bring himself to glance at the boy's face. When he did so, he was astonished to find its expression changed. The smiling eyes were blue in the sunlight and the mouth showed its fine teeth. Charles in this mood was as good-humouredly greedy as a child in a pastry-cook's shop.

The reason was not far to seek. Following his son's gaze, the squire saw Lucy riding towards them. So that was why Charles was out, was it? And she expecting to meet him! He was filled with wrath against her – that horse, that saddle, the groom who rode behind her – they had been Laetitia's! So soon… How could her own brother enjoy such a sight? Had he no memory, no decent feeling? What was that fool of a girl's mother about to allow such a thing? But his anger did not last long. 'It's natural,' he thought bitterly. 'The world's selfish. And nowadays they haven't even the good breeding to conceal it.'

'Hello!' said Charles.

'Fancy meeting you!' exclaimed Lucy. 'I've had such a lovely ride, Uncle Charles, on this dear, dear creature.' She patted the horse's neck. 'And now meeting you – quite unexpectedly – has made my enjoyment perfect.'

The groom grinned, for Lucy was not looking at her uncle

as she spoke. She was dimpling pink and white as apple blossom and leaning towards Charles. But there was little they could say in that company. Soon, with a wave and a laugh, she rode on.

Not until she was gone, did Charles look again at his father. Then the former gloom settled on his face.

'I – I hope you didn't mind,' he said. 'It's been devilish hard on her sitting indoors all day in a house of—' He left the sentence unfinished and began to stutter. 'She's so considerate, so – so – I had to suggest at last – she was growing devilish pale – and Aunt Emily agreed—'

'Yes, yes, yes,' said the squire, striking at last year's withered bracken with his cane. 'Of course. I quite understand. Life must go on.'

Charles stared at him as though he had pronounced words of great enlightenment.

'Yes, sir,' he exclaimed gratefully, 'that's just what I think. I mean – what you've said – it means such a lot. I've been thinking of the future—'

'That's a gift of the young,' said the squire.

But Charles, having begun, rushed on. He was brick red from stock to hat brim, and, before he had done speaking, his face was moist with sweat. 'Could I – could you spare me a few minutes in the study tonight, sir? I've wanted for a long time – but of course after all that has happened—'

'Yes, yes, yes,' said the squire for the second time. 'Ride after her, and say I'll put no obstacle in the way of your happiness – if you imagine you can be happy with her.' He looked resentfully after the girl who had dared to ride in his daughter's saddle, and strode on. 'Damn you!' he exclaimed a moment later, his self-control snapping like that of an old dog that has been worried too long by a puppy, 'don't follow me, gaping and stammering. Go and do as I bid you.'

Left alone on the bleak hillside, he remembered that he'd have to make a marriage settlement. That was all the young people wanted from him, his money. No doubt they wished him dead. They'd most likely ask to be set up in the dower house, too –wouldn't care to live with him in his old age. They liked, these days, to be independent, if you please – independent at someone else's expense! His sister would marry again. He'd be neglected and forgotten, at the mercy of dishonest servants, with no woman of his own to control them, ashamed to go abroad in the county where this hideous scandal in his family had been the gossip of butcher, baker, and candlestick maker. So he'd grow older, and sadder each year.

Thus, among the waste of hills where there was no human being to befriend him, Squire Wingfield walked on, envying little children whose troubles hadn't begun. The land beneath his feet was his by right of inheritance. He was about to exercise his authority in turning out one of the families which had their home upon it. Yet his chin was sunk in his cravat and his eyes looked only at the path he was treading. Round and round in its little circle of anxieties went his mind. Was he being cheated? Had he obtained full value for his money? Were not those who owed him deference, gratitude, obedience, defrauding him of his due? Why had they refused him their love – those two women, mother and daughter, from whom most assuredly he had a right to demand it? His spirit was weary of it all.

Coming at last to the summit of the hill, where jutted up the rocks that hid Tinygraig from his sight, he heard the blows of an axe falling upon wood. Monotonous and dreary, an accompaniment to his thoughts, the noise drew him on. He rounded an outcrop of stone as big as a house, and came suddenly on a young woman who was standing on its farther side. She was looking intently into the little enclosures that surrounded the cottage; but, at the squire's appearance, she turned, startled, and faced him, her grey eyes wide open and her lips parted. A simple, honest, stupid peasant, he thought her, and tried hurriedly to remember about whose ailments she would expect him to enquire. This must be Elizabeth Evans of Alltgoch, he decided, and prepared to address her with that degree of condescension which the daughter of so civil a tenant deserved. But the appropriate words were not spoken. She was looking straight at him as a woman might look at a man whose equal she was in age and station, and whose sorrows were not hid from her compassion. Humiliated by the mute pity she seemed to offer, humiliated yet more by the knowledge that his mood invited and his heart desired it, he jerked his head away, forgetting his mission to Tinygraig, urged only, like a hurt wild beast, to escape from observation. Behind him he heard a stifled, timid exclamation as though, having realised her offence to his wounded pride, she were both asking his forgiveness and begging him to stay. He hesitated. He glanced over his shoulder. She was no longer looking at him. Had all this been in his imagination, then? he asked himself, as she dropped him a curtsy and murmured: 'Good evening, sir,' just as any farm girl might who was too shy to raise her eyes to him. Had he imagined it all – the sympathy, the friendliness, the desire to welcome him, above all the tact, so unexpected in one of her order, which had won his heart?

'Good evening, my dear,' he said. Then, finding that his throat was tight and his eyes smarting, he trusted himself to say no more. 'Good evening to you,' he repeated, and swung round, cursing himself for a susceptible fool. His way home was long and solitary, but he did not remember that day to inspect the hedges of Tinygraig.

II

When the 'poor old lonely man' had gone his way, Elizabeth turned again to her contemplation of Peter in the field below. His coat was off and hung upon a gate nearby her. In his shirt and breeches, collarless, with sleeves rolled up and feet planted wide apart, he hacked away at an apple tree. It quivered beneath his giant blows, began to sway, and crashed to the ground. Standing amid a pile of chips, he looked at the havoc he had wrought. Wherever he had been in the orchard were broken boughs and felled trees. Having stared at them with prolonged satisfaction, he shook himself and stretched his tired limbs like a dog after a fight, and, with a sweep of his forearm, wiped the sweat from his face.

'Now as he has taken the life from something, he'll feel kinder,' Elizabeth told herself, and, going down to the orchard gate, laid a hand upon it. But her hope was vain. He had not yet expended the hatred in his heart, and took up his axe again.

The interlude of sunshine had been as little noticed by him as by his enemy. Presently clouds came sweeping low over the ridge that stretched beyond Tinygraig rocks to a darkened horizon, and a squall of wind whipped the rain into Elizabeth's face. To seek shelter would have been to turn away from Peter. 'And maybe he'll need me to comfort him when he's stood out there in his poor, hurted anger till he's starved,' she thought. So long as he chose to inflict suffering on himself, she knew that it was inevitable that she also should suffer, and, having accepted this fact, she felt happiness well up in her heart.

She wondered, as any one seeing her might have done, what there was in her life to make her so happy. The wind bit through her threadbare clothes; her feet and ankles were chilled in the sodden grass; when she looked down at her hands, with which she had been butter-making in cold water all the morning, she saw that they were chapped across the knuckles and were oozing blood. And Peter, for whom she had waited so long, pretended to be blind to her, lest her love should hinder his act of vengeance.

Nevertheless, her joy increased, so warming her mind that it received no longer the hurts of her body. 'For nothing can stop me to love him,' she thought, 'and in that is my delight. And if I wait long enough, surely I shall be able to serve him in the end.' For now, as on the first night when he came courting her, she perceived that her peace of soul was not at his mercy, nor to be destroyed easily as is the peace of lovers who demand that their love be paid in kind.

Searching in one of the big baskets which she was bringing home from market and had set down at her feet, she drew forth a dozen spoon cakes wrapped in a handkerchief. These she forced into the pocket of his coat where it hung upon the gate. 'That'll be a small little surprise when he do come to fetch it, for I can see 'tis no manner o' use my staying on here now. Hate is too strong yet, workin' through him like yeast just, same as it was in Susan Jones.'

She remembered her last glimpse of Susan, being driven in the squire's luggage cart to Llangantyn station on the morning after the discovery. How tortured and how vindictive the white face and bitten lips had been! 'Poor gel,' Elizabeth mused. 'She were a hissy sort – soon up an' over. Long after such love as ever she had is dead, she 'ull go keeping the hurt of it alive through anger, God forgive her … And her poor dead lady and her sweetheart as was more afeared to live than to die, God forgive them too … God forgive the old squire as is shutting his heart, up, an' my dear, foolish Peter there, thinking as he'll find balm for hisself by doin' another a mischief.' She clasped her hands and whispered: 'Lord Jesus, who died for them, do thou draw the poison out o' their hurted spirits as has had a part in this sad story.' And she added, because there was more she needed to say for which she had no words of her own, 'And have mercy upon all men, Amen. Amen.'

When she had said this, she became aware again of her own body, that it was cold. Casting once more a wistful glance upon Peter, she turned about and blew upon her numbed fingers until they were able to do their work. Then she gathered her shawl about her, and picked up her baskets. They were heavy, and she was tired. Nevertheless, she must make haste if the men and beasts at Alltgoch, who depended upon her for their comfort, were not to be kept in want, and she went forward bravely in the teeth of the wind.

Welsh Women's Classics

Series Editor: *Jane Aaron*

Formerly known as the *Honno Classics* Series, now renamed and relaunched for Honno's 25th Anniversary in 2012.

This series, published by Honno Press, brings back into print neglected and virtually forgotten literary texts by Welsh women from the past.

Each of the titles published includes an introduction setting the text in its historical context and suggesting ways of approaching and understanding the work from the viewpoint of women's experience today. The editor's aim is to select works which are not only of literary merit but which remain readable and appealing to a contemporary audience. An additional aim for the series is to provide materials for students of Welsh writing in English, who have until recently remained largely ignorant of the contribution of women writers to the Welsh literary tradition simply because their works have been unavailable.

The many and various portrayals of Welsh female identity found in these authors' books bear witness to the complex processes that have gone into the shaping of the Welsh women of today. Perusing these portrayals from the past will help us to understand our own situations better, as well as providing, in a variety of different genres – novels, short stories, poetry, autobiography and prose pieces – a fresh and fascinating store of good reading matter.

"*[It is] difficult to imagine a Welsh literary landscape without the Honno Classics series [...] it remains an energising and vibrant feminist imprint.*"
(Kirsti Bohata, *New Welsh Review*)

"*[The Honno Classics series is] possibly the Press' most important achievement, helping to combat the absence of women's literature in the Welsh canon.*"
(*Mslexia*)

Titles published in this series:

Jane Aaron, ed.	*A View across the Valley: Short Stories by Women from Wales 1850-1950*
Jane Aaron and Ursula Masson, eds,	*The Very Salt of Life: Welsh Women's Political Writings from Chartism to Suffrage*
Elizabeth Andrews,	*A Woman's Work is Never Done* (1957), with an introduction by Ursula Masson
Amy Dillwyn,	*The Rebecca Rioter* (1880), with an introduction by Katie Gramich
	A Burglary (1883), with an introduction by Alison Favre
	Jill (1884), with an introduction by Kirsti Bohata (forthcoming in 2013)
Dorothy Edwards,	*Winter Sonata* (1928), with an introduction by Claire Flay
Margiad Evans,	*The Wooden Doctor* (1933), with an introduction by Sue Asbee
Menna Gallie,	*Strike for a Kingdom* (1959), with an introduction by Angela John
	The Small Mine (1962), with an introduction by Jane Aaron
	Travels with a Duchess (1968), with an introduction by Angela John
	You're Welcome to Ulster (1970), with an introduction by Angela John and Claire Connolly
Katie Gramich and Catherine Brennan, eds,	*Welsh Women's Poetry 1460-2001*
Eiluned Lewis,	*Dew on the Grass* (1934), with an introduction by Katie Gramich
	The Captain's Wife (1943), with an introduction by Katie Gramich
Allen Raine,	*A Welsh Witch* (1902), with an introduction by Jane Aaron (forthcoming in 2013)
	Queen of the Rushes (1906), with an introduction by Katie Gramich
Bertha Thomas,	*Stranger within the Gates* (1912), with an introduction by Kirsti Bohata
Lily Tobias,	*Eunice Fleet* (1933), with an introduction by Jasmine Donahaye
Hilda Vaughan,	*Here Are Lovers* (1926), with an introduction by Diana Wallace
	Iron and Gold (1948), with an introduction by Jane Aaron
Jane Williams,	*Betsy Cadwaladyr: A Balaclava Nurse* (1857), with an introduction by Deirdre Beddoe

Clasuron Honno

Honno also publish an equivalent series, *Clasuron Honno*, in Welsh, also recently re-launched with a new look:

Published with the support of the Welsh Books Council

ABOUT HONNO

Honno Welsh Women's Press was set up in 1986 by a group of women who felt strongly that women in Wales needed wider opportunities to see their writing in print and to become involved in the publishing process. Our aim is to develop the writing talents of women in Wales, give them new and exciting opportunities to see their work published and often to give them their first 'break' as a writer.

Honno is registered as a community co-operative. Any profit that Honno makes is invested in the publishing programme. Women from Wales and around the world have expressed their support for Honno. Each supporter has a vote at the Annual General Meeting.

To receive further information about forthcoming publications, or become a supporter, please write to Honno at the address below, or visit our website:

www.honno.co.uk

Honno
Unit 14, Creative Units
Aberystwyth Arts Centre
Penglais Campus
Aberystwyth
Ceredigion
SY23 3GL

All Honno titles can be ordered online at
www.honno.co.uk
or by sending a cheque to Honno